KATANA SANDAN

THE CODE OF BODHIDHARMA

THE KATANA SERIES
BOOK THREE

KEN WARNER

For David,
who instilled in me
a love of reading and learning.

Without him, these books would not exist.

Think neither of victory nor of yourself,
but only of cutting and killing your enemy.

-Miyamoto Musashi

CONTENTS

KATANA SANDAN

PROLOGUE

JAPAN, EDO PERIOD

Kushan walked down the temple steps. He took the same path he always did, rounding the small hill that hid the temple from view. He stopped at the water's edge, breathing in the clean salt air as he gazed out over Suruga Bay and the ocean beyond. It was a ritual with him, coming here at dawn to practice. He never missed a day, regardless of weather. When the ritual was over, he would return to the temple and spend the rest of his day training young monks. Until then, this solitude was his sanctuary.

He bowed to the sun and began his first kata. He felt the grass beneath his feet as he hit each stance, punching and kicking invisible opponents. He sensed his chi beginning to flow. When he was done, he turned and faced distant Mount Fuji. Bowing to the mountain, he began his second kata.

They really were his kata; he had designed the whole art of kempo. *Kempo—Law of the Fist,* he thought to himself. In its archaic form, the character for fist meant "strength of the base of the mountain." Ultimately, his art was named for the mountain. This made him smile.

"I bow to you, Fuji," he called out as he finished the kata.

"You're losing your mind, old man," said a voice from behind him. "You're talking to the Earth."

"And it responds," Kushan replied without turning. "Perhaps if you spent more time in meditation, you would hear the mountain as I do, Jaaku. That is what they call you now, you know."

Kushan turned slowly, and saw exactly what he expected to see. His sanctuary had suddenly become rather crowded: a dozen samurai warriors faced him from behind black armor, helmets and masks. At their center stood a single warrior whose armor was brilliant white: Jaaku. It was he who had spoken.

"This is your last chance, Kushan. You will give me the secret. Or you will die."

"You never learn," Kushan replied quietly.

Jaaku raised one arm, then let it fall. Swords raised, the warriors behind him charged forward, straight at Kushan. Jaaku strode forward behind them.

As the warriors converged on Kushan, he extended one hand and shouted "YASH!" There was a sound of rushing air, and they all flew back off their feet as if swatted by some giant, invisible

2

hand. They landed flat on their backs, a dozen feet behind their leader—who was somehow unaffected.

Jaaku lunged forward and thrust his sword at Kushan's chest. Kushan leaned slightly to one side. The blade missed him by inches.

One of the other samurai regained his feet and charged again at Kushan, who stepped to one side and wrapped an arm around the warrior's neck, dropping him to the ground. He drove one knee into the man's chest plate, pinning him to the ground, and plucked the sword from his hands.

Jaaku thrust again with his sword. Kushan rolled out of the way, sword in hand.

"You cannot defeat me, Jaaku," he said, standing.

Three more warriors charged at Kushan. Again he threw out one hand and launched them into the air with some unseen force.

"You are not invincible," said Jaaku, and lunged forward a third time. Kushan parried, and the two engaged in fierce combat, swords glinting in the morning sunlight.

Every few seconds, another warrior would charge forward and attempt to join the fray, but each time Kushan merely held out his hand and sent the attacker stumbling backward.

But finally, as Kushan repelled one warrior, another came in from behind and grabbed him around the waist. Two more rushed in, each grabbing an arm.

Jaaku stepped forward and held the tip of his sword against Kushan's chest.

"The secret, old man. Now."

"You cannot take immortality from me," said Kushan. "So be it."

CHAPTER 1
THE MASTERS COUNCIL

CALIFORNIA, PRESENT DAY

J ordan Nash, the Headmaster of the Hall of the Dragon, sat at the head of the long table in his conference room. A large picture window to his left overlooked the Zen rock garden behind the school. A sunbeam flooded through the glass, casting a warm glow on the old books and scrolls piled up on shelves along the adjacent wall. The other masters sat around the table, their laptops open in front of them—Sam, Daniels, Osaka and Nelson Fu, who'd recently accepted a position at the Hall.

"Now for the last item on our agenda. Katana." Nash looked around at his colleagues. "I've spoken with the headmaster of Shaolin again since our last meeting, and I have come to a decision."

"You are set on this course of action, then?" asked Osaka. "We're going to comply with the headmaster's demands after all?"

"I don't see that we have a choice," Nash replied. "If we are going to continue to be a part of the temple network, then we have to abide by the Code of Bodhidharma. And the code says that if a disciple can perform three of the chen do and attain third degree in any art, then..."

"Oh please, surely the Code of Bodhidharma was not meant to apply to fourteen-year-old girls!" said Master Daniels. "This is ridiculous. What are we doing here? First we're teaching that 'sport karate' garbage at the oldest hall of traditional martial arts in the country, and now we're going to let a *fourteen-year-old*..."

"She's almost fifteen," said Sam with a twinkle in her eye. "You're not still upset that you couldn't catch her when she levitated out of your reach, are you Brock?"

Master Daniels opened his mouth to argue, but Osaka spoke first. "No, nobody ever intended the Code of Bodhidharma to apply to a fourteen-year-old." Sam looked at him in surprise as he continued. "The Code of Bodhidharma is old and obsolete. And the rule for disciples who can do three chen do has *never* been used—there is absolutely no precedent for this action. Not to mention the fact that the Hall of the Dragon has *never* used the disciple system in the first place."

"You mean you're opposed to this?" asked Sam. "I figured that you of all people would support Katana having a shot at..."

"Samantha, I support Katana in her every endeavor. But this

is lunacy. There are things going on here that you are simply not aware of. I can think of nothing, *nothing* that could be more detrimental to Katana's well-being at this time," said Osaka.

"I discussed your concerns with the headmaster," said Nash, with a very conciliatory tone, "and he has agreed to keep this matter as private as possible."

"To believe that this will remain secret strains all credibility," said Osaka. "If the Shaolin Temple implements some archaic provision from the Code of Bodhidharma, word will spread throughout the temple network—and beyond. And even if it does not happen, the other headmasters will already be aware of the situation."

Sam looked at Osaka with a frown, then asked Master Nash, "What ever happened to the headmaster's paranoia about Katana knowing dim mak? Is he still pretending to be concerned about that?"

"What?!" asked Master Fu. "The headmaster of Shaolin thinks Katana knows dim mak?"

Master Nash let out a long sigh. "The headmaster never really believed Katana was a dim mak master, I am sure. However, he does remain quite curious about our having *four* students who can do two—or more—of the chen do."

"What does that have to do with dim mak?" asked Master Fu.

"We found out that when Jaaku recruits a new Arashi, he takes their prenatal chi into his own dantian. That forms a link between him and the individual—a connection he can use to perform the death touch at a distance, and to compel the Arashi to do his bidding. But he can also use that link to transfer power to the individual. That is why, for example, all of the Arashi can fade even if they could not do so before becoming Arashi," explained Master Nash. "The headmaster's man, Liang, insinuated to Samantha when she visited Shaolin earlier this year that perhaps that was how the other students here could do two of the chen do. He suggested that Katana might be using dim mak to transfer power to them the same way Jaaku shares power with his Arashi. It is, of course very rare for students so young to learn even *one* chen do. Yet we have three students, in addition to Katana, who can do *two*. And all three of them have been very close to Katana."

"That's insane..." said Master Fu. "How on earth could she have learned dim mak?"

"Undoubtedly it was no more than a ploy on the headmaster's part," said Master Nash. "He was hoping I would allow Katana to go to Shaolin to prove to him that she was *not* in fact a dim mak master."

"Yet that is very curious indeed," said Master Daniels. "Do you think there is some correlation between those students having two chen do and their relationship with Katana?"

Osaka looked sharply at Master Nash. But Nash merely held up his hands, shrugged his shoulders and said, "Coincidence?"

"Katana doesn't know about any of this yet, does she?" asked Sam. "About the headmaster's plan?"

"No, she does not," said Nash. "And I think it would be best to keep it that way, for now. It is still possible, after all, that it will not come to fruition."

"We're going to have to tell her what's going on at some point," said Sam. "We can't let her go into this blind, without any preparation..."

"No, of course not," replied Nash. "Once the decision is finalized, we'll let her know. We will discuss this more at our next meeting. Unless anyone has any further questions... then that concludes our business for today."

The masters closed their laptops and got up to leave. Master Daniels stayed behind to talk to Master Nash, but Osaka followed Sam and Master Fu out into the hall.

"Osaka," began Sam tentatively as they walked down the corridor, "why are you so concerned about the headmaster's plan? The whole thing is silly, I'll grant you, but you truly think it could be dangerous for Katana somehow?"

"Samantha..." said Osaka, and heaved a long sigh as they stopped in front of the door to his apartment. "I know with every fiber of my being that this course of action is *wrong*. I cannot elaborate right now, but suffice it to say, I fear Jordan is making a grave mistake."

"But you heard what he said—if the headmaster is pushing the stupid code, what choice does Nash have? The only alternative would be to break away from Shaolin altogether."

"Then that is what he should do," said Osaka. And with that, he walked into his apartment and closed the door.

"Wow," said Fu as he and Sam continued down the hall. "You're right, he does seem different."

"I told you," said Sam. "Ever since he went to Vermont, he

hasn't been himself. It's like he keeps his guard up all the time. I don't know what it is..."

"Maybe Adrian's death affected him more deeply than anyone realized," suggested Fu.

"Yeah... you're probably right," said Sam thoughtfully.

CHAPTER 2
SUNRISE

Katana made her way down the gravel path to the beach. She could feel goose bumps forming on her arms in the chill morning air—she was wearing no more than a white sports bra and an old pair of shorts. The white material of the sports bra contrasted sharply against her dark brown skin, and her shorts, originally red, had faded with time and weren't really red anymore. They used to say "Angel" across the rear end, but were so old that the letter "L" had long since peeled off.

"Idiot," she said to herself. Clearly it wouldn't be as warm out at quarter to five in the morning as it had been the previous afternoon. She made a mental note to wear something warmer tomorrow. She pulled the towel she'd draped around her neck down over her shoulders and jogged the rest of the way to the beach to try to warm up a little.

The path met the shoreline at a large outcropping of boulders that jutted into the ocean. Katana walked farther down the beach to an area that was less rocky and spread her towel out on the sand. Then she bent over to let her long, black hair swing free, and pulled it back in a ponytail.

She walked a bit closer to the water, and stood with her feet shoulder-width apart. She dug her toes into the sand, bent her knees slightly and relaxed her shoulders, letting her arms hang freely at her sides. Already she could feel her chi flowing, up from her feet and down her arms, causing the familiar tingling sensation in her fingertips.

"Any minute now," she said. Standing there, she could feel her body getting warmer as her chi strengthened its flow.

The moment for which she'd been waiting finally arrived. As the edge of the sun cracked the horizon, Katana dug her feet a little farther into the sand, bent her knees a little deeper and raised her arms in front of her ever so slowly. She pretended she was a marionette and the puppeteer was lifting her hands by strings attached to her wrists. She kept her shoulders, elbows and fingers totally relaxed.

She executed this first posture excruciatingly slowly. She raised her arms before her and straightened her knees only as fast as the sun rose above the horizon. Her jade green eyes blazed in the sunlight.

"Wu chi," Katana said to herself, "gives birth to tai chi." She remembered how Master Nash had explained that wu chi was supposed to be the state of the universe before it split into yin and yang. Thus in the form she was doing now, wu chi was the name of this first posture, the only one in which the weight was planted firmly on both feet. For every subsequent posture, the weight shifted slowly from one foot to the other.

Katana brought her arms up to shoulder height and straightened her knees completely only as the bottom edge of the sun rose above the horizon. Then she sank back down in her stance, lowering her arms to waist level.

As she shifted her weight to her right leg, she raised her right arm to shoulder level again, keeping her left hand by her waist, palm-up. She formed a ball of fiery red chi energy between her hands. And before the rising sun she moved through all 108 postures of the long form.

She had been doing this every single morning since the term had ended at The Hall of the Dragon the previous month. Although she was now discovering that practicing tai chi on the beach at dawn was vastly more invigorating than doing it in the backyard of her aunt's house back in Croton.

Katana thought she could feel the energy of the entire ocean flowing through her, so strong was her chi this morning. She began to time each yang, or advancing move to the crashing of the waves and each yin or retreating move to the lapses between crests.

By the time she was halfway through the form, the fireball between her arms was the strongest she'd ever achieved. She decided she'd definitely be coming back every morning this week —this was the most exhilarating sensation she'd ever felt.

Katana was so totally focused on her form that only when she was done did she notice her best friend, Sara Brown, lying on the towel behind her.

"Hey!" said Katana, walking over to sit next to her.

"Morning," said Sara with a yawn. Sara's curly, shoulder-length brown hair looked disheveled. Katana guessed that she'd just rolled out of bed. "Was that the long form?"

"Yeah," said Katana, finding she was soaked in sweat.

"That was amazing—I've never seen you get the ball that strong before."

"I know! You should come with me tomorrow—doing tai chi by the ocean is really intense," said Katana.

"I don't wanna be up this early!" Sara replied, looking offended that Katana would even suggest such a thing.

"You're up this early now!"

"Yeah, but that's only because I still have jet lag. My body clock is all sorts of screwy right now," said Sara with a frown. "I hope this doesn't go on all week…"

"Well, if it does," said Katana as she got up off the towel again, "you might as well come practice with me."

"Where are you going?"

"To finish my workout," said Katana, walking away. "Grab my towel?"

Sara stretched and yawned, then got up and swiped the towel from the sand. She followed Katana to a short retaining wall farther along the beach.

Katana jumped up to the sidewalk atop the wall. She began bouncing up and down on the balls of her feet.

Sara caught up and sat with her legs dangling over the edge of the wall. "You've been doing this every morning?"

"All summer," said Katana.

"Why?"

"You remember what Hua always used to say. Do this a thousand times a day to get your jumps higher."

Sara just stared at her, mouth wide open. "Kat, your calves already look like they were chiseled out of stone... I wish mine were like that. Do you really need to get them any stronger?"

"If I wanna jump as high as Jelly, I do, yeah."

"Good point... It *is* ludicrous that that midget can jump higher than you."

"Hey, did you talk to him last night?" asked Katana.

"Yeah, for a while online, after you fell asleep," Sara said with a sigh.

"And?"

"I guess we're done. He doesn't want to keep going out because we won't see each other all summer."

"Aw," said Katana. "I'm sorry, Sara."

But Sara smiled and said perkily, "I'm young—I'll adjust."

Katana snorted at her and kept jumping.

"Chris and Olivia are still together, aren't they?" Sara asked tentatively a minute later.

"Yeah, they are," said Katana. "He talks to her *every day*."

Once Katana had finished jumping, she reached down and placed her hands on the sidewalk, kicking her legs into a handstand. She held it for a few moments, then swung her legs down and stood up again.

"Can you do me a favor? Hold my legs so I can do this?" asked Katana.

"Um... do what?" asked Sara, getting to her feet.

"Watch," said Katana. She went into a handstand again. Sara grabbed her ankles and held her steady. Katana began doing pushups in that position.

"Are you kidding me?" asked Sara.

Katana did about twenty, then said, "That's good." She landed on her feet when Sara released her ankles.

"I didn't know you could do that..." said Sara in admiration.

"Dana suggested doing them to build arm strength. She says it helped her spin the chains faster. I can only do it against a wall, unless someone holds me steady like that. You should see Dana though—she just holds her handstand and pumps them out."

"Wow..."

"Of course, I don't have my own set of chains, so I haven't been able to practice all summer. But at least if I keep working on this, I'll be stronger by the time we get back to school."

Katana took her hair tie out and shook her head to let her hair swing free, then bent over and tied it back in a ponytail again. "I'm so sick of all this hair," she said.

"You're not really going to cut it off... are you?"

"Oh yes I am. When we go to Portland today, we're stopping at that hair salon we saw on our way here."

"Katana, your hair is so beautiful, I wish I could grow mine out like that," said Sara. "Why not just trim an inch or two..."

"No way. I'm chopping it," said Katana firmly. "All right, I think I'm done," she added.

The girls walked back up the beach and along the gravel pathway to the cottage where they were staying.

"It was nice of Mrs. Boyd's friend to let us use this place," said Sara.

"Yeah," Katana agreed. "I came here with them once when I was little. I guess it's a timeshare, and they couldn't use their week this year. They had a wedding to go to or something."

The front door of the cottage opened into a large room, half of which served as a living room, the other half a dining area. The kitchen was around the corner. Katana could smell bacon the moment she opened the door.

"Good morning, girls," said Mrs. Boyd with a smile. She and Mr. Boyd were bustling around the kitchen making bacon and eggs and pancakes. Mrs. Boyd was still in her bathrobe.

"Morning," Katana and Sara replied.

"Is Chris still asleep?" added Katana.

"Yes," said Mrs. Boyd with a frown. "Could you go get his lazy butt out of bed? Breakfast will be ready in a few minutes."

The girls went down the hall to Chris's room and barged right in. Chris was indeed asleep, gangly limbs sprawled out on top of the covers.

"Wake up," said Sara halfheartedly, plopping down on the end of the bed.

"Huh," Chris grunted without opening his eyes.

Katana walked over, pulled the pillow out from underneath him, and smashed him in the head with it.

"Hey!" said Chris grumpily. He grabbed the pillow from Katana and turned over to face the other way.

"That worked," said Sara with a smile.

"Hey, can I use your laptop?" asked Katana, and then said,

"Okay, thanks," before Chris could reply. She sat at the table in the corner of the room and turned on Chris's computer.

Chris sat up finally, and looked at Sara with one eyebrow raised.

Sara simply shrugged. "Whatcha doin', Kat?"

"Hmm?" asked Katana absently. "Oh, just research."

Sara frowned, walking over to sit next to her at the table. "What kind of research?" she asked. She turned to look at Chris, who rolled his eyes.

"Well..." began Katana hesitantly. "I've been trying to find out more about Jaaku and dim mak and the Arashi... We don't know much about them. And..."

"I told you," said Chris. "She's been obsessing about this all summer."

"I'm not obsessing!" said Katana, turning to glare at him. "I need to learn everything I can about Jaaku and dim mak because..." She didn't finish her sentence.

"Because you still think you're going to face him someday, don't you?" asked Sara quietly.

"No. I don't *think* I'm going to face him, I *know* I am, Sara," said Katana. "Look, I know you think I'm crazy..."

"I don't think that," said Sara.

"But he *killed my parents*," Katana continued as if Sara hadn't spoken. "He killed Hua... And we know he's way more powerful than any of the masters, even Nash. I've got to do *something*—I'm nowhere near strong enough to face him now..."

"But Kat," said Chris delicately, "it's not like you're going to run into him here, in Maine... Can't you just, I don't know, take the week off?"

Katana felt frustrated. Chris had been telling her all summer that she was going off the deep end and needed to chill out. But he didn't understand. She knew—even if she didn't understand how she knew—that someday in her future, she'd have to confront Jaaku. This scared her more than anything ever had before, but it also toughened her resolve. She had time. If she started learning everything she could about the enemy, then maybe when that day arrived...

"Come on, kids," called Mrs. Boyd from the kitchen. "Breakfast is ready!"

Katana shut down the laptop. The three of them went out to the dining room.

"We'll probably head into Portland around three or so, so you kids can hang out at the beach all day until then," said Mrs. Boyd as they dug into their food. "Just make sure you're back in time to shower and get ready."

"Can we stop at that hair salon we saw yesterday?" asked Katana. "I need to do something about this," she said, holding up her ponytail.

"Yeah, definitely," said Mr. Boyd. "And while you're there Chris can follow your lead."

"Mmm," Chris agreed through a mouthful of bacon. "I think I will actually. My hair really is too long."

"You're finally consenting to a haircut?" asked Sara. "We've been telling you for a year that it looks like you've got a shrub growing on your head..."

Mr. Boyd had chosen the wrong moment to take a swig of his orange juice—he started to laugh and nearly spit the juice out all over the table.

"Maybe *Olivia* said something to him about it," suggested Mrs. Boyd with a smile.

"No!" said Chris, turning a bright shade of red. "I just decided I don't like it long anymore."

The kids finished breakfast and went to change into their bathing suits. They grabbed the suntan lotion and a Frisbee and ran down to the beach.

As always, Chris applied an enormous amount of sunscreen all over himself—his pale skin didn't fare well in the sunlight. They threw the disc around for a while and went for a swim, then came back to lie out on their towels.

"So... What have you been able to find out?" asked Sara.

"Huh?" asked Chris.

"Not you, dummy. Katana—your research. What have you learned?"

Katana sighed. "Next to nothing."

"But Chris said you've been doing this since we got out of school," replied Sara.

"I have. But I haven't been able to find a single thing. There's some stuff about dim mak, but it's obviously fake. I mean, the Arashi are a *secret* society, right? So I guess it's not too likely that anyone who *really* knows dim mak is going to write about it on the internet."

"'Those who know don't talk, those who talk don't know,'" said Sara.

"What?" asked Katana.

"It's an old Taoist saying. You're right, though—the people who know dim mak aren't going to go blabbing about it on the internet.

"Well, we know some stuff. We know that Jaaku was a samurai warrior in the beginning," said Sara.

"Yeah, and Jaaku can't be his real name," said Katana with a frown.

"Why not?"

"Jaaku is Japanese for 'evil.' I don't exactly think anyone names their kid 'Evil,'" said Katana sarcastically.

"You're right," said Sara. "You know, I knew that was the Japanese word for 'evil,' but I never put two and two together before."

"Hmm," said Chris. "Maybe that's what Billy's mom shoulda named *him*!"

"Chris!" said Katana. "That's so not nice—he's been *way* better this summer."

"Who's Billy?" asked Sara.

"He's this kid who goes to Sensei Mike's," replied Chris. "You'll meet him next week."

"Anyway," said Katana. "We know that Jaaku wasn't his real name, he started out as a samurai warrior in Japan, and he was born two hundred and ninety-one years ago."

"And we know he went to China to learn dim mak," said Chris.

"We also know that at some point he went back to Japan," Katana added.

"We do?" asked Chris.

"Yes, we do!" said Sara. "Remember, Sam told us right after the first Arashi attack that the Arashi were Jaaku's inner circle. And she said something about the Japanese government shutting down his temple after he died…"

"Oh, right," said Chris. "Chow and that Ching guy went to Japan to fight him."

"It was Chang—Chow's successor," Sara corrected him. "The story was that Chow died killing Jaaku."

"Yeah, only Jaaku didn't die," said Katana. "Even though everyone *thought* he was dead."

"So where was he from the time the Japanese government shut down his temple until the time he sent the Arashi to steal the scroll?" asked Chris.

"No idea," said Sara.

"We also know that Jaaku killed the Immortal Master," Katana continued. "And that's why Chow went to Japan—to get revenge. Sam said Chow left the Hall in 1868—which makes sense. That was the year Chang took over as headmaster, according to the portraits in the tai chi dojo."

"How do you remember all that stuff?" asked Chris.

"But that's just a legend," said Sara doubtfully. "We don't know if the Immortal Master was real."

"True…" said Katana. "But when Sam told us that it was only a legend, she still thought Jaaku was dead. So it *might* be real."

"We also know that Jaaku showed up in Hawaii…" Chris added quietly.

"Yeah," said Katana. "He turned up in Hawaii right after I was born, long enough to kill my parents and leave again."

"Which is how Osaka knew he was still alive," Sara added.

"Exactly," agreed Katana. "He was there... Everyone else thought Jaaku was dead, but Osaka knew better. I wonder why he never told Sam?"

"Maybe he didn't tell *anyone* because he wanted to make sure *you* didn't find out," said Chris. "He didn't want you to know that your parents were murdered."

"I bet Nash knew," said Sara. "It seems like him and Osaka are really close—I'm sure Osaka would have told him. But that's pretty much everything, right? Do we know anything else about Jaaku?"

"No," said Katana. "That's all of it."

"What about dim mak?" asked Sara.

"We've learned even less about that," said Katana with a sigh. "We know you can use it to cause pain—I can speak from experience on that one. And you can cause temporary paralysis, or stop someone's heart."

"And we know the chen do is taking someone's chi," said Chris.

"Right," Katana agreed. "And Jaaku can use the chen do to take a person's prenatal chi and control them..."

"Or to do the death touch, and take *all* of their chi," Chris finished for her.

"Anything else?" asked Sara.

"No," said Katana.

"Well, when you guys come to Japan later this summer, we

can talk to my dad about everything. I know he knows some stuff, about the Arashi at least."

"Sara," said Chris, "what exactly does your dad do?"

"I'm not sure," answered Sara. "I know he works for the FBI —that's why I always moved around so much. He kept changing assignments. But I don't know what he does for them."

"Do you think he's *allowed* to tell us anything?" asked Katana.

"He always tells me everything I want to know."

"Yeah, and when he doesn't, you eavesdrop..." said Chris.

The three of them headed up to the cottage and had some lunch, then showered and got ready to drive up the coast to Portland. Mr. and Mrs. Boyd dropped them off at a large shopping plaza. Mrs. Boyd handed Chris a big wad of cash through the window. "You can use that if you or the girls find anything you want to buy. Then meet us back here at six and we'll go for dinner. Your father and I are going to do some shopping—call the cell if you need us for anything."

"Okay, Mom."

The girls spent the next couple of hours going through all the stores and little shops looking at clothes. Chris had his earphones on the whole time. He tagged along, bearing it the best he could. Finally they went to the hair salon at the end of the plaza.

Sara looked pleadingly at Katana as she sat down in the chair. "Kat, come on. Don't do it. You're going to regret it."

"Well if I do," said Katana, "I can always grow it out again."

Despite Sara's repeated admonitions, Katana refused to be swayed. The stylist chopped off her long hair and, as Katana requested, left it only just below her ears. Katana thought Sara was going to cry.

Chris got his hair cut as well and Katana and Sara agreed that he looked much better. "Olivia will be very happy," chided Katana.

"You know, it looks a lot better than I thought it would, Kat," said Sara as they walked out of the salon.

"I'm not sure I know how to take that," Katana replied.

"No, really," said Sara. "You look older now... More sophisticated."

"More *sophisticated*?!" Chris repeated. "Whatever! She just looks like Katana... with shorter hair."

"Hey, look!" said Katana, pointing to the other side of the road. "Let's go check it out."

"Lassater Karate Academy," Chris read from the sign at the top of the building. "Sure, why not."

They ran across the street and went inside. Plate glass windows formed the front of the school, and the doors opened into a large waiting room. The dojo itself was separated from this area by a wall with several large Plexiglas windows.

The waiting room served as a store as well—loads of uniforms and T-shirts were hanging from the walls and there were shelves piled with sparring gear and various martial arts weapons. Katana saw a lot of nunchucks and kamas and other sport karate weapons, but there were also a couple of Chinese broadswords, and a set of whip chains.

"Check this out," said Chris, reading from a poster between two of the Plexiglas windows. "Master Griffin Lassater, seventh degree black belt, six-time national kata champion, four-time national sparring champion." The poster featured a photo of the man who was inside the dojo at that moment, teaching several adults.

Griffin Lassater looked to Katana to be as tall as Sensei Mike. He had bright orange hair and a friendly face. He was a little on the chunky side compared to Sensei Mike, though. Katana thought he looked substantially younger in the photo.

The kids watched the class for a few minutes. Master Lassater was working with his students on kata—Katana recognized all of the forms they were doing. Some of the moves were a little different, but they were definitely the same kata that she and her friends practiced at the Hall of the Dragon.

Master Lassater came out a few minutes later. "Hey kids, are you interested in lessons?"

"Oh, no," said Sara. "We do karate already, we were just at the plaza across the street and wanted to come check the place out."

"Oh, I see. Where do you train?"

"We go to a school in California," said Sara.

"Well, you've come a long way! Which school do you train at in Cali?" he asked.

"The Hall of the Dragon," said Sara. Katana could tell from the look on her face that she was wondering if Lassater would've heard of it.

"Ah, yes," said Lassater. "So you guys must compete at the Golden Gate Classic every year."

"Yeah! How'd you know?" asked Sara.

"I'm a judge on the tournament circuit," explained Lassater.

"I'm on the judges committee too, so I try to get around to as many of the big regional events as I can."

"Hey, do you know where nationals are gonna be this year?" asked Chris.

"Sure do!" said Lassater. "We just chose the location last week. It's going to be at the Presidential Hotel in Washington, D.C. You're going to love it—the place is way bigger than the hotel in Eureka—we were rather cramped there this year."

"Oh!" said Katana suddenly. "Can I buy that set of chains you have over there?"

"Sure," said Lassater. "Do you train with those?"

"Yeah," said Katana. "I just started last year."

"That's a tough weapon," said Lassater as he went to retrieve the chains from the shelf. "I don't practice chains myself. One of my students was cross training at a wushu school nearby a few years ago, so I got a couple of sets. I played with them a little... But I gave up after I hit myself in the face a few times!"

Chris paid for the chains with the money his mom had given him.

"Well, I'd better get back to my class. Maybe I'll see you kids at Golden Gate!" said Master Lassater.

"He seems pretty nice," said Sara once he'd gone back in the dojo.

"How does he get to Golden Gate?" asked Katana. "Don't all the regional tournaments happen at the same time?"

"Nah, they stagger them, I think, so that they have enough judges to go around to all of them," explained Sara.

"He does look kinda familiar," said Chris. "I think we mighta seen him at nationals last year."

KATANA WENT to the beach again the following morning—this time dressed in sweat pants and a hoodie—and took Sara along with her. Katana was very excited to practice with a set of chains for the first time all summer.

"I can't believe I let you drag me out of bed at this hour," Sara complained.

"You were awake anyway," said Katana, rolling her eyes.

Katana started teaching Sara the long form, then went through the whole thing on her own. She was warm enough by the end that she didn't need the hoodie anymore.

After that she practiced her whip chain set for a while. She couldn't do the full body jumps, as the bottom chain got stuck in the sand, but she was able to do everything else.

She started with flowers. She did them standing still, whipping the chains as fast as she could. She also did them walking along the beach, turning in circles as she went. Next she did neck wraps—which entailed letting one chain wrap around her neck as the other circled behind her, then whipping her head around to throw the chain off her neck in the other direction. She also did leg wraps—they were similar to neck wraps, but less scary as the chain didn't have to pass so close to her face.

She was also able to do a series of butterfly kicks around in a circle, letting one chain pass underneath her on each kick as the other one circled above. That was everything she'd learned from

Dana and Master Hua the previous year. She was eager to get back to the Hall and start working with Dana on some harder moves.

"I think your strength training is paying off," said Sara. "It definitely looks like you're spinning them a lot faster."

The kids enjoyed the rest of the week at the beach, and Sara went to work out with Katana every morning at sunrise. They couldn't get Chris to join them, however. He wanted nothing to do with being up that early during vacation. At the end of the week they packed up the Boyd's Jeep and headed back to Croton.

CHAPTER 3
DOC

Katana woke up Monday morning and went out in her backyard to practice. She felt like this was a poor substitute for doing tai chi on the beach.

She went through the long form, holding a ball of energy between her hands the entire time, then worked more on her whip chain set. She tried doing the full body jumps again, but this didn't work any better on grass than it had on the beach.

After that, she jumped on the balls of her feet a thousand times and did pushups from a handstand. She tried this again without anything supporting her feet, but didn't quite have the balance to pull it off. So she did them against the back of the house instead, with her feet touching the wall.

She stretched when she was done with the workout. She finished by holding a front split on each leg for a full minute, then a straddle split.

She was soaked with sweat by the time she got inside, and jumped in the shower before doing anything else. Once she'd dried her hair (which was much easier, she realized, since her hair-cut) and dressed, she sat down at the computer in the living room. She was careful not to disturb Sara, who was still asleep in the foldout bed.

Her aunt emerged from her room, and said, "Goo... Goo... Good morning, Kat," through a big yawn.

"Morning, Leanna."

"I still can't get used to you being up before me!" said Leanna as she went into the kitchen to put on the coffee. "Quite the change from last summer."

Katana resumed her online search. As usual, she couldn't find a single reference to Jaaku—other than the Japanese word. She did find some more information about dim mak this time, though.

She found one site about a tenth degree "grandmaster" who'd learned martial arts from a French legionnaire. "What on earth is a legionnaire?" Katana asked out loud.

"What, Katana?" asked her aunt as she ran around getting ready for work.

"Oh, nothing," said Katana. "I was talking to myself."

"Well I'm going... I'll be picking you kids up at karate tonight." She came over and gave Katana a kiss before heading out the door.

Katana went back to the website, and read out loud. "A member of an elite unit in the French military..." She realized that

32

the person claimed to have learned his entire system of martial arts in the three weeks he'd visited France.

She scrolled as quickly as she could past a picture of the man with his shirt off—bad call in Katana's opinion, as he was very hairy and had a big beer belly. Then she read that he had awarded himself his tenth degree for creating a new kata. The only trouble was, she thought, that he'd only been a second degree before that. By this time she was feeling extremely skeptical, and when she read that he'd learned dim mak in a dream, she stopped reading.

She found another site about a man who claimed to be the youngest tenth degree in history. He had earned the promotion at the age of thirty-four.

"Thirty-four?" she said. "Nash is in his seventies and he's a fifth degree..."

She read more and discovered that this individual had somehow managed to get himself promoted every six to eight months, ultimately going from first degree to tenth degree black belt in only five years. She kept looking and finally found the part about dim mak. The man claimed to have learned it in a book.

"Oh, I'm sure you can go to your local bookstore and find that..." said Katana, quite frustrated now. She decided to give up her search for the day. Sara woke up as she was shutting down the computer.

"Hey," said Sara, as she sat up and stretched. "How's the research going?"

Katana sat down on the end of the bed. "Just great. I found one guy who says he learned dim mak in a dream." Sara snorted at this, and Katana continued. "I found another guy who says he learned it in a book."

"Bought that at the local Barnes & Noble, did he?" asked Sara sarcastically.

Sara got up and showered, and the girls sat down at the kitchen table for breakfast.

"Oh, I got this letter from Lincoln yesterday," said Katana, pulling the paper out of the envelope. "It says we have to decide what math class we're doing this year."

"What are the choices?" asked Sara, but there was a knock at the door before Katana could reply.

Katana ran downstairs and returned with Chris. "What are you doing up this early?" asked Sara.

"My dad made me get up," said Chris grumpily. "He says I'm sleeping too much."

"Did you get one of these?" asked Katana, holding up the paper.

"Oh, yeah," said Chris. "Something about what math class we're doing this year."

"Well, it says we can either do algebra two with trigonometry, or we can do regular algebra two," Katana read from the sheet.

"What difference does it make?" asked Chris.

"I think we have to do it with trig if we want to do calculus junior year," said Sara. "Otherwise we do pre-calc junior year, and don't do calculus until senior year."

"Calcu-what?" asked Chris, totally dumbfounded.

"Calculus," said Sara. "Isaac Newton made it up. He was doing physics, and figuring out gravity and stuff, but the math they had back then wasn't good enough. So he had to take a break from that and invent calculus. Then he was able to go back and finish his work on physics."

"He invented... *a new kind of math*?" asked Chris, clearly impressed. "Who the hell *does* that?!"

"We should definitely do the one with the trig," said Sara. Katana shrugged and said, "Okay."

"Why do I get the feeling I'm not going to do so well in math this year..." said Chris.

The girls told Chris about the websites Katana had found while they finished their breakfast. Then the three of them went to Turtle Beach to hang out until it was time to go to Sensei Mike's dojo. The dojo was in the center of Croton, about a twenty-minute walk from the beach.

"Hey guys," said Mike with a big smile as they walked in. "How was Maine?"

"It was awesome," said Katana. "I worked out every day on the beach..."

"And dragged me with you!" said Sara accusingly.

"Not a chance!" said Chris when Mike looked at him. "They were up at the crack of dawn! Of course I didn't go with them—I know that's what you were going to ask!"

Mike laughed at him. "Yeah, your mom was telling me the other week how you're sleeping your summer away."

"That's what summer's for!" said Chris

The kids got changed and went into the dojo—they were wearing their karate pants and T-shirts. While they stretched, they told Mike about their week in Maine.

"Hmm... Griffin Lassater, huh?" he said when they were done. "He's one of the people in charge of setting up all the big tournaments."

"Yeah, he said he was on the judges committee," said Sara.

"He grew up in Croton," said Mike.

"Really?" said Katana and Chris at the same time.

"Yeah—I used to hang out with his nephew when I was in high school. He told me all about him."

They finished stretching and Mike ran them through their kata. They knew a total of fourteen forms now, the last two of which they needed to go for their third degree black belts. Mike made minor corrections to some of the moves, but said, "Those are really sharp," when they were done. "You three are definitely well on your way to third degree, at least as far as your kata are concerned."

They did their combinations next, which were prearranged sets of moves, including strikes, kicks and various kinds of take-downs, that were used to defend against all kinds of attacks. Finally they did attack drills, wherein they had to defend freestyle against a series of attacks, without knowing in advance whether the other person would try to punch, kick, grab or tackle them.

"Where are you three with the chen do now?" asked Mike when they had finished. "It seems like every time I talk to Osaka, one of you has another one!"

"We can all deflect intent and project our chi," said Chris, "and Katana can levitate."

"Wow, Kat, so you're like the chen do master, aren't you?" said Mike.

"Yeah," said Katana, rolling her eyes, "something like that."

"Have you gotten any of them yet?" asked Sara.

"Nah," said Sensei Mike, "but certainly not from lack of trying. I've been working on that standing chi kung exercise, but I don't seem to be getting anywhere."

"Let me see you do it," said Katana. "I might be able to help."

Sensei Mike stood with his weight on one foot, the ball of his other foot touching the mat in front of him. He formed a circle with his arms, one hand at shoulder level, the other by his waist.

"First, relax your shoulders more," said Katana. "Good, now turn your right foot out a little more so it's at the same angle as your knee."

Sensei Mike did what she said. Katana stepped back and looked up and down at his posture. "Tuck in your tailbone a little more," she suggested.

"Do what?"

"You're sticking your butt out!" she said. "You have to rotate your pelvis under, like this," she said, showing him the correct posture.

"Oh, I see what you're doing." He held the position this way for a few moments, but nothing happened.

"Hmm," said Katana. "Try this—pretend you're standing on the beach, and torque your right foot a little, like you're trying to dig it into the sand."

"Okay..." said Mike, starting to sweat now.

"Good," said Katana, "but keep your shoulders relaxed still..."

And then it happened. A faint ball of energy formed between Sensei Mike's hands.

"Whoa!" he said. "That's it—I'm finally getting it!"

"Yes!" said Katana. "Now try to feel the energy flowing up from your feet, and down your arms into the ball."

He was able to hold the ball for a minute, and it grew a little stronger, but then he lost it.

"What happened?" asked Katana when he got out of the stance, shaking his right leg.

"I got a cramp!" he complained. "So who taught you all that posture stuff? That made a huge difference."

"No one really taught me," Katana replied with a shrug. "I just kinda figured it out. When I was doing tai chi on the beach last week, it felt different. I had to change my stance and dig my feet into the sand to keep my balance. I could feel it making my energy flow stronger."

"Wow," said Mike.

He resumed the same stance, this time on his left leg, and held his hands out to form a circle. This time he was able to create the ball of energy on his own.

"Chris," said Katana, "go stand over there. I'm gonna have him try to throw it at you."

Chris walked in front of Sensei Mike. Katana said, "Now take a step toward Chris and throw your hands forward."

Sensei Mike tried it, but the energy faded away as soon as he moved. Katana spent the next several minutes trying to help him get it, but every time Sensei Mike took a step or moved his arms, he lost the fireball.

"Well, that's still helpful—I was never able to form the ball before," said Sensei Mike. "Osaka tried to teach me when he was here a couple of weeks ago, but I wasn't getting anywhere."

"How much do you train with Osaka now?" asked Chris.

"Not very often, unfortunately," said Sensei Mike. "This was the first time he was able to get out here since last summer."

"That must be hard," said Sara. "How do you keep learning?"

"Well, earning mastery is more a matter of practicing than it is learning anything new," he explained. "You have all the material and all the concepts when you get your fourth degree, but to become a master, you have to get it in your bones. Osaka says that your every movement has to be an expression of the art."

"Doesn't that get boring, though?" asked Chris. "Practicing the same stuff over and over again without learning anything new?"

"Sometimes," Mike replied. "But I've been doing some cross training to mix things up a little. I met this guy down in Burlington who does Brazilian jiu jitsu, so I've been working out with him once in a while."

"*Brazilian* jiu jitsu?" asked Katana. "I thought jiu jitsu came from Japan."

"It does, but Brazil has its own separate style. I don't know the history of it, but they do mostly ground grappling and stuff. I guess traditional Japanese jiu jitsu does a lot of joint locks and throws, kind of like aikido. They work primarily on takedowns to get your opponent to the floor. But the Brazilian stuff really starts once you're on the ground," explained Sensei Mike.

"But if you already got the guy down, what else do you need to do?" asked Chris.

"Well, if you knocked him down and you're still standing, you're set," said Mike. "But what if you end up on the ground with him? None of the stuff we do on our feet works in that situation. Most of what they do involves gaining a superior position, so you can control your opponent. Then you can choke him out or get him in an armbar or something."

"You actually choke each other out?" asked Sara. "Like to the point of unconsciousness?"

"No," said Sensei Mike. "When they get you and you know you can't get out, you submit. You tap them or tap the ground to let them know that you give up. Well, in a real fight you'd hold the choke until they passed out. The guy could attack you again if you let him out of it!"

"Can you show us some of this stuff?" asked Chris.

"Yeah, definitely," said Mike. "Here, lie down on the mat."

"Okay..." said Chris uncertainly.

"No, on your back," said Mike—Chris was lying flat on his stomach.

"Oh," said Chris, turning over.

Mike got down on his knees and straddled him. "The most common position is the mount. When someone's on the ground, if you get on top of them like this, there's a whole lot you can do."

Mike dropped to his elbows. He wedged his hands under Chris's neck, and brought his head down next to his, almost like he was giving him a hug. "Try to get out of this," he said.

"Um... yeah, right." Chris struggled to get out from underneath. Katana thought he had no chance, until finally he managed to squirm over onto his stomach.

"Don't do that," said Mike. "You never want to turn your back to the opponent."

"Why not?" asked Chris. His voice was muffled, as he was talking into the floor.

Mike snaked one arm around Chris's throat, and grabbed his other arm, which was against the back of Chris's neck. "That's why," he said, as he applied the chokehold and Chris made a gurgling sound.

"This is when you tap," said Mike.

Chris made another gurgling sound and tapped the mat frantically with one hand. Sensei Mike let him out of the hold, and got back to his feet. Chris rolled onto his back—his face was red and he was drenched in sweat.

"You don't even look tired," Katana said to Mike.

"I'm not—I wasn't really doing anything. I was just lying there and letting him waste his energy," said Sensei Mike. "That's what a lot of this stuff comes down to—wearing down your opponent."

"Is there a way out of the mount?" asked Chris.

"Yeah, lots of ways. Here, watch," he said, and lay down on the mat. "Sara, come here and straddle me."

"Um... What?" asked Sara, suddenly turning red.

"Get on top of me, on your knees," said Sensei Mike. Sara did this, and Katana heard her mutter, "This isn't awkward at all..."

"Now put your hands on my throat like you're trying to choke me," said Mike. He grabbed her arm with one hand, her head with his other hand, and pushed over with one leg. This caused Sara to roll over to one side and land on her back, Sensei Mike on top of her. Sara squealed.

"That's the most basic way to get out of it," he explained as he got back to his feet again. "It almost never works against someone who's good at grappling, though, because there are a lot of ways to counter it. But it'll help you understand how to move from one position to the next."

For the next twenty minutes Mike helped them with this move. Katana discovered that there were several variations of the technique. She started to get the feeling that, much like sparring or pushing hands, grappling was almost like a chess match. There were countermoves to every hold, and counters to those as well.

"Can you teach us that choke you did on me?" asked Chris once they had achieved some proficiency at escaping the mount.

"Sure," said Mike. He demonstrated on Chris, and Katana and Sara tried it on each other. Katana had always assumed that choking someone out entailed blocking the air passage. But Sensei Mike explained that it was actually a matter of applying pressure to the neck at just the right point to block the blood flow along the arteries to the brain.

When Sara did it on her, Katana almost felt like her head was going to explode. She understood immediately how this could be quite effective in making someone submit.

"Does Brazilian jiu jitsu have a chen do?" Chris asked thoughtfully.

"Yeah, they learn how to fade," said Mike.

"But fading is the chen do of aikido," Sara replied.

"I asked Osaka about this," said Mike. "Apparently a lot of different arts have the same chen do. I guess that fading is the chen do for aikido and jiu jitsu, and judo, and he mentioned some others, too, that I'd never heard of before."

"Is there a temple or something like the Hall of the Dragon in Brazil?" asked Katana.

"There is," said Sensei Mike. "It's called the Hall of the Tiger. It's in Rio de Janeiro—or near there, anyway. Osaka said it's only been around for like twenty years or so. It's the newest temple in the Shaolin network."

"Did your friend train there? The guy from Burlington?" asked Chris.

"Oh, no, he trained in Brazil, but not at the temple. He doesn't do any of the chen do or anything. But he's been competing a lot since he came to the U.S. He does pretty well, apparently."

"They don't do jiu jitsu at the tournaments we go to," Sara observed.

"No, the grappling tournaments are a whole separate thing," said Mike. "Listen, I'm gonna have to wrap this up for today. Billy's coming in for a private lesson in a few minutes. Some kid from school has been picking on him, so we're going to work on some anti-bullying stuff."

"Aw, poor Billy," said Katana.

"Are you guys gonna be around for classes tonight?"

"Yeah," said Chris. "We're here all night."

"Great, if I give you some cash, can you go get me a grinder at Anthony's?"

The kids went across the street to Anthony's, which was, in Katana's opinion, the best pizza place in Croton. They sat down and ordered a pizza for lunch. When they were done, they got the grinder for Sensei Mike and went back to the dojo.

Billy's mom was sitting in the lobby when they walked in. Billy was in the dojo for his lesson.

"Hi, Mrs. Webster," said Katana.

"Oh, hi, Katana!" she answered. "Hi, Chris."

Katana introduced her to Sara and asked, "What's been going on? Sensei Mike said some kid's been picking on Billy?"

"Yes," said Mrs. Webster with a frown. "He's older than Billy, and he's a lot bigger. He goes to some other karate place somewhere. But he found out that Billy does karate, and he tried to pick a fight with him at the bus stop every morning for the last several weeks of the school year."

"Was the kid hitting him or anything?" asked Chris.

"He wasn't at first, he was just teasing him. Billy tried to ignore it, but this kid wouldn't leave him alone. It was to the point where he'd push Billy and tell him if he really knew karate, he'd defend himself. The last week of school, he grabbed Billy around the neck and threw him on the ground.

"I talked to the school about it, but they wouldn't do anything. And Sensei Mike called the boy's instructor, but he didn't seem to care. And now Billy's going to camp next week, and we found out this kid is going to the same camp."

"Why didn't Billy do something when the kid grabbed him?" asked Katana. "He definitely knows how to get out of that."

"I know," said Mrs. Webster with a sigh. "He's so good-natured, he wouldn't hurt a fly." Chris looked at Katana. She knew Chris was thinking about the previous summer when Billy had bit him. "We always tell him he's not allowed to use his karate on anyone unless they're hurting him, and he gets that. But he gets it too well, I'm afraid. He won't use karate even when someone *is* hurting him! That's why Sensei Mike suggested we come in for a few privates. He's working with him on being more assertive. I think if Billy would stand up to this kid, he might think twice before he picks on him again."

Sensei Mike finished up with Billy, and they both came out of the dojo.

"Sensei Katana!" said Billy, running over to give her a hug. Sara raised her eyebrows at Katana and smiled.

"Hey, Billy!" said Katana.

"He talks about you *all* the time," said Mrs. Webster. "I think he has a crush on you," she added in a whisper.

Katana was touched and a little embarrassed by this, but was immediately distracted when Billy asked, "Katana, do you want a kitten?"

"Um... What?"

"Oh, our cat had kittens, six or seven weeks ago," said Mrs. Webster. "Billy has been working very diligently to give them away—we don't need any more animals in the house right now. But we've only found two takers so far."

"Please, Katana, please, please, please..." said Billy, jumping up and down.

"Um..." said Katana, trying to find the heart to turn him down. She knew her aunt wouldn't approve. Leanna would be stuck with the responsibility since Katana would be away at the Hall of the Dragon most of the year.

"Aw, you should take one, Kat," said Sara. "It would be so cool if we had a cat in our room this year."

"We're allowed to have pets at the Hall?" asked Chris, sounding surprised.

"We can't have dogs," said Sara. "But cats are allowed, or fish. This girl had a big ragdoll cat my first year there. He was kind of like the hall mascot. It would be awesome to have a cat on the hall again."

"Well, all right then," said Katana, still not certain this was a good idea. "I'll take one, Billy."

"YAY!" said Billy. "Chris do you want a kitten?"

"No, not me!" said Chris. "My mom's allergic to cats. She'd kill me if I brought one home!"

Billy wanted to go get one of the kittens right then and there, but Mrs. Webster talked to Katana and they agreed that she would come back after the teens class that night instead.

"So where does this kid train who's picking on Billy?" asked Chris, once Mrs. Webster had managed to get Billy out the door.

"Milton Karate Academy," said Mike with a scowl. "Jeff Conroy is the head instructor. He's pretty active on the tournament circuit. Big into sparring. He trains his kids to be super aggressive."

"And you tried to talk to him about the kid who's bothering Billy?" asked Katana.

"*Tried* being the key word," said Mike. "I gave him a call, but he didn't care. He said the kids should settle it themselves."

"Me and Katana should go take care of the kid," said Chris. "Nobody messes with our students and gets away with it!" Katana thought Chris looked ridiculous, punching one hand with his fist.

"Yeah, Chris, that's a great idea," said Sara sarcastically. "Go beat up some eight-year-old. That really proves how tough you are."

Katana, Chris and Sara helped Sensei Mike with the kids class, then participated in the teens class after that. Katana was exhausted by the time they were done, as this was her third workout of the day.

Mrs. Webster came back at the end of class with Billy and one small, orange tabby kitten in a cat carrier.

"His name is Doc!" said Billy excitedly.

"Doc? How'd you get that name?" asked Chris.

"There were seven kittens in the litter," explained Mrs. Webster. "So Billy decided they should be named after the Seven Dwarves. This one seemed like the leader, so Billy named him Doc."

"Chris, are you *sure* you don't want one?" asked Sara. "Because Sleepy would be *perfect* for you!"

"Oh, ha-ha," said Chris sarcastically.

"We already gave Sleepy away. Sorry, Chris," said Mrs. Webster, patting Chris on the shoulder.

The kids went outside and got in Leanna's car. "Katana, what is that?"

"It's Doc!" said Katana brightly, knowing that her aunt wasn't going to be happy about this.

"And who's going to take care of Doc?"

"I am!" said Katana.

"Katana, this is a big responsibility. I wish you had asked me first. Once you go back to school..."

"I can take him with me!" said Katana.

"We're allowed to have pets there," Sara contributed.

"Well... all right," said Leanna with a sigh as she pulled out of the parking lot. "But next time please ask me first before you come home with any more animals."

They stopped at the store to get cat food, a litter box and some cat toys before they dropped Chris off at his house. When they got back to Katana's house, the girls spent the rest of the night playing with Doc. And when Katana finally went to bed that night, the kitten curled up next to her pillow, lulling her to sleep with his purr.

CHAPTER 4

JAPAN

Sara spent the rest of the week with Katana and Chris. On Saturday, Mrs. Boyd drove her to the airport; Katana and Chris went along for the ride. "I'll see you guys in a few weeks," Sara said as she went to board her plane back to Japan.

Katana worked out in her backyard at the crack of dawn every day for the rest of the summer. She kept practicing the long form and as much of the double whip chain set as she could manage in the grass. She continued with the conditioning exercises as well, and after a few more weeks could do pushups in a handstand without anything to stabilize her.

She felt like the pushups were definitely helping her spin the chains faster. And the jumping exercise seemed to be helping her get higher on her tricks as well. She had started working on all the various tricks in her repertoire, including back handsprings, aerials and front flips. But her favorite tricks were the ones based on the backflip. She had a very high flash kick—which was like a backflip except she kept her legs straight, and kicked one leg over before the other. And her favorite trick of all was the gainer flash. That was a flash kick where she walked forward to launch it, instead of going from a round-off.

She also tried to think of a way to add more tricks into the whip chain set, but nothing came to mind. Like Dana, she always started the form with an aerial or a flash kick. But once the chains were moving, she didn't know how she could possibly add anything else.

Much to Chris's dissatisfaction, Katana also spent a large amount of time every day on the internet, trying to find out more about Jaaku and dim mak. Katana didn't understand why it upset him so much. Sara hadn't had a problem with it. But Chris insisted it wasn't healthy for her to be "obsessing" about it as much as she was.

Katana continued to feel that he didn't understand. *His* parents were still alive. He didn't have to wonder what his life might be like if a power mad monster hadn't murdered them. Katana had spent much of the first couple of weeks of their summer vacation talking to her aunt about her mom and dad. Katana had always been curious about them when she was growing up—she'd always wished she could have known them. But she'd never dwelled on her loss. She'd had Leanna and Mr. and Mrs. Boyd and even Osaka around to look after her—she often felt as if she had *extra* parents. But since finding out that her mom and dad had been murdered instead of having simply been victims of a tragic accident, her entire perspective had changed. Instead of merely being curious about the parents she'd never known, she'd started to feel like someone had taken something vital away from her, and she wanted desperately to take it back, although she knew that was impossible. She even began having nightmares about the night they'd died, imagining what it would have been like for them to be in that car as it flew over the cliff. Of course, Katana hadn't been there, and wouldn't have remembered it if she had—she was only five months old at the time. But her subconscious brain had no problem supplying the details for this terrible vision.

But it wasn't just her parents. Jaaku had killed Master Hua. And from what Katana had heard, Jaaku had killed countless others in his insane quest to prolong his own horrible life. He had been doing this for nearly three hundred years.

Katana knew, somehow, that one day it would be up to her to put a stop to it all. She knew that she was nowhere near powerful enough to confront Jaaku now, but one day, she would be. This was almost all she thought about as she practiced tai chi every morning. She focused with her entire being on increasing the flow of her chi. She knew that this was the path to greater power. This, ultimately, would be the path to defeating the enemy.

By the time Katana and Chris packed for their trip to Japan, however, Katana had given up all hope of finding anything useful or accurate about Jaaku or dim mak on the internet. She decided she would wait until they returned to the Hall of the Dragon. She would talk to Sam—Katana was sure Sam knew more about Jaaku that she hadn't told the kids before. And Katana also reminded herself that Sara's dad knew at least some things about the Arashi.

When the day of their journey arrived, Mrs. Boyd brought the kids to the airport in Boston. They had to take a plane to Houston, Texas, then switch planes to Tokyo, where Sara and her dad met up with them.

"Katana, Chris!" yelled Sara as they left the gate. She came running over and grabbed them both in a hug. "I'm so psyched you're here!"

"Hi, kids," said Mr. Brown, extending his hand to each of them in turn. "I'm Mitch Brown, Sara's dad. It's nice to finally meet both of you. Sara talks about you all the time."

Katana thought she could see Mr. Brown's face in Sara's as she looked at the two of them standing next to each other. He was much taller than Sara, and Katana thought he looked rather beefy, like he'd probably been a weight lifter at some point in his life.

Mr. Brown guided them through the terminal to a train station. "We'll take the local to the bullet train, and that'll take us to Kumamoto City," he explained.

The bullet train was unlike anything Katana had seen before. "How fast are we going?" she asked a few minutes after they left the station.

"Not that fast here," said Mr. Brown. "Once we clear the city though we'll build up to about 180 miles per hour." Katana was amazed a train could move that fast.

Chris had passed out the moment they sat down, but Katana didn't feel like sleeping. She was looking out at the passing scenery, chatting with Sara about the sightseeing they planned to do in the coming days.

Eventually, though, Sara drifted off to sleep as well.

"Train rides and long car rides always put her to sleep," said Mr. Brown. "I'm surprised you're still awake—it's almost two in the morning by your body clock!"

"I don't know," said Katana with a shrug. "I don't feel sleepy yet."

"Katana..." said Mr. Brown hesitantly, "I never had an opportunity to thank you for what you did for Sara earlier this year..."

"What did I do?" asked Katana, feeling confused.

"Well, with Sara's eating disorder, if you hadn't talked to Mrs. Boyd..." said Mr. Brown. Tears welled up in his eyes. "It's just good to know that she has someone to look out for her."

"It was nothing, Mr. Brown," said Katana, somewhat embarrassed. "Mrs. Boyd was the one who did everything. She set up the counseling sessions..."

"Yes, but you are the one who went to Mrs. Boyd in the first place. Because of you, Sara got the help she needed. And Sara was extremely grateful that you went with her to the counseling sessions at Lincoln. She was terrified to talk to the counselor alone.

"You and Chris are the closest friends she's ever had. I changed assignments pretty frequently when Sara was growing up, so we never stayed in one place very long. I don't think Sara ever had a chance to feel grounded anywhere. I wonder sometimes if that's part of what led to her problem in the first place..." Mr. Brown paused to blow his nose in his handkerchief.

"I feel like it might have been my fault," he continued. "Maybe if I hadn't changed assignments so many times, if we had stayed in one place, she would have had roots. Maybe then she wouldn't have grown up feeling so insecure about herself.

"It's important to have friends, Katana," he said, "people you can trust, and people you can turn to when you're in trouble. Patty and I are very grateful that Sara has someone like you in her life finally. And if there's ever anything we can do for you, to repay the kindness you've shown our daughter, just say the word."

Katana felt overwhelmed by this speech. She was at a loss for words, and felt herself tearing up now as well. "Thanks, Mr. Brown," was all she could manage at that moment.

The train arrived in Kumamoto City several hours later. A car was waiting for them. Katana was famished by the time they arrived at the Brown residence thirty minutes later. She was grateful that Mrs. Brown had dinner ready for them.

Mrs. Brown was only a few inches taller than Sara. She had long, curly brown hair that went past her shoulders. "Katana!" she said as they walked into the dining room, and pulled her into a big hug. "It's so good to meet you. I cannot tell you how grateful Mitch and I are for everything you've done for Sara..."

"Mother!" said Sara, looking utterly distressed. "You're embarrassing me!"

"Tough," said Mrs. Brown. She walked over to Chris. "Hi, Chris, I'm Patty Brown."

"Just shake his hand, Mom; you'll embarrass him if you give him a hug..." said Sara, but it was too late. Katana could see Chris go red when Mrs. Brown pulled him into a hug, too.

Mrs. Brown had prepared a variety of traditional Japanese dishes, including different kinds of fish and a lot of rice. "Sara told me you're not crazy about sushi, Chris, so I decided to stick to things that were cooked."

"That's okay," said Chris. "I eat sushi now—hanging around these two all the time, I didn't have much choice!"

Chris went straight to bed after dinner, but as Katana still wasn't sleepy, she stayed up talking with Sara and her dad.

"I don't know how you haven't passed out yet," said Sara. "The jet lag kills me every time I come home."

"It's probably all the tai chi," said Mr. Brown. "Jordan never has a problem when he's here, either."

"Do you still do tai chi, Mr. Brown?" asked Katana. Sara told her once that he'd practiced tai chi with Nash when Nash lived in Japan.

"After a fashion," said Mr. Brown. "I muddle my way through the form every morning, but I haven't had any formal training in many years. Not since Master Nash left Japan."

"You used to do kempo, too—didn't you?" asked Sara.

"Yes, but not since I was very young," said Mr. Brown. "My dad was in the military, stationed in Okinawa the whole time I was growing up. Jordan used to run a dojo there. He taught a lot of kids with military parents back then. I started doing kempo with him when I was eight."

"I always forget that Nash knows kempo, too," said Katana. "I just think of him as the tai chi master."

"Well, he started with tai chi," said Mr. Brown. "He grew up in New York, right in the city. He trained with a master in Chinatown when he was very young—Master Li—he was the last headmaster at the Hall of the Dragon.

"Jordan's family moved to Hawaii after that—he started kempo there. Eventually he went to the Shaolin Temple, and that's where he tested for master in tai chi.

"Once he left Shaolin, he came to Japan. He taught in Okinawa for many years—that's when I started training with him. He used to train at Shaka-In as well, and I think that's where he made master in kempo. That was back before Headmaster Miyagi passed away."

"That's where Terry-san is from, isn't it—Shaka-In?" asked Katana.

"Yes, that's right," said Mr. Brown. "Oh, Tanaka was not happy when Terry-san left to work for Nash. You kids will meet Tanaka later this week—we're going to visit the temple on Friday. Master Tanaka was very interested in meeting you, Katana, when he found out you were coming to Japan."

"Really?" asked Katana, surprised that anyone from the other temples would have any interest in her.

"Well, it's not every day that a student your age learns *three* of the chen do," said Mr. Brown. "You've earned yourself a reputation in certain circles."

This news made her uncomfortable—she didn't like the idea of random people wanting to meet her for this reason.

"Well, I think I'm going to head to bed," said Mr. Brown. "You kids should come practice tai chi with me in the morning. Maybe you can help an old man brush up on his moves a little."

"Um, no!" said Sara, looking at her father askance. "I'm not getting up that early—you're up at dawn every day."

"I think I'll join you," said Katana. "Something tells me I'll be awake anyway."

Sure enough, Katana awoke before dawn the next morning. She walked down the hall to use the bathroom and saw that the light was on in Chris's room. She opened the door and poked her head in.

"What are you doing awake this early?" she asked.

Chris was lying in bed, playing video games on his laptop. "I've been up for over an hour already," he said grumpily.

"I guess jet lag is the only way you'll ever see this hour during vacation," said Katana. Chris glared at her. "I'm gonna go do tai chi with Sara's dad, you wanna come?"

"Might as well," said Chris with a sigh.

The two of them went downstairs to the kitchen, where they found Mr. Brown. They followed him outside. There was a small wooden outbuilding in the back of the yard, near the woods. Katana realized it was a dojo, complete with tatami mats. It wasn't very big, but there was enough room for the three of them to practice tai chi.

Katana went through the form once with Mr. Brown. Chris watched—he didn't know the long form yet. Then Katana helped Mr. Brown make some corrections to his stances. She made some of the same adjustments to his posture that she'd shown Sensei Mike.

"That does feel stronger," said Mr. Brown. "Did Jordan teach you all of this?"

"No," said Katana. She explained that she'd learned it doing her form on the beach.

"Well, Jordan told me you were a natural born master—now I know what he means," said Mr. Brown.

They practiced for a while longer, and Katana taught Chris the beginning of the long form. After that, they went back up to the house. Sara and her mom were up. Mrs. Brown was busy making breakfast.

"Patty's going to take you kids sightseeing today," said Mr. Brown as they sat down at the table. "After that you'll be going with Sara to her karate class tonight. Her sensei tells me he has something special planned for you, Katana."

"For *me*?" she said. "Why—what is he going to do?"

"I don't actually know," he replied. "But he heard about your success on the American circuit. He's excited to have you in his class."

"What success? I was disqualified at nationals..."

"For getting levitation," Mr. Brown said with a grin. "A note-worthy disqualification, I'd say. And you were undefeated in the *boys' division* before that. Like I said, you've acquired something of a reputation."

"Great," said Katana, feeling anxious now. "But I won't understand a word he says; the class is taught in Japanese, isn't it?"

"Don't worry," said Sara. "It's like Sam's class... only a little more formal. You'll be able to follow along, no problem."

Mrs. Brown acted as tour guide, showing the kids around Kumamoto City. They visited Kumamoto castle, which reminded Katana of a cross between the Hall of the Dragon's main building and a traditional, European castle. They also went to Suizenji Park, a formal Japanese garden that reminded Katana of a Zen rock garden, only with actual trees and bushes and grass instead of boulders and gravel. At the end of the day, they went back to Sara's house, and grabbed a quick bite to eat before changing into their karate uniforms.

Mrs. Brown drove them to Sara's karate school. Katana was stunned as they walked inside. It looked almost identical to Sensei Mike's dojo back in Vermont, right down to the tatami mats, the scrolls on the walls and even the little bamboo plant on the altar at the front of the dojo.

But the atmosphere was totally different—Sara was right, this was much more formal. Sara had instructed Katana and Chris on the drive over that they weren't allowed to talk, and that they should follow her lead.

So when Sara knelt down upon entering the dojo, Katana and Chris copied her every move. Sara got down on her knees and placed both hands on the mat in front of her, forming a triangle with her thumbs and index fingers. She bowed down and touched her head to her hands. Katana and Chris imitated her the best they could.

They stood up and walked to one side of the room. They knelt down along the wall with a dozen other students waiting for class to start. Katana noticed one boy across the room from her who was very tall, and built like Sensei Mike. She thought to herself that he'd be the perfect person to use her gainer flash against in a sparring match.

After a few minutes, a tall Japanese man with a shaved head and dark mustache approached the entrance to the dojo. A shorter Japanese woman accompanied him. She wore glasses and had her hair pulled back in a ponytail. They both wore traditional karate uniform tops and what looked to Katana like long, black skirts. They knelt down and bowed upon entering the dojo, exactly as Sara had done.

They walked to the front of the room and the man shouted one word in Japanese. The whole class lined up immediately in two lines.

The first part of class was very similar to what Katana was used to back home in Vermont, and at the Hall. The woman led the class through warm-up exercises and stretches. But the class was conducted in total silence. This made Katana feel a little awkward; Sensei Mike, Sam and Master Osaka had always allowed quiet conversation.

The male instructor took over the class again once they were done with their stretches. He took them through basics. These, too, were nearly identical to what Katana had done all her life. They got into horse-riding stances and threw a variety of punches and kicks at the instructor's command. Katana couldn't under-stand the names of the strikes he called out, but she was able to follow along, just as Sara had said.

They went through kata next—this was a little difficult, as

they didn't seem to be going in any particular order. Katana never knew which form they were doing until the students around her did the first couple of moves.

After they'd completed several kata, the instructor had them sit along the walls again. He called them up individually. When it was Katana's turn, she was worried that she'd have no idea what he was asking her to do. But the instructor was clearly aware of the language barrier. He demonstrated the first few moves of the kata he wanted Katana to perform.

It was Kata Fourteen, her newest form, and one of two she would need one day to test for her third degree. Once Katana had completed the kata, the instructor had her repeat a section from the middle. He made a small correction to one of the stances. Then he motioned for her to have a seat again.

Sara gave her a thumbs-up as Katana sat down next to her.

Once everyone had had a turn, the instructor began talking to the class in Japanese. Katana didn't know what he was saying, but started to worry when she distinctly heard her name. Then the instructor held his hand out toward her and smiled. Sara gasped.

Katana looked at her in alarm—she had no idea what was going on. But Sara, who also looked worried now, simply pointed, indicating that Katana should get up and walk to the middle of the dojo. Katana saw the large boy she'd spotted at the beginning of class getting up as well. She thought she might know what was happening after all.

The instructor said something to them in Japanese. He motioned for her to follow the boy to one corner of the room to put on a set of sparring gear.

Yes, Katana knew exactly what was coming.

Sara joined her with the pretense of helping her with her gear. But she whispered in Katana's ear, "Be careful—that boy's the Japanese national sparring champion!"

Sara ran back to retake her seat. Katana gave the boy a side-long glance; her heart jumped into her throat.

The two of them finished putting on their gear and returned to the center of the room. The instructor bowed; Katana and the boy bowed to each other.

Katana didn't know if the rules were the same as what she was used to back home, but had to assume that they were. One point for a punch, two points for a kick and two points for a takedown. The instructor shouted a command and the match began.

Katana circled around for a moment, waiting to see what the boy would do. She didn't have to wait long. He moved in with a series of kicks to her head. Katana dodged the first of these, then dropped down and swept out his other leg. The boy fell to the mat.

The instructor kiaied. They both got up and squared off again. The instructor said something in Japanese and pointed two fingers at Katana.

The match began again, and the boy was a little more cautious this time. Katana moved in with her own series of kicks, but the boy dodged these with ease. Then he caught her in the head with a roundhouse kick. It was so strong that it knocked her right on her butt. She hadn't seen it coming.

She got back to her feet, and the instructor held out two fingers toward the boy.

The match resumed. They traded a few kicks. Katana tried to keep her distance so she wouldn't be caught off guard so badly again. Finally the boy moved in with a side kick. Katana figured he was going for the leg scissors takedown. She dropped down and swept his leg again. She had earned two more points.

When they started again, the boy came at her much more aggressively. Katana realized that he must have been toying with her at first, because she was totally incapable of defending against this onslaught. The boy landed another kick with ease.

Katana now understood that she was badly outmatched. When they started the next round, she knew what she had to do. She lunged in, faking a punch to launch her gainer flash. The boy lifted his guard—exactly as he should, Katana thought to herself—but Katana was already in the air. She kicked out hard, slamming her foot into his chest—the boy reeled as she flipped herself over backwards.

The last time Katana had used this technique successfully in a sparring match had been at the Golden Gate Classic tournament several months earlier. The crowd had erupted in cheers. This time, only silence greeted her. Katana thought it was a very strange sensation—she had no way of knowing what anyone might be thinking of her performance.

The instructor pointed two fingers at her and came over to hold her hand in the air. The boy looked stunned for a few seconds. The instructor had them bow to each other. They lined up again, and class was over.

As the students filed out of the dojo, the female instructor came over to Katana. She motioned her into the conference room. Katana looked at Sara, but Sara only shrugged.

They entered the room and the woman closed the door behind them. "Please have a seat, Katana," she said. Her English was perfect.

Katana figured she would be in trouble for using the gainer flash. But as the woman sat down, she said, "Master Sakamoto wanted me to tell you that he is most impressed with your skills."

Katana felt relieved. "Oh—thank you!"

"He also says that anytime you are in Japan, you are welcome in his dojo," the woman added with a smile. "I understand you are here with Sara Brown all week?"

"Yes," said Katana, "that's right."

"I hope you will return again before you leave. It was a pleasure having you in class—and instructional for our students, I think."

They returned to the waiting room. Sara and Chris both raised their eyebrows at her. But Katana waited until they were outside in Mrs. Brown's car to tell them what had just happened.

"Well, that was nice of her," said Chris.

"Chris, that boy she fought is the Japanese national sparring champion!" said Sara.

"Are you kidding me? You mean... Let me get this straight... Katana beat the *Japanese national champion*?"

"I got lucky," said Katana. "It's obvious he wasn't trying very hard at first. He woulda crushed me if I didn't use the gainer."

When they got back to the house, Katana and Chris ran inside with Sara to tell her dad what had happened at class.

"You mean to tell me that Katana beat Komatsu?!" asked Mr. Brown when they had finished the story. He laughed out loud. "I don't imagine Komatsu had ever seen a gainer flash in a sparring match before!"

"Well, it was the only reason I beat him," said Katana. "He was clearly *way* better than me."

"Sakamoto doesn't usually do sparring in that class—he coaches Komatsu privately," said Mr. Brown. "But I guess this must have been his plan—I bet he was hoping you'd put Komatsu in his place. You know, deflate the old ego a little."

"I was thinking about it," said Katana. "And I don't understand—how exactly did he find out about me? We've never heard about any foreign competitors at the Hall, so it seems strange that a coach here would follow the American circuit."

"I'm sure Tanaka has told him *all* about you," said Mr. Brown with a smile. "Tanaka's not one for keeping his mouth shut. Sakamoto still trains with him at Shaka-In on a regular basis."

Once again, Katana found herself feeling uncomfortable with the notion of people she'd never met taking such an interest in her.

"Dad, when did Ms. Nakamura make master?" asked Sara. "She was wearing hakama tonight."

"Is that the skirt thingy they had on?" asked Chris.

"Yeah," said Sara. "But it's not a skirt—they're pants with really wide legs. You're allowed to wear them here when you become a master."

"I'm not sure," said Mr. Brown, in reply to Sara's question.

"It was fairly recently, I think. Tanaka was telling me the other day that she's going off to Bangkok to train with Master Chatri soon."

"Bangkok?" asked Katana. "What do they do there?"

"Thailand is known mostly for muay thai, which is a form of kickboxing," said Mr. Brown. "It's similar to the sparring you guys do, but they use a lot of kicks with the shins. They do a lot of elbows and knees, too. It's pretty brutal.

"Chatri Benjawan, the headmaster at the temple in Bangkok, does muay thai, but he's also a hsing-i master. That's what Nakamura's going to do with him, according to Tanaka."

"Sing-what? What on Earth is *that*?" asked Sara.

"It's pronounced *sing-ee*. It's similar to tai chi," said Mr. Brown. "Tai chi, hsing-i and pakua are considered the three jewels of the Chinese martial arts. They're all internal arts, meaning that even their external techniques work directly with your chi."

"I've never heard of the other two," said Chris.

"Tai chi is definitely the most widespread," said Mr. Brown. "I've never seen the other two myself, but I've heard Jordan talk about them.

"Well, congratulations on beating Komatsu, Katana. I've got to be getting to bed—I have to catch an early train up to Tokyo tomorrow."

"How long are you gonna be gone?" asked Sara.

"Just a couple of days," said Mr. Brown. "I should be back on Thursday. You kids have fun!"

Mr. Brown gave Sara a kiss on the forehead—"Dad!" said Sara with a stern look—and went upstairs to bed.

Finally Katana decided to ask Sara the question that had been on her mind since they'd arrived. "Sara, do you think we can ask your dad what he knows about the Arashi when he gets back?"

"Oh—definitely," said Sara. "I forgot about that."

"Katana sure didn't," muttered Chris.

CHAPTER 5
MASTER TANAKA

Mizuki struggled to open her eyes. Her forehead was throbbing. Something was trickling down her face —it tasted like blood. Everything was dark; where was she?

There was some light, high above. Not enough to see anything. She tried to stand up, but discovered she couldn't. She was sitting in a chair, her arms tied behind her back. It felt like the chair was up against a metal pole.

Then she remembered. She'd been walking by the bay. Some crazy guy in samurai armor had yelled at her. She'd run...

Mizuki screamed.

No one answered. She screamed again, thrashing against her bonds. Her voice echoed in the distance.

Time went by; it must have been hours. Then she heard a noise—a clang. There it was again... Someone turned on a light.

She was in a warehouse. Enormous crates were piled up all around her. She heard voices—someone was coming around the corner, up the aisle.

Mizuki screamed again. It was the crazy guy in the armor. No—there were two of them. The second one was dragging something. They stopped in front of her. It was a woman being dragged. She was older, filthy. Unconscious.

The two men removed their helmets and facemasks. One of them crouched in front of Mizuki. "Maybe we won't bring this one to the master, eh?" he said to his partner. His breath stank. "We could keep her for ourselves."

Mizuki spat in his face. The man straightened up and slapped her. There was a flash of light behind him; suddenly a blade protruded from his chest. Mizuki screamed. The man looked down in surprise. The blade disappeared and he fell to his knees. Blood spurted from his wound. He slumped over in Mizuki's lap. There was nobody behind him—who had stabbed him?

The second man looked around frantically, shouting. He ran around the corner, out of sight. Mizuki heard him scream, but the scream was cut short. Something came rolling up the aisle.

Mizuki realized it was the man's head.

MRS. BROWN TOOK the kids to do more sightseeing for the next couple of days, and they stopped at Sara's favorite sushi restaurant for lunch one time. They also went back to Sara's dojo for class on Thursday night. Katana was worried she'd have to spar with Komatsu again—and that he'd be looking to get back at her for using the gainer flash. But Komatsu wasn't there this time.

Mr. Brown was home by the time the kids got back from class. Katana and Chris followed Sara into his home office.

Katana was amazed at how large this room was—it looked more like a small library than an office. Three of the four walls were lined with bookshelves, nearly from floor to ceiling, many of them overflowing with books. Against the fourth wall was a large desk, which hosted a computer system with three enormous monitors. Mr. Brown was scanning through a series of pictures that looked to Katana like police mug shots on one of the monitors when they walked in. He seemed very engrossed in his work.

"Dad," said Sara, "can we talk to you for a minute?"

"Oh—what?" asked Mr. Brown, startled to see them standing there. "Sure, what's on your mind?" he asked, closing his files.

"Katana was wondering..." Sara began, but when Katana looked at her in alarm, she said instead, "well, *we* were wondering what you know about the Arashi."

"The Arashi?" asked Mr. Brown, looking surprised. "Funny you should mention them... Well, come in and have a seat, kids."

The three of them walked over to the couch and chairs set up around a low glass table at the other end of the room. "So why this sudden interest in the Arashi?" asked Mr. Brown, sitting at one end of the table.

Sara looked at Katana, and Katana could tell she wasn't sure how she should answer this question. Katana was relieved that Sara didn't mention her belief that she'd have to face Jaaku someday. She was getting to like Mr. Brown, and didn't want him to think she was crazy.

"I've been trying to find out everything I can about Jaaku and the Arashi... since... well, since I found out that Jaaku killed my parents," Katana said quietly.

"Ah," said Mr. Brown, nodding his head slowly. "Jordan told me about that. I'm so sorry, Katana. It so happens there have been some very interesting things happening with the Arashi lately."

"Like what?" asked Katana.

Mr. Brown paused for a moment. "Look, before we go any further, I need you three to understand that I shouldn't *really* be talking to you about this at all. It's official FBI business, and it's confidential."

"But Dad, Jaaku *murdered* Katana's parents!" said Sara. "She has a right to know about this, doesn't she?"

Mr. Brown looked at Katana for a long moment. She was sure he was thinking back to their conversation on the bullet train a few days earlier.

"All right," he said with a sigh. "But I can't name names, or get into too many specifics.

"The FBI has been working on the Arashi for ages because the Arashi are heavily involved in organized crime. But recently, we discovered they're being targeted by an assassin. We found out about the seventh victim this week, in fact."

"Wait—someone's killing off the Arashi?" asked Sara in total surprise.

"Yes, that's exactly what they're doing," said Mr. Brown.

"But how is that possible?" asked Katana. "I thought they were a secret society and nobody knew who any of them were?"

"That's correct, Katana. And we don't know how the assassin has been able to figure out their identities. We don't have any leads on the assassin, unfortunately.

"The bureau has been tracking Arashi activity for decades now, so *we* know who some of them are. Several weeks ago, we were getting ready to bust a human trafficking ring they were running. But the assassin killed two of the Arashi who were running the operation, and the others fled. There was no one left to arrest after that."

"Human trafficking... What does that mean?" asked Chris. Katana wasn't sure if she wanted to know.

"Basically they were abducting people and selling them into slave labor camps," said Mr. Brown. "But we're pretty sure some of the victims were being brought to Jaaku so he could take their chi."

"That's horrible," said Katana. "I knew Jaaku had to keep stealing chi from people but I never thought about where the people were coming from..."

"We think the Arashi were mostly taking homeless people from the larger cities in Japan at first. Most of these would have gone unnoticed, though, as they had nobody to report them missing. But then they started taking young runaways," said Mr. Brown, shaking his head. "And those definitely got noticed."

"Runaways—you mean kids?!" asked Sara with a look of horror on her face.

"Yes. Kids," said Mr. Brown. "We only caught on to this last month. We had suspected for some time, since Jaaku came back, that the Arashi were abducting the homeless. There were wild stories going around, stories about men in samurai armor appearing out of nowhere, and abducting people right off the street. In fact, my assistant in Tokyo used to give money to a homeless man there on a daily basis. The guy used to panhandle right outside his apartment. But then one day, he was gone. We became suspicious, so we sent a team to go talk to the others at the homeless shelter where the man used to stay. Nobody there knew anything, though. The man had just vanished.

"But then the local authorities in Osaka contacted us. There was a missing girl—she had run away from home initially—and one of her friends said she saw *her* being dragged off by someone in samurai armor."

"I thought the FBI could only work on stuff in the U.S.?" asked Chris.

"The bureau coordinates with foreign authorities on a wide variety of cases," said Mr. Brown. "But you're right, Chris, the crime has to have some connection to the U.S. for it to fall under our jurisdiction. But the Arashi operate very heavily in the States. One of their main activities for several decades has been selling stolen jewels—diamonds, mostly—on the black market in the U.S.

"The Arashi operate across international borders. They are active in several different countries, and those governments are only too happy to let us head up the efforts against them."

"So the Arashi were active before Jaaku came back?" asked Katana.

"Oh, yes," said Mr. Brown. "We only found out that Jaaku was still alive when Osaka tracked him down, a little over a year ago. But the bureau has been actively investigating the Arashi for as long as I've been working for them—longer than that, actually. The Arashi may have started out as Jaaku's inner circle, but they've been heavily involved in organized crime for a long time as well."

"Does anyone know where Jaaku was before Osaka found him?" asked Katana.

"I'm not sure," said Mr. Brown. "All I know is that he started out as a samurai warrior here in Japan. Tanaka knows a lot more about the early days of Jaaku and his Arashi than I do, though. Maybe we can get him to talk about it when we go up to Shaka-In tomorrow."

"That would be great," said Katana.

"Dad... I remember when I was little, hearing stories about Jaaku. You remember that time when the girl at school told me that Jaaku was going to steal my chi if I didn't give her my lunch money?" Sara asked.

"Yes," said Mr. Brown. "I always thought myself that Jaaku was probably something of a folk legend—just some crazy monster parents used to frighten their children. An old colleague of mine used to tell his kids they couldn't stay outside after dark because Jaaku would come and get them.

"But when the Arashi started becoming more active in China two years ago, I talked to Tanaka. He told me that Jaaku had been a real person, and that he could use the death touch to steal chi from people. When Osaka finally found him, there was no

75

longer any doubt that he was real, and still alive after all these years."

"Mr. Brown, what exactly do you do for the FBI?" asked Katana.

"I'm the director of the Tokyo field office," he replied.

"So you're in charge?" asked Chris.

"That's correct," said Mr. Brown. "They have me set up here with a secure computer linkup, so I can do a lot of work from home. But I end up in Tokyo for a few days at a time every couple of weeks.

"We should probably get to bed, though," he said, getting up from his chair. "We're leaving at first light to go up to Shaka-In."

Katana found it very difficult to get to sleep that night. She kept having a nightmare that Jaaku was creeping around outside of Sara's house, trying to find a way in. She would wake up and realize it was only a dream—but then it would start again the moment she fell back to sleep. When Mr. Brown knocked on her door in the morning, she jumped out of bed—her brain had incorporated the knocking into her dream, and she thought that it was Jaaku at her door.

The kids got ready and had a light breakfast. They went outside with Mr. Brown and got in the car that was waiting for them in the driveway.

Chris yawned. "How far away is the temple?"

"It's about a half hour drive," said Mr. Brown.

"Good—someone wake me up when we get there," he said, closing his eyes for a nap.

"Then it's another hour on foot," added Mr. Brown.

Chris opened his eyes. "An hour *on foot?*"

"The temple itself is way up in the hills—there's no road that goes up there. We'll be stopping at a little village at the base of the mountain, then hiking the rest of the way up to the temple," said Mr. Brown with a smile.

Katana could tell that Chris was wishing he'd stayed in bed.

They arrived at the village. The kids followed Mr. Brown along a well-trodden path through the woods, up into the hills. A little over an hour later, they climbed the crest of a hill and Katana could see the temple—all gray and black with a sloping roof—poking out of the trees ahead.

They got to the top of the next hill and walked under a huge torii gate that marked the entrance to the temple complex. Katana could see several monks dressed in gray robes tending the grounds. She was surprised to see several other structures spread out around the main temple—she had assumed that Shaka-In consisted of a single building.

One of the monks came over and talked to Mr. Brown in Japanese for a moment, then led them to the main building. As they began climbing the steps to the entrance, one of the doors burst open and a short, fierce-looking Japanese man with a goatee came trotting down the stairs to greet them.

"Ah, Mitchell—so good to see you again," the man said, extending his hand to Mr. Brown.

Mr. Brown shook his hand and said, "Good morning, Master Tanaka. You know my daughter, Sara..."

"Hello again, Sara," said Master Tanaka, shaking her hand rather vigorously.

"This is Chris Boyd and..."

"Katana," said Master Tanaka, ignoring Chris completely. Katana extended her hand, but Master Tanaka grabbed her head in both of his hands instead. He scrunched up his face, staring into her left eye, then her right. Katana was taken totally off-guard—she had no idea what was going on. She felt like Master Tanaka was trying to stare right into her brain.

"Are you in there, Musashi? Or you, Master Kosho?" he asked. Katana was at a loss for words, unsure whether to feel afraid or amused. She could see Sara staring at this spectacle with her mouth wide open. Katana was sure this was the most awkward thing that had ever happened to her. Master Tanaka let go of her face and said, "No, you are just Katana."

"Um..." said Katana. From the heat in her face she knew she must have turned a bright shade of red.

Mr. Brown tried to keep a straight face. "Master Tanaka has heard about your skills, Katana, and he has speculated that perhaps you are a... well, a reincarnation of one of the ancient masters..."

"A girl of only fourteen years who can do *three* of the chen do?" said Master Tanaka. "If ever one of the ancient ones were to come back, surely this is how we would know. Young they would appear, but deep would their power flow. But hers is a young soul —I do not see any of the ancient ones in her eyes."

Katana was stunned at this pronouncement—she was certain that this was the strangest man she had ever met.

"I am not so sure I believe in reincarnation anyway," said Master Tanaka with a frown. "No matter—come with me, our disciples are very eager to meet you." He turned and trotted back up the steps.

Katana looked at Mr. Brown with her eyebrows raised. Mr. Brown winked, and said, "After you, Master Musashi!"

They followed Master Tanaka into the temple. He led them down a long hallway, and around the corner to an enormous dojo. The room had stone walls and a vaulted ceiling. The tatami mats covering the floor were old and worn.

There were forty or fifty monks arranged in several lines, all going through a series of chi kung exercises. A tall monk with a shaved head at the front of the dojo was leading the group.

Master Tanaka led them to the back of the room and said to the kids, "Please, we would be honored if you would join our morning workout. Just follow along with Master Suzuki."

"Um..." said Chris.

"We don't have any... robes, or uniforms, or whatever..." stammered Sara. They were wearing shorts and T-shirts.

"No matter," said Master Tanaka briskly, herding them into the end of the last line.

Katana had thought they were just coming for a visit—she didn't know they'd be training with the monks. But she got in line with Sara and Chris and they followed Master Suzuki through the next few chi kung exercises.

Master Suzuki took the class through basics next. The monks did these with much lower horse stances than Katana was used to. Her thighs were burning after only a few minutes.

The monks went through several kata together after that— Katana was thankful that she recognized them. She didn't know what arts they practiced at Shaka-In. Apparently kempo was one of them.

After they were done with kata, Master Suzuki called up one of the monks and walked to the center of the dojo with him. All the other monks gathered around them in a circle. Master Suzuki demonstrated a self-defense technique on the monk that wasn't quite like anything else Katana had ever seen. When the monk punched, Master Suzuki stepped to the side, and caught the monk's wrist with his left hand. He brought his right hand under the monk's arm, and Katana could tell that he was pushing up on the back of the monk's elbow from the way the monk went up onto his toes. But then Master Suzuki switched hands, grabbing the monk's wrist with his right hand, and pushing on his elbow with his left. At the same time, he kicked the monk's front leg out from underneath him, dropping him to the mat.

The monk got back to his feet, and bowed to Master Suzuki. The rest of the monks spread out into groups of two or three to practice the technique.

Katana tried it with Sara and Chris but didn't understand exactly what Master Suzuki had done when he switched hands. Mr. Brown was standing with his arms folded on his chest, deep in conversation with Master Tanaka. But when Tanaka saw they were having trouble, he came over to help. He showed them how to apply the technique for the next few minutes, then went back to talk to Mr. Brown again.

Master Suzuki taught several more techniques. Each involved using joint manipulations to take the opponent to the ground. At the end of the class, everyone lined up. The monks spent several minutes sitting with their legs crossed, their hands palm-up, one on top of the other in their laps, and their eyes closed. The kids followed along, but Katana wasn't sure what they were supposed to be doing. She assumed this was some form of meditation.

Master Suzuki called something out in Japanese, and the monks got up and began to file out of the dojo. But as Katana tried to make her way over to Mr. Brown and Master Tanaka, several monks accosted her, bowing and shaking her hand. She didn't know what this was all about—but finally she was able to work her way to the back of the dojo.

Tanaka had left the room. Katana was disappointed—she'd been hoping to talk to him about Jaaku's history.

"I guess you're something of a celebrity here, Katana," said Mr. Brown with a smile. "Apparently Master Tanaka has told them all about you. They were very excited to meet the American girl who can do three chen do."

"Oh, great..."

One of the monks joined them as they walked outside. He gave them a tour of the grounds. He explained that the building from which they'd emerged was the main training hall, but housed only the large dojo, a smaller dojo that the monks used for private lessons, and a couple of small conference rooms.

He showed them the dormitory and the archive building. Near the edge of the grounds, he pointed out the charred remains of a structure they'd used to store food and supplies. He explained that the Arashi had torched it when they attacked the temple many months earlier, looking for information about the

Scroll of the Five Masters. They completed the tour, and the monk left them at the path leading to the village.

"Mr. Brown, were you able to ask Master Tanaka about the stuff we talked about last night?" asked Katana as they started out down the hill.

"No, actually," said Mr. Brown. Katana felt her heart sink. "But he's invited you to come back tomorrow and meet with him privately."

"WHAT THE HELL was up with that guy?" asked Chris when they got back to Sara's house. The kids were hanging out in Sara's room; Chris was sitting on the floor next to Katana.

"He was *not* that weird last time I met him," said Sara, lying on her stomach on her bed, looking over the edge at the other two. "Well, he was weird, but not *freaky* weird."

Chris turned suddenly and grabbed Katana's head, imitating Master Tanaka. "Are you in there, my sushi?"

Katana pushed him away, but laughed along with him. "I couldn't tell if he was joking or not," she said. "He was either really funny, or really scary."

"At least they didn't make you spar with anyone this time—I was certain that was coming next," Sara said.

"Tell me about it," said Katana. "I'm betting your dad was right though—your instructor heard about me from Tanaka for sure."

"Yeah," said Sara. "He seems to be telling *everyone* about you. I thought those monks were going to ask for your autograph."

The kids took it easy for the rest of the day. Katana slept well that night, free of nightmares. She got up early the next morning and went with Mr. Brown back to Shaka-In. Chris and Sara had thought they were going, too, but Mr. Brown informed them at breakfast that Tanaka wanted to meet with Katana alone.

"You mean I got up this early for *nothing*?" Chris had muttered grumpily as he went back upstairs.

When Katana and Mr. Brown arrived this time, Master Tanaka himself was waiting for them under the torii gate. He escorted them inside the main building and they went into one of the small conference rooms. "I'll be waiting for you outside," said Mr. Brown. He closed the door behind him. Katana sat down at the table across from Master Tanaka.

Master Tanaka seemed perfectly normal this morning, and in a mood to get right down to business. "Mitchell tells me you want to learn more about Jaaku and his Arashi," he said. "This is very wise. Sun Tzu said 'If you know your enemies and know yourself, you will not be imperiled in a hundred battles.' What do you wish to know?"

Katana wasn't sure where to begin. "Um..." she said, trying to gather her thoughts. "Well, I know that Jaaku started out as a samurai warrior here in Japan... but his real name could not have been 'Jaaku,' right?"

"That is correct," said Master Tanaka, "though nobody remembers his true name. We know Jaaku grew up in a powerful samurai family, but little else is known now about his early years. We do know that he left Japan and traveled to China, where he learned dim mak. He returned to Japan in 1800 and established himself at Taiyou. We have detailed records of those years here in our archives."

"Taiyou—what's that?" asked Katana.

"The Temple of the Sun," said Master Tanaka. "Shaka-In was the first Shaolin temple to be built in Japan. It was constructed by Master Kosho in 1420. Master Kosho was himself a samurai warrior—he was an extremely powerful martial artist. It is said he was able to do all five of the chen do at a very young age.

"Master Kosho traveled to China and trained at the Shaolin Temple in Henan Province for many years. When he came back to Japan, he built Shaka-In, and taught the chuan fa he'd learned in China."

"Chuan fa...?" asked Katana.

"Yes, that is the Chinese term for kempo. It means 'Law of the Fist,'" said Master Tanaka. "Today, kempo is considered a type of karate, although each art had a very different history.

"True karate started in the Okinawan islands—they are a part of Japan today, but used to be their own separate kingdom. A fisherman from Okinawa was once lost at sea for many years. When he came back, he taught what became known as karate. He had learned his art somewhere in China—possibly at one of the temples.

"Kempo had a similar history. Kosho had already mastered jiu jitsu, like all the great samurai masters. He went to China and learned Shaolin boxing, and combined this art with jiu jitsu to create kempo.

"During the centuries after Master Kosho's death, several other temples were established in Japan. Taiyou was one of those.

It was located outside of Tokyo. I do not know much about its early history, but by the time Jaaku came back to Japan in 1800, it had been abandoned. Jaaku took it over and taught his Arashi there for decades—until the government drove him from Japan."

"That was in 1868, right?" asked Katana, feeling like she was finally getting some concrete information.

"In fact, Jaaku was driven from Taiyou in *1869*," said Master Tanaka. "Master Chow came here, with his successor, Chang, and aided the headmasters of Shaka-In and the other temples in Japan in defeating Jaaku. It was a bloody battle; many monks lost their lives that day. And in the end, the temple at Taiyou was destroyed. The headmaster of Shaka-In tried to find the dim mak manuscript first—it was believed that Jaaku possessed this evil book and kept it at Taiyou. It is said that the dim mak manuscript contained all the secrets of that art, including the death touch. But the headmaster could not find it anywhere. He then ordered the monks to destroy the temple to make sure Jaaku could not recapture it."

"Chow left the Hall of the Dragon in 1868—at least that's what it says on his portrait in the tai chi dojo," said Katana. "But the story I always heard was that he left the hall specifically to fight Jaaku. Do you know why the battle didn't happen until a year after he left?"

"No," Tanaka said, furrowing his brow. "But I thought Chow left California in 1869."

"Hmm... That's strange," said Katana. "Well, whatever year it was, I know that everyone thought Jaaku was dead. Sam—the kempo master at the Hall—told us that Chow died killing Jaaku."

Master Tanaka paused for a moment, and took a deep breath. "Yes, that is the common belief. But Chow did not actually die at Taiyou, either."

"What?" Katana asked.

"Very few people know this part of the story," said Tanaka. "But the headmaster here at Shaka-In at the time was old friends with Master Chang. Chang told him that they faked Chow's death."

"But... Why?" asked Katana, totally mystified.

Tanaka shrugged. "Chow wanted to go into hiding. Chang helped him do it."

"Then what really became of Chow?"

"No written record tells of Chow's activities after the battle at Taiyou. Master Chang took over as headmaster of the Hall of the Dragon and Master Chow was never heard from again, as far as I know."

Katana was baffled. Not once had she questioned Chow's death in the fight against Jaaku. Now it turned out that *neither* of them had died.

"There is a legend at the Hall of the Dragon that Master Chow decided to kill Jaaku because Jaaku had killed Chow's teacher, the Immortal Master," said Katana. "Do you know if *that* is true?"

"Hmm," said Master Tanaka, stroking his goatee. "I have not heard that story before."

"Was the Immortal Master real?" asked Katana.

"I do not think so," said Master Tanaka. "At least I doubt that he was immortal. Master Chow's teacher was probably an old tai chi master in China. He was likely very old, having extended his life through the practice of tai chi. But I have never heard any stories about him—other than his being Chow's teacher."

"Where did Jaaku go after he left Japan?" asked Katana.

"Nobody knows," said Master Tanaka with a frown. "Everyone thought Jaaku was dead. And even had we known that he'd escaped Taiyou alive, we would have thought him long dead anyway. He had to have been very old by that time."

"When the Arashi attacked the Hall, Master Osaka told us that Jaaku was two hundred and ninety years old," said Katana. "If that's true, then he would have been... one hundred and forty-eight when he left Japan?"

"Yes," said Master Tanaka. "Some of the old tai chi masters lived to be one hundred and twenty... But one hundred and fifty? We never would have believed that Jaaku could have lived any longer than that, no matter how much chi he stole. It seemed certain that he was gone. But then I understand he showed up in Hawaii and murdered your parents?"

This question startled her. "Yes," she said, surprised that he would know about this.

"Master Nash has told me the story," said Master Tanaka. "Jaaku's appearance in Hawaii was the first time anyone had any contact with him after he disappeared from Taiyou in 1869."

Master Tanaka spent the next hour or so talking mostly about the history of Shaka-In after Jaaku left Japan. When they were done, he walked Katana out to the torii gate to meet Mr. Brown. "It has been a pleasure, Katana," he said. "I will be seeing you again very soon, I think."

He would? Katana didn't know what that was supposed to mean.

She told Sara and Chris about her meeting when she got back to the house with Mr. Brown.

"He said he's going to see you again?" asked Chris. "I can't imagine when he thinks that's going to happen—we're going back to Vermont tomorrow..."

"I don't know," said Katana.

"Well, he definitely knew loads of useful stuff about Jaaku," said Sara.

"We still don't know *that* much more than we did before," Katana replied, frustrated.

"I wanna know what happened to Chow, if he didn't die fighting Jaaku," Chris said.

"I don't know where we're going to find out any more stuff," said Sara with a sigh. "It sounds like *nobody* knows where Jaaku was for all those years."

"I wanna talk to Sam when we get back to the Hall," said Katana. "I'm betting she found out loads of stuff when she went to the Shaolin Temple."

CHAPTER 6

RUPTURE

K atana and Chris flew back to Vermont. While Chris spent the entire trip napping and playing video games, Katana kept going over in her head everything she knew about the history of Jaaku and his Arashi. She still didn't feel like she had the complete picture.

They had only one week left before their return to the Hall of the Dragon. Katana spent most of the time working out and playing with Doc. She was up at dawn every day to practice in her backyard, and she went with Chris to the dojo every afternoon. Sensei Mike worked with them more on the Brazilian jiu jitsu he'd learned, and Katana continued helping him with the chen do. Sensei Mike was able to form a stronger ball during the standing chi kung exercise, but still couldn't throw a fireball by the time Katana left that weekend.

Mrs. Boyd dropped the kids off at the airport on Saturday

morning. They checked their baggage before going to the gate. "It's okay, Doc, plane rides aren't that bad," Katana said to her kitten. She stroked his head with one finger through the metal grate at the end of the cat carrier.

"Although *you've* never had to ride in the cargo hold," said Chris sarcastically.

Gerald picked them up at the airport in Eureka. They rode in the limo to the Hall of the Dragon. He dropped them off in front of the enormous torii gate. Katana and Chris grabbed their bags —and Doc—and walked across the courtyard.

"Hey! Katana!" someone yelled as they passed the fountain.

Katana looked up to the balcony on the second floor of the north wing in time to see Jelly vault over the railing, pumping his arms like he was trying to fly. He hit the ground and ran over to them.

"Hey, Jelly!" said Chris.

"Hey, Chris—Katana..." He stopped mid-sentence and looked at her with a curious expression. "Hey, you look different..." he said, as if he couldn't quite figure out *what* had changed.

"Ya think?" said Katana, running her hand through her hair.

"Hello, captain obvious," said Chris.

"Hmm... Well, whatever, you have to come with me, *right now*!"

"What—why?" asked Katana. "What's wrong?"

"Nothing's wrong—but you have to get a double backflip!"

"Are you kidding me?" asked Katana.

"No, come on! We're both gonna do it in the demo this year!" said Jelly, jumping up and down.

"I made the team?!" asked Katana. She'd forgotten about the possibility of making the performance team over the course of the summer.

"Yeah!" said Jelly. "And I talked to Fu and if you can get the double back, we're both doing it together in the demo! Just like that other dumb team we saw at nationals!"

"What's a Fu?" asked Chris.

"Fu's not a what, Fu's a who!" said Jelly.

"What's a Hu?" asked Katana.

"Fu!" said Jelly.

"What?" said Katana.

"No—WHO!" said Jelly.

"Jelly, what the hell are you talking about?" asked Chris.

"You called Fu a what—but Fu's a who! Master Fu! He's the new wushu teacher, ya big dummy!"

"Oh!" said Katana and Chris together.

"Katana!" said Jelly suddenly, as if he were seeing her for the first time. "I know what's different—you cut your hair!"

"Very good, ya stupid midget..." said Chris, shaking his head in disbelief.

"I don't know..." said Jelly, looking at her appraisingly. "It kinda makes you look like a boy!" He ducked just in time to avoid getting smacked in the head by Katana's hand. "You missed!" he said and stuck his tongue out at her.

"Come here!" yelled Katana, lunging to smack him again. But Jelly ran off and called back, "You can't catch me!"

Katana tore off after him, chasing him all the way across the courtyard. When Jelly got to the north wing, he sprang like a cat, and vaulted over the railing onto the second-floor balcony. "Oh! Now what!" he called down to Katana.

But Katana jumped up herself, landing right next to him. "Oh crap!" Jelly yelled, running into his room to get away from her. "I forgot you could do that too!"

"Get back here you midget!" shrieked Katana as she bolted through his room after him. "Oh, hi Scott," she added. Jelly's roommate was lying in the bottom bunk, watching them run through as if this were an everyday occurrence.

"Hey, Kat," he said calmly.

Katana was in hot pursuit, mere feet behind Jelly, down the hall, and down the stairs into the central atrium. Jelly got halfway across the atrium and leaped up to the balcony on the second floor. Katana was right behind him, only inches away from grabbing his feet mid-flight.

Jelly hurtled through the door into the wushu dojo, Katana hot on his heels. He ran across the room, vaulted onto the springboard floor and dashed across it. He skidded to a stop just before the foam pit, turned and said "Uh-oh!"

Katana caught up to him an instant later and tackled him, sending them both tumbling into the foam. She grabbed him around the neck with one arm and gave him a noogie to the head. "I do *not* look like a boy!"

"I know," said Jelly, laughing. "I only said that cuz I knew it'd piss you off! It looks really good—you look older with short hair."

They climbed back out of the foam pit and Jelly said, "Now

seriously. You *have* to get a double backflip, as soon as possible. Like right now, in fact."

"How am I supposed to get it that fast?!" asked Katana. "It took you months!"

"Yeah, but *I* couldn't levitate yet when I learned it—you can. That makes it way easier!"

"If you say so..." Katana replied doubtfully.

"No, seriously—try it, and if you aren't high enough to make it around, you can levitate instead of going SPLAT!" said Jelly. "Just DO IT already!"

"Okay!" said Katana. "Just do it..." She ran down the floor, did a round-off, jumped as high as she could, and tried to rotate twice before landing. As she began her second rotation, she could see that she was way too close to the floor to land it—so she bounced her chi off the mat and arced up, landing on her feet.

"I'm not getting around fast enough," she said.

"No, you went plenty fast," said Jelly. "You started too late—you have to start turning as soon as you come out of the round-off."

Katana tried it again. She got farther around this time, but still couldn't get her feet underneath her before she landed. She had to levitate again to avoid crashing.

Chris and Scott wandered in after she'd tried it a few more times.

"You're welcome," said Chris grumpily.

"Um... for what?" asked Katana.

"For what... You left your bags and your cat sitting out in the middle of the courtyard!"

"Oh crap!"

"Don't worry," said Scott. "We brought everything upstairs for you."

"Thanks, guys," said Katana.

"So did you get the double back yet?" Scott asked.

"Not exactly," said Katana. "How'd you know that's what we were doing?"

"Jelly's been freaking out since we got here. He's been obsessed with getting you to do it. I was worried his head would explode if you didn't get here soon."

"Yeah!" said Jelly. "But now you're here, so come on—do it again!"

"All right..." said Katana, "but this time I wanna do it into the foam pit. If I keep levitating at the end, I'll never know what it's supposed to feel like."

She did it into the foam pit several times. She could land on her knees finally, so she knew she was almost there. But she couldn't get around fast enough, or jump high enough to get her feet underneath her before hitting the foam.

Sara walked in a minute later with Jimmy in tow. "Here you guys are!" she said. "I've been looking all over for you. I didn't think we were allowed to use the wushu dojo outside of class?"

"Nah," said Jelly. "Fu's nice. He said we can use it for tricks because it's safer than the other dojo."

"Well that's cool," said Sara. "Look, I'm starving, are you guys ready for dinner?"

"Hell yes," Katana replied.

They left the dojo with Jimmy and Sara. "So how was your summer, Katana?" asked Jimmy as they walked down the stairs.

"It was good," she said. "I worked out a lot, and Chris and I went to Japan for a week to visit Sara."

"That's cool," he said. "My summer was pretty slow. I missed you... er... everyone a lot."

"Yes!" exclaimed Sara when they got to the cafeteria. "I've missed this so much!" she said as she and Katana headed toward the sushi bar. The boys got in line for the buffet.

"Sara, you ate sushi all summer!" said Katana.

"Yeah, but nobody makes rolls like Terry-san."

"Konichiwa," Terry-san greeted them as they sat down on their stools. "Did you girls have a good summer?"

They told him about Katana and Chris's visit to Japan as he prepared their sushi.

"Terry-san," said Katana, "Master Tanaka was... well, strange. Like he grabbed my face when I met him and it felt like he was trying to stare into my brain."

"And he said he thought she might be a reincarnation of some old master or something," added Sara.

Terry-san chuckled softly. "Master Tanaka is quite eccentric," he said. "I think he was joking around with you. He has a unique sense of humor."

"You know, he also said he was going to see me again very soon," said Katana. "But that was the day before we left. Do you know what he was talking about?"

"No, I do not," said Terry-san, shrugging his shoulders.

"I thought the headmasters told their sushi chefs *everything*!" chided Sara.

"Usually, they do," Terry-san said with a frown. "However, this summer, Master Tanaka and Master Nash have both become much more tight-lipped than usual. I think something is going on, but I don't know what it might be."

Sam came over and sat down next to Sara. "Hey girls, welcome back!"

"Hi Sam!" they both replied.

They talked briefly about how their summer had gone, then Katana asked, "Sam, do you think I can talk to you for a few minutes?"

"Yeah, sure, Kat," said Sam. "I'm going to go say hello to everyone else—come get me when you're done eating."

The girls dug into their sushi. Terry-san entertained them with stories about Master Tanaka's antics.

As she was listening to Terry-san, Katana saw Sam sit down at the table with Chris, Jelly and Jimmy. But a minute later, she and Chris got up and walked out of the cafeteria. Katana wondered what that was about.

Terry-san told the girls about an incident involving a monk at Shaka-In who was testing for master. Tanaka had dressed up as a ninja. He'd gone into the dormitory in the middle of the night with two samurai swords. He'd jumped on the monk's bed, holding a sword to his throat. "It's time," he'd said when the monk awoke.

"Master Tanaka dragged him out of bed, and started his test right then and there," concluded Terry-san.

"What a whacko," said Sara, shaking her head.

"So it sounds like he's always been a little... off," said Katana.

"Oh yes," said Terry-san. "I think he's mellowed in his old age."

The girls finished their sushi, and Katana went to look for Sam. "I'll catch up with you later," said Sara.

Chris, Jelly and Jimmy had already left. Sam had returned, and was now sitting at a table with some older kids whom Katana didn't know.

"Hey, Kat—you're done?" asked Sam, getting up from the table. "I'll see you guys at orientation tomorrow," she said to the others. She walked out of the cafeteria with Katana.

"You wanna go down to the beach and talk?" asked Sam when they got to the atrium. "It's such a beautiful day out, we might as well enjoy it."

"Yeah, sure."

Katana told Sam about her summer as they walked across the grounds and over the pedestrian bridge across Highway 101. She maneuvered carefully around the real reason she wanted to talk to Sam, however. They sat down on one of the benches at the top of the cliff, not far from Master Hua's memorial stone. Katana mostly discussed her trips to Maine and Japan, and Master Tanaka's weirdness.

"Yes, Master Tanaka is quite eccentric," said Sam with a smile. Katana decided that "eccentric" must be the word adults liked to use to describe someone really weird in a nice way. "Hua and I met him when we stopped at Shaka-In on our way to China earlier this year."

They sat in silence for a moment, watching the sun descend in the sky and listening to the waves crash on the beach far below. "So what's really on your mind, Kat?"

Katana didn't feel entirely comfortable talking to Sam about this after all. She felt like she was doing something wrong. But her desire for knowledge overcame her discomfort.

"I'm trying to find out everything I can about Jaaku and the Arashi," she began. "I searched all over the internet, and couldn't find a thing. I finally learned some stuff from Sara's dad and from Master Tanaka... But I still don't know very much. I was hoping... well, I was thinking that you probably heard a lot when you were at the Shaolin Temple..."

"Katana," said Sam, and paused for a moment to collect her thoughts. "Chris talked to me during dinner. He's worried about you, Kat. He says..."

"I know—he thinks I'm obsessing about this too much. But he doesn't get it!" Katana got to her feet and started pacing back and forth. Sam watched her with a look of growing concern.

"Sam, Jaaku *killed my parents*! I'll never know what my life might have been like because Jaaku took them away and I can never get them back." She pointed at the memorial stone. "He killed Master Hua..."

"I know," said Sam quietly. "I was there."

"How much longer can this go on?! How many more people is Jaaku going to kill before someone stops him? He's been at it almost three hundred years, and nobody's stopped him yet! It's going to be me, Sam, I know it's going to be me. And I have no idea how to do it, I'm not nearly strong enough and..."

"Katana, why do you think that?" asked Sam. "Where are you getting the idea that you're the one who has to stop Jaaku?"

"I don't know!" said Katana. "You probably think I'm crazy now—that's obviously what Chris thinks!"

"Nobody thinks you're crazy, Kat, I'm just worried..."

"Well, I don't know *how* I know, *I just know*!" said Katana. "When I first found out I was going to the Hall of the Dragon, I had this weird feeling, like I'd always known I'd end up here. I'd never heard of the place before, but when Osaka told me about it... It was like I'd lived here my whole life. I was able to picture the Hall in my mind, even though I'd never seen it—how is that possible?"

Sam didn't answer.

"It's not possible," said Katana. "But I've had the same, exact feeling about Jaaku ever since Osaka told us that he killed my parents—like somehow I'd always known it. And I realized my entire life is leading me to him. Why can I do *three* chen do when I'm only fourteen? Why is my chi so much stronger than anyone else's? It's because I'm *meant to face him*. Someday, it's going to be me. And I am terrified because I have no idea how to beat him."

"Katana, I will grant you, you seem to have... an intuition, I don't know what else to call it. I remember when you came to me after the kidnapping—when you asked me to help you get a chi hit. You seemed *certain* then that you were going to face the Arashi again—and then you did. I thought you were just scared. But then you really did face the Arashi.

"So yes, you seem to have a sense of things that I can't explain.

99

But you cannot let that consume you. Chris says you spent every waking hour worrying about this all summer. That's not a healthy way of dealing with it..."

"It wasn't 'every waking hour,'" said Katana, sitting down on the bench again. "That's an exaggeration."

"Perhaps," said Sam. "But it sounds like it wasn't *much* of an exaggeration. Chris said he tried talking to you on the plane ride here, and it was like you were in another world. You didn't hear him.

"Katana, I can't blame you for trying to learn about Jaaku. But the way you're going about it isn't healthy. You're young— you should be enjoying life. And the fact is that *nobody* knows very much about Jaaku, so you can obsess your life away and you still won't learn much more than you already have. Your parents wouldn't have wanted to see you like this..."

"My parents!" said Katana. She got back to her feet and started pacing again. "That's just it—we don't know *what* my parents would have wanted because they're DEAD!"

"Katana!" said Sam, getting to her feet as well. Katana thought for a moment that Sam was going to strike her—but she merely pointed a finger in her face. "Adrian Kahanu was the best friend I ever had. And I am telling you he would have been heartbroken to see his daughter *consumed* the way you are."

Sam walked a few feet away from her, then turned around. "You're young, Kat, these are going to be some of the best years of your entire life. *Enjoy them!*"

"I can see them, Sam," said Katana, a tear sliding down her cheek.

"What?" asked Sam quietly.

"I can see them dying. I've been having nightmares about it all summer. They were in a car. Jaaku showed up right in front of them—he threw a fireball at them. My mom screamed. She swerved—but the car went out of control. My dad tried to grab the wheel but it was too late—the car was already going over the cliff. Then he tried to grab my mom—I think he was trying to pull her out or something—but he couldn't reach her. I saw them die, Sam..."

"That's not possible..."

"I saw the car smash into the rocks and explode—I saw the fire..."

"Katana, that's impossible—you weren't there! You were only a baby..."

"I KNOW! But I'm telling you, I saw it—I see it in my nightmares over and over again!"

Katana sat down on the bench, her elbows on her knees and her hands over her face. She was crying uncontrollably. She felt Sam sit down next to her and put her arm around her.

"Katana..." whispered Sam and kissed her on the head. "Look at what this is doing to you. You have to let this go. Yes, your parents are dead, and yes, Jaaku killed them. I feel your pain, Kat, I do—I was devastated when Adrian died. Everyone who knew him was. But you need to know this. Adrian and Kristine were two of the happiest people I have ever met. They lived in pure joy every moment they were together. And when you were born, if it's possible, they were even happier. It would have crushed them to see you like this. We can't get them back, Kat, but you can honor their memory by *living your life*."

They sat there for several minutes, Sam holding her and Katana crying into her chest. Finally Katana calmed down. She sat up and sniffled. "I miss them, Sam. I never knew them, but I miss them *so much*."

"Listen, Kat, I'll make a deal with you," said Sam. "I'll tell you anything I can about Jaaku, but you have to promise that you're going to let this go. You're back at school; you're with your friends. You need to stop this, and start living your life again. If you're going to face Jaaku someday, you're going to need your sanity when you do it!"

"Deal," said Katana.

Katana told Sam everything she'd learned so far. "I still don't know what Jaaku's real name was—I don't know anything about him before he went off to learn dim mak. I just know he was a samurai. Where did he train? Why did he leave Japan? Where did he learn dim mak?"

"None of us knows anything about Jaaku's early days," said Sam.

"But Osaka knew exactly how old he was," said Katana. "To the year—he must know at least *some* stuff."

"You know, you're right," said Sam pensively. "I forgot about that. Osaka *is* the big history buff, it might be worthwhile to talk to him about this at some point.

"I *can* tell you where Jaaku learned dim mak though," she added. "When we were at Shaolin, Master Liang told us a lot about the temple's history. He said that dim mak was created at the Shaolin Temple."

"Dim mak came from Shaolin?!"

Sam nodded. "Master Tong was a tai chi master there, and he'd mastered the healing arts as well. He spent many years secretly developing the techniques of dim mak. He's the one who discovered the death touch. Liang said he left Shaolin and set up his own temple out in the desert of Xinjiang Province.

"When Jaaku went to China, he found Tong, and that's where he learned dim mak. Once he'd learned everything, Jaaku killed Tong. The monks from Shaolin went to the temple and tried to recover the dim mak manuscript—apparently, Tong had written down every technique as he developed it. But the manuscript was gone. Liang says Jaaku must have taken it."

"That's interesting..." said Katana. "Master Tanaka said that Chang tried to find the manuscript at Taiyou, but it wasn't there either. Do you think Jaaku still has it?"

Sam shrugged. "I assume so, but I don't know."

"What about the legend that Jaaku killed the Immortal Master?" Katana asked. "I know that Chow left here in 1868, and attacked Jaaku's temple in 1869. But the legend says that Jaaku killed the Immortal Master. Nobody seems to know anything about that, though. Did Jaaku really kill him?"

Sam shook her head. "I remember hearing that story when *I* was a student here. Allegedly Jaaku sought out the Immortal Master because he wanted to become immortal. But the Immortal Master refused to teach him, so Jaaku killed him. Master Chow left the Hall of the Dragon to 'avenge his teacher's death.' That's how the legend goes anyway—but I've always assumed that the whole story was just that—only a story. But who knows—I never knew that Chow survived the battle at Taiyou, so I guess anything is possible."

"Sam, when Jaaku killed Master Hua," Katana said quietly, "he did it with lightning. How does that work?"

Sam let out a long sigh. "Nobody understands it, Kat. It's like the jet of fire he used against Sato. To do either of those skills, you have to use your shen to control the surrounding field of chi. But *that* is supposed to be impossible. Nash can't do it, nor can the headmaster of Shaolin, nor anyone else—except Jaaku. Somehow, Jaaku has found a way to extend his shen into the field of energy around him, and manipulate that chi as if it were his own."

"And how did Jaaku learn *that*?" asked Katana.

"Nobody knows."

"Is it part of dim mak?"

"Nobody knows," Sam repeated with a shrug.

They walked back to the Hall. When they got inside, Sam reminded Katana about the promise she'd made. "No more obsessing, right?"

"I'll try," said Katana with a smile.

"All right then," said Sam, pulling Katana into a hug. "Goodnight, Kat—I'll see you tomorrow."

They went their separate ways—Sam off to the south wing to her apartment, and Katana to the north wing. She walked up to her room, but found it dark and empty. She turned on the light and heard Doc meow from the cat carrier, which was sitting in the middle of the floor next to her suitcases. The door to the carrier was wide open, but Doc was curled up inside.

"Hey, buddy!" said Katana, bending down to pet him.

She sat in one of the chairs. Doc jumped into her lap, and curled up to go back to sleep. Katana thought about her conversation with Sam.

Sam was right, of course. Katana *had* been letting her fear consume her all summer. But how could she not? How was she supposed to live her life and be happy, when she was certain that a confrontation with Jaaku stood in her path—however far off it might be?

And come to think of it, how was it Chris's business to talk to Sam in the first place? Although Sam was worried about her, she'd still acknowledged that she didn't blame Katana for trying to learn everything she could. Master Tanaka had even said it was wise to learn everything possible about the enemy.

Yet Chris had been on her case about it all summer. And now he was interfering—he'd had no right and no reason to go to Sam like this.

Katana gathered Doc to her chest—he meowed forlornly at her—and got up, placing the cat back on the chair. She walked downstairs to Chris and Jimmy's room and barged in without knocking.

Chris and Jimmy were sitting on the couch, playing a video game. Sara was reclining in a chair next to them. They turned to look at Katana.

Jimmy dropped his controller, got up and said, "Hi, Katana," with a big smile.

"Get out," said Katana.

"Um..." said Jimmy, and started moving toward the door.

Chris stood up and glared at Katana. "Sit down, you idiot—this is *your* room!"

Jimmy stopped in his tracks, looking confused. "Okay..."

"GET OUT!" Katana screamed.

Sara got up, grabbed Jimmy by the elbow and walked him out of the room. She closed the door behind her.

"What is your problem?" demanded Katana. She and Chris stood there glaring at each other.

"I'm not the one with a problem, Kat."

"What'd you have to go running to Sam for?"

"You've been obsessed—all summer, you sat on that stupid computer looking stuff up, and the whole time we were in Japan all you did..."

"Why do you not get this?!" Katana yelled. "Jaaku *murdered my parents*! You have no idea..."

"No, you're wrong, Kat—I have every idea. I get it; he killed your parents. But you never *knew* them! You grew up *knowing* they were dead—but now, all of a sudden, you're obsessing..."

"Nobody ever told me they were MURDERED!"

"But that doesn't *change* anything—they're dead either way! The only thing that changed is YOU!"

"How can you possibly understand?! Your parents are STILL ALIVE—you don't have to wonder what your life might have been like..."

"What my life might have been like if my parents weren't

dead? No, I don't. But I *do* have to wonder what my life might be like if *your* parents were alive!"

Katana was stunned. "What the hell does that mean..."

"Think about it, Katana—if Jaaku hadn't murdered your parents, I never would have met you. You would have grown up in Hawaii and I still would've been in Vermont. And Osaka never would have come to Vermont either, and I probably never would have started karate—my mom only had me start because Leanna was signing *you* up!

"My whole life would be different if you didn't come to Vermont—everything I care about, everything I know wouldn't EXIST! But you're going around all summer like you wish everything was different. You know what—I don't WANT anything to be different! I'm GLAD you came to Vermont, and I'm GLAD I started karate..."

"Stop right there," said Katana, advancing on him. "You stop right there—are you trying to say you're GLAD Jaaku killed my parents?!"

Chris glared at her for a moment, then finally muttered, "No, of course not." He looked down at the floor.

"THAT'S EXACTLY WHAT YOU'RE SAYING!" Katana screamed.

She could hear her heart pounding in her ears. Her hands were shaking. For the first time in her life, she felt the urge to hurt Chris. It took every ounce of self-control she possessed not to strike him. Instead, she turned around, stormed out of the room and slammed the door behind her.

CHAPTER 7

RECONCILIATION

Katana ran down the end of the hall. But instead of going upstairs to her room, she went downstairs, and through the short hallway to the atrium. She stopped for a moment and looked around before running right out the front doors.

She had no idea where she was going; she ran past the fountain, then stopped. She was crying—tears of rage and pain. She wanted to run back upstairs and hurt Chris and make him feel what she was feeling. But she didn't understand *what* she was feeling anymore. She had never wanted to hurt anyone in her entire life—least of all Chris.

She stormed back inside the Hall, across the atrium, and out the back doors to the Zen rock garden.

Katana felt like she was losing her mind. This rage had been simmering inside of her since the day she found out that Jaaku had killed her parents. It was the engine driving her search for knowledge, for power. But now it was boiling over. Never before had she felt emotions this intense.

She walked around the perimeter of the garden three times, trying to calm herself down. Finally, she sat down on one of the benches and stared at the large boulder in the middle of the gravel.

"I don't know what I'm doing anymore," she said out loud a few minutes later. She got up to go back inside. She'd expected to find Sara and Jimmy in her room, but it was empty, exactly as she'd left it. Doc was curled up inside the cat carrier again.

Katana unpacked her suitcases—throwing things haphazardly in drawers. Finally she went out on the balcony and sat down in one of the deck chairs. The sun had set; the sky was getting dark.

She had to admit that Chris was right. Her parents' absence while she was growing up had always made her sad. But that's the way it was, the way it had always been. The knowledge of how her parents had really died *had* changed her.

And she felt like the more that she learned about Jaaku, the angrier she became. The more she felt the loss of her parents—the more she wanted revenge.

Was that truly what this was about? Revenge? She'd been telling herself that she'd have to confront Jaaku someday to stop him from taking chi from others. But deep down was it just about revenge for her parents' deaths?

Katana reminded herself this was precisely the reason Osaka had kept the truth from her for so long. He'd never allowed her to know that a monster had murdered her parents because he hadn't wanted her to grow up with a desire for vengeance. Yet here she was, consumed by that very thing.

Chris was right. She'd changed—but this wasn't who Katana wanted to be.

She went back inside, changed into her pajamas and climbed into the top bunk. After a minute, she heard Doc meowing at the base of the ladder. She climbed down to bring him up to bed with her. Katana curled up in fetal position, her kitten lying in front of her.

As she scratched Doc between the ears, she suddenly felt an overwhelming sense of guilt for the way she'd treated Chris. He had not deserved that.

Katana thought about what he'd said. He was right—his life would *not* have been the same if Katana hadn't come to live in Vermont. She wished her parents hadn't died, but perhaps things had happened the way they had for some greater purpose. She realized that there was nothing about her life that she would want to change. She'd grown up happy and healthy—exactly as Osaka had wanted. And she couldn't imagine her life without Chris.

Katana drifted off to sleep eventually. She dreamed about her parents again. But this time the dream was very different. She didn't see them dying—she saw them alive and well, smiling down at her as she slept. And she never had the nightmare of their deaths again.

WHEN SHE WOKE up the next morning, Katana was nervous for a moment because Doc wasn't in bed anymore. She found him asleep in the cat carrier. How had he gotten down from the top bunk?

"You crazy cat!" she said. "You can go anywhere in the whole room, but you keep going in the stupid carrier."

She looked at the clock. It was after eight—this was the first time in months that she hadn't woken at the crack of dawn. Sara hadn't returned—her bed was still made, as perfectly as it had been the night before.

Katana felt like she'd been beaten up—she was sore all over and had a huge headache. She changed out of her pajamas and walked down to the cafeteria. Sara was sitting at a table with Jelly, Dana and Paul.

"Hey," said Sara tentatively. "How are you feeling?"

"Awful. Where's Chris?"

Sara pointed across the room. Katana looked over to see him sitting with Olivia, her sister, Sierra, and some of their friends.

"He was really upset last night," said Sara, without making eye contact. Katana got the impression that Sara was afraid she'd start screaming at her, right there at the breakfast table. The other three watched them in silence.

"I was a real bitch to him," said Katana. "He didn't deserve that. I feel horrible."

They sat in silence for a moment, then Katana got up to get some food. When she returned, Sara was alone—Jelly, Paul and Dana had left.

Katana started eating. "What happened, Kat?" asked Sara. "I've never seen you like that before."

"I don't know," said Katana. She told Sara about her conversation with Sam. "I felt this overwhelming rage at Chris for talking to Sam about me. I don't know where it came from. It's like my fear of Jaaku and my anger about my parents' murder were building all summer... and everything exploded last night. Chris and I never had a fight like that—ever. Not in all the years we were growing up."

"He felt awful, Kat. I dragged Jimmy down to Dana's room, but we came back after we heard you slam the door. Chris was in tears. You didn't really think he was glad your parents were dead... Did you?"

"I know that's not what he meant," said Katana. "But I was so angry—that was all I was hearing. I need to talk to him," she added as she watched Chris walk out of the cafeteria with Olivia.

"Yeah, you do," said Sara. "But he's hanging out with Olivia all day. So it's gonna have to wait till tomorrow."

"Hey, where were you last night? You never came back to the room."

"I figured you needed to be alone," said Sara with a shrug. "I slept on the floor in Chris and Jimmy's room. Oh, Dana wants you to meet her in the wushu dojo when you're done eating so you two can start working on chains. I guess Master Fu talked to her about some new move he wants you to do this year."

Katana sighed. "Yeah, that's cool. It'll help me get my mind off things."

"I think I'm gonna go with you," said Sara. "I gotta work staff like crazy if I'm gonna be ready for practice this week."

"You made the team too?!" asked Katana.

"Yeah—that's right, I didn't get a chance to tell you. Master

Fu told me I'm on the team. I'm gonna be doing staff with Jelly and Tim. He wants me to start trying that release skill that Jelly always does. I'm so psyched! This year is gonna be awesome!"

"Wait a minute," said Katana. "Master Fu has talked to you, Jelly and Dana—all about plans for the demo this season... and I haven't even met him yet!"

"He was looking for you," said Sara. "But you were out with Sam."

The girls went up to their room. Katana tried to remember where she'd tossed her chains when she unpacked the previous night. Once she'd found them, they went to join Dana in the wushu dojo. Jelly and Scott were there, too. The three of them were working on tricks.

"Hey, Kat—you okay?" asked Dana.

"Yeah, I'll be all right."

"Listen, I was talking to Master Fu, and he wants us to try to add that move back into the set that me and Kelly did two years ago for nationals," said Dana excitedly.

"Oh—wow, okay," said Katana. She remembered the move clearly. Dana had swung both chains in opposing circles with one hand while lifting her foot over her head with the other hand. After several rotations she'd fallen down into a split, holding her foot the entire time.

Sara went to grab a staff and started practicing with Jelly and Scott—she and Jelly worked on staff while Scott went through his broadsword set.

"Have you ever fallen into a split like that before?" asked Dana. "Holding your foot overhead the whole time?"

"No, definitely not," said Katana warily. "Does it hurt?"

"No, but it's wicked scary the first few times," said Dana. "Come on, let's do it on the springboard floor first—it's a little less scary that way."

Katana followed her up to the floor. Dana showed her the correct hand position for the move. Katana had to grab the inside of her left foot with her left hand, then lift it up over her head. She was able to do it, but was scared to fall into a split without letting go of her foot.

"Go ahead and let go of it the first few times," suggested Dana. "It'll help you get over the fear."

Katana tried it. She held her foot up, then started falling over. She let go about halfway down. She dropped her foot to the floor, then slid the rest of the way into her split. After several more tries, she held her breath, grabbed her foot and held on all the way down.

"Yeah!" shouted Dana. "That's it—that wasn't so bad, was it?"

"No!" said Katana in surprise. "It looks way scarier than it really is."

"Now for the hard part..." said Dana.

"You mean *that* wasn't the hard part," Katana asked apprehensively.

"Um... no, unfortunately not," said Dana. "Get your chains."

Katana and Dana jumped off the springboard floor. Dana picked up one chain in each hand. "You have to start by spinning both of them forward in a circle—we'll do this out of the flowers. Now, bring your hands closer and closer together, so the chains are crossing each other's paths—be careful not to smash them."

"Okay," said Katana, following along with her chains.

"Good, now put both handles together in your right hand," said Dana. She did so herself, continuing to spin both chains.

Katana followed her lead, but her chains smashed together. "How are you doing that?!"

Dana hit the chains on the floor to stop them. "I told you this was the hard part. It's one of those things where you just have to get a feel for it—there's no real trick to it."

"Right," said Katana. She tried the move several more times. She got it for a couple of rotations once or twice, but couldn't keep them going longer than that.

"Don't worry," Dana reassured her. "Keep doing it and you'll get it eventually."

"Do you know if there's any way to put more tricks into the set?" asked Katana. "I know we start with a flash kick or an aerial, but I was trying to think of something we could add in the middle."

"That's the problem," said Dana. "Once the chains are moving, you can't do any more tricks. Although... Master Hua was telling us once about this kid who did a butterfly twist... But I can't do that trick, so we never tried it."

"A butterfly twist..." said Katana. "That's that thing where you roll over sideways in the air, right?"

"Yeah," said Dana. "Jelly can do them—let's have him show us."

They walked over to where Jelly was practicing with Scott and Sara.

"Hey Jelly," said Dana, "show Katana a butterfly twist."

Jelly did one, without bothering to put his staff down. He started out like he was going to do a butterfly kick, but once his first leg was off the ground, he rolled over sideways in the air, then landed and said "Tada!"

"How do you do that with the chains spinning?" asked Katana.

"I don't know," said Dana with a sigh. "Master Hua never explained it."

"I've seen someone do that before!" said Jelly. "This kid at my school back home used to do it."

"He did it in a double whip chain set?" asked Dana.

"Yeah! He spun them around like he was going into a butterfly kick, but then as he rolled over, the chains spun around with him, and he landed in a split. It was *wicked* cool!"

"I'm having trouble picturing how that would work," said Katana.

"Yeah, me too," said Dana.

"I think my friend might have a video of it," said Jelly. "I'll message him later. Can you two do a butterfly twist already?"

"Nah," said Dana. Katana shook her head.

"Then it's time to learn!" said Jelly, bouncing with excitement. Katana felt like Jelly's two favorite things were learning new tricks, and teaching other people new tricks.

He had the girls do a couple of butterfly kicks first. "Those were high, but in a twist you don't want to let your first leg go higher than your head. As soon as you're in the air, you have to bring your legs together and twist over hard with your shoulders."

Katana and Dana both tried it, and both landed on their rear ends. "You're not twisting early enough. You have to twist right away, like this," he said and demonstrated the trick again.

"Okay," said Katana. She tried it again, twisting as soon as she began the move—but this time she crashed even more dramatically than she had the first time. "That was definitely wrong," she said in frustration.

"That time you never got your leg in the air," said Jelly. "You still have to kick your first leg way up, but you have to start twisting right away too."

Dana tried it again with no more success than Katana. But when Katana tried it a third time, she landed it.

"That's it!" said Jelly. "Now we gotta figure out how to do it with chains..."

"And how to do it into a split," said Dana.

"Ooh, yeah," said Jelly. "I've never tried that... That might hurt."

"Are you three done yet?" asked Sara, walking over to them with Scott. "I need a shower."

"Yeah, we are," said Katana. "Jelly, we should go see if your friend has that video."

They went upstairs. Katana and Dana followed Jelly and Scott to their room. Jelly sat down at his computer. "Oh, good—he's online!" He had his friend e-mail him the video, then they gathered around the screen to watch it.

As Jelly had said, the boy in the video started the move as if he were going to do a butterfly kick, spinning one chain underneath him and the other above. But suddenly he twisted over, pulling his hands in close. The chains spun around as he rolled over sideways. He kept his left leg forward to land in a split, and extended his arms out again, hitting the chains into the floor.

"I think I get it now," said Dana. She walked around in a circle, pretending to go through the move. "Yeah, I definitely get this. Katana, we're gonna have to try it tomorrow."

"I'll meet you in the wushu dojo after orientation?" Katana suggested.

"Yeah, definitely," said Dana. "All right, I'll see you guys later —I need a shower, too."

"Yeah, so do I," said Katana. She walked out with Dana.

Katana got to her room—and saw Chris sitting on the couch with Doc in his lap. Sara was in the shower.

"Hi," said Katana quietly. She sat down in one of the chairs.

"Hey," Chris replied, without looking at her.

"I thought you were spending the day with Olivia?"

"I was."

"What happened?"

"She knew I was upset. She said she didn't want to see me again until I talked to you and patched things up," said Chris.

"Oh Chris, I'm sorry—I don't want to screw things up between you two..."

"No, it's not like that," said Chris. "She's not pissed or anything, she just knows me and you need to talk."

"Yeah, we do," Katana agreed. "I didn't mean what I said last night. I know you're not glad my parents are dead..."

"I know," said Chris. "But look, Kat, I need you to understand me on this. My life would *not* be the same if it weren't for you. You're like my best friend and my sister rolled into one, but I never woulda met you if you hadn't come to Vermont. I never would've started karate, or met Osaka, and I definitely wouldn't have come to the Hall. Do you understand? Everything in my life is the way it is because you came to Vermont when you were a baby."

"I know," said Katana.

"I'm not glad your parents died—I feel terrible about that. But the thing is, when something bad happens, good stuff can still come out of it, ya know?"

"Yeah, I do," said Katana.

"And it sucks that your parents died, especially now that we know the truth about *how* it happened. I get that. But a lot of good came from you moving to Vermont, especially for me."

"I know," said Katana. "I'm sorry for screaming at you the way I did. I don't know what came over me. Everything was building up over the summer, and it all came out last night. Unfortunately, you were the target.

"But you know me better than anyone else, and you were right. You kept telling me I needed to chill out. Everyone else fed me information, but you knew what was really going on.

"I promised Sam I'd stop obsessing about Jaaku—but I didn't get why that promise was so important. For the first time in my life, I wanted to hurt someone, and it was you—of all people, it was you."

"I know," said Chris, cracking a smile. "I thought you were about to kill me."

Katana smiled back, then looked down at the floor. "I almost did. But that's what made me realize that you and Sam were right. The very thing Osaka was afraid of was coming true: I started wanting revenge."

"But now you don't?" asked Chris.

Katana took a deep breath. "No, I don't. But I need you to understand, I still know I'm going to face him..."

"I know, Katana."

"Do you?"

"Yeah, I do," said Chris. "Ever since that night when we found out what really happened, to your parents, I mean. When you said you were going to have to face him someday, I knew exactly what you meant, because I felt it, too. I'm scared for you, Kat. I don't want to lose you."

They both stood up at that moment. Chris pulled her into a hug. Katana felt tears streaming down her cheeks. "I love you so much," she whispered.

Sara came out of the bathroom a moment later, stopped dead in her tracks, looked at the two of them and said, "This is SUPER AWKWARD! I'm standing here in nothing but a towel, and you two are hugging!"

"You're just jealous," said Katana over Chris's shoulder.

"Yeah, I am," she said. She walked over and hugged the two of them together. "Are we better now?"

"Yeah, we are," said Katana. She and Chris sat down again as Sara went to put on some clothes.

"Well, don't let Jimmy see you two hugging like that," Sara called out from the bathroom.

"What? Why?" asked Katana.

"Jimmy's decided he's in love with you," Chris said with a smirk.

"Oh no... Well that explains why he's been weird around me since we got back..."

"You should go out with him, Kat," said Sara as she came out of the bathroom again. "He looks great this year—his acne cleared up a *lot* over the summer!"

"Um, no," said Katana. "I did the boyfriend thing *last* year—that's the last thing I need right now!"

CHAPTER 8

MASTER FU

K atana spent the rest of the day on Sunday lounging around, trying to relax. She felt physically and emotionally drained after everything that had happened on Saturday.

She got up Monday morning before dawn, though, and got dressed to go find somewhere to practice tai chi. She was heading to Sam's dojo by default, but decided instead that she wanted to practice outside. She stopped in the atrium just inside the front doors—she figured she would go down to the beach, but then she changed her mind.

She walked across the atrium, out the back doors to the Zen rock garden, and across the field. It took a minute, but she found the path that led into the forest, and soon arrived at her destination: the old stone foundation she'd discovered the previous year.

Katana half-expected to meet Osaka there again, but she was

alone. The stone was glowing with the energy of the masters who'd practiced there over a hundred years ago. She could see it more clearly than ever.

She walked to the middle of the foundation, and started the form. She bent her knees in the opening stance and thought of sinking her chi down to her feet. From wu chi, she formed a ball of energy between her arms and continued to the next posture.

As she went through the form, Katana could feel her own energy reverberating against that of the forest around her. It was totally different than what she'd felt on the beach in Maine. There, although she could feel the energy of the ocean, it was constant, like the drone of a motor. Here, in the forest, the energy of the trees had a subtle melody, as if it were moving, dancing from tree to tree.

Katana also felt that her own energy was different this morning. All summer she'd focused on building her chi. Now she was much more relaxed, letting her body flow from one posture to the next, for the pure joy of motion.

She went through the form twice more, then did her conditioning routine—including bouncing on the balls of her feet and doing pushups in a handstand. She finished with a series of stretches.

Katana felt great as she jogged back to the Hall. Her mind was clearer than it had been in months, and she felt like herself again. When she got back to her room Sara was in the shower, so she sat out on the balcony, watching the sky grow brighter. When Sara got out of the bathroom, Katana went to shower herself. The two of them went down to the lounge for orientation at nine.

The room was crowded. The girls went to sit with Chris, Jimmy, Jelly, Scott, Paul and Dana. Katana looked around. Nash and Osaka had their heads together at the front of the room, and Nash appeared to be listening carefully to something Osaka was saying to him.

Sam was with a group of younger girls that Katana didn't recognize at the back of the room, and a man she didn't know was near Sam, talking to Tim and Donnie from the wushu team. Katana assumed this must be Master Fu. She wondered for a moment if Donnie was still on the team.

Master Daniels was on the other side of the room, his arms folded across his massive chest. He surveyed the room through beady little eyes.

"Is that Fu?" asked Katana, indicating the man next to Sam.

"Yeah," said Sara, but at that moment Master Nash called the room to attention.

"Good morning, everyone," he began as he beamed around at them. "To our new students, welcome to the Hall of the Dragon; to everyone else, welcome back.

"My name is Jordan Nash and I am the headmaster here at the Hall. This is Master Osaka, who will continue as our kempo master this year; that is Master Samantha Malloy, our tae kwon do master and coach of the sparring team," Nash continued as he held his hand out toward Sam. "Master Daniels will continue as our aikido master, and it is my great pleasure to introduce to you Master Nelson Fu..."

When Nash got to Master Fu, several of the kids broke out in loud cheers and whistles—Katana realized that Jelly, Sara and

Dana were clearly not the only ones he'd talked to over the weekend. He already seemed to have quite a fan club. Master Fu pumped his fist in the air in response to all the noise, and everyone cheered even louder.

"Master Fu will be taking over this year as our wushu master and coach of our performance team," Master Nash continued once the noise had died down.

"I am also pleased to announce some very special additions to our calendar this year. To begin with, Master Malloy has succeeded in her campaign to convince the tournament committee to add a girls' team sparring division..." The room broke out in cheers again.

"If I could please have Katana Kahanu, Sierra and Olivia Gomez and Michelle Summers rise for a moment," asked Master Nash. Katana got to her feet uncertainly. She spotted Sierra and Olivia across the room, both of whom she recognized—although she still couldn't tell them apart. A short black girl with long braids got up as well. Master Nash continued, "These four girls will make up our inaugural team in this new division. Let's give them a big hand." Again, the room broke out in cheers and shouts.

Katana sat down again and said to Sara, "I'm on the wushu team *and* the sparring team?! How am I going pull *this* off?"

"Also, the masters and I are pleased and honored to announce that we will be hosting some very special visitors at the Hall of the Dragon this year. In September, Headmaster Kim from the Temple of the Crane in Korea will be staying with us. The headmaster teaches tae kwon do and hapkido. He will be conducting a seminar for our entire student body while he is here.

"In October, we will have an extremely rare visit from Headmaster Nang from the Hall of the Silent Buddha in Tibet. The temple in Tibet has been independent of the Shaolin temple network for hundreds of years, and this will be the first time a headmaster from Tibet has *ever* visited the Hall of the Dragon.

"Headmaster Nang will not be conducting a seminar. However he will be giving the entire student body a demonstration of his unique and very rare art, known as chi tao.

"In November, Headmaster Santos from the Hall of the Tiger in Brazil will be visiting. The Hall of the Tiger is the newest temple in the Shaolin network and lessons with Headmaster Santos are in high demand all over the world. He will be conducting a seminar on Brazilian jiu jitsu during his stay."

"Hey, Kat—isn't that the place Sensei Mike was talking about?" whispered Chris.

"Yeah—you're right!" said Katana.

"Finally, in December," continued Master Nash, "Headmaster Chatri Benjawan from the Temple of the Golden Arhat in Thailand will be staying with us. Headmaster Chatri is a master of muay thai, which is a form of kickboxing indigenous to Thailand, and he is also a master of hsing-i, which is one of the three great internal arts, along with tai chi and pakua. You will be very fortunate to participate in a hsing-i seminar with one of the most powerful internal masters in the whole world."

"Hey!" said Sara. "That's the guy Master Nakamura was going to go train with, remember?"

"You're right," said Katana. "I wonder if she's coming with him—she was really nice."

"You will be going over to Lincoln Academy for orientation after breakfast this morning. Classes at Lincoln start tomorrow and your regular lessons here at the Hall will commence tomorrow afternoon. Our morning tai chi practice will begin next Monday at five. You will find four complete student uniforms in your closets—I remind you that full uniform is required for all regular lessons, but casual dress is allowed for our morning tai chi practice and, at your coach's discretion, for the team practices as well.

"Finally I remind you that you are required to maintain honor roll status at Lincoln Academy in order to continue your training at the Hall of the Dragon. Master Fu wanted me to announce that he will be making himself available for private tutoring sessions in the evenings should any of you require extra help in your classes.

"Now, if you will see Francine for your schedules, you may then proceed to breakfast," Master Nash concluded.

The whole room erupted in noise and chaos as everyone swooped down upon Francine. Katana grabbed her schedule and joined the throng heading into the cafeteria.

"You're on the wushu team *and* the sparring team?" asked Dana as they sat down with their food a few minutes later.

"Yeah," said Katana. "How am I going to do both?" she asked pleadingly to the table in general.

"Easy," said Paul. "They're not at the same time."

"Yeah, but I was exhausted after the sparring team practice

every week last year," said Katana. "I don't know how I'm gonna have the energy to do both practices back to back like that."

"What am I doing," said Sara, looking down her schedule. "It says here performance martial arts on Mondays and Wednesdays, tae kwon do on Tuesdays and Thursdays, private class with Osaka on Thursdays and performance team on Fridays. What's 'performance martial arts'?"

"I don't know," said Dana, "but that's what it says on my schedule, too. That must be what they're calling the wushu program now."

"I made the sparring team!" said Chris suddenly as he read his schedule. "YES!" He got up and punched his fist in the air, knocking his orange juice all over the table in the process.

"Hey, dummy!" said Jelly, who'd moved out of the way only just in time to avoid being splattered.

"Oops!" said Chris, grabbing all the napkins in sight to clean up the mess.

"I don't have tae kwon do class anymore," said Katana. "I have wushu with you guys on Mondays and Wednesdays, but then I have tai chi on Tuesdays and Thursdays. It says here I have a private with Sam on Tuesdays, and the private with Osaka on Thursdays."

"You got into the tai chi class?" asked Paul, looking impressed. "Nash only takes the top students in that program—the class only has like six kids in it."

"Looks like getting up at dawn every day is paying off," said Sara.

"So it's me, you and Tim on staff," Jelly said, pointing at Sara.

"And Katana and Dana are doing chains... so who's on broadsword with Paul and Scott?"

"Donnie," said Scott through a mouthful of toast.

"Oh!" said Jelly. "I didn't think he was on the team anymore."

"Donnie's awesome on sword," said Paul. "He just wasn't very good at chains."

"You're telling me?" asked Dana sarcastically.

"So what's the deal with these other headmasters coming here this year?" asked Katana.

"Yeah, that's weird," said Sara. "I've never heard of that happening before."

None of the others could explain it, either.

They finished their breakfast, then loaded onto the buses that were waiting for them beyond the torii gate. They arrived at Lincoln and Katana went into the auditorium with Sara and Chris to find the line for sophomores.

"Kahanu, let me see, dear," said the older woman behind the table when Katana got to the front of the line. "All right, you elected to take algebra two with trigonometry, I see... And you have AP biology, French two, honors English, tech ed, and world religions. Good luck with the trig, dear—my son was a math whiz until he got to trig. He failed math that year!"

"Great... thanks," said Katana halfheartedly.

"What was with that lady?" asked Sara as they went down the hall to find their classrooms.

"Did she tell you about her son failing trig, too?" asked Katana.

"Yes!"

"Yeah, I'm not feeling so good about this trig thing, you two," said Chris apprehensively. "And what's with the AP biology? What exactly does 'AP' mean?"

"Advanced placement," said Sara. "It means you get ready to take a special test at the end of the year, and if you score well on that, you get college credit for the class."

"College credit? What do we need that for? We're only in tenth grade!" said Chris with a scowl.

Suddenly Katana felt someone tousle her hair. She ducked and pushed the person's arm away, then turned around to see that it was Ed Golia. "That's a great haircut, Kahanu," he said. "Now everyone can *definitely* tell you're a boy."

Sara grabbed Ed by the throat with one hand and shoved him into the lockers. Ed's sidekick, Tommy Cosgrove, took a step toward Sara, but a third boy who was with them held him back.

"You know, Golia," said Sara, her face only inches from Ed's, "I was hoping we'd run into you today. Just so you know, I'm not putting up with any of your *crap* this year. So you and idiot number two better stay away from us."

Sara walked away. Katana and Chris stared at her for a moment, then looked at each other in amazement before running to catch up with her.

"Wow," said Chris.

"What was that about?" asked Katana.

"I wanted to start things off on the right foot this year," she said perkily. "Come on, you know what they say," she continued, when Katana stared at her, "the best defense is a good offense."

"I guess..." said Chris. "Hey, who was that Chinese kid with the moron twins? He looks familiar, but I can't place where I've seen him before."

"I don't know," said Sara thoughtfully. "You're right, though, he does look very familiar."

"I recognize him from somewhere, too," said Katana, "but I don't think it's from Lincoln."

They found their classrooms and got their books, then took the bus back to the Hall. Katana and Sara dashed up to their room to drop off their books. Katana grabbed her chains and they ran up to the wushu dojo. Jelly, Scott and Tim were already there.

"KATANA!" yelled Jelly as they walked in.

"JELLY!" Katana shouted back at him.

"It's double backflip time!"

"Ugh," said Katana. "I was worried you were gonna say that."

"Come on," Jelly insisted. "You were this close the other day," he said, holding his thumb and index finger an inch apart.

The two of them went to the end of the springboard floor, by the foam pit. "Here it goes," said Katana. She did a round-off into her double backflip. She landed in the foam on her knees, not quite making it far enough around. She tried it repeatedly, Jelly urging her on the whole time. Finally she was able to get her feet underneath her one time before she hit the foam.

"YEAH!" yelled Jelly. "Now do it on the floor!"

"No," said Katana, "that was only once. I wanna get it way more consistent before I try it without the foam."

Dana walked in then anyway, so the two of them went over to talk to her. As they jumped down from the spring-board floor, Katana saw Sara and Tim working on the release skill for staff. Sara threw her staff straight up into the air, did a standing backflip, and caught the staff without a problem.

But then Tim threw the staff up, tried to do a standing backflip, but landed on all fours instead. The staff crashed down on his head.

"OW!"

Jelly ran over to them. "Don't think about the staff while you're jumping, you idiot!"

"I'm not!" Tim retorted. "I can't do a standing backflip!"

"Sure you can!" said Jelly. "Give me the staff, and show me one!"

Jelly grabbed Tim's staff out of his hands. Tim jumped up and did a backflip, landing on his feet with ease.

"See!" said Jelly. "You're thinking about the staff while you're going over—I had the same problem the first time I tried this. You can't think about the staff until your feet are on the ground—otherwise you're gonna fall."

"That looks like it's going well," Dana said to Katana.

"Yeah, Jelly's got it under control."

For the next half hour, Katana and Dana worked on their whip chain set. Katana could now fall into a split with her foot over her head, and she was even able to spin both chains in one hand for several rotations before they smacked together. She knew she now needed to keep the chains spinning this way as she lifted one foot up. But putting the moves together proved more difficult.

Katana kept working on it though, and finally Dana said,

"That's getting better. I'm sure you'll have it down in time for the tournament in Eureka."

Jelly came back then and asked, "Hey, have you two tried the butterfly twist with the chains yet?"

"No," said Dana. "That's right, I wanted to work on that more today. I have to get the twist down first, though."

They practiced the trick. Katana could already do it nearly as well as Jelly. Dana wasn't even close. "I can't get around in time," she said in frustration after a few minutes.

"You really gotta start rotating earlier," said Jelly. "You're going fast enough, and you've got enough height, but it looks like you're just doing a butterfly kick. You're not turning until the very end."

Jelly continued helping Dana, so Katana went off to work on her own. She wanted to get this move down with her chains— she'd been trying all summer to think of a way to add more tricks to the set. This was a good start. She needed to do the twist into a split first though.

She walked through it a couple of times, not actually doing the twist, but walking around in a circle, then jumping into the air and landing in a split. She'd done a front aerial into a split the previous year with Master Nash. This shouldn't be much more difficult, she decided.

She gave it a try for real. She went into the twist, then kicked her legs out as she came down, landing in a full split.

"Yes!" she said out loud. She picked up her chains and decided she was going to get this, right now.

She spun her chains and stepped around the way she did for a butterfly kick, then twisted over hard. And sure enough, as she pulled her arms in, the chains continued to spin around her as she rolled over sideways in the air. She landed in the split and the chains fell limply by her sides.

"You got it already?!" yelled Dana. Katana realized that everyone else had stopped to watch her. "That's SO not fair! I can't even do the twist yet!"

Someone started clapping; it was Master Fu—he'd been watching from the doorway. "Nicely done," he said, walking over to Katana. "I'm Nelson Fu, nice to finally meet you, Katana."

Katana got up and shook his hand.

"I was friends with your parents and Samantha back at UH," he said. "I haven't seen you since you were a baby!"

"You knew my parents?!" asked Katana, totally surprised by this news.

"Oh yes," said Master Fu. "I was going out with your mother's roommate our freshman year. Kristine introduced me to your father and Osaka. She knew I was big into wushu, and Adrian was training with Osaka, of course. That's how I first got started in kempo.

"So, you girls have the monk move in the chain set now?"

"The monk move?" asked Katana uncertainly.

"Oh, yeah, I call it that. The move where you hold your foot up, spin both chains in one hand, and drop into a split. The first time I ever saw that done was by this monk at Shaolin. I've called it the monk move ever since," Master Fu explained.

"We haven't put it in the set yet, but we've both been practicing it," said Dana.

"Well let's try it," said Master Fu. "Go through your set from the beginning, and put that in at the end of the flowers."

"How do you want us to start?" asked Katana. "I've never done this in the demo before."

"Oh, right," said Master Fu. "Well, let's do this—you can both flash kick?" The girls nodded. "I'm going to have you two flash kick past each other diagonally across the stage, throw the chains out at each other, and go into flowers. You're not going to be able to walk forward very far, so when you do the neck wrap and the leg wrap, you're going to have to do it almost in place. Go into the monk move facing each other, and fall into the splits in opposite directions. You can swing your back leg around and lie down for the body jumps, then kick up and get off stage."

"All right," said Dana. Katana lined up with her to start the set.

They ran past each other and each did a round-off into a flash kick, then threw out the chains and went through the set exactly as Master Fu had described. Dana was going full speed through the flowers, and Katana was pleasantly surprised to find that she was able to keep up. They got to the monk move, and Katana focused on maintaining the rhythm of the chains as she brought both handles together in one hand. She lifted her foot in the air very carefully with her left hand, keeping the chains going in her right. She had done it—she stalled the chains as she fell into a split, and landed at the exact same time as Dana. Both of them swung their legs around, did several full body jumps, and kicked to their feet.

"Yes, girls, that was great!" exclaimed Master Fu when they were done.

"Sifu, is there any way we can add a butterfly twist to the set," asked Katana—then looked at Dana and added, "if we can both get it down?"

"Katana, first of all, do *not* call me 'Sifu'!" said Master Fu with a stern look. "Please, call me Nelson—it is my name after all. And yes, if you can both get the twist down with the chains, I'm sure we can work it into the set. It doesn't take as much room as the butterfly kicks, so we can probably fit both of you on stage doing that move at the same time. Can you both do a twist already?"

"NO!" said Dana. "I can't land it to save my life!"

"Let me see you try it," said Master Fu.

He spent the next several minutes helping Dana with the twist. Katana went off and did it with the chains a few more times. She thought about where she could add it to their set.

Even with Master Fu's help, Dana wasn't able to land the butterfly twist. He had her start doing it without going completely sideways, so she could get a feeling for how to land it. Dana did it keeping her body almost totally vertical the whole time.

"Once you can get it horizontal, then we'll do it with the chains," said Master Fu.

"Jelly, Katana," he continued, "let's see the double backflip."

"Um..." said Katana, feeling anxious, "I haven't been able to land it yet!"

"That's okay," replied Master Fu. "You can levitate, right?"

"Yeah," said Katana. "I get it—just do it, and levitate if I'm going to crash."

"Good, let's see it then. I want you to do it side by side, so start over here, and run toward the springboard floor."

Katana went over to the edge of the floor with Jelly. They looked at each other and nodded, then ran into a round-off. Katana was determined to land the flip without levitating. So she jumped as high as she could, and started going over backwards the instant she was in the air. Her feet hit the ground first—but she stumbled over backwards and landed on her butt.

"Nicely done," said Master Fu, clapping and coming over to them. "Sam told me you were stubborn, Katana—you were really fighting for that landing. Keep working on this together. I want that move in the demo as soon as possible."

"Sara and Tim, let's see the release skill."

"Together?" asked Sara.

"Absolutely."

Sara and Tim went out on the floor, nodded to each other, threw their staves in the air and did standing backflips. Sara landed perfectly and caught the staff, but once again, Tim landed on all fours. He covered his head with his arms just in time to protect himself from the staff.

"Tim—you can't think about the staff while you're flipping!" said Master Fu. "Flip first, then worry about the staff!"

"That's exactly what Jelly said," Tim muttered.

Sara sat down with Katana, Dana, Scott and Jelly, and they watched Master Fu work with Tim for a few minutes. "He's really nice," said Sara.

"Yeah, he reminds me of Sam, like a lot," Dana said. "He's wicked focused, that's for sure. He knows exactly what he wants!"

"Our demo's gonna be awesome this year," said Jelly with a big grin.

With Master Fu's help, Tim was finally able to do the release skill with a clean backflip.

"All right kids," said Master Fu as he walked off the floor, "I want you to keep practicing your moves this week. We have our first team practice this Friday and I want to get the demo together as soon as possible.

"Scott, I want you to keep practicing sword the way you have it now—we might be adding something more to that set, but I haven't decided yet. I'll let you know on Friday.

"Have a good week, everyone," he said with a smile, and walked out the door.

"Yeah, I'm done for today," said Dana. "I'll see you guys later."

Katana and Sara got up to leave with Dana, but Jelly said, "Not so fast, you two!"

"I'm exhausted, Jelly, I'm not doing anything else today," Sara complained.

"Oh yes you are—I still have to work on the chen do!"

"You can levitate on your own," said Katana. "You don't need us."

"No, I'm not talking about levitating, I wanna get a chi hit and deflect intent."

"Good luck," said Sara. "Kat's the only one who can do three of them."

"Not for long!" said Jelly. "I'm gonna get them both this year if it kills me."

"You guys have fun," said Scott. "I'm outta here." He ran out the door before Jelly could stop him.

Jelly walked back to the springboard floor. "Here's what I wanna do. I'm gonna stand at the edge of the floor, and I want you two to hit me with your chi."

Katana and Sara looked at each other in total disbelief. "Are you kidding me?" said Sara. "You're gonna stand there and *let* us hit you?"

"Yeah!" said Jelly. "I figure, if I wanna deflect it bad enough, and not get hit anymore, then this is the best way to do it!"

Katana thought this idea was ridiculous. But she quickly discovered it was an immense amount of fun to throw fireballs at Jelly while he stood there and took it.

Jelly stood at the edge of the floor, and the girls took turns hitting him with their chi. Every time a fireball hit him, he flew through the air and landed in the foam. Then he climbed out and got ready again.

Katana had a lot more energy left than she'd thought; she and Sara became creative. Katana did an aerial one time, and threw her chi at Jelly while she was upside down. Sara tried it too, and squealed when Jelly flew into the foam. "This is the most fun I've ever had in my entire life!"

They took turns, trying to throw the fireball from different tricks. Katana tried it from a double backflip—she threw the fireball at Jelly as she started her second rotation, and landed the flip without falling over this time.

They did this for another half hour, but as far as Katana could tell, it was accomplishing nothing—other than amusing her and Sara. Jelly was no closer to deflecting intent than he'd been when they started.

"That didn't work," he said as he climbed out of the foam pit the last time.

"No, maybe not," said Sara, "but it sure is a lot of fun!"

"Well, I wanna try it again next time," said Jelly. "I'm convinced it should work. Maybe we'll try it without the foam pit though, cuz then it'll hurt more and I'll want to block it REALLY badly!"

Katana was beginning to think Jelly was insane.

CHAPTER 9
BREAKING AND PERFORMANCE

Osaka walked into Nash's conference room and took a seat. Nash was sitting at the head of the table.

"What news from Shaolin?" Osaka asked.

"The headmaster heard from Supomo. There was an attack at the temple in Indonesia."

"The assassin?"

"That remains unclear," Nash said with a sigh. "One of their monks was patrolling the perimeter of the grounds. Someone grabbed him from behind, and tried to use him to get inside the temple. The monk refused to help."

"And he lived to tell the tale?"

"Apparently. The attacker roughed him up trying to get him to comply. But in the end he let him go, and disappeared. The monk wasn't able to get a look at him."

Osaka took a deep breath.

"There must be an Arashi among Supomo's people."

"*If* this was the assassin, then I would have to agree," said Nash.

"Who else would do this?"

"It could be anyone—someone with a personal grudge against one of the monks, perhaps. There's no evidence pointing to the assassin. And in any event, Supomo isn't one of the headmasters coming here, so this doesn't affect us."

"I find it unlikely that this is a coincidence. And if there's an Arashi in Indonesia, there could be one inside any one of the other temples as well."

"Anything is possible," Nash admitted.

"This only underscores the danger we face. Having the headmasters and their entourages here is bad enough. Should any member of their parties prove to be an Arashi..."

"I know," said Nash. "But that's hardly likely."

"The risk is too great," said Osaka, shaking his head. "I still think we should cancel these visits."

"The risk would exist whether the headmasters came here or not. We cannot afford to leave Shaolin."

Osaka leaned back in his chair, letting out a long sigh.

"I hope we don't live to regret this."

"We'll do everything in our power to protect Katana," said Nash. "Have faith, old friend."

KATANA WOKE up before dawn on Tuesday. She found a birthday card from Sara sitting on her desk. She'd forgotten that it was her birthday—the events of the past few days had driven it completely from her mind.

She got dressed and went out to the old dojo in the forest to practice tai chi. Again she half-expected and hoped that she would find Osaka there. But again, she was alone. She wondered where Osaka was; he'd told her when she first found the place that he practiced tai chi there every morning.

Katana went around to her classes at Lincoln that day and, unlike any of her friends, found that she was glad to be back in school. She'd always loved learning of any kind, whether it was academic or martial arts.

Chris, on the other hand, was not feeling good about the new school year. He kept shooting apprehensive looks at Katana as their math teacher went over the syllabus. Katana knew she could look forward to many an evening helping Chris with his homework.

When Katana got to the tae kwon do dojo for her private lesson that afternoon, Sam was arranging piles of wooden boards around pairs of cinder blocks spread out around the room.

"What are these for?" she asked.

"We're going to be doing some board breaking this week," said Sam with an odd expression on her face, as if she didn't approve of the idea.

"Why are we breaking boards?"

"Well, a lot of tae kwon do schools do it for demonstrations —to show how much power you can generate in strikes and kicks. I've never had much use for it myself... If you ever find yourself being attacked by a tree, you should probably run," she said sarcastically.

"Then why are we breaking boards?" Katana asked again.

"Oh, well Headmaster Kim is coming soon and I have a feeling he's going to try to make us look bad. He has this arrogant attitude that if you aren't doing tae kwon do in Korea, then you're not *really* doing tae kwon do. So if there's anything we're *not* doing in our program, he's sure to cover it in his seminar, to point out our weaknesses," Sam replied as she carried a pile of boards over to the last set of cinder blocks.

Jason Beecher walked in. "Hey, Kat—hi, Sam. Oh cool, we're doing board breaking?" Katana had felt a little awkward around Jason ever since they'd broken up several months before. But if Jason shared any of her discomfort, he didn't show it.

"Yeah," said Sam, rolling her eyes as she walked over to them.

"Van Heldon did this with us my first year here," said Jason. "It was right after that Kim guy came—he had us do some board breaking in his seminar, but we'd never done it before. Kim made a big deal out of it. So after he left, Van Heldon did nothing but board breaking for like the next month!"

"See?" said Sam to Katana. "I don't plan on giving him that same satisfaction; I'm covering all the bases before he gets here.

"All right, let's get started," she said. She took them through some stretches. When they dropped into a front split, she asked, "So are you feeling any better, Kat?"

Katana was mortified that she was bringing this up in front of Jason. "Yeah, definitely," she said, hoping Sam would leave it at that.

"I'm glad," said Sam. "It should be easier to keep your mind occupied now that school's started. It's good to stay busy."

Jason looked at them quizzically for a moment. But much to Katana's relief, he didn't ask what they were talking about, and Sam didn't pursue the subject any further.

"Who wants to go first?" Sam set up a board across the two cinder blocks closest to them.

"I'll go," said Jason. He walked over and got into a low horse stance right in front of the cinder blocks. He reached back with his right hand, and chopped straight down, right through the board with the edge of his hand. The board split in half with a loud cracking noise.

"Piece of cake," said Sam, setting up the next board. "Your turn, Kat."

"How do I do this, exactly?" Katana asked uncertainly. She'd never tried to break a board before.

"It's easy," said Sam. "You're actually breaking with the grain of the wood—the structure of the wood is very strong, so it's almost impossible to break across the grain. But when you break with the grain it splits easily. Try it with a knife hand strike, like Jason did. Focus on striking *through* the board, as opposed to hitting it on the surface."

"Okay," said Katana tentatively. She got into a horse stance in front of the cinder blocks like Jason had done. She reached back, focused on hitting through the board, and brought her hand down as hard as she could. She was shocked at how easily the board broke—it felt as if she'd hardly touched it.

"Wow!" she said, "that was easy—I thought it was going to hurt!"

"It only hurts when you don't go through," said Sam. "The energy from your strike has to go *somewhere*. If you do it right, the energy goes into the board. If you don't focus through it, though, your hand absorbs the force—and that hurts!

"Let's try two boards," she said, setting them up for Jason.

Jason broke two just as easily.

"Your turn, Kat," said Sam. "You have to do the same thing with two boards you did with one—focus on your hand going right through."

"So it's kind of like the unbendable arm exercise?" asked Katana.

"Yes," said Sam, nodding her head, "it's exactly like that. Visualize your hand moving right through the boards as if they weren't there."

"Okay," said Katana, feeling like getting through two boards was going to be infinitely harder. She did the break. Again, it felt like she'd hardly touched the wood.

Sam continued increasing the number of boards until it was Jason's turn to try five. Sam talked him through it. Jason brought his hand down a few times in slow motion before going for the actual break. Then he shouted out a loud kiai, and smashed through all five boards.

Katana did this as well, and asked, "Sam, it almost feels like the whole stack is breaking just as my hand touches the top board—is that really what's happening?"

"It is," Sam confirmed. "Wood is flexible—it bends a bit

before it breaks. So when you put the boards right on top of each other like this, they all start to flex when your hand comes in contact with the top of the pile. It's the *bottom* board that's breaking first, so by the time your hand gets down that far, it's already broken. That's why it feels like the whole stack is breaking when you hit the first one.

"Now we're going to try it with spacers, though," Sam continued. "This is going to be harder for exactly the same reason. The boards aren't going to be touching each other, so the bottom one will not break until your hand gets there."

This was exactly the opposite of what Katana would've expected—without Sam's explanation, she'd have been certain that breaking the boards *without* spacers would've been much tougher.

Sam set up five boards again, this time with pencils stuck in between each board, one on each edge. Jason went first; he couldn't quite do the break. The top four broke, but the bottom one bounced off the cinder blocks, quite whole.

"Ow!" he said, shaking his right hand. "That one hurt!"

"Yeah, it hurts when you miss one," said Sam. She set up five more boards, with spacers again, and invited Katana to take her turn.

"Remember, Kat," said Sam, "you have to focus on your hand going through to the bottom. Make sure you put all of your weight into the strike—drop your stance a bit as you do it, and hit with your whole body, not just your arm."

Katana focused as hard as she could on the space underneath the bottom board. She rose up in her stance, and mimed the break a few times. "Here it goes," she said finally. She hit down as hard as she could, driving her hand through all five boards.

"Well done!" said Sam with a smile.

"That was definitely a lot harder with the spacers," said Katana. Her hand didn't hurt, exactly, but it felt like she'd done way more work than she had without the spacers.

"That's enough for today," said Sam. "I'll be doing this with all the classes this week, and we're going to move onto bricks next."

"Bricks?!" asked Katana. She almost thought that Sam was kidding.

"Bricks!" Sam repeated. "They're not that bad. Breaking one brick is about the same as breaking five boards without spacers. It's totally different when you stack them, though. Bricks don't bend, so it's the opposite of stacking wood. When you stack bricks without spacers, it's *much* more difficult. Either they all break, or you break your hand! But when you put spacers between them, unlike with wood, it's actually easier. When you break the top brick, the force of the break carries down into the second brick, and so on.

"Don't worry," she continued when she saw the apprehensive looks on their faces. "We'll work up to that."

"I don't know about bricks," said Jason. "Van Heldon only ever had us break wood!"

Katana and Jason helped Sam clean up the broken wood, then Katana ran upstairs for her first tai chi class. When she arrived, she discovered that Paul had been right—there were only five other students in the enormous dojo.

"Good afternoon, everyone," said Master Nash with a smile as he lined them up. "I would like you to welcome Katana to our group," he continued. "She learned the long form with Master Osaka last year, so her transition into this class should be a smooth one."

He introduced Katana to each of the other students—whom Katana was sure were all seniors—and started class. They went through a series of chi kung exercises first, most of which Katana had done in the morning tai chi class during her previous two years. Next, he had them do the standing chi kung exercise Katana had done with Sensei Mike over the summer. Only one of the other students was able to form a ball of energy between his arms—a tall boy named Ryan. Katana vaguely recognized him as one of the students who had helped Master Nash with the morning tai chi lessons the previous year.

Master Nash went around to each of them in turn to correct their stances. But when he got to Katana he merely watched her for a moment, with an approving nod. "Mitchell told me you had been doing some interesting work with your posture. I understand you figured this out from doing tai chi on the beach?"

"Yeah," said Katana a little nervously as she came out of her stance. She'd had a little more contact with Master Nash the previous year than she'd had the year before that, but she still found him intimidating. She could see his aura glowing brightly around him. "I had to change my stances to keep my balance. I could feel it making my chi flow stronger, too."

"That it does," said Master Nash. "You are aligning your meridians in a way that does indeed allow the chi to flow more directly. I never thought of using sand as a way to teach the posture before—perhaps we'll go to the beach and practice some afternoon."

Master Nash went around to everyone again and made some of the same corrections to their stances that Katana had made for Sensei Mike and Mr. Brown.

They went through the long form together next—only Katana, Master Nash and Ryan were able to hold a ball of chi as they did this—then Master Nash had them pair off to work on pushing hands.

Nash paired off with Ryan, and Katana went with a girl named Betsy. Katana stood facing Betsy, with one foot in front and the other behind, her front foot next to Betsy's. Katana had gained a deep appreciation for this exercise the previous year, but found very quickly that she was no match for Betsy.

Katana could see Betsy's shen—her intent, which manifested itself as faint, wispy tendrils of energy extending from her aura. This allowed her to sense where Betsy was going to push. But Katana couldn't feel Betsy's center of mass. As Katana adjusted her arms to get ready to push, Betsy made a slight adjustment to her posture. Katana no longer had anything to push against.

After a few minutes, neither of them had been able to push the other over. Master Nash came over to watch. "Katana, I would like you to proceed with your eyes closed," he said with a smile.

"But I won't be able to see her shen!"

"Exactly," said Master Nash. They did the exercise again, and Betsy was able to push Katana over three times in a row. Katana hadn't felt the pushes coming, and was still totally unable to find Betsy's center.

"You can see Betsy's shen, so you were, of course, relying on that to sense where she was going to push," said Master Nash when Katana gave up in frustration. "By doing the exercise with your eyes closed, you had to rely on more mundane methods of detecting her intent."

"But I couldn't feel *anything*," said Katana. "I couldn't find her center."

"Observe," said Master Nash. He assumed a stance, and indicated that Katana should join him. Katana got into her own stance facing him, and brought her hands up in light contact with his. "As I get ready to push, you can feel through your contact with my hands that I am doing so," he said. At the same time he shifted his weight slightly, and indeed, Katana could feel that shift through her contact with his hands. She adjusted her own stance to prepare to redirect his energy.

"Now, if we do that again—please close your eyes, Katana— but this time I disengage my arm from my shoulder—in other words, I leave my arm totally relaxed and in the same position as I advance, you cannot feel my weight shift." Master Nash pushed again. This time Katana couldn't feel a thing; Nash was able to knock her right over.

"Because of your ability with the chen do, you are able to *see* your opponent's shen even if you cannot *feel* their center. By doing the exercise with your eyes closed, you are forced to pay more attention to the feeling," Master Nash explained.

"So that's why I could never find her center?" asked Katana. "Because she was disengaging her arm?"

"That is correct," said Master Nash.

"Then there's no way to feel where she's going to go?"

"Observe," said Master Nash. "Betsy, if you will?" Master Nash assumed his stance again, and Betsy got in position to do pushing hands with him. Nash closed his eyes, and they began. Yet even with his eyes closed, Nash was able to redirect Betsy's every push, and knock her over.

"How are you doing that?!" asked Katana.

"Betsy is very good at masking her intent," said Master Nash. "But as you increase your touch sensitivity, you will be able to feel very slight and subtle shifts in her position."

They repeated the exercise as Nash went to work with the other students. Katana continued doing it with her eyes closed. She tried to relax and focus completely on feeling little changes in Betsy's position, but was no nearer being able to do this by the end of class.

"That was amazing," said Katana as she and Betsy walked down to the cafeteria for dinner together. "How'd you learn to do that so well?"

"I don't really know," said Betsy with a sigh. "I started doing it a couple of years ago in the morning tai chi classes. Master Nash did pushing hands with me one day, and I was able to knock him over. So the next year he added me to the regular tai chi class. He's been helping me get it better ever since."

Katana decided she wanted to do pushing hands with Betsy as

often as she could—maybe some of her skill would start to rub off.

"How'd tai chi class go?" asked Paul when Katana sat down next to Sara with her food.

Katana told them about the class. "Betsy's really good at tai chi," said Paul. "She competes with the short form at the tournaments and always wins first place."

"How was tae kwon do?" asked Katana.

"We had to break boards!" said Sara, as if she were offended by the very idea. "Who does that?"

"I guess Master Kim does," said Katana.

"That guy who's coming from Korea?" asked Chris.

"Yeah," said Katana. She explained what Sam had told her. "So I guess she wants us to know how to do it in case Kim decides to be a jerk."

"Well board breaking sucks," said Sara with a frown. "I hope we're not gonna be doing this all year."

"You're just mad cuz you couldn't break four boards," said Chris.

"Psh, so what?" said Sara. "At least I didn't keep hurting myself trying to do five!"

"At least I tried!" Chris retorted. "You gave up after you missed four the first time."

"How many did you break, Kat?" asked Sara after she'd glared at Chris.

"Five," said Katana around a mouthful of spaghetti.

"You broke five?!" asked Jimmy, dropping his fork. "*Nobody* was able to get five in our class!"

"Really?" asked Katana. "It wasn't too hard."

"Not too hard..?" asked Chris in disbelief. "You musta been using your chi or something. I couldn't get through five no matter how hard I hit."

Katana had difficulty concentrating at school the next day—she was eager to get to their wushu class. She was not alone, either—she overheard at least half a dozen other students from the Hall talking excitedly about the new wushu master.

When they arrived at the wushu dojo, Master Fu was greeting everyone personally at the door as they walked in. "Hi, Katana, Sara—you're Chris, right?"

"Yeah," said Chris, shaking his hand. Katana had the distinct impression that Master Fu already knew nearly everyone in the class—not only the kids from the wushu team.

Master Fu started class and ran warm-ups and stretches much the same way that Master Hua always had. Katana felt great satisfaction at having done all the conditioning work all summer—it had paid off. She was jumping as high as Jelly now.

Next, Master Fu took them through the short form Katana had learned the previous year, and had everyone go through it on their own while he worked with the beginners. After that he had everyone make two lines on the springboard floor and ran them through various tricks.

Katana and Jelly had the most extensive repertoires. Everyone cheered loudly when Master Fu called them up to do side-by-side double backflips. Katana was a little nervous about this—she'd only successfully completed the trick once so far. But she landed it perfectly, right next to Jelly.

Master Fu asked them both to demonstrate levitation, the chen do of wushu. Katana did another double backflip. But just before she landed, she bounced her chi off the floor, kicked one leg over hard and did a front aerial.

When it was Jelly's turn, instead of doing a trick, he ran up the wall. He went all the way to the ceiling before jumping down again, landing gracefully on the springboard floor.

Master Fu then explained that the four basic weapons in the wushu program were staff, broadsword, spear and straight sword. He had a different student come up to demonstrate a form with each weapon—Sara did staff, and Scott did broadsword.

Finally Master Fu had everyone sit down again. "As you may have noticed on your schedules, we have renamed the wushu program this year. From now on it will be called 'performance martial arts.' The reason for this is that we will be adding a whole new dimension to the curriculum this year.

"I started my career as a wushu artist, but then when I was in college, I began training in kempo—with Master Osaka, in fact, back when he was teaching in Hawaii. Over the years I have also become more involved with sport karate.

"I know you participate in the tournaments every year as part of your training here at the Hall, so you will have seen sport karate before. The Okinawan and Japanese weapons you see people perform at those events—kamas, nunchaku, bo staff, samurai sword—those forms come from sport karate.

"Now I want to reassure you, we *are* going to continue doing wushu—you will test for rank in wushu, and we will still be teaching all the different wushu weapons. But now you will have a choice—if you want, you can start learning some of the sport karate weapons in addition to the wushu you're doing.

"The two styles have a very different background, a very different history, but both styles, ultimately, also have a lot in common. Both are very heavily grounded in performance—so there is a certain way you carry yourself, a certain energy that you project in both that is very much the same. Eventually, as some of you get better with these new weapons, I plan on adding some sport karate elements to our team demo."

Katana looked over at Dana when Master Fu said this—she remembered only too well how Dana had reacted when Master Nash took over as coach of the wushu team the previous year. Dana had balked at what she perceived as his "tampering" with Master Hua's demo, even though Nash had followed Hua's plan.

But it looked to Katana like Dana was taking this in stride—she was nodding in agreement to everything Master Fu was saying.

Finally Master Fu asked if anyone had any questions. An older girl raised her hand and asked, "How can you change one of the programs like this? The Hall of the Dragon has been teaching the same five arts for like a hundred and fifty years, hasn't it?"

"Actually not," said Master Fu. "For example, aikido was only added back in the 1940s—it did not exist for long before that. Like Master Nash always says, the martial arts have to evolve, or else they will die. Change doesn't happen overnight, but even at the Hall of the Dragon, there have been many changes to the curriculum over the years. This is the next step in that evolutionary process."

Master Fu concluded his speech and had a small black boy named Nathan come up to demonstrate a nunchuck form. Katana had never seen him before, and assumed from his size that he was new to the Hall this year.

Katana was dazzled by this performance—Nathan did many of the same moves with the weapon that she'd seen Becca Stratton do at the tournaments the previous year. He rolled the weapon around his fingers as fast as lightning and released them spinning into the air, catching them again flawlessly.

Master Fu himself performed a set with a samurai sword which also had many different spins and release skills. Katana thought that if she were ever going to learn a sport karate weapon, that was probably the one she'd want to do. Her father's sword—that Sato had given her two years ago—still sat in its stand on her desk. Every time she looked at it, she thought about learning how to use it someday. She knew that the performance weapon wasn't the same as a real samurai sword, but she figured that at least some of the movement would be similar.

Master Fu reminded the kids from the performance team to practice their new moves for Friday, then dismissed them for the day.

"Did you see that kid do chucks?!" asked Jelly when they got to dinner. "That was *awesome*! I definitely wanna learn that!"

Katana watched Dana carefully as Sara said, "What, you mean you don't wanna do staff anymore?"

"No, of course I wanna keep doing staff! But you heard him, I can do both!"

"Dana, what do you think about the new weapons?" Katana asked as delicately as she could.

Dana thought for a moment. "Well, I still like chains the best, but it'd be neat to learn samurai sword. You can do a lot more with that weapon than you can with broadsword. And we wouldn't have so much trouble adding new tricks into the set, either."

As they ate, Katana thought to herself that Master Fu must be a genius. She realized that by getting to know all the kids to some degree, and giving everyone on the wushu team new things to work on *before* he announced the new curriculum, he'd already won them over. Otherwise, Katana was certain that Dana would've had a very strong, negative reaction to the idea of adding sport karate to the wushu program.

CHAPTER 10

TEAM TIMES TWO

All day Thursday Katana found she was very much looking forward to her private lesson with Osaka that afternoon. She'd gone out to the old dojo in the forest to do tai chi every morning this week, hoping to run into him there. But not once had he turned up.

Osaka had been like a father to her while she was growing up, and had been her karate teacher for as long as she could remember. It was different now, in the summer, not having him around in Vermont. Katana liked Sensei Mike, but it wasn't the same. She had a connection with Osaka that she didn't feel with anyone else —even Sam, although she came the closest. But since her return to the Hall, the only time Katana had seen Osaka was at orientation on Monday.

Sara and Katana ran up to their room right after school, got changed into their uniforms, then went downstairs to collect Chris. The three of them walked to the kempo dojo together.

Osaka looked older to Katana somehow, more careworn than ever before. And he got right down to business—he had them stretch on their own for a few minutes and said, "This year we will be working to get the three of you ready to test for your third degree black belts in kempo."

"You mean we're going to test... *this year*?" said Chris in total shock.

"Yes, Chris," Osaka said with a smile. "I have discussed your progress with Sensei Mike—and with Master Sakamoto," he added with a nod to Sara, "and we are in agreement that preparing you three for the test in June is a reasonable goal.

"You are going to have to work extra hard to achieve this—third degree is a very big step in your martial arts careers. This is considered the first step toward becoming a master."

He began their lesson. They went through their kata first, and Katana could tell from the look on Osaka's face that he was satisfied, maybe even impressed with their forms.

They each took a turn doing self-defense combinations next. Other than making a few small corrections, Osaka seemed happy with their progress in this area as well. Finally they did attack drills.

Katana took her turn in the middle first and Sara and Chris took turns attacking her. Katana quickly achieved the state of mind where she didn't consciously know how she was going to respond to each attack—her body was simply reacting. She'd learned long ago that allowing her conscious mind to interfere in this process was a mistake. Every time she'd ever done so, she'd found herself fumbling her defense. But she made no errors today. By the time Katana had finished her turn, she couldn't recall a single technique she'd used against either Chris or Sara.

Osaka was apparently very happy with her performance. He patted her on the back and said simply, "Excellent, Katana" when she was done.

Sara had her turn next; she started out very strong. Chris attacked first—he threw a punch, and Sara sidestepped, hit him in the ribs with an elbow, then turned, grabbed his arm and flipped him over onto the mat.

Katana had to position herself so that Chris would not be in the way of her attack. She dove in to tackle Sara the moment Chris hit the mat. Sara lunged back and pushed down hard on the back of Katana's neck, sending her sprawling on the mat.

Chris had positioned himself directly behind Sara, however. He grabbed her in a bear hug the moment Katana was down. But Sara simply grabbed his arms and flipped him over onto the mat again. Katana had to scurry out of the way to avoid Chris falling on top of her.

Katana got back to her feet, and threw a punch at Sara's head. Sara deflected this with ease. She kicked Katana in the ribs, hit her in the head, then grabbed her neck and pulled her into a knee— knocking the wind out of Katana.

"Oh Kat—I'm sorry!" said Sara the moment she realized what she'd done.

Katana caught her breath. "I'm fine." She prepared to attack again, but Osaka stopped them.

"Sara, that was very good—but you lost control," he said. "You must react in the drills without trying to consciously anticipate the attack, but kempo is still about control. And to get your third degree, you must be able to maintain enough control, even during attack drills, to temper your response..."

"And not hurt my friends," added Sara.

"Exactly," said Osaka, "Please continue."

Katana and Chris each took a few more turns attacking Sara, but Katana could tell she was no longer focused. Sara fumbled the next couple of attacks and couldn't regain her composure.

Osaka had them switch, and put Chris in the middle. Chris also started out very strong, and defended perfectly against the first half-dozen attacks. But then one time, when he'd just thrown Katana to the mat, Sara came in with a punch to his head before he was ready. Chris dropped down and threw out his hands. Katana could tell that he'd deflected Sara's intent—she crumpled down on all fours.

"Very good, Chris," Osaka said with a grin, "but for this round, I wanted you to use only external techniques, not the chen do!" Chris muttered something about Sara sneaking up on him.

Osaka had Katana take another turn in the middle. "This time, Katana, please use *only* the chen do—I will attack in Chris's place, of course." Katana had discovered in the middle of her black belt test two years ago that she and Chris couldn't use the chen do against each other. She'd tried to do so—without knowing what she was doing at the time—during an attack drill. While it had worked fine on several other students, it had had no effect on Chris. Master Osaka had explained later that because Katana and Chris had been so close for so many years, their chi had mixed. This made it impossible for them to use the chen do against each other.

Osaka and Sara took turns attacking Katana, and she deflected their intent with ease every time—they couldn't get close to her. Chris and Sara each had a turn when Katana was done.

"That is good for today," said Osaka when Sara had finished. "You are just about where you need to be with your kata and your self-defense combinations. The attack drills are always the hardest area to maintain control as they are obviously more stressful than simply repeating the movements by rote. That is where all three of you can use the most work."

He dismissed them, but when they got into the atrium, Katana remembered that she'd wanted to ask him something. "I'll see you guys at dinner," she said to Sara and Chris, and went back into the kempo dojo.

"Osaka, can I talk to you for a minute?" she asked.

"Yes, Katana, what's on your mind?"

"I was talking to Sara's dad and Master Tanaka and Sam about Jaaku's history, and none of them knew very much about his early years—before he went to China to learn dim mak. But I remembered that you knew exactly how old he was, so I figured you probably knew a lot more than they did…"

"Katana, I want you to stop pursuing this line of inquiry," Osaka said, suddenly very stern. "Samantha told me you were becoming consumed with Jaaku, and I agree with her that you need to let this go. It is not healthy."

"I promised Sam I wouldn't obsess about it anymore, and I haven't been—I swear—I haven't thought about it all week. Sam was the one who said that I should talk to you..."

"Katana," Osaka interrupted, "I must insist. Pursue this no further." And with that he turned and walked out the door.

Katana was stunned—Osaka had never refused to talk to her about anything. She'd always felt like he was one person she could always turn to. What had just happened? Why was Osaka so adamant that she not try to learn any more about Jaaku's past?

Katana got to the tai chi dojo as Nash was starting the class. He was reviewing the short form with them today, as they'd be helping the rest of the students with that form the following week at their morning tai chi lessons. But Katana was hardly paying attention—she kept going over her conversation with Osaka, trying to figure out if she'd said something wrong.

She told Sara and Chris at dinner about what had happened, but neither of them had any explanations either.

"So he just shut you off?" asked Sara.

"Yeah," said Katana with a sigh.

"He's never refused to talk to you about *anything* before," said Chris. "Are you sure he wasn't just worried that you were still obsessing about it?"

"I don't know," said Katana doubtfully. "I don't think so, though. It wasn't like when I talked to Sam—she wanted me to stop going crazy about it, but she was still willing to tell me what she knew. Osaka didn't want to talk about it under any circumstances."

"'Those who know don't talk...'" said Sara with a shrug.

"Yeah, that's just it," said Katana. "He clearly *does* know something—if not everything."

All Katana could think about during school the next day was her conversation with Osaka. Clearly, he did know a lot about Jaaku, but just as clearly wouldn't be discussing any of it with her anytime soon. She raced up to her room after school to change into a pair of shorts and a tank top, then ran back down to Sam's dojo for the sparring team practice.

Katana felt a slight twinge of annoyance when she walked in. Jimmy looked her up and down then immediately came over to talk to her. She liked Jimmy fine as a friend, but she had no interest in having a boyfriend this year. She decided she was going to have to talk to him sometime soon and make it clear that she wasn't interested.

"Hi, Kat! You look pretty today..." said Jimmy with a slight blush.

"Jimmy... I look a mess!" said Katana.

Jimmy started to stammer a response, but just then Sam came over with the other girls. "Katana, you know Sierra and Olivia already, right?" she asked, pointing them out in turn.

But the girl she'd introduced as Sierra raised her hand slightly and said with an embarrassed smile, "I'm Olivia, she's Sierra."

"Girls—I'm so sorry," said Sam. "I *cannot* tell you two apart... Anyway, Katana, this is Michelle Summers."

"Hi," said Katana.

Michelle held out her hand with a very big smile. "Hi, Katana —I'm so pleased to meet you! I saw you compete at Golden Gate last year and I'm really excited to be on the team with you!"

Katana thought Michelle was probably the friendliest girl she'd ever met—she wondered if she'd be aggressive enough to do well in sparring.

Katana walked over to the end of the room to stretch. She looked around to see who else was on the boys' team. Chris had walked in while Katana was talking to Sam, and he was sitting with Jimmy. Katana recognized Jeff Smith and Matt Kennedy from the previous year—they were talking to Jason Beecher. And there was a new boy Katana didn't recognize. He was extremely tall, but looked very young.

Sam had them line up and kneel down. "All right you guys, this year is going to be very exciting. For the first time ever we'll have teams entered in two separate divisions—well, this'll be a first for everyone else, too, as there's never been a girls' division before.

"You met the girls at orientation the other day, and if you don't know them already, this is Chris Boyd and Greg Mukon.

"Girls, you will be competing in the fourteen- to fifteen-year-old division individually, but they're not separating the points for the teams into different age categories. All the teams will be grouped together this year. As the division starts to grow, in the future they'll probably divide it up like they do with the boys.

"For the boys, Jason, Jeff and Matt will be in the sixteen- and seventeen-year-old division, and Chris, Jimmy and Greg, you'll be in the fourteen- and fifteen-year-old division. This will give us even coverage again this year.

"For the sake of our practices, you'll all be sparring together." Katana heard Sierra—or Olivia, she wasn't sure which—groan at this, but Sam continued. "I know, Sierra, but it will be good for you to spar with the boys in practice. They're bigger, and they have more experience at the tournaments.

"Jason will be the team captain this year, and I've decided to have one captain for the whole team, rather than having separate captains for the girls' and boys' teams.

"All right, let's get started. I want you to pair off with a partner, and spread out around the room. Do some light sparring to warm up. I'll be calling you up for matches two at a time."

Everyone put their gear on, and Katana paired up with Olivia. As they walked down to the end of the dojo, Olivia asked, "So you and Chris straightened everything out?"

"Yeah, we did," said Katana with a sigh. "He didn't do anything wrong, I was in a crappy mood and I kinda took it out on him. He didn't deserve it."

"He was really upset that day, but he felt a lot better after you two talked."

Katana and Olivia sparred lightly for a few rounds, then Sam called Katana and Michelle.

As Sam had them bow to each other and square off, Katana wondered why Sam had added Michelle to the team. She wasn't very tall, and she didn't seem like she'd be very aggressive. But Katana understood Sam's reasoning the instant Sam yelled "Fight!"

Michelle underwent an instantaneous and very frightening transformation. She suddenly had the meanest look on her face Katana had ever seen—like she was about to kill someone—and she let out a kiai that was more of a scream as she charged at Katana with a barrage of punches. Katana was stunned and managed to do no more than cower in the face of this onslaught —she took one of the punches right to the face.

Sam stopped the match. Michelle backed up and squared off again—smiling in a way that made her look very sweet and innocent again.

"One point Michelle," said Sam. "Any more doubts, Katana?"

"None," she replied.

Sam started the match again. This time Katana kept her weight on her back foot, ready to snap her lead leg to Michelle's head if she charged in. But Katana realized that Michelle played a smart game. Michelle danced around her initially, then faked a charge again. Katana snapped her kick out, but Michelle hadn't committed her body weight. Michelle timed Katana's kick perfectly—the moment Katana extended her leg, Michelle lunged in, landing another punch before Katana could get out of the way.

When the match started again, the girls circled around each other for a few moments, each trying to gauge the other's response by faking with their kicks. When Katana faked with a roundhouse kick and saw Michelle move her arm to block it, she knew what she was going to do. She moved in with a roundhouse kick again, but then snapped her foot the other way for an axe kick. But Michelle wasn't there—suddenly Katana found herself flat on her back with Michelle's foot in her face. She realized that Michelle had dropped to sweep out her leg the moment she'd snapped her leg out for the axe kick.

Michelle won six to zero.

Katana definitely felt like she'd done Michelle a disservice to underestimate her so badly. She promised herself she wouldn't make that mistake again.

Sam spent the rest of the practice calling them up two at a time to run matches. She lined them up at the end of the hour. "Good practice, everyone. Today I wanted to see where you're at, and next week we'll start working some different techniques to get ready for Eureka. Have a great weekend!"

Katana took off her gear and bolted up to the wushu dojo. She was thankful that today's practice had been pretty easy, but she knew that wouldn't last long. She remembered how grueling the sparring practices had been the previous year once Sam hit her stride.

Katana got to the wushu dojo to see that Master Fu had already lined everyone up.

"Come on in, Katana," he called out. Katana got in line with everyone else—and saw that they were wearing full uniform. She was mortified—everyone had worn shorts or sweats to the wushu team practices the previous year, so she had assumed this would be the case again. Clearly shorts and a tank top were not going to cut it.

"We were just discussing the uniforms," said Master Fu with an amused twinkle in his eye.

"I'm *so* sorry," said Katana. "I didn't realize..."

"It's all right, just make sure to wear the full uniform from now on. I'm ordering everyone traditional, heavyweight karate uniforms that we'll be using for the tournaments this year. They're going to be really nice—they'll have the school logo embroidered on the back and on the chest.

"We're still doing straight wushu in the demo this year, but most of the circuit does sport karate. And most of the judges are expecting to see sport karate, and karate uniforms. So to some extent we have to meet their expectations. I think the new uniforms will help make for a sharper looking performance all around.

"All right everyone, warm up and stretch, and I'll be looking at your sets one at a time to start with."

Katana was already quite warm from the sparring team practice, but she went with Sara and Dana while they got ready.

"What are you doing, Kat!" said Sara when they went over to the side of the dojo. "It said right on our schedules that Fu wanted us in uniform!"

"Oops," said Katana. "I missed that somehow..."

Broadsword went first. Katana heard Master Fu tell them that he was going to leave the set alone after all. "We'll probably be replacing this set with samurai sword next year," he said.

He called up staff next, so Sara went up with Tim and Jelly. Katana went with Dana to warm up on chains. Katana was feeling pretty confident with everything by the time Master Fu called them up.

"Girls, let's see what you've got," he said. Katana lined up across the floor from Dana.

They ran through the set exactly the same way they had the previous weekend. At the end, Katana kicked her right leg around and lay flat on the mat for the full body jumps. After the last jump, she kicked back to her feet and turned to see what Master Fu wanted them to do next.

"Excellent job, both of you," said Master Fu, walking over to them. "I think what we're going to do is keep this set last and build a new closer for the demo around your ending.

"I want you both to try this—do the body jumps again, and when you kick to your feet, start doing flowers facing the audience. Bring your chains together in one hand again, but instead of picking up your foot, you're going to move forward toward the audience. I want you to walk under your chains, and hit them on the ground behind you."

"Walk under the chains?" asked Dana. "How do you mean?"

"Here, watch," said Master Fu and took Dana's chains from her. He spun them forward, and brought them together in his right hand. He walked forward, with the chains spinning in front of him. Then he brought his right hand up over his head, stepped forward, and slammed the chains to the ground behind him.

Katana and Dana both tried this move and realized it wasn't difficult. So then they tried the whole ending, from the body jumps.

"Yes, that's it," said Master Fu. "As you're both doing that, I'm going to have the rest of the team getting into formation behind you for the closer." He closed his eyes for a minute and

Katana had the impression he was visualizing the demo in his head. "Yes, that's exactly how I want to do it."

Master Fu looked at everyone's sets once more, then had them line up. "Awesome job tonight, everyone. Next week we're going to put the whole demo together.

"I'm going to do a movie night up in my apartment tonight, and I'd like you all to come. We're going to review the video of some of the other teams out there who we're likely to face at nationals this year, including Supernova. So go get showered and everything, and come up to my apartment in an hour or so."

"Can we bring friends?" asked Paul.

"Um… no, let's have just the team this time," said Master Fu. "We'll do another one that's more social soon. Tonight I want to focus on the other team performances."

Master Fu dismissed them, and Katana and Sara went up to their room to get ready.

"How'd staff go?" asked Katana.

"Great," said Sara. "Fu wants me and Tim to work on a standing flash kick for the release skill."

"Was Tim able to get the standing backflip this time?" asked Katana.

"Yeah, with Fu's help—he only missed it once."

The girls both showered and got dressed. Chris and Jimmy showed up as they were about to leave.

"Hey," said Chris, "where are you two going?"

"Fu's doing a movie night," said Sara.

"Oh cool—can we come?" asked Jimmy.

"No," said Katana, grateful for the excuse not to have to bring

Jimmy, but feeling bad that Chris couldn't come, either. "Fu said this one's only for the team."

The rest of the team was already there when the girls got up to Master Fu's apartment.

"Hey you two, come on in and get some food, and we'll get started," said Master Fu.

Katana and Sara helped themselves to some of the sushi that Master Fu had laid out on the table in his sitting room, and went into the den with everyone else.

"Here we go," said Master Fu as he started the first video. "This is a team from the same region as Supernova—you probably remember them from nationals this year."

"Hey!" said Jelly. "This is that really bad team that had the two kids do the double backflips!"

Master Fu chuckled. "Yes, that's the team. Let's watch, and then I want you to tell me *why* they're bad."

They watched the whole demo and Katana still thought the two double backflips were the only good part.

"Jelly, tell us why you think that's not a good demo," prompted Master Fu.

"Um... I dunno, they just suck!" said Jelly. Everyone laughed.

"There was no choreography," said Sara. "The whole demo was one kid at a time coming out and doing a form or a weapon set."

"Right," said Master Fu. "How was the actual karate?"

Katana thought about it for a moment. "Their karate was good. But it was boring as a demo to have one thing at a time like that."

"Exactly," said Master Fu. "Every set they did was solid as far as their martial arts goes. But this is what I want you to start understanding—there is a lot more that goes into a good demo than just good karate.

"Let's watch Supernova and we'll talk more."

He played the next video. "What do you think?"

Paul smiled and shook his head. "They're amazing."

"Why?"

"They have so much energy," said Paul. "And *their* choreography is good."

"What about their choreography made them so good?" asked Master Fu.

"They had things going on between sets," said Dana. "It wasn't just one person coming out and doing a form, then leaving again. All the tricks happened between sets, and there was no downtime—there was something happening on stage like every second of the whole demo."

"Yes, exactly!" said Master Fu. "You guys hit the nail on the head.

"First of all—and this is probably the most important thing —their energy level *is* amazing. They're not just going through the moves, they're doing it with this powerful stage presence. If you were to walk into a room and there were twenty demo teams doing their routine, you probably wouldn't notice the other ones if Supernova was there. They have so much energy, you have no choice—you have to watch them.

"That's what we need to shoot for this year.

"And Dana is right—they also have great choreography. It's

not real complicated, either—but there's always *something* going on as one set leaves the stage and the next one comes out. They have great transitions. But the energy level is still the thing that's made them national champions so many times."

They watched video from several more teams, but Katana thought that Supernova was the best. And Master Fu's enthusiasm was contagious—Katana couldn't wait for their next team practice. She was eager to bring their demo up to that level.

CHAPTER II

THOSE WHO KNOW

Katana spent a good chunk of her day on Saturday doing all the homework she'd racked up during their first week. Chris was already struggling with math, so Katana helped him with their problem sets, then worked with Sara on their biology project.

She felt like her brain was fried by the time she got to the wushu dojo that afternoon. But she was very excited to practice her whip chain set with Dana after their movie night with Master Fu the previous evening.

Sara worked with Tim on their staff set, but Chris, Jelly and Scott spent the whole time working on tricks. Chris had perfected his backflip the previous term, so now Jelly was teaching him how to do a flash kick.

Katana and Dana went through their whip chain set together several times. Katana also worked on her double backflip—she wanted to make sure she could land it consistently before the next team practice. Finally she did the butterfly twist with her chains several times while Jelly tried to help Dana figure out how to do the twist in the first place.

When they were done Katana asked Sara if they were going to Sam's for dinner that night.

"You know, I have no idea," said Sara. "I haven't talked to her about it."

"She's expecting us," said Chris. "She told me after you left sparring practice, Kat."

The kids went up to their rooms to shower, then to Sam's apartment to join her for dinner.

"So how did your first week of tenth grade go?" asked Sam as they sat down around the table in her sitting room, which was loaded with some of Terry-San's latest creations.

"Don't ask," said Chris.

"I take it algebra two with trigonometry's not going so well?" asked Sam brightly.

"I think biology's going to be a lot harder," said Sara. "It's an AP course, and those are the toughest classes you can take."

"Math was always my worst subject," said Sam. "I had no problem with AP bio, but trig... Trig was rough. Hey, so how do you guys like Nelson so far? Master Fu, I mean?"

"I think he's a genius," said Katana.

Chris and Sara both looked at her quizzically. Sam asked, "How do you mean, Kat?"

"Well, he announced this week that he's going to be adding sport karate weapons to the curriculum," said Katana.

"Yes, I knew he was doing that," said Sam. "We were worried about how some people were going to take it—not everyone deals with change very well."

"Well that's just it," said Katana. "I think he planned it perfectly. He went around and talked to all the kids on the wushu team before orientation, and had us start working on new stuff for the demo. And it sounds like he made sure to meet most of the kids in the whole wushu program and get to know their names before we even had our first class. So by the time he announced the sport karate stuff, everyone already liked him, so no one had a problem with it—even Dana! I was *sure* she was going to freak when she found out."

"Yes, I was worried about Dana's reaction, too," said Sam. "But she was okay with it?"

"She said she wants to learn samurai sword," replied Katana.

"Wow," said Sam. "Well, I can tell you, Nelson was very worried about how people would react. He wasn't sure of himself at all—he was losing sleep over it."

"Really?" asked Sara. "He seemed pretty confident when he announced it in class."

"I'm sure he did," said Sam. "As you now know, Nelson is all about presentation—even if he's terrified of something, you'll never see it in the way he carries himself. You know, he has severe stage fright. He gets nervous in front of a big class."

"Sam, do you know if something is... well, I don't know, if something is wrong with Osaka?" Katana asked after they ate for a minute.

"Wrong—how?" asked Sam.

Katana told her about what had happened after her private on Thursday, the way Osaka had refused to discuss anything about Jaaku's history with her.

"I know he was worried when he found out how consumed you'd become," said Sam. "I spoke to him after you and I talked last weekend."

"But Sam, I haven't obsessed about it since we talked, I swear —I didn't think about it until our private on Thursday. And the only reason I thought of it then was because you said Osaka's the big history buff. I know he doesn't want me to obsess about it, but it was more than that. I got the feeling that he *does* know a lot about Jaaku's history, but doesn't want *me* to know about it no matter what."

"Katana, I don't know what's going on there. Osaka thinks of you as a daughter, I can tell you that much. I think he's afraid of losing you the way he lost your father," said Sam.

"But how is he going to lose me by telling me about stuff that happened hundreds of years ago?" asked Katana.

"I don't have a good explanation for it, Kat," said Sam with a sigh. "But maybe he's just being a little over-protective. While he may not be your real father, most fathers do get that way when their daughters start growing up."

Katana finished her sushi in silence while the others talked. She hadn't considered this—as much as she had come to think of Osaka as the father she'd never had, she'd never thought about how that relationship would feel from his perspective.

Katana woke up on Monday morning at quarter to five, and jumped down from the top bunk to find Doc. Every night she brought him up to bed with her, and every morning he was gone again. She still couldn't figure out how he was getting down—it seemed like a long way for such a small kitten to jump. But at least Doc had stopped sleeping in the cat carrier—Katana had put it away in the closet.

She walked around for a minute, but couldn't find the cat anywhere. Finally she went to use the bathroom—and found Doc curled up in the sink.

Sara's alarm clock went off. When it had failed to wake Sara up after a few minutes, Katana dragged her out of bed and they made their way up to the tai chi dojo.

Only a few other kids were there yet, waiting in the hallway that ran the length of the front of the building. Katana looked in one of the doorways and saw that Nash and Osaka were inside. The two of them were standing about twenty feet apart. Each was in the same stance as the standing chi kung exercise—all the weight on the back foot, the ball of the front foot just touching the mat. They both held their hands in a manner similar to the standing chi kung exercise as well, except that instead of turning them inward, as if grasping a ball, they had their palms turned outward, toward each other.

In addition, Katana could see tendrils of energy extending from each man's aura, reaching out and circling around the other. It appeared that they were doing pushing hands, except that they were doing it with their shen instead of their hands. Little pulses of light were traveling along the tendrils, sometimes exploding in a flash of light when they came in contact with each other.

"What on Earth..." said Sara, watching in awe.

Katana realized that there was a slow, subtle wavelike quality to the flashes—they would start happening closer to Osaka then slowly shift back toward Master Nash. Katana had absolutely no idea what was going on, but she was intrigued.

She'd been able to see people's shen since the previous year, and she'd seen Nash send a pulse of chi along his shen to knock down an opponent during pushing hands. But she'd certainly never seen anything quite like the display in front of her now.

Chris walked in a few minutes later. "Hey Kat—what the hell?"

"You can see it?" asked Sara, still watching the spectacle as if entranced.

"I can see something..." said Chris uncertainly. "Like these little flashes of light in between Nash and Osaka—what are they doing?"

"Not a clue," said Katana.

Finally an intense series of flashes traveled in an arc from Osaka to Master Nash and the exercise was apparently over. They bowed to each other, and walked forward to shake hands.

"Well done," said Nash.

"I'll see you tomorrow morning," said Osaka. He turned to leave through the door at the other end of the room.

Katana walked into the room with everyone else, and Master Nash began class. They started out with a series of chi kung exercises, then went through the short form together once. When Nash had them work on their own, Katana, along with the other students from her tai chi class, went around and helped the new kids with the first few postures.

"Everyone please line up," called Master Nash at the end of the class. "This weekend, we will be welcoming Master Kim from the Temple of the Crane in South Korea. As I mentioned at orientation, Master Kim is a master of tae kwon do and hapkido. He will be conducting a seminar for the whole school on Saturday at three o'clock here in the tai chi dojo. You should be here ahead of time so you can stretch and warm up and you should wear full uniform for this event."

With that he dismissed the class. But as Katana started to walk out with Sara and Chris, Master Nash came over to them. "Katana, can I speak to you for a moment?"

"Yeah, sure," said Katana.

Nash waited until everyone else had cleared out of the dojo. "Thank you for helping this morning."

"No problem," said Katana. "I like teaching; it was fun."

"Katana, I need to discuss a few things with you. If you wouldn't mind joining me for dinner this evening, we could talk over sushi. Terry-san has some new creations he is eager for me to try," said Master Nash.

"Oh, um... Yeah, sure," said Katana.

"Excellent. Then come up to my apartment when you are done with your classes this evening."

For the rest of the morning Katana tried to figure out what "things" Master Nash wanted to discuss with her. She had a feeling it might have something to do with her conversation with

Osaka. Did Nash also believe that Katana was worrying about Jaaku too much?

"What did Nash want this morning?" asked Chris when they sat down for lunch at Lincoln later that day.

"I don't know," said Katana. "He wants to talk to me about something. I'm going up to his apartment for dinner tonight."

"Hmm..." said Sara. "Maybe he's going to tell you more about Jaaku's history. I bet he knows at least as much as Osaka."

"Maybe," said Katana. "I was thinking he was going to say the same thing Osaka did—to *stop* trying to figure out Jaaku's history."

"Nah," said Sara. "He coulda told you that this morning. If he invited you to dinner, he has a *lot* more to say than 'Stop obsessing.'"

"I guess..." said Katana.

Just then Ed Golia walked up behind Sara and kicked the leg of her chair, causing her to dump her juice all over the place. "Oh, I'm sorry fatty, I didn't see you sitting there!"

Sara got up and lunged at Ed. But Chris, who had been sitting next to her, got up at the same time and threw his arm around her waist to hold her back.

"Aw, isn't that sweet, Chrissy-poo," taunted Tommy Cosgrove, "giving your new girlfriend a hug. Did you break up with Kahanu when you realized she's a boy?"

Now it was Sara's turn to hold Chris back. But then the Chinese boy who had been with them last time grabbed Tommy by the arm. He pulled him away, saying, "Leave them alone guys, come on."

Ed stood and stared for a moment as the boy walked away with Tommy. "You spilled your drink, fatty," he said to Sara before finally moving off himself.

Katana saw Ed give the Chinese boy a shove as they arrived at their own table. Then she heard him yell, "What's your problem, Fisher?"

Sara and Chris sat down again. Sara mopped up the juice that was now dripping off the table. "I'm going to kill those two, I swear I am."

"Kat, I figured out who idiot number three is—it's the Fisher kid you were sparring at nationals when you got levitation!" said Chris. "Picture him with a sparring helmet on."

Katana leaned over to get a better view of their table. "Hey—you're right!"

"He must have moved here this year," said Sara. "He couldn't have been from our region last year or we woulda seen him at Golden Gate, too."

"Well he's probably a jerk if he's hanging out with those two," said Katana. "I could've forgiven him for messing up my gainer flash at nationals if he weren't friends with the moron twins!"

For the rest of the afternoon Katana tried to figure out what Master Nash wanted to talk to her about. Sara was probably right, though—if he were going to tell her to stop trying to find out more about Jaaku, he could have done that after class. Maybe he really was going to tell her what she wanted to know. Maybe she was finally going to learn *everything* about Jaaku.

After school, Katana spent her entire wushu class working on chains with Dana. When Master Fu dismissed them she ran up to Master Nash's apartment in the south wing.

"Your timing is impeccable—Gerty just got here with the sushi," said Nash as Katana sat down next to him at a large conference table. Master Nash's apartment appeared to Katana to be quite a bit larger than those of the other masters. It looked like he had another large room next to this one and she assumed he still had the sitting room, den and bedroom she'd seen in the other suites. Katana looked around at the old scrolls and books on the shelves that lined two of the walls and wondered what secrets they might contain.

"Katana, this weekend, in addition to the seminar on Saturday, Master Kim would like to meet with you privately on Sunday," began Master Nash.

"Privately—why?" asked Katana, realizing she hadn't been on the right track at all regarding the subject of this meeting.

"He will be evaluating you, putting you through a test basically," said Master Nash.

"What is he testing me for?" asked Katana.

Katana had the impression that Nash was choosing his words very carefully. "He will not be testing you for any kind of rank, if that's what you're wondering. Katana, it is extremely unusual for a student to reach your level of skill at such a young age. Your abilities have attracted the attention of the other headmasters, and truthfully, this is the reason they are coming to the Hall of the Dragon this year. They will be conducting seminars while they are here, but you are the real reason for their visits."

"You've got to be kidding me..." said Katana, feeling totally overwhelmed at this news. Tanaka's attention was one thing—she'd assumed he only knew about her because of Terry-san. But to find out that several other headmasters wanted to meet her as well... "But I'm not the only one who's been able to do three chen do so young—my dad got a third one while he was here. Did the other headmasters want to meet him, too?"

"No, Katana, they did not," Nash replied with a slight frown. "But from what Osaka tells me, your father didn't learn his third chen do until a few days before graduation. He was moving on from the Hall by that point and word did not spread to the other temples.

"And in actuality, there is a boy at Shaolin who has three of the chen do now as well."

"Are the other headmasters going to be evaluating *him*, too?" asked Katana.

"In fact, they are," said Nash.

This made Katana feel a little better—at least she wasn't going to be the only one on display. "What exactly am I going to have to do for Master Kim?"

"That I don't know," said Nash. "It is up to Master Kim. But I anticipate that he will put you through a test similar to what we do here. He will probably want to see you perform some of your forms, maybe do attack drills—that sort of thing. And he will certainly want to see you perform the chen do. Beyond that, it's anyone's best guess."

"Who are the other headmasters that are coming again?" asked Katana. "You said the one from Brazil... and someone from Thailand?"

"Yes," said Master Nash. "Master Nang from Tibet will be coming next, in October. Master Santos from Brazil will be here in November and Master Chatri from Thailand in December.

"Katana, you will also be going to see Master Tanaka in Japan again..."

"So that's what he meant!" said Katana. "When I met him this summer, he said he would be seeing me again very soon! Wait a minute—why couldn't he evaluate me when I was there the first time—and why isn't he coming here like the other head-masters?"

Nash chuckled softly. "Master Tanaka is quite eccentric. He hasn't left Shaka-In in many years. You will have to go to him because he refuses to come here.

"And in hindsight, it would perhaps have been easier for you to have your evaluation with him when you were there the first time. But that visit was somewhat informal—and it was arranged by Mitch Brown, who didn't know at the time that the head-master of Shaolin was scheduling the evaluations..."

"The headmaster of Shaolin is behind this?!" asked Katana.

"Oh, yes. He will be coming here himself in February. He will be bringing the boy who can do the three chen do so that *we* may appraise *him*. In all likelihood you will be going through the eval-uation with the boy so that the headmaster may see you as well, while he is here," said Master Nash.

This was almost too much for Katana to believe. She was going to be evaluated by the Headmaster of the Shaolin Temple? She shook her head and smiled.

"What is it?" asked Nash.

"I thought you were going to tell me to stop obsessing about Jaaku," said Katana. "Boy was I wrong!"

"Ah, yes," said Nash. "I've heard about your research."

"And do you think I should stop?" Katana asked. "Osaka made it clear he doesn't want me looking into Jaaku's background *at all* anymore. I know he must know lots of stuff about Jaaku's early days, but it seems like he thinks telling me about it is going to hurt me somehow."

"Be patient with Osaka, Katana. You are very dear to him. I think he fears for you like any father would fear for his only child."

"But how can finding out about stuff that happened hundreds of years ago possibly hurt me?"

"Katana, you've been through a lot since you arrived here two years ago—you've grown very quickly in that time. You confronted the Arashi at the end of your first year, learned a *third* chen do last year, and now the evaluations with the headmasters this year... I think Osaka sees you growing up so fast and wants to slow it down a little."

"But I still don't see how finding out about Jaaku..."

"It may not make much sense, but Osaka feels very strongly about this."

"It's not fair though," Katana insisted. "I've been trying *so hard* to find out about this, and he has the answers! He's never refused to talk to me about anything before. I don't see why..."

"Okay, okay," Nash said with a smile, holding up both hands. "I surrender! Samantha is absolutely correct when she says you are the most stubborn pupil she has ever taught. I know everything Osaka knows, so I will share some information with you under one condition."

Katana felt herself getting very excited now. "Anything."

"Don't tell Osaka I told you!" Nash said with a wink.

"I promise."

"What have you been able to figure out so far?"

Katana went through it all. "I know that Jaaku started out as a samurai, went to China to learn dim mak from Master Tong, then killed Tong and stole the dim mak manuscript. Then he went back to Japan and set himself up at Taiyou, and trained the Arashi there. Chow and Chang and the other headmasters fought him at Taiyou, and he wasn't heard from again until he showed up in Hawaii when I was a baby.

"But I still don't know anything about Jaaku's early years— before he went to China. And nobody can tell me if the legend is true—that Jaaku tried to get the Immortal Master to teach him the secret to immortality..."

"But that he killed the Immortal Master when he refused," Master Nash finished for her.

"Yeah!" said Katana. "Is it true then?"

Master Nash let out a long sigh. "Katana, there is much information about Jaaku, and about the Immortal Master that has been known only to the headmasters of the Hall of the Dragon.

"You see, Master Chow really was a student of the Immortal Master." Master Nash pointed to the scrolls and books that lined the walls. "Master Chow left behind extensive memoirs about his training and experiences. Some of this material recounts the history of the Immortal Master and Jaaku."

"So the Immortal Master was real?!" asked Katana. "Was he really immortal?"

"I don't know if he attained true immortality, but he was at least as old as Jaaku is now when Chow trained with him," said Nash.

"He wasn't... He wasn't a dim mak master, was he?" asked Katana. "He didn't live so long by stealing people's chi... Did he?"

"No," said Nash. "Definitely not. He must have found some other means to extend his life."

"And did Jaaku really try to get him to teach him the secret?"

"Oh yes," said Master Nash. "On more than one occasion, according to Chow's memoirs. Jaaku and the Immortal Master were archenemies. Jaaku tried to get the Immortal Master to teach him the secret to his longevity before he ever went to Master Tong to learn dim mak. In fact, it was only after the Immortal Master refused to teach him that Jaaku went to China."

"Did Jaaku really kill the Immortal Master?"

"No," said Master Nash. "That story has been told from one generation of students to the next here at the Hall since the days of Master Chow himself. But it's not true; Jaaku did not kill the Immortal Master."

"Then is the Immortal Master still alive—is he still out there somewhere?"

Master Nash looked at her for a moment. "He may be, Katana... He may be. No one has ever had any contact with the Immortal Master—not since Chow trained with him."

"And what about Master Chow?" asked Katana. "What

happened to him after the battle with Jaaku? Tanaka told me that Chang helped him fake his own death."

"Chow's memoirs end the day he left the Hall of the Dragon," said Master Nash. "He disappears from the pages of history after that."

"And where was Jaaku after he left Taiyou? Where was he during all those years before... before he turned up in Hawaii?"

"Unfortunately, *nobody* knows the answer to that question," said Nash.

"What about Jaaku's early days? What was his real name? And how did he find out about the Immortal Master in the first place—was the Immortal Master from Japan? And..."

Master Nash laughed quietly and held out his hand as if to say "Stop!" "That is as far as I can go, Katana—if Osaka finds out I told you even this much, he will not be pleased. The answers to all of your questions are here, in these documents. I am sure that one day Osaka will relax, and we'll be able to get him to consent to giving you more information."

When they were done with their sushi, Katana said, "Master Nash, can I ask you one more question—what on earth were you and Osaka doing this morning?"

Master Nash smiled. "Ah yes, I should've known you'd be able to see that. It is called 'chi fa.' It's similar to pushing hands, but you have no physical contact with your opponent and you use only your shen to push back and forth."

"Wow..." said Katana.

"You recall when you and I did pushing hands last year, and you blocked my shen?" he asked.

"Yeah—but you were able to push me over anyway!"

"Don't worry, Katana, you will get there. Blocking intent the way you did is the defensive side of chi fa. To play offense, however, you need to be able to send small pulses of chi along your shen—that is much more difficult to master. We'll work on it during your tai chi classes. I think you will be a formidable chi fa player once you learn the skills."

Katana ran up to her room when she was done with Nash. She found Sara and Chris sitting out on the balcony when she got there.

"Well?" asked Sara as Katana sat down with them. "What did he want?"

Katana told them what Master Nash had said about the other headmasters.

"Are you serious?" asked Chris when she'd finished. "So they're coming here to test you?"

"That's what it sounds like," said Katana with a sigh.

"That must be what Tanaka was talking about, when he said he'd be seeing you again soon," said Sara.

"Yeah, exactly," said Katana.

"So he didn't tell you anything about Jaaku's history after all?" asked Chris.

"Oh—I forgot—yeah, he did!"

"You forgot?" asked Sara, incredulous.

"Well, that's not why he wanted to talk to me, but I asked him anyway," said Katana. She told them everything she'd found out.

"Wait a minute..." said Sara, a look of dawning comprehension on her face.

"What?" asked Katana.

"The Scroll of the Five Masters... Chow left it behind and it was supposed to hold the secret to immortality. And now we know the Immortal Master was real. So even if he didn't teach Jaaku the secret, he *must* have taught it to Chow!"

"That's true," said Katana. "If Chow hadn't known the secret to immortality, he wouldn't have been able to leave the scroll. But then again, the scroll was blank..."

"Yeah, I still don't understand that," said Sara with a frown. "How is a blank piece of paper supposed to teach you *anything*?"

"We'll never know, will we?" said Chris. "Osaka incinerated it."

"Did Nash know where Jaaku went after he left Japan—before he showed up in Hawaii?" asked Sara.

"No," said Katana. "It seems like *nobody* knows that."

"Nobody but Jaaku," said Chris. "And we can't exactly ask *him*."

"And we know almost nothing about Jaaku and the Immortal Master," Katana replied.

"It seems like the more we learn, the more we realize we don't know..." said Sara.

"Yeah," said Katana. "You're right. And it's all right there in Nash's conference room. I wish I could look through that stuff."

CHAPTER 12

FISHER

When Katana got to the tae kwon do dojo for her private the next afternoon, Jason was already there. Katana could see that Sam hadn't been kidding about breaking bricks next. The cinder blocks were arranged in pairs around the room again, but this time there were piles of large gray bricks piled up around them. Sam had also placed beach towels underneath the cinder blocks.

"Hey Sam," said Katana. "What are the towels for?"

"Oh, the bricks make a lot of dust when you break them. It's *impossible* to clean out of the tatami. This way I can just pick up the towels when we're done," she explained.

Katana and Jason stretched out, then Sam brought them over to a set of cinder blocks. She placed a brick across the top, and put a small towel on top of it.

"And what's the little towel for?" asked Jason.

"It's to make sure you don't cut yourself," said Sam. "The brick shatters when it breaks and without the towel there, you can get a shard in your hand."

"Ouch," said Katana.

"Jason, you're first. I want you to use a palm heel this time—so you're going to drive straight down instead of chopping," said Sam.

"Right," said Jason. He got in a horse stance, but this time turned on an angle so he could drive straight down with the heel of his palm. He brought his hand down slowly a couple of times, then let out a loud kiai and smashed through the brick.

"Well done," said Sam.

"That was hard," said Jason. "That was a lot tougher than the boards."

Sam set up another brick for Katana. "Remember, Kat, you have to drop your weight into the strike," said Sam, "and focus *through* the brick."

"Got it," said Katana. She brought her hand down in slow motion a couple of times. "Here we go." She dropped her weight down into her strike as hard as she could, and smashed right through the brick.

"Yeah, that is a lot harder than wood," she said, nodding to Jason.

"Now we're going to try two bricks with spacers," Sam said, setting them up.

"I don't know, Sam," said Jason apprehensively. "Going through *one* was pretty hard."

"You'll be fine," said Sam. "Go ahead, try it."

"Okay…" said Jason, setting up for the break again. He went through the motion a couple of times, then smashed down hard —he broke both bricks.

"Wow, that wasn't too much worse," he said.

"See?" said Sam. "It's not too bad with the spacers in there. The force from the first brick breaking helps you get through the second one."

"Yeah, I could feel when the second one broke, and it didn't feel as hard as the first one," Jason agreed.

"Kat, you're up," said Sam when she'd set up two more bricks.

"Okay," said Katana. She set up again, and brought her hand down slowly twice. She let out a kiai and smashed her hand through the bricks.

"You're right, the second brick does break easier than the first."

"Now for the hard part," said Sam. "Two bricks—no spacers." She set it up and said, "Who's first?"

"I'll try it," said Katana.

"This is going to be a *lot* harder, Kat," said Sam.

Katana set up again and brought her hand down slowly a few times. She slammed her hand down again with all her might—but nothing happened. "Ow! That hurt!"

"All yours, Jason," said Sam.

Jason looked at Katana for a moment, then at the bricks. "I'll give it a shot," he said, setting up for the break. But he wasn't able to get through it either. "That's pretty painful when you don't go through," he said, caressing his right hand with his left.

"Let's try this. You're going to do it with an elbow strike instead," said Sam.

Jason looked from his elbow to the bricks and said, "Won't we break our arm that way?"

"Not if you do it right," said Sam. "You're not going to use the point of your elbow. You're going to use the flat," she added, pointing to a spot a few inches up from the tip of her own elbow.

"Watch," she said, getting down on one knee in front of the bricks. She reached back and circled her elbow around a couple of times. Then she kiaied loudly and smashed through both bricks.

"Wow," said Katana. "I'll try it."

Sam set up two more bricks. Katana dropped to one knee, like Sam had done.

"Okay, Kat," said Sam, "just like before, you have to focus through the bricks. And remember, do *not* use the point of your elbow—use the flat."

"Got it," said Katana, going through the motion a few times. She reached back, dropped her weight and slammed her elbow down as hard as she could. She did it—the bricks shattered in a cloud of dust.

"That's hard," she said. "I don't think I'd be able to do more than two."

"No, we won't be doing any more than that," said Sam. "Jason, you wanna try it?"

"Nah, I'm good," he said, "My hand is still hurting from my first try."

"Yeah, mine too," said Katana, opening and closing her fist.

"Well that's good for today," said Sam. "We should be ready now, no matter what Master Kim throws at us this weekend!"

She dismissed them for the day and Katana ran up to the tai chi dojo.

Master Nash started the class and took them through the long form, then had them pair up for pushing hands again. Katana went with Betsy, and didn't feel like she was doing any better than she had the previous week. As long as she could see Betsy's shen, they were a perfect stalemate. Katana couldn't find Betsy's center, and thus couldn't push her over; but neither could Betsy knock *her* down, as Katana could see her shen every time.

But as soon as Katana repeated the exercise with her eyes closed, she didn't stand a chance. Betsy dropped her to the mat every time.

Master Nash came over to them a few minutes later. "Katana, it's time for some chi fa."

Katana was quite excited for this—she'd wanted to have a chance to try it since talking to Nash the previous night. Nash instructed Katana to get into the same stance as the standing chi kung exercise. He had her make a circle with her arms, but turn her hands out, facing him. Nash assumed the same stance twenty feet away and said "Begin."

Suddenly, Katana could see a web of tendrils extending out in all directions from Nash's aura. She didn't know if she was doing the same thing herself or not. She tried to maintain an awareness of the whole field instead of focusing on any one spot.

Katana could see a pulse of light coming toward her along one of the tendrils. She deflected it with her own energy, but there was another one coming toward her along a different path. She tried to keep her focus on the whole field and deflect whatever came at her. She lasted a couple of minutes like this, but finally found it impossible to keep her attention so broad. She deflected one pulse of light, and three others hit her, knocking her to the mat.

"Very good, Katana," said Nash, coming over to help her back to her feet. "I say again, once you learn to play offense, you are going to be a very strong chi fa player."

"How do you play offense?" asked Katana.

"It's rather subtle," said Nash. "You have to learn to focus your chi into a very small area—it is much more nuanced than throwing a fireball. As you continue building your chi, it will come to you eventually. I have no doubt."

"That was cool," said Betsy as they walked down to dinner together. "It looked like what Nash was doing with Osaka the other morning."

"You can see it, too?" asked Katana.

"I can," said Betsy with a sigh, "but I still can't do any of the chen do. Do you really have three of them?"

"Yeah," said Katana. "But I wish I could do what Nash does in that chi fa thing."

"That's *really* advanced, I guess," said Betsy. "Nash told us last year that only tai chi masters are able to do it."

They moved through the buffet line in the cafeteria, and Katana went to sit with her friends.

"Hey," said Sara as Katana sat down next to her. "How was tai chi?"

"It was so cool—Nash had me try that thing we saw him doing with Osaka!"

"Seriously?!" asked Chris. "Can you do it?"

"I can do defense—sort of. But I can't throw anything back. And I'm not even that good at defense—he was going *way* easier on me than he was on Osaka.

"How was tae kwon do? Did Sam have you guys break the bricks?"

"Yeah she did," said Sara, rubbing her right hand with her left. "I couldn't do it. I tried like three times, but I couldn't get through it."

"I couldn't do it with a palm strike," said Chris, "but I got through with an elbow."

"How'd you do?" asked Sara.

"I was able to get through one with a palm strike, but I had to use my elbow to get through two."

"Two... with spacers?" asked Chris.

"Nah, I did that with my hand," said Katana. "But I had to use my elbow to do it without the spacers."

"You got through two bricks—*without spacers*?!" asked Jimmy, who had been listening quietly to their conversation.

"Yeah, it was hard though," said Katana. "I don't think I could've done more than that."

"Well, I can't wait till Sam gets over this phase," said Sara. "Breaking hurts. Hey, are we gonna go to the dance on Friday?"

"They're having the first dance already?" asked Katana.

"Yeah," said Sara. "I think I wanna go. I'm hoping to get a chance to talk to that Fisher kid."

Katana and Chris looked at each other. "You don't like him, do you?" asked Katana.

"Come on, Kat, you can't tell me you don't think he's cute," said Sara.

"Yeah, I guess, but he's hanging out with the moron twins—that's never a good sign."

"But you heard him—he told them to leave us alone. If he just moved here, maybe he doesn't know any better yet. And I still think I know him from somewhere..."

"We figured that out already," said Chris. "Katana sparred with him at nationals, remember?"

"No—I mean besides that. I think I've seen him somewhere else, too—like a really long time ago."

The rest of the week flew by and it was Friday before Katana knew it. She ran up to her room after school—and remembered to change into uniform this time—then back down to the tae kwon do dojo.

"Hey, Katana," said Sam when she walked in. "You don't have to wear full uniform for this, you know."

"I know, but Fu wants it for the wushu practice."

Sam lined them up and took them through a few warm-ups and stretches. "All right everyone, based on what I saw last week, I can say that you're doing very well with your kicking combinations, and going from sweeps to kicks. What I want to spend some time on today is distancing. You saw how Michelle was able to beat Katana last week—that was in part because Katana underestimated her..."

"I won't do *that* again!" said Katana, giving Michelle a high-five.

"You'd better not," said Sam, "but part of it was due to Michelle's skill at distancing. She grew up with two older brothers in the house who were both a lot taller, and we can learn something from that. Jason, please come up."

Sam and Jason bowed to each other and squared off.

"Watch—Jason, please throw a roundhouse kick to my head," said Sam. Jason threw the kick. Sam backed up a few inches and said, "Throw it again."

Jason threw the kick again and was only just able to reach her this time. "Here, he can still reach me, right?" said Sam. "Now watch—Jason, please throw that kick one more time."

This time as Jason threw the kick, Sam leaned back slightly and Jason was no longer able to reach her.

"This is where you want to be," said Sam. "If you can dance at the edge of your opponent's range, and keep your weight on your back foot as you circle around, you can lean out of the way and avoid his kicks. But, with your weight on your back foot, you can also lunge forward instantly for a kick of your own.

"One more time, please, Jason?" she said.

Jason threw the kick at Sam's head again. Sam leaned out of range, then pushed off with her back foot and kicked him in the chest with her lead leg.

"Everyone pair off with a partner, I want you to try that."

Katana went with Olivia. They traded kicks back and forth, working on the technique Sam had taught them. After a few minutes, Sam had them switch partners. Katana went with Jimmy this time.

Finally Sam had them get their gear on and she brought them up two at a time to run matches. Katana went against Michelle again. Now that she knew what Michelle was doing, Katana fared far better than she had the previous week. She pulled out a win five to three.

Sam mixed the boys with the girls on their next turn, and Katana ended up going against Jason.

"We haven't done this in a while," he said with a wink as they squared off.

They traded kicks back and forth and the match went to 4-4 very quickly. Then Katana decided to use her gainer flash. Jason raised his hands to block when Katana faked with a punch. Katana took to the air and kicked him square in the ribs to flip herself over backwards.

"I knew that was coming," said Jason as they bowed to each other.

"Now Katana, remember, you're probably not going to have a chance to use that in competition this year—I don't think you're going to go up against any girls who are nearly big enough," said Sam. "But—I want you to save it for nationals even if you do... just in case."

"Got it," said Katana.

Sam finished them up for the night and Katana ran up to the wushu dojo.

Master Fu was wasting no time. He took them through warm-ups and stretches for about three minutes before he had them spread out to work on their weapon sets. "This is it, people, we are putting our demo together *tonight,*" he yelled. Katana had done chains with Dana only twice by the time Master Fu called everyone to the front of the room.

"We're going to piece the weapon sets together first, then we'll work on an opener and a closer. Broadsword, you guys are going to be first. When you're done, I want Donnie and Scott to aerial out to the back corners. Sara and Tim, you two are going to aerial on stage right past them—so you are facing each other, upside down in midair."

"Wow," said Sara, but Jelly asked, "What am I doing?"

"Aha," said Master Fu. "I have a special project for you and Paul. Come over here."

"Jelly," he said when they got to the middle of the floor, "you are going to do a butterfly twist right to the center of the stage. And Paul, you are going to do a diving front roll over him as he twists."

"Um... You're serious?" asked Paul, looking very apprehensive.

"Yes, I am," said Master Fu. "Jelly is short enough—"

"Hey!"

"—that you should be able to get over him."

"Uh... But he's got that stick in his hands, too..." said Paul.

"Yes, but he's going to keep that up against him as he rolls over—it won't be sticking out," Master Fu assured him.

"Okay..." said Paul.

"Let's do this..." said Master Fu. "Jelly, do a butterfly twist, right here. Paul, I want you to pay attention to how high he goes."

Jelly did the twist, and Master Fu said, "Sara, come here. I want you to hold your staff by one end, straight out in front of you. Good, now, Paul, I want you to tell Sara how high to hold the staff—I want her to hold it as high as Jelly went in his twist."

"He was about here," said Paul, adjusting Sara's staff.

"Good—now, can you do a diving front roll over that?"

"Yeah, easily."

"Do it," said Master Fu. Paul dove over the staff.

"If you can dive over that, you can get over Jelly's twist. Let's try it. The only issue is going to be timing, because obviously Jelly's moving... unlike Sara's staff."

It only took a few tries for Paul to get the move. "That's a lot easier than I thought," he said.

"Good... now, for chains," said Master Fu. "You guys on broadsword are going to come out again and trick while staff leaves the stage. Katana and Dana—you're going to go to your corners, like we've been practicing. Katana—you'll be in the front right corner, and Dana, you'll be at the back left. You two are going to run past each other, and Kat—you're going to do the double back, while Dana flashes past you."

"That's not exactly symmetrical, is it?" asked Dana.

"No, but Jelly's going to be in the front left corner. He's going to go at the same time, and he's going to double back as well."

"Wait," said Jelly, "you mean all three of us are going to run across the stage at the same time? What if we crash into each other?"

"Don't!" said Master Fu. "Jelly, you don't need as much runway for the double back as Katana does. I want you to time it so you're going across the girls' line *immediately* after they pass each other into their round-offs. You have to do your round-off as you cross that line."

Katana thought this was going to be very difficult to time correctly—and she was right. They totally missed it the first few times, and Katana and Jelly ran into each other once. But finally they got it, and Master Fu videotaped it so they could see how it looked.

"That is *so* awesome," said Jelly. "It's better than that other team because there's *three* things happening at once—two double backs *and* a flash kick!"

"Yeah, and it goes right into chains," said Dana. "I can't wait to do this in the tournament—we're gonna blow those judges away this year!"

Master Fu had them do it again, and this time had the girls go right into their set with chains. "Remember, girls—at the end of the body jumps, you're going to do the monk move walking forward toward the audience. Then walk under the chains and smash them to the floor behind you."

Once they had gone through the set, Master Fu had the team do the full demo from the beginning.

"Good work tonight, everyone. We don't have time to put the actual closer together, but we'll do that next week. Have a great weekend!"

Katana and Sara ran up to their room right after dinner to shower and get ready for the dance. They met up with Olivia and Sierra, and went downstairs to get Chris. They took the bus over to Lincoln. Olivia dragged Chris out on the dance floor the moment they got inside the auditorium.

"Come on," said Sara. "I wanna find Fisher."

Katana followed Sara around the room, but it didn't take long. Sara turned around at one point and walked right into her quarry. "Sorry!" she said, then backed up and realized who it was. "Fisher!"

"Oh—hi," said Fisher, looking embarrassed. "That's me—call me Sean, though."

"Sean—so tell me why, out of all the people at Lincoln, you are hanging around with the moron twins?" asked Sara.

Sean laughed. "The moron twins? Yeah, I guess that's an appropriate name. They are pretty stupid. I'm sorry about the way they treated you at lunch the other day. I tried to get them to stop..."

"Yeah, we heard," said Katana. "But why are you hanging out with those two?"

"Hey, cut me some slack!" said Sean. "I just moved here from Denver a couple months ago, and I don't really know anyone yet. I met those two at my new karate school..."

"You go to U.S.A. Tae Kwon Do?!" Sara asked.

"Yeah, that's right," said Sean. "Right in downtown Eureka. Why—is that not a good school?"

"Well, Sebastian's kind of a jerk, isn't he?" said Katana.

"Nah, he's okay," said Sean. "He's kinda young—I guess he graduated last year. But he's a decent teacher."

Katana and Sara looked at each other. "He hasn't been using any dim mak on his students?" Katana asked.

"What's that?" asked Sean.

"Like when he grabs you and hits you in the chest," said Sara, jamming her hand into Sean's sternum, "and does something to your chi so it feels like your heart is going to explode?"

"Um..." said Sean, giggling. "No, he hasn't done anything like that. Anyway, he's not the main teacher. This Sato guy is the master there."

"Sato's teaching now?" asked Katana.

"Sometimes. He's not always around, though. He's been going away a lot—he was gone again on Monday when I went to class. Why—how do you two know Sato?"

"He used to be the aikido master at the Hall of the Dragon," said Sara.

The girls told Sean the whole story of Jaaku and his Arashi, and how Sato had helped the Arashi steal the Scroll of the Five Masters during Katana's first year.

"Wow," said Sean when they finished. "Well, I wouldn't have guessed anything like that. He seems pretty nice."

Just then Katana had a sinking feeling in her stomach, as if she'd missed a step going down a flight of stairs. An overwhelming sense of panic came over her. She had no idea why she was feeling this way, but forgot about it a moment later. Olivia stormed past them, Chris only a few steps behind her.

"Olivia—I'm sorry! Olivia, wait..." He stopped right next to Katana, hitting himself in the forehead with the palm of his hand.

"Um... What's going on?" asked Katana.

"You're not going to believe me if I tell you..." said Chris, shaking his head.

"Chris, what happened?" Sara asked.

"I made out with Sierra..."

"WHAT!?" said Katana and Sara at the same time.

"Chris, what were you *thinking*?!" replied Katana.

"I thought it was Olivia!" said Chris frantically. "But it wasn't! Then Olivia came over and pulled us apart and slapped me... And well, you saw her running out of here! What do I do?!"

"But they're not even wearing the same outfit!" Katana said, totally exasperated.

"Oh..." Chris replied, bewildered. "Yeah, I thought something was different..."

"Why would Sierra make out with you—she knows you're going out with her sister..." said Sara.

"I don't know! Guys, help me out here, what do I do?!" asked Chris, panic-stricken.

"Wait here," said Sara, "we'll go talk to her." Sara grabbed Katana's hand. The two of them went to look for Olivia. They found her outside, sitting on one of the benches, crying.

"Hey," said Sara quietly.

Olivia looked up. "Hey guys."

"Chris told us what happened," said Katana.

"Why would he do that?" said Olivia. "Why would he kiss my *sister*?!"

Sara sat down on the bench next to Olivia. "Chris thought it was you—you two *are* pretty difficult to tell apart sometimes."

Katana sat down on the other side of Olivia and asked, "I want to know why *Sierra* would do that—obviously she didn't mistake Chris for anyone else..."

"She only did it because I made out with *her* last boyfriend," said Olivia, sniffling.

Sara looked at Katana and raised one eyebrow. "Um... Why did you do that?"

"Because she made out with my last boyfriend, too!" said Olivia. "I don't know how it started—we've been doing crap like this to each other since we were little. I guess it's kinda stupid..."

"Olivia, you can't be mad at Chris, then—if Sierra was pretending to be you, it's her fault, not his," said Katana, feeling glad at that moment that *she* didn't have a twin.

"Yeah, I know. I just saw them and I got really pissed off."

"Hey, do you two have that thing where you can like... feel what the other one's feeling?" asked Sara.

"Sara!" said Katana. "That's ridiculous!"

"No—seriously," said Sara. "I was friends with two twins when I was little—in San Francisco. Madison was at school one day, but her sister Melissa was sick, so she stayed home. Well, Madison got in a fight that day, and Melissa knew it as soon as it happened. She said she could feel that Madison was scared."

Katana thought this sounded very unlikely, but Olivia said, "Yeah, that happens to us, too. One time, when we were little, I went to the store with my mom, but Sierra stayed home. All of a sudden, I got really scared, and I had this image of a dog barking. When we got home I found out that the neighbor's dog got loose and chased my sister up a tree." Olivia giggled. "I wish I could find that dog now—I'd like to set it loose on her again!"

They walked back into the auditorium to find Chris—he was still talking to Sean. Olivia pulled Chris into a hug. "I'm sorry for slapping you—I know it was Sierra's fault. I'm gonna kill her one of these days."

Chris mouthed "Thank you" to Katana and Sara over Olivia's shoulder.

Olivia led Chris onto the dance floor. "Come on, you two," said Sara. "I wanna dance." She dragged Katana and Sean out as well.

Jimmy came over to dance with them a while later. When the DJ played a slow song, and Sara went to dance with Sean, Jimmy danced with Katana.

Katana felt uncomfortable; she knew how Jimmy felt about her, and she hadn't had a chance to talk to him yet. She didn't want to dance with him, but thought it would be more awkward to pull away.

After a minute, however, Jimmy started kissing her neck. She decided that pulling away would be decidedly *less* awkward.

"Jimmy, no," she said, and immediately felt horrible—Jimmy looked crushed when she backed away from him. "Come on, we need to talk." She grabbed him by the hand and led him outside to the same bench where she'd been sitting with Olivia and Sara.

"Jimmy, I'm sorry, but I don't want a boyfriend right now. I like you, as a friend, but... well, that's it. Just as a friend."

"Oh..." Jimmy looked like he didn't know what to say next. "Why don't you want a boyfriend?"

"I'm no good at the boyfriend thing," said Katana. "I went out with Jason last year and I screwed it all up."

"You won't mess anything up," said Jimmy. "Katana, I'm in love with you. Ever since you and Sara helped me out when I was smoking with Ed and Tommy two years ago..."

"Jimmy, come on—you can't possibly be in love with me..."

"Why not?! Katana I swear, I've been in love with you almost since the first day you came to the Hall...."

"Then why didn't you ever say anything before?"

"I wanted to last year, but you were going out with Beecher... and I started going out with Sierra..."

Katana was starting to feel awful. "Jimmy, I'm so sorry. I can't go out with you—I just can't. It's not you—I don't want to go out with anyone right now. I've got too much going on—between the sparring team and the wushu team and... I have a whole lot on my mind right now."

"I know, Chris said you've been upset lately," said Jimmy, a sad expression on his face.

"We're still friends, though—right?" asked Katana.

Jimmy got up and started walking away. But he turned around and said, "Yeah, Kat, of course we are. We're still friends."

Jimmy walked back inside. Katana didn't feel like being around a lot of people anymore. She stayed where she was, sitting on the bench until Sara, Chris and Olivia came out again.

"Here you are," said Sara. "We've been looking for you. We wanna head back, are you ready?"

"Yeah, definitely."

Chris went with the girls up to their room when they got back to the Hall. The three of them went outside to sit on the balcony.

"So I figured out where I know Fisher from," said Sara.

"Where?" asked Katana.

"We did karate at the same school when I lived in Denver. In fact, he was my very first boyfriend!"

"You've gotta be kidding me—how old were you then? Like six?" asked Chris.

"Seven!"

"You had your first boyfriend when you were *seven*?!" asked Katana, shaking her head.

"Sure did!" said Sara. "And now I'm going out with him again!"

Chris looked at Katana and laughed. "You're one of a kind, Sara."

"Hey, so are you and Olivia good now?" Katana asked.

"Yeah, we're fine. Thanks for that, you guys. She was *so* pissed at me at first. I've got to find a way to tell those two apart. Oh, did Jimmy ask you out?"

Katana sighed. "No. I didn't give him the chance."

"Aw, Kat, I hope you let him down easy," said Sara.

"I tried, but he was pretty upset. He says he's been in love with me since I first got here—like two years ago!"

"He has been," said Chris. "He told me that, too. He wanted to ask you out last year..."

"I know—but then I was going out with Jason, and he was going out with Sierra by the time me and Jason broke up."

At that moment Katana saw one of the school limousines pull up in the driveway beyond the torii gate. Gerald got out to open the back doors, and Master Nash got out of the front seat.

Katana saw a very tall Asian man in a business suit get out of the limo, followed by two other men dressed in jeans. Gerald opened up the trunk and helped the other two men with the suitcases as the tall man walked toward the Hall with Nash.

They got to the front doors, and it looked to Katana like Master Nash was hanging back a couple of steps. The tall man got to the doors first, opened them both wide, and strode through.

"That must be Master Kim," said Katana. Master Nash held the door open for the other two men.

"Yeah—and now we know he's not an Arashi," said Sara.

"What do you mean?" asked Chris. "How do we know that?"

"He was able to open the doors," Sara said with a shrug. "If he were an Arashi, they wouldn't have opened for him."

CHAPTER 13

MASTER KIM

Katana was not looking forward to the seminar with Master Kim. Maybe it was because she was feeling rather apprehensive about the evaluation she was going to have to endure with the man the next day. Or perhaps it was because of what Sam had told her about him during her private lesson the previous week.

"He did seem to have an arrogant air about him, the way he walked through the doors last night," said Sara when Katana discussed her feelings about the seminar with her.

"Yeah, he did, didn't he?" said Katana. "Almost like he thought he owned the place or something."

The girls went to get Chris and Jimmy a little before three and the four of them went downstairs together. "So this should be interesting," said Jimmy. Katana could hear the note of sarcasm in his voice.

"How do you mean?" she asked.

"Jason was telling me about the seminar he did with Master Kim the last time he came to the Hall," he said as they walked through the short hallway to the atrium. "He says he was kind of a jerk."

Katana took one step into the atrium then stopped dead—she couldn't believe her eyes. Chris walked right into her and she stumbled forward.

"What are you doing—Oh!" said Chris. Standing on the other side of the atrium, outside the doorway to the south wing, were Nash—and Master Sato. Nash had his arms folded across his chest, and the two of them seemed deep in conversation.

"What the hell is *he* doing here?" Sara asked.

"I don't know," said Katana. "But Nash doesn't exactly look unhappy to see him, does he?"

Nash shook hands with Sato a moment later and walked him over to the main doors.

"That's weird," said Sara. "We're definitely asking Sam about this."

They joined the stream of kids making their way up to the tai chi dojo. Katana walked into the room and went with Sara and Chris to stretch and get ready for the seminar. Katana noticed several piles of wood and bricks lined up along the front of the dojo; she thought that Sam had been very wise in her decision to introduce them to breaking.

Sam herself walked in a minute later and came over to them. "Hey, guys—we're gonna have to postpone sushi until tomorrow

220

night," she said. "We have a meeting with Master Nash after the seminar tonight."

Katana did not get a chance to reply however, as Nash walked in with Master Kim a moment later. His two assistants were dressed in traditional tae kwon do uniforms—which were much like karate uniforms, but with pullover tops. Master Kim was wearing a business suit. This struck Katana as a little strange. She'd never seen anyone teach martial arts in a suit before.

Master Nash walked to the front of the room with Master Kim and his two assistants, and had the students line up. "Good afternoon, everyone," he began. "It is my great honor to introduce to you Headmaster Kim from the Temple of the Crane in Korea. Assisting Master Kim today will be Master Park and Master Lee. Let's please give them a warm welcome."

Everyone clapped for the three masters, but Katana thought the response was rather lukewarm. Katana watched Master Kim for a moment, expecting that he would say something or start the seminar himself, but he merely held his hand out to Master Park and nodded. Master Park, in turn, had everyone get in a horse stance to do basics.

They spent the next twenty minutes throwing a variety of strikes and kicks—they were doing essentially the same workout Katana had done in every tae kwon do class she'd ever taken. This seemed silly—why would they come all the way from Korea to run everyone through this? Master Park finished with basics and Master Kim walked to the front of the class.

"Basics strong, very good," he said, pacing back and forth in front of them. "Today we do much traditional tae kwon do. As art spread through whole world, some tradition lost. Masters here very good, much experience. But not everything teach like in Korea."

Master Kim motioned to Master Park again. Katana saw Master Park, Master Lee and Sam, Osaka and Master Daniels move to the front of the room, each of them taking up position next to a pile of wood.

"We break today, use to train power and focus. Make five lines. Go!" commanded Master Kim.

Katana got in one of the lines with Sara and Chris. As the first boy in their line went up for his turn, Katana saw that Master Lee was holding a single board by the edges, his arms locked out in front of him. He instructed the boy to break the board with a palm heel strike.

Katana got to the front of the line and smashed her hand through the board when Master Lee yelled "Go!" They went through the line again and this time Master Lee was holding two boards for Katana to break, one flat against the other.

"I'm glad Sam had us do this in class," said Sara when she got back in line behind Katana after her second turn. "I don't know if I would've been able to do it otherwise."

Apparently Master Kim was satisfied with their breaking skill. He didn't give them a third turn, and did not so much as talk about breaking for the rest of the seminar.

Instead, he had Master Park bring an enormous punching bag to the center of the room, and instructed everyone to gather around him. "Flying kick also important part of traditional tae kwon do training," he said to the whole room. "Please watch Master Lee."

Master Park held the punching bag steady. Master Lee took a running start, then leaped into the air—nearly as high as Master Park's head—and kicked the bag with a side kick. Katana thought that if he'd gone much higher, he would have sailed right over the bag—and Master Park.

"Please go back to lines, and do flying side kick on bags," said Master Kim. Each of the masters set up a punching bag, and Katana got back in line with Sara and Chris.

"I've never really tried this before," said Katana.

"It's not that hard," Sara assured her. "We did flying side kicks with Van Heldon my first year here. You'll probably nail it considering how high you can jump."

Katana got to the front of the line, and did the kick exactly as Master Lee had demonstrated. She realized Sara was right—this wasn't very hard.

Once everyone had had a turn, Master Kim instructed them to watch Master Lee again. "This time kick both feet," said Master Kim, holding his hand out toward Master Lee. And sure enough, Master Lee ran forward, and went totally horizontal in the air. He kicked the bag with both feet, knocking Master Park and the punching bag back several feet, and landing on his side on the mat.

"This one looks kinda painful," said Chris apprehensively as they got back in line again. Katana could tell that people were having quite a bit more difficulty with this kick—kids at the front of each line were taking several attempts to work up the nerve to try it. She saw Olivia (or it may have been Sierra, she couldn't be sure) jump too late and face-plant right into the bag.

Katana got to the front of her line, took a deep breath, and ran forward. She launched like she had for the flying side kick, but then kicked out with both feet as hard as she could. She landed on the mat and saw that she'd managed to knock Master Lee into the front wall.

Sara did the kick as well, and said, "That was cool!" when she got back in line with Katana. Chris, however, did not fare as well. He got scared when he started to jump, and tried to bail out. He put his hands down, and ended up doing an awkward sort of handstand instead. Master Lee made him try it three more times before he gave up and sent him to the end of the line.

"This kick is stupid," Chris complained. "When would you ever use this?"

Once everyone had had two turns, Master Kim gathered them together in the center of the room again. "In Korea, flying kicks very important. Learn tae kwon do outside Korea, not learn as much whole art. Lose tradition. Watch again Master Lee."

This time Master Lee started with a flying side kick, but twisted over in midair when his first foot connected with the bag. He swung his other leg around, hitting the bag with the back of his heel. Master Kim directed everyone to get into their lines again, and Sara said, "That kick looks cool as hell!"

"Oh yeah, really cool," Chris replied angrily. "Half the room couldn't do that last kick, what makes him think we're gonna be able to do this one?"

Katana did get the impression that Chris was right—it almost seemed like Master Kim was setting them up to fail. He didn't bother explaining to them *how* to do the kick. He'd had Master Lee demonstrate it only once; he couldn't possibly expect people to do it without any instruction. And sure enough, Katana watched everyone in her line totally fail to do anything resembling the kick that Master Lee had demonstrated.

Katana thought about the kick as she waited for her turn. She didn't understand how it was possible to turn over like that once she was already in the air. But suddenly she realized it might work something like her gainer flash in sparring. Maybe when she did the first kick with her right foot, she could use that to push against the bag, and turn herself in the air for the second kick.

She tried it when she got to the front of the line. She ran toward the bag, and jumped as high as she could. She pulled her knees up to her chest, and kicked out with her right foot. The moment she felt her foot connect with the bag, she twisted to her left, extending her other leg. It worked—her left foot hit the bag and she knocked it right out of Master Lee's hands.

When she got to the end of the line, she saw Master Kim at the front of the room, pointing at her and talking to Master Nash.

"How did you do that?" asked Sara. "I landed flat on my face!"

Master Kim had everyone take several more turns trying the kick, but offered no instruction. Katana explained it to Sara and Chris in between turns. Sara was able to do it on her third try, but it didn't look like anyone else was coming close.

Katana liked this kick—although she couldn't think of any

situation in which she'd be able to use it. She couldn't imagine a flying kick working in a sparring match. And even if it did, she thought the second kick would probably take the person's head off—it had that much power.

Finally Master Kim had everyone gather around the center of the room again. Katana wondered what ridiculous thing he was going to have them try next. She thought for a moment that Master Kim was going to demonstrate something himself—he took off his suit jacket and handed it to Master Lee.

But Master Kim didn't demonstrate anything. He talked at them more instead.

"Flying kicks very important part of tae kwon do," he said, pacing back and forth. He unbuttoned the cuffs of his shirt and rolled up his sleeves. "Must train all facet of the art to be complete. Breaking, sparring, flying kicks, kata—without all of these, cannot attain perfection of art. When art is complete, art is perfect. Only can master art if master complete art, only reach perfection if master *complete* art!"

At this point, he held out both of his arms and Katana could see that he had a tattoo of a dragon on his left forearm and a tiger on his right. "When master complete art, you attain perfection. I am perfection—I have dragon and tiger of Shaolin—yin and yang. Just as yin and yang achieve perfect balance in universe, mastering complete art of tae kwon do achieve perfect balance in body. Without complete art, without tiger *and* dragon, never achieve perfection!"

And with that pronouncement, Master Kim rolled his sleeves down, and took his suit jacket back from Master Lee.

From the looks on people's faces, Katana could tell that nobody else had any better idea what he was talking about than she did. Master Kim's speech met with stunned silence, until Nash and Sam began clapping for him. Everyone else clapped halfheartedly, and Nash lined them up again.

"What the hell was he babbling about?" asked Chris once Nash had dismissed them and they were headed to their rooms to get ready for dinner. "The tiger and the dragon and the perfection —did he really just say that he was perfect?"

"Yeah, he sure did," said Sara, rolling her eyes. "He's a perfect pain in my ass!"

"Pain in *your* ass?" asked Katana with a laugh. "*I'm* the one who has to go through an evaluation with him tomorrow!"

Katana was now looking forward to that evaluation even less than she had been to the seminar. If Master Kim would intentionally make all of the students in the school look bad like that, what would he have in store for her?

She went back to the tai chi dojo at ten the next morning. She was surprised to find that only Nash and Master Kim were there. Neither Master Park nor Master Lee was present, and Master Kim was wearing a traditional tae kwon do uniform this time—gaudy, but traditional. The top of his uniform had gold and black trim, and there was a gold stripe running down the outside of each pant leg.

"Ah, Katana—good morning," said Master Nash. "Are you ready?"

"Um... I guess," she replied uncertainly.

"You'll do fine," said Master Nash with an encouraging smile. "Master Kim has decided to keep things rather informal today."

"We start with breaking, please come with me," said Master Kim. He led her over to one side of the room, where Katana saw that he had set up five boards on two cinder blocks. "Please break with any strike you wish."

"Now?" Katana asked.

"Yes, now," Master Kim replied.

Katana set up in her horse stance for a palm heel strike, like she'd done with Sam. Five boards did not seem nearly as daunting now that she'd broken two bricks. She didn't bother going through the motions this time—she wound up, let out a loud kiai and smashed right through all five boards.

"Good," said Master Kim. He went to the pile of bricks along the wall and brought one over. He set it up on the cinder blocks and said simply "Again."

Katana noticed that he hadn't bothered to put a towel down on top of the brick. She moved through the break slowly a couple of times first. Then she took a deep breath, kiaied as loud as she could and smashed her hand through the brick.

Master Kim then placed two bricks, without any spacers, across the two cinder blocks. "Again," he said.

"Can I do it with an elbow?" asked Katana.

"Any strike," Master Kim said with a nod.

"Okay..." Katana had done this only once. She was starting to feel nervous now, but she got down on one knee and set up her break. She reached back with her whole arm, and swung her elbow in slow motion several times. Finally she kiaied, and slammed her elbow down with all her might. To her surprise, this didn't feel quite as hard today as it had when she did it with Sam —but she still didn't think she'd be able to get through more than two bricks.

But Master Kim did indeed set up three bricks next. "Again," he said.

Katana was beginning to get the feeling that no matter how many bricks she could break, Master Kim would have her try even more. She didn't think she was going to be able to get through them. But she set it up and focused through the bricks. Then she kiaied and brought her elbow down with every ounce of strength she possessed. But it was no good. The bricks were quite as solid as they'd been a moment ago. Katana now had a sharp pain in her arm, and her fingers were numb.

Master Kim said nothing about her failure, but nodded and said, "Come with me." He walked to the center of the enormous dojo. Katana followed him, opening and closing her fist to try to get the feeling back in her fingers.

"Now we spar," said Master Kim. "Please use chen do."

Katana didn't like this idea very much. She was certain he was going to try to make her look bad—and she had no idea which chen do he could do. But she didn't have any time to think about it—they bowed to each other and Master Kim yelled "Fight!"

The instant they started, Katana could see from his shen that Master Kim was gathering his energy for a chi hit. She deflected his fireball. He followed up immediately with a series of kicks. Katana used the distancing exercise she'd done with Sam during their team practices. Master Kim was very tall, so this proved to be a useful strategy.

Katana was able to keep away from his kicks. The moment he backed off, she threw a fireball of her own. But Master Kim deflected it as easily as Katana had.

She launched at him with a combination of three kicks—she feinted with a front kick then turned her body slightly to snap a roundhouse kick to his head—which she could barely reach. Master Kim leaned out of the way of the roundhouse kick and Katana snapped her leg around the other way for an axe kick—but Master Kim dropped down and swept out her other leg. Katana fell to the mat.

Master Kim jumped—he was going to land on her if she didn't move. She scrambled to get her feet underneath her, and using levitation, shot out of the way. She threw her chi at him, from midair this time, but Master Kim turned around in time to deflect it. Katana was floating back to the mat, but Master Kim jumped into the air to engage her mid-flight—apparently he could levitate as well. He brought his foot around for a kick to her head. Katana blocked by kicking his shin before he got his leg to full extension.

Katana landed on the mat and got ready for his next attack. But when Master Kim landed a moment later, he gathered his energy for another chi hit. In the split second that it took Katana to see this, she formed a powerful ball of energy between her arms. She caught his fireball with her own energy, spun around and threw the flaming mass back at him. The fireball streaked toward Master Kim like a comet. He tried to deflect it—but had clearly not been expecting this technique from Katana. The fireball hit him in the chest and knocked him halfway across the room.

Katana looked at Master Nash, who had been watching the match from the front of the room. He smiled and winked at her. Master Kim got up and walked back over to Katana. He seemed a little shaken, saying only "Very good." They bowed to each other and Master Kim shook Katana's hand.

Katana ran back to her room when Master Nash dismissed her. Chris and Sara were waiting for her.

"That didn't take very long—how'd it go?" asked Sara.

Katana told them about her evaluation. "It definitely seems like he was trying to make you fail," said Chris. "I bet if you broke the three bricks, he woulda made you try four!"

"Oh, no doubt," agreed Katana.

"Too bad you didn't knock him out with that fireball the way you did to Jason last year," said Sara. "That woulda put him in his place!"

"Psh, Katana put him in his place anyway," said Chris with a smile. "I bet he didn't think she could hit him with her chi."

The three of them went to the wushu dojo after lunch. Once Katana had recounted the story for the rest of their friends, they spent the remainder of the afternoon tricking and working on their sets for the demo.

Katana was feeling very confident with everything—she could land her double back consistently now, and she went through the opening for their chain set with Jelly and Dana several times. Jelly was goofing around and levitated right over Katana's double backflip once, but other than that they nailed the sequence every time.

Katana also felt extremely good with the double whip chain set itself. Jelly said he thought they were both going faster than Dana had when she competed individually the year before. Katana spent a lot of time spinning both chains in one hand—like Dana had said, all it took was practice. She could do over two dozen revolutions now; considering they only did five in the demo, Katana felt pretty comfortable with the move.

Once they'd tired themselves out, Katana went back to her room with Sara. They both showered then went with Chris up to Sam's apartment for dinner.

"I hear the evaluation went pretty well," Sam said as they sat down to eat.

"I guess," replied Katana. "But I get the feeling Master Kim was determined to make me look bad."

"Yeah, he does that," said Sam with a sigh. "It's like I told you that day—he feels very strongly that you are not doing the true art unless you do it in Korea, preferably with him."

"Sam, what the hell was he babbling about with that tiger and dragon and perfection crap the other day?" asked Chris.

Sam rolled her eyes. "He's referring to the rite the Shaolin Temple used to use to test monks for master. You had to fight the headmaster's bodyguards first, then a bunch of other monks, and *then*, if you made it through that, you had to go through the Hall of Wooden Men."

"Wooden men?" asked Sara.

"There's this tunnel that goes out through the back of the

temple," Sam explained, "and it's rigged with these mechanical men—there's 108 of them and they're made of wood. They're triggered by your body weight—so as you walk on the stone in front of a dummy, it launches at you with some kind of attack. Some of them come at you with a wooden arm or leg, but others have weapons—spears or swords."

"And they're real—they're sharp?" asked Chris.

"Oh yes," said Sam. "The Hall of Wooden Men was often lethal. Anyway, if you made it through *that* then came the hardest part of the test."

"You mean the dummies attacking you with real spears wasn't the hard part?" asked Sara.

"No," said Sam. "At the very end, there was this enormous urn blocking the exit from the tunnel. They loaded the urn with burning coals—the thing allegedly weighed five hundred pounds. The monk had to lift the urn and move it out of the way to escape."

"And how are you supposed to do that?!" asked Chris. "Nobody can lift that much weight!"

"I don't know," said Sam. "I think the whole idea was that it was almost impossible to become a master—but you could only leave the temple if you could pass the test. That's why you rarely saw any Shaolin masters outside of Shaolin. But they don't do that anymore—I think they stopped a few hundred years ago."

"Wait—I still don't get what this has to do with the tiger and the dragon..." said Sara.

"Oh—right!" said Sam. "Well, there were these carvings on each side of the urn, right where you had to put your arms to lift the thing. There was a tiger on the right side, and a dragon on the left. So if you lifted the urn, the images of the two animals were burned into your forearms forever, marking you as a Shaolin master.

"The dragon and the tiger are the two most powerful animals in the Chinese zodiac. They've been the symbol of the Shaolin Temple since its founding. The dragon represents wisdom and the tiger strength—yin and yang. The idea was that strength without wisdom would be bad—if you had the strength of a Shaolin master, but not the wisdom..."

"Then you'd be like Jaaku and steal people's chi just because you could!" said Katana.

"Exactly," Sam agreed.

"Wait—so did Master Kim test at Shaolin?!" asked Sara.

"Hardly," said Sam, rolling her eyes. "Master Kim got the tiger and the dragon tattooed on his forearms. He never trained at the Shaolin Temple."

"Psh, so much for being perfect," said Sara sarcastically.

Suddenly Katana remembered another question she wanted to ask Sam tonight. "Sam, what was Sato doing here? We saw him talking to Nash on our way up to the seminar."

"Sato is working for us now," Sam answered simply.

"But he's an Arashi!" said Chris.

"He took the Scroll of the Five Masters!" said Sara. "And brought Jaaku into the Hall—how can you possibly trust him?"

"And Jaaku took Sato's chi," said Katana. "How can Sato come here without Jaaku knowing about it? He could be spying for Jaaku."

"I don't think so," said Sam. "Sato has been giving Master Nash a lot of information about what the Arashi have been up to. And Nash isn't stupid—he's not telling Sato anything that would be useful to Jaaku, just in case. I'm not sure how Sato can come here without Jaaku's knowledge, but between Sato and Master Lu, Jaaku won't be able to sneeze without our knowing about it."

"Master Lu," said Sara. "Wasn't he the guy we thought was the new dim mak master, before we found out Jaaku was?"

"Yes," said Sam. "He's also the one who figured out where Jaaku hid the Scroll of the Five Masters last year. Without his help, we never would've found it."

"Sam..." said Katana tentatively, "what exactly is Jaaku doing now? I know last year he kept trying to figure out the scroll, but now that's gone..."

"Well, as you heard from Sara's dad, there's an assassin out there killing the Arashi," said Sam. "Sato told us that Jaaku isn't doing much of anything because of it. I'm sure he's trying harder than anyone to figure out who the assassin is, but he's holed himself up at the temple in Shanxi and has very little contact with most of the Arashi."

"Why is that?" asked Sara.

"We don't know for sure," said Sam. "Nash thinks Jaaku might be afraid the assassin will target *him* next, using one of the Arashi to get close to him. But I don't see how anyone could possibly kill Jaaku like that—he's much too powerful."

Just then Master Fu barged into the room. Sam smiled at him and said, "Hi Neslon."

Master Fu was not smiling. "You're not going to believe this," he said. He grabbed the remote off the table and turned on Sam's television. He tuned in a news channel and Katana saw what looked like a hundred police officers moving people away from a gate at an airport.

"We're live at San Francisco International Airport," said the reporter on the television. "As you can see behind me, police have now roped off the gate where witnesses report the attack took place. Earlier reports we were getting said that someone had been shot—now we're hearing that in fact it was not a shooting, but that the victim was stabbed with a sword of some kind. Witness accounts are very sketchy however—people are saying they could not see the attacker. They only saw the victim fall down, and he was bleeding heavily from the chest. As you can imagine, there was a lot of panic and confusion and it seems like nobody saw the attack take place, they only saw the man lying on the floor..."

"That's horrible!" said Sam. "How did someone get into SFO with a sword?"

"Sam—it's Master Lee!" said Fu. "Someone killed Master Lee as they were waiting to board the plane back to Korea!"

Sam got to her feet. "Master Kim's assistant! You've got to be kidding me..."

"That's not all—I just talked to Nash. He heard from Mitch that Lee's body vaporized. The FBI are taking over the investigation and trying to keep that little detail as quiet as possible," said Master Fu.

"Wait a minute—his body vaporized?!" asked Katana. "I thought that's what happens when Jaaku does the death touch..."

"Yeah, exactly," said Master Fu. "Lee must have been an Arashi. Jaaku already had his prenatal chi..."

"If Jaaku senses that one of the Arashi is dying, he uses the connection to take their chi," Sam explained. "The headmaster of Shaolin found that out from Master Lu."

"Wait a minute... If Lee was an Arashi, does that mean the killer was the assassin?" Sara asked hesitantly. "Was Lee the assassin's eighth victim?"

"Ninth," said Master Fu. "Well, the ninth that we know about anyway—hang on—you know about the assassin?"

"My dad told us about it when Kat and Chris came to visit us in Japan," said Sara. "When was the eighth victim?"

"Monday night—during Katana's meeting with Master Nash," said Sam. "Nash found out about it from your father, Sara, right after he finished talking with Katana. It was in Tokyo —apparently it was one of the people who had been in charge of the human trafficking ring."

"But if Lee was an Arashi, how'd he get into the Hall of the Dragon?" asked Katana.

"Nash held the door open for him—remember?" said Chris. "Kim walked in first, but then Nash held the door for the other two."

"Osaka is flipping out," said Master Fu. "He's in Nash's office right now. He's saying this is exactly what he was worried about."

"Osaka was worried about an Arashi getting into the Hall?" asked Katana. "Why would he be worried about that? Osaka destroyed the Scroll of the Five Masters—what else could they want here?"

"I don't know," said Sam. "Nelson, are you sure that's what he meant—that he was worried about an Arashi getting in? Kat's right, that doesn't add up."

"I just assumed that's what he was referring to," said Fu. "What else would he have been worried about?"

Sam glanced at Katana. She looked away immediately and said, "I don't know. He *was* pretty unhappy about the headmasters coming here. But I don't see what that has to do with the Arashi."

"Sam, why did Kim have to go to SFO?" asked Sara. "Doesn't the temple in Korea have its own jet, like the Hall of the Dragon?"

"No, Sara—definitely not. Only the Hall of the Dragon has a jet and a Ferrari."

"And a Porsche!" said Chris.

"I never thought about that before," said Katana. "How does the Hall have so much money if the other temples don't?"

"You know, I don't know for sure," said Sam. "But the Hall of the Dragon has always been extremely wealthy, even back in Master Chow's day."

"Oh—I almost forgot, Nash has called a Masters Council in five minutes," said Master Fu.

"Right," said Sam. "Sorry kids, we're going to have to cut the evening short."

They finished their sushi, and the kids went back up to Katana and Sara's room.

"I can't believe Lee was an Arashi," said Chris. "Do you really think Osaka was worried about an Arashi attack?"

238

"No," said Katana. "That doesn't make any sense. I don't know what Osaka was thinking, but I guarantee it's got something to do with me."

"How do you know that?" asked Sara.

"Sam said that Osaka was unhappy about the headmasters coming here. And we know they're only visiting so they can evaluate *me*. On top of that, Osaka's been worried about me knowing too much about Jaaku..."

Chris shook his head. "So are you saying... you think Osaka was worried that an Arashi was going to sneak into the Hall with one of the headmasters and... I don't know, give you information about Jaaku?" he said sarcastically.

"No, obviously that's not it, wise-ass," said Katana. "I don't know what it might be, but it seems like it's all connected somehow."

CHAPTER 14
CHI TAO

Life at the Hall of the Dragon returned to normal for the next couple of weeks. Katana didn't hear about any further attacks by the Arashi assassin. Nor was she able to find out what Osaka had been so worried about.

The teachers at Lincoln Academy hit their stride. Katana was now spending most of her evenings in the lounge helping Chris with math. Sara was thrilled that Sam's classes had gone back to normal—they didn't break any more boards or bricks after Master Kim's visit. She did spend one class teaching everyone how to do the flying kicks that Master Lee had demonstrated, but after that went back to a lot of sparring and chi kung practice.

Katana continued to work on pushing hands with Betsy and chi fa with Master Nash, but didn't feel like she was making any progress with either endeavor. She thought the wushu demo, on the other hand, was coming along very nicely. Master Fu seemed to agree with her. The kids were nailing their sets like never before. Master Fu declared one Friday evening at the end of practice that he thought they had a good shot at defeating Supernova at nationals this year.

Katana, Chris and Sara spent much of their time with Master Osaka every Thursday working on attack drills. Sara and Chris were both getting stronger and more consistent. Osaka told them he felt confident that all three of them would be ready to test in June.

Katana practiced chains with Dana every weekend. She finally figured out a way to add the butterfly twist into her solo set. She was feeling more and more like this was going to be her year—she had made it to nationals in sparring the previous year, but had been disqualified for (accidentally) using a chen do during her match with Sean Fisher. But she was feeling so good with chains she thought she might have a shot in the weapons division as well as sparring this year.

Dana kept trying to get the butterfly twist—and managed to land it a couple of times—but couldn't do it consistently. "I can go over backwards all day long, but rolling over sideways like this feels *wrong!*" she complained on their way down to dinner one Saturday after a particularly long practice session.

And Katana, Sara and Chris kept trying to help Jelly get another chen do. Jelly had them take turns hitting him with their chi one afternoon in Sam's dojo. But he decided rather quickly that it hurt too much to keep landing on the mat so hard. They went back to punting him into the foam pit in the wushu dojo instead. And Katana also tried to help him form a ball of energy in the standing chi kung exercise—she'd been inspired by her success with Sensei Mike over the summer. But no matter what they tried, Jelly didn't seem to be getting any closer to doing any more of the chen do.

Much to Katana's dismay, Jimmy seemed to focus on nothing more than trying to get her to go out with him—even though she'd made it very clear to him that she didn't want a boyfriend this year. When the next dance at Lincoln came around, Katana went with Jelly to avoid dealing with Jimmy's advances all night. Chris and Olivia went together, and Sara met up with Sean Fisher at Lincoln. Katana was getting to like Sean. He started sitting with them at their lunch table every day and Sara talked to him online whenever she could in the evenings.

By the beginning of October, Katana had all but completely forgotten about the Arashi assassin and Jaaku and the other head-masters who were coming to visit—until one Friday morning when Master Nash made an announcement at the end of class.

"Next week we will be hosting Master Nang from the Hall of the Silent Buddha in Tibet. This will be the very first time a head-master from the temple in Tibet has ever visited the Hall of the Dragon. Master Nang is a master of the very rare art of chi tao. He will be giving us a demonstration during our tai chi class on Monday morning. I would like you to please wear full uniform for this occasion."

Master Nash dismissed the class, and asked Katana to stay after for a moment.

"As you know, Master Nang will be evaluating you during his

stay here," he said. "But you will be happy to hear that Master Nang has chosen a format for his evaluation that is rather different from Master Kim's."

"Different... how?" asked Katana.

"Master Nang will be teaching you privately, Katana. This is an extremely unusual and special opportunity for you—Master Nang has been quite secretive about his art. He even refused to share his style with the masters at Shaolin. You will be joining him in Samantha's dojo every morning next week, starting on Tuesday, in lieu of our morning tai chi practice."

Katana felt much more excited about Master Nang's visit than she had about Master Kim's. For one thing, she was thrilled that she would not be going through a true evaluation this time. And getting private training in a rare and secret art that nobody had seen in centuries was right up her alley.

That Monday morning Katana woke up, as always, without an alarm at quarter to five. She dragged Sara out of bed. They were two of the first ones up to the tai chi dojo. Master Nash invited them inside. Katana saw that the other masters were here for this demonstration as well.

"Katana Kahanu, Sara Brown, this is Headmaster Nang," said Nash. Master Nang was wearing brilliant white robes. He was an inch or two shorter than Katana, and looked very old. His head was totally bald, and he was very wrinkly. But when he smiled and shook Katana's hand, she thought he had a very peaceful and serene look about him.

Master Nash lined up the class once everyone had arrived. He introduced Master Nang. Master Nang smiled and waved to the whole room, and motioned for them to sit along the back wall.

He walked to the center of the dojo and bowed, as if he were going to start a form. And in fact, he proceeded to drop into a low horse stance and do what looked like some form of chi kung for several moments.

Suddenly, though, he jumped into the air and did a perfect double backflip. He landed on one foot, holding his other foot over his head—like Katana did in her whip chain set. But Katana noticed that he hadn't only landed on one foot—he was standing on his toes.

Katana joined the rest of the room clapping and cheering for Master Nang. Abruptly, he levitated straight up into the air—almost to the ceiling—and faded, reappearing instantly on the mat where he'd just been standing.

Next, he motioned for Sam to join him. "We spar now," Katana could hear him say. "Please use chen do."

Sam and Master Nang bowed to each other. Sam got into a fighting stance. Master Nang, however, merely stood there, one hand behind his back and the other hand extended in front of him, palm-up.

Sam circled around him for a moment, then threw a roundhouse kick at his head. It appeared to Katana that Master Nang only tapped her foot. But Sam flew through the air as if some invisible giant had tossed her by the leg. She landed on the mat a few feet from where Katana was sitting. Everyone gasped.

Sam got up and walked back to Master Nang. This time she threw a chi hit at him. Master Nang turned his hand over again, and tapped the fireball the same way he'd done to Sam's foot. Yet the fireball bounced off his hand and shot at Sam. It hit her in the chest and knocked her down.

Katana was amazed—she knew how to catch someone else's chi hit and throw it back at them. But Master Nang hadn't caught it—he had *bounced* it. Katana had no idea how this was possible—she was certain it was totally different from the skill she'd mastered.

Sam got to her feet, held up her hands and yelled, "I'm good —you win!"

Everyone laughed. Master Nang smiled and bowed to her.

He motioned to Master Daniels next. Daniels lumbered over to the center of the room, and bowed to Master Nang. Master Nang continued to stand there, but this time held both hands behind his back. "Please push," he said.

Master Daniels walked forward and placed one hand on Master Nang's chest. He appeared to push—but succeeded only in pushing himself back.

He tried again, and this time got into a good horse stance. He pushed harder and harder—it looked like he was putting all of his considerable weight into it. But Master Nang didn't budge.

"How is he doing that?" asked Chris. "Nang's smaller than us, and Daniels must weigh a ton!"

Master Daniels gave up and bowed to Master Nang. Everyone cheered, but Master Nang said, "Now I push."

Master Daniels looked confused, but stood there, waiting for Master Nang to push him.

"Get in good stance, do not let me push," said Master Nang.

"Okay..." replied Master Daniels. He stood in a horse stance sideways to Master Nang. Master Nang tapped Master Daniels in the chest—and sent him flying through the air. Daniels landed with a loud thud.

Everyone broke into uproarious applause this time.

Master Nang motioned for Master Fu to join him. Master Fu ran out to the center of the dojo. He was carrying a spear.

Master Nang bowed to him and said, "Please try to stab."

Master Fu held the spear in both hands. He lunged in, jabbing the spear at Master Nang's chest—and it connected. Everyone gasped—Master Fu looked stunned—but the spear bounced off of Master Nang. He appeared unharmed.

"Again," he said. Master Fu stabbed at his stomach this time and again, the tip of the spear bounced right off of him.

Finally Master Nang took the spear, and held it with the tip up, so the base was on the mat. "Please hold base," he said. Master Fu knelt down and grasped the base of the spear with both hands, holding it firmly against the mat.

Master Nang brought the tip of the spear down on an angle, and stood directly in front of it. He leaned forward and put his throat on the tip. He then took his hands away so that it was clear that he was supporting himself—by the throat—on the tip of the spear.

Everyone cheered loudly again. From the chatter, Katana could tell that everyone else was as awestruck by this performance as she was.

"That was *amazing*!" said Chris when they got down to

breakfast twenty minutes later. "Did you see him throw Daniels across the room?!"

"What about that spear in his throat—how did he not impale himself?" asked Paul.

"You'd better teach me everything you learn this week, Kat," said Sara.

"Yeah—me too," Chris agreed. "I can't believe you get to take privates with him—you're so lucky!"

Katana couldn't wait to get to her first lesson the following morning—it was all she could think about at school that day.

She woke up extra early on Tuesday and ran down to the tae kwon do dojo. She worried at first that she would be *too* early, and Master Nang wouldn't be there yet. But when she walked in the door, she saw him sitting on a short table with his legs crossed in full lotus position, his hands palm-up in his lap, one on top of the other.

Master Nang opened his eyes and smiled at her. He unfolded his legs and got to his feet—and Katana realized he hadn't been sitting on a table. He had been levitating in place—she'd assumed that his long white robes had been concealing a table of some sort.

"Master, how can you levitate in place like that—I thought you could only bounce your chi off the floor..."

Master Nang held up one hand and Katana stopped talking immediately. "Yes, when you levitate, you bounce your chi off floor. But you can also hold your chi outside your body," said Master Nang with a smile. "Please try."

"Uh... okay," said Katana uncertainly. "Should I sit to try it...?"

"Sit or stand," said Master Nang, appearing to grow a few inches taller. Katana thought he was on his tiptoes until he pulled up the bottom of his robes. She could see that he was actually standing a few inches off the ground.

"Wow..." She focused on sending her chi through the bottom of her feet, and promptly jumped several feet into the air.

She landed and Master Nang said, "You must relax and bounce your chi very slowly—then hold it there. Bounce your chi too fast and you jump!" And with those words he jumped several feet himself.

He landed next to Katana and smiled. "Sink your chi very slowly through your feet, and push against the floor. Try again, please."

Katana remembered how she'd had to dig her feet into the sand to keep her balance when she practiced tai chi on the beach. She thought that maybe this worked in a similar way. So she focused on sinking her energy down through her feet, and imagined pushing against the mat with her chi.

Suddenly it worked—she rose a few inches off the ground. "This is so cool!"

"Yes, very cool," said Master Nang with a smile. He rose up a few inches again himself.

"Can you go any higher like this?" asked Katana.

"No," said Master Nang, shaking his head. "You can only push your chi short distance—extend it slowly and you can hold yourself up. Extend it quickly and you jump. But you cannot do both. Please try sitting now."

"All right," said Katana. She sat down on the mat and folded her legs into full lotus position. Again, she focused on sinking her chi down, this time right through her rear end, and pushing against the mat. And suddenly she was floating there, several inches off the floor. "This is amazing."

"Now please do handstand," said Master Nang. He placed his hands down on the mat, and kicked his legs up into a handstand.

"Okay," said Katana, and did so herself.

"Now lean, and push your chi to stay up," said Master Nang. He tilted over on a forty-five degree angle. He looked like he should have been falling flat on his back.

Katana tried it, and actually fell. "Where do I push my chi?" she asked, getting back in a handstand to try it again.

"Through your hands," said Master Nang. He leaned over the other way.

"Through my hands," Katana repeated. She tried to focus on extending her chi through her hands into the mat. She started leaning backward. And suddenly she could feel the mat with her chi; she was able to hold herself that way without falling.

"Now push to your feet," said Master Nang. He pushed off the mat with his hands, jumping into the air and landing on his feet. Katana copied him with ease.

"Now we will flip to standing. Please watch," said Master Nang. He leaped into the air—clearly using levitation, based on the incredible height he achieved—did a triple backflip, and landed on one foot. But this time Katana could see that he hadn't really landed—he was levitating on one foot a few inches off the ground.

"Please try," said Master Nang with a smile as he continued to stand there, several inches off the ground.

Katana leaped into the air, flipped over backward for three rotations—this part was easy, she thought—and tried to sink her chi through her feet as she landed. But she landed for real, with a loud thump. "Oops."

"Try again," said Master Nang.

Katana tried it a few more times. Finally she was able to land on her feet, then immediately levitate in place. But she couldn't get herself to land without really landing.

"This is good for today—again tomorrow morning, please." said Master Nang.

"Yeah, definitely!" said Katana. She'd already decided this was about the coolest lesson she'd ever had.

All through school that day, she kept trying standing levitation—she found this was quite easy now. When she grew bored in algebra, she levitated a few inches off her chair. Sara looked at her suddenly, saw what she was doing and hissed, "How the hell are you doing that?!"

And as Katana walked through the halls, she kept doing back-flips to try landing without landing. She finally got it as they made their way up to study hall for their last period.

"That's the coolest thing I've ever seen," said Chris. "You've *got* to teach us how to do that this weekend."

Katana raced down to Sam's dojo again the next morning, eager to see what she was going to learn next.

Once again, Master Nang was levitating in full lotus position when she walked in. He opened his eyes and smiled at her.

"I can do it," said Katana. "I can flip and land without landing!"

"Please show me."

Katana shot into the air and did a triple backflip. She landed without ever touching the mat, holding herself a few inches in the air.

"Very good," Master Nang said, beaming at her. "Today we will bounce fireballs."

"Oh, cool," said Katana.

Master Nang walked a few steps away from her, held his hand out toward her and said, "Please throw your chi."

Katana hurled a fireball at him. And to her ongoing amazement, the fireball bounced off Master Nang's hand. It hit her square in the chest, knocking her right over.

"How do you do that?!" she asked, getting back to her feet.

"It is levitation," said Master Nang with a smile.

"Levitation?! How do you do that with levitation?"

"You bounce your chi against fireball instead of floor," he said. "But you must bounce *fast* this time."

"That's incredible," said Katana, realizing this made perfect sense. "Can I try?"

"Yes," said Master Nang. "You are ready?"

Katana held out her hand in front of her, like Master Nang had done. "Yes, I'm ready."

Master Nang threw his hand out and launched a fireball at her. Katana focused on bouncing her chi against the fireball exactly the same way she always bounced it against the floor to levitate. And it worked—the fireball ricocheted off her hand and flew back at Master Nang. But he held his hand out as well; the fireball bounced back at Katana, knocking her off her feet again.

"Hey!"

"Oops," said Master Nang with a mischievous smile. "Try again?"

"Yes!" said Katana. She threw a fireball at him. He held out his hand and bounced it back at her, and Katana did the same—they spent the rest of the lesson passing the fireball back and forth to each other. They did it from standing first, then while running around the dojo. They even did it as they levitated up the walls, and while flipping through the air.

Katana was starting to feel like Master Nang might be the coolest teacher she'd ever had.

"You passed the fireball back and forth?!" asked Chris incredulously when Katana got to breakfast a little later.

"Yeah!" she said. "It was the coolest thing ever—it's like levitating, but you bounce your chi against the fireball instead of bouncing it off the floor!"

"We're trying this on Saturday," said Jelly. "I may not be able to do a chi hit, but I *can* levitate—so I should be able to get this!"

Katana got down to Sam's dojo on Thursday morning and once again found Master Nang levitating in full lotus position. But today she also saw that he had a stack of four bricks set up on two cinder blocks.

"Good morning," he said with a smile as Katana walked in.

"Are we working on breaking today?" Katana asked. She thought she was done with that after Master Kim's visit.

"Yes, breaking," said Master Nang. He walked over to the pile of bricks.

Katana joined him, and he said simply, "Please break."

"Four?! I can't break four—I hurt myself trying to break three!"

"Use levitation and you will not hurt," said Master Nang. He tapped the top brick very lightly with his right hand—all four bricks shattered.

Katana was amazed. "How on earth..."

"Bounce your chi against brick," said Master Nang. "But you must bounce *very* fast!"

He set up four more bricks for Katana. "Please try."

She held her hand several inches above the bricks for a moment. Then she tapped the top brick, concentrating on bouncing her chi through her hand. It worked—all four bricks shattered. "This is so cool!"

Master Nang waved his hand at the dust that now filled the air. "Very cool. Very dusty."

He set up four more bricks. "Now break only top brick, please."

"Only the top one—how?" asked Katana.

"Do not bounce chi so far."

"Oh," said Katana. That made sense. She tried it, and broke the top two bricks.

"Almost," said Master Nang. He cleared off the broken bricks and added two more to the pile. "Please try again."

Katana did it once more, and bounced her chi a little less forcefully. This time she succeeded in breaking only the top one.

Master Nang replaced the brick. "Now break only bottom one, please."

"Are you kidding me?"

"No kidding," said Master Nang with a smile.

"But how can I do that—if I bounce my chi farther again, won't all four of them break?" asked Katana.

"Bounce your chi *before* your hand touches," said Master Nang.

"Before..." she said. She held her hand about a foot over the top brick, then bounced her chi against the bricks as she dropped her hand. When her hand touched the top brick, the bottom two broke.

Master Nang had her play with this for the rest of the lesson. By the time she was done, her control was good enough that she could break any one of the bricks in the pile. She had only to focus on how fast she bounced her chi, and how soon she did it before she came into physical contact with the top brick.

Katana was amazed that she could use the exact same chen do that she used to levitate to do so many other things. It all came down to bouncing her chi just outside of her body. How far and how quickly she bounced it determined the effect it would have on the object she bounced it against.

When she arrived on Friday morning, Master Daniels was there as well. Katana thought he looked quite grumpy. Master Nang smiled as she walked over to them. "Please stand, and sink your chi into floor."

"Do what?"

"Sink your chi through your feet slowly, but do not push *against* floor—instead, push *through* the floor," said Master Nang.

"Uh... right," said Katana. She tried it, but pushed herself a few inches into the air. "No..." She tried again. This time she imagined digging her chi *into* the mat, instead of pushing against it.

She didn't feel like anything had happened. But Master Nang came over, placed one hand on her sternum and pushed. She could tell that he was pushing very hard, but it didn't move her. She felt like he was pushing her feet more firmly into the floor.

"Master Daniels, please push," said Master Nang.

Master Daniels came over, placed his hand on Katana's sternum and pushed with all his might. And the harder he pushed, the more firmly Katana was rooted to the floor.

"Thank you," said Master Nang. "Now, please push Master Daniels."

"Push... how, exactly?" asked Katana. "Like he did to me?"

"No," said Master Nang. "Like this." Master Nang tapped Daniels on the chest and sent him flying across the room. He landed in a heap on the floor, then got up and walked back over to them. He looked much grumpier now.

"Be careful," said Master Nang with a smile. "Push like you push off floor to levitate—not like you push to break bricks. Otherwise, you break Master Daniels."

"Wait a minute—what?" said Master Daniels, suddenly

looking quite alarmed. "What do you mean, 'break Master Daniels'?!"

But before Master Nang could answer, Katana tapped him in the chest. Master Daniels sailed across the room.

"*That* is cool," said Katana.

"Very cool," said Master Nang with a smile.

Master Daniels shuffled back over to them and Katana heard him mutter something about getting out of bed this early to be humiliated.

"Now, please use levitation to lift," said Master Nang.

"Lift?" asked Katana uncertainly.

"Yes, lift," said Master Nang. He grabbed Master Daniels by one arm and lifted the man off the ground. Master Daniels squealed like a pig.

Master Nang put him down again. Master Daniels said, "Now wait a minute..."

Katana interrupted him. "How did you do that?!"

"Think, please" said Master Nang.

"You didn't toss him across the room this time... So do I push against him with my chi slowly—like when I hold myself up off the floor?" asked Katana.

"Please try," said Master Nang.

"Now hang on!" said Master Daniels. Katana grabbed him by one elbow and pushed her chi against him slowly. And to her astonishment, she was able to lift him right off the floor. Master Daniels let out a sort of muffled yell. Katana returned him to the floor.

"Are we done now?" asked Master Daniels.

"Yes, done," said Master Nang. "Thank you very much."

Master Daniels stomped out of the dojo. Master Nang smiled at Katana, held up his hand and said, "High-five, please."

Katana gave him a high-five. She decided Master Nang was absolutely the coolest teacher she'd ever had.

"You tossed Daniels across the room?!" asked Jelly after Katana had told her friends about her lesson a little while later at breakfast.

"Yeah," said Katana, stifling a giggle. "He wasn't very happy about it."

"I've gotta learn how to do that," said Jelly. "Then next time he yells at me for levitating, I can levitate *him*!"

Saturday afternoon, Katana did indeed try to teach Jelly, Sara and Chris everything she had learned with Master Nang. But Jelly was the only one who was able to do any of it.

"I've always been able to hold myself in the air a few inches," he said.

"Really?" Katana asked.

"Yeah—you remember," he said. "The first time I got levitation in the rock garden—I was meditating on the bench. I opened my eyes and I was just floating there!"

"Oh, right," said Katana, thinking back. "And then you levitated over the bed in the infirmary that time. I remember now."

Katana taught him how to extend his chi to push someone. After a few tries, Jelly was able to toss Chris across the wushu dojo into the foam pit.

"That looks like fun!" said Katana. "I want a turn!"

"Great," said Chris, bracing himself. But when Katana tried it on Chris, nothing happened.

"Of course you can't do that, Kat," said Sara. "It's still a chen do—you know you can't do them on Chris."

"Yeah, you're right," said Katana. "I didn't think of that." Then she lunged at Jelly, tapped him on the chest and sent him sailing through the air. "But I can do it to the mighty midget!"

Jelly yelled "Wee!" as he crashed into the foam.

"I wanna try to bounce the fireball," said Sara. "Throw one at me?"

"Yeah, all right," said Katana. She threw her chi at Sara, and Sara tried to bounce it off her hand. But it smashed into her, knocking her to the floor.

"That didn't work!" she said.

"Of course not—you're not gonna be able to do *any* of this stuff cuz you can't levitate!" said Jelly, who had run back over to them. "I should be able to do it, though—Kat, throw one at me!"

Katana threw her chi at Jelly, and sure enough, he was able to tap it with his hand and send it back to her. The two of them ran around for the next few minutes passing the fireball back and forth.

"This is so not fair," said Chris. "I've *got* to learn levitation now!"

"Hey—remember how Nang blocked Sam's kick and threw her across the room?" said Sara. "Did he teach you how to do *that*?"

"Hmm," said Katana. She thought about it for a minute.

"No, he didn't teach me that exactly, but I think I know how to do it. Jelly, throw a kick at me?"

Jelly threw a roundhouse kick at her. She tapped his foot with her hand, bouncing her chi against him the same way she had when she'd thrown him into the foam pit. It worked—Jelly went flying again.

"How about that thing he did with the spear?" asked Chris. "You didn't do that?"

"No!" said Katana. "I forgot about that."

"How would that work?" asked Sara. "I get how the rest of this stuff comes down to levitation—but what about that? You're not exactly bouncing your chi off the spear—are you?"

"No, I don't think so," said Katana. "I don't think I wanna try that one. I like not having a hole in my throat."

Katana went with Chris and Sara to Sam's for sushi later that evening and told Sam about her lessons with Master Nang.

"Yes, Master Nang was interesting. I never realized you could do so many different things with levitation," said Sam.

"You know, what I don't understand is how I was able to do all of it so easily," said Katana. "I mean, it took me months to get a chi hit, but I was able to do everything Master Nang taught me the first or second time I tried it."

"That's true," said Sam. "But everything he showed you was based on a chen do you'd already mastered. You were just using the skill in different ways. If you hadn't already known how to levitate, it would've taken you ages to learn that stuff."

"Yeah... That makes sense," said Katana.

"Oh, and Katana, you're going to be interested in this—Master Nang also solved part of our mystery for us."

"What mystery?" asked Katana.

"The mystery of where Jaaku was after he left Japan," said Sam with a mischievous smile.

"So where was he already?" demanded Sara.

"Yeah, come on—tell us!" said Chris.

"We still don't know where he was for the *whole* time," said Sam.

"Whatever—tell us what you know!" said Katana.

"Well, the temple in Tibet was independent of the Shaolin network for hundreds of years," she said. "After Jaaku came back, there were talks, and Nang decided to bring the temple back into the fold.

"Apparently when Nang first went to Shaolin to meet the headmaster, they talked about Jaaku. It turns out that Jaaku went to Tibet when he left Japan. He arrived in 1869 and tried to get the headmaster at the Hall of the Silent Buddha to teach him. But the headmaster could tell immediately that Jaaku wasn't someone he wanted in his temple."

"Yeah, I don't think I'd want someone who looked like a walking skeleton training in my temple, either," said Sara.

"That's just it—he didn't look like that back then. He was an old man, but he hadn't been stealing chi long enough to have the appearance he does now," said Sam. "But the headmaster sent him away, and I guess Jaaku set up his own temple in Tibet, near the Hall of the Silent Buddha.

"Over the years, he was able to entice some of the monks to

join him. He taught them dim mak in exchange for the secrets of the Tibetan monks."

"So Jaaku knows how to do everything Master Nang taught me this week?" asked Katana.

"He sure does," said Sam.

"How long was Jaaku in Tibet?" asked Chris.

"Only for about thirty years," said Sam.

"So that doesn't solve very much of the mystery, does it?" said Sara with a frown. "There's still almost a hundred years unaccounted for."

"It's better than nothing," said Katana.

CHAPTER 15

THE ARCHIVES

Over the next couple of weeks Katana practiced everything she'd learned from Master Nang at every opportunity. She tried every trick she could think of without landing. She even did the butterfly twist into a split with the chains one time without ever contacting the floor—she held her split a few inches off the mat.

"Don't do that at the tournament," Dana scolded her. "You'll get disqualified again!"

Katana started sneaking up on Jelly during their weekend practice sessions and using her chi to punt him across the room into the foam pit. Jelly retaliated, but didn't confine the shenanigans to the weekend practices. Katana was walking down an empty hallway to lunch at Lincoln one day and suddenly found herself flying through the air—Jelly had hit her from behind. She had to levitate to stop herself from crashing into the lockers at the end of the hall.

Of course, the chen do were supposed to be a secret—Jelly only hit her when no one else was around. But Katana didn't let this deter her from tossing Ed Golia across a hallway one afternoon on her way to study hall. She'd stopped at her locker to put some of her books away. Ed came by and grabbed her in a headlock. "Oh, sorry—I thought you were Tommy!"

Tommy was standing right next to him, laughing stupidly. Katana elbowed Ed in the ribs—bouncing her chi into him. Ed flew through the air and crashed into the lockers on the other side of the hall.

"Oh sorry—I thought you were Jelly!" Katana said before running off.

Katana also found that sinking her chi into the floor added a whole new dimension to her tai chi form practice. She felt more rooted than ever and wondered if doing it like this on the beach would work better than physically digging her feet into the sand.

As Halloween approached, Jimmy tried to talk everyone into going trick-or-treating.

"What's his deal?" asked Katana. "He didn't want anything to do with this last year!"

"Yeah, but he knows *you* were into it last year. He's hoping to get some time alone with you if we go again," said Chris.

This made Katana not want to participate in any Halloween activities. And in fact, when the rest of them went with Gerald the Saturday before Halloween to get their costumes, Katana stayed behind.

Halloween fell on a Monday night, so when Jimmy tried to get her to go trick-or-treating with them despite her lack of a costume, Katana used her homework as an excuse. "I'm feeling overwhelmed this year," she said. "I've gotta spend some time studying tonight!"

"Liar!" whispered Sara as she walked out of the room with Jimmy.

Naturally, Katana was not feeling remotely overwhelmed with her schoolwork. But she did spend most of the evening reading ahead in their algebra text, teaching herself the next few weeks of work.

When everyone else returned, they ganged up on her, insisting that she come play hide-and-seek in the tunnels. Katana finally gave in, but made Sara promise to help keep Jimmy away from her.

Sara was "it" first. Katana ran by the classrooms that they'd used two years prior, trying to find a good hiding place. Suddenly a thought occurred to her. She'd found the Hall's archives in an old storage room last Halloween. She'd only casually perused one box of old scrolls—she hadn't looked any further once she'd realized they were in Chinese. But if the scrolls and manuscripts in Master Nash's office held the entire history of Jaaku and the Immortal Master, what secrets might be hiding in the archives, just waiting to be discovered?

Katana was able to remember exactly where she'd found the storage room the last time—even though she hadn't been down here since Golden Gate. She ducked inside the room and closed the door behind her.

She pulled out a box and started unrolling various scrolls. This was probably a waste of time—she still couldn't decipher any of the documents.

But finally she found one that had a diagram of a human body. It was covered with what she guessed were meridian lines, drawn in fine detail. She'd learned from Nash the previous year that chi traveled through the body along meridians, much like blood flowed through vessels, or electrical impulses were carried along nerves.

Katana could see a point a little below the navel on the diagram that she was sure was the dantian—the center of the chi in the body, and the location of the prenatal chi. All the meridian lines in the diagram flowed out from this point.

Suddenly the door burst open. Sara came running over. "Gotcha!"

"Sara—check this out!" said Katana.

Sara squatted down next to her. "Wow—meridians?"

"Yeah—but I can't read any of the labels."

"I can," Sara replied.

"I thought this was Chinese, not Japanese," said Katana.

"It is," Sara confirmed. "But a lot of the characters they use in Japan came from China originally." She pointed at one meridian line that ran from the dantian up to the left shoulder. "That's the heart meridian."

"It looks like it runs right through the spot where Ed did that dim mak move on me at the tournament last year!" said Katana.

"Hmm..." said Sara. "What else is in here?"

The girls spent the next half hour going through several

boxes. Sara wasn't able to read some of the texts and scrolls *entirely*, but was able to glean enough from each to determine its subject matter. They set aside things that looked interesting.

Finally Chris ran into the room and yelled, "Found you!"

"We're not playing anymore, you idiot!" yelled Sara. "Get over here and help us bring this stuff upstairs."

"Um... no way," said Chris. "We're not supposed to be down here—we're gonna get in a ton of trouble if we start carting stuff up to our rooms!"

"We won't cart it to *your* room then," said Katana. "I don't want Jimmy to know what we're doing anyway."

Chris reluctantly agreed. The three of them brought up a whole box of the most interesting-looking stuff they could find. When they got up to the girls' room, Sara started going through everything more carefully. Katana showed Chris the meridian diagram they'd found.

"Hey—check this out!" said Sara a few minutes later.

"What is it?" asked Katana. Sara was holding a leather-bound manuscript that appeared to devote a page or two to each meridian.

"It's about this kind of chi kung, I think," said Sara. "The instructions next to each diagram talk about how to increase your chi flow along the given meridian."

Katana flipped through the manuscript for a moment. She stopped at a page that showed the heart meridian.

"Here, what does this one say?" she asked.

"Um... mostly it says to stand like the dude in the diagram," said Sara, her brow furrowed in concentration. "Then you have to exhale slowly, hold your left arm out like in the diagram, and focus on your chi flowing from your dantian up to your left shoulder."

Katana stood like the figure in the diagram, holding her left arm out parallel to the floor, at a slight angle forward. Then she exhaled and tried to feel her chi flowing up from her dantian along her heart meridian.

Suddenly she felt her heartbeat accelerate. "Whoa! It's working—it feels like I've been working out or something. My heart's beating like crazy!"

"I wanna try!" said Chris.

Katana talked Sara and Chris through the exercise. They were startled at how well it worked.

"I can feel my chi flowing," Sara observed. "This is kinda neat!"

"My heart's beating a mile a minute now," said Chris.

Katana and Chris went through the manuscript for a few more minutes while Sara went through some of the other materials they'd brought up.

Katana was able to figure out a couple more exercises from the diagrams despite her inability to read the text. She talked Chris through one that made him start sweating profusely. Then she did one herself that enhanced her vision.

Sara said, "I don't believe it!"

"What is it?" asked Katana. She sat next to Sara to see what she'd found.

"I'm not certain, but this looks like a memoir—and I think it's Master Chang's!"

"No way!" said Chris, going over to look as well.

"It's a lot of text though. I can't figure it all out. But this part's definitely about Chow asking him to go to America to start a new temple."

"It's long," said Katana. "Do you think you can translate the whole thing?"

"Not a chance," said Sara. "But I know someone who can!"

"Who?" Katana and Chris both asked.

"Sean's fluent in Chinese. His mom's from China. She insisted that he grow up bilingual," Sara explained.

"But Sean doesn't go to the Hall of the Dragon," said Chris.

"No, really?" Sara replied sarcastically. "I'll put this in my bag and bring it to school tomorrow. I can give it to him at lunch."

"I don't know," Chris protested. "This is kind of like stealing, isn't it? It's bad enough we brought it up *here*—now you wanna take it to Lincoln? We're gonna get in a lot of trouble if we get caught."

"It's not like we're gonna do anything bad to it," said Katana. "And we'll put it back when we're done. But Sara, you've gotta make Sean promise not to tell *anyone* about this—especially Ed and Tommy!"

"No worries," said Sara. "He doesn't hang out with the moron twins anymore. I made sure of that!"

Sara gave Sean the manuscript the next day. She decided to wait until their study hall, though, as too many people were watching at lunch.

"You cannot tell *anyone* what this is," said Sara, "or where you got it!"

"And you have to get it back to us as soon as possible," added Katana.

Sean flipped through the manuscript. "This is really long, you two. I can read it fine, but translating it and writing it down is going to take a long time."

"Well... summarize it then," Sara suggested. "Translate any interesting parts, and then write an outline of the rest."

That night, Katana, Sara and Chris locked themselves in the girls' room. They looked through more of the documents they'd brought up from the archives. It turned out that a lot of it was not terribly interesting—they found some recipes, and some papers that looked like work orders from the days when the Hall was being built.

They stayed up much later than usual that night. Katana was feeling sleepy by the time she arrived in the wushu dojo the next afternoon. But she livened up immediately when Master Fu announced that he was going to allow anyone who was interested to start learning one of the sport karate weapons. Katana and Dana were both solid with their double whip chain set, so Master Fu let them start working with samurai swords.

"You two are going to love this weapon," he said. "Flexible weapons like whip chain limit you to some degree—you have to keep the chains moving, and they won't change direction very fast, so there's only so much you can do with them. With a sword, especially this kind of sword, you have a lot more versatility. I'm going to start you off with some basic cutting patterns."

First he showed them how to hold the swords correctly. Next, he taught them a sequence of slices and stabs with the blade and left them to practice.

Katana liked this weapon right away—it felt good in her hands. It was much lighter than her father's sword. And while Katana knew that this particular sword was only a performance weapon, it still felt like something she could use in combat— unlike whip chain, which was clearly *only* for performance.

Master Fu came back after he had worked with some of the other kids. He seemed satisfied with their progress.

"Now we're going to try a release skill," he said. "I want you to hold the sword in your right hand and slice it across your body to the left. Good—now turn it over and start to swing it the other way, but then release. You're going to let it spin in the air, horizontally for two full rotations, then catch it by the handle again." He demonstrated the skill.

Katana was able to spin the sword, but caught it badly—she grabbed it by the blade instead of the handle.

Master Fu helped them with the release until they could both do it correctly. "I want you girls to practice with the sword as much as you can. A large part of the learning process is going to be getting comfortable with the weapon and becoming more fluent with it. So don't be afraid to play with it and freestyle a little."

When class was over, Katana went with Sara and Chris for a quick dinner. They ran up to the girls' room as soon as they were done to dig into more of the materials from the archives.

Katana looked through more of the meridian manuscript while Sara combed through some of the other documents. Using the diagrams, Katana found that she could control the flow of chi through all of the meridians in her body. She could speed up or slow down her heartbeat, increase her lung capacity, augment her hearing—she could control virtually any bodily function through the flow of her chi. Chris tried the exercises, too.

Sara finally found another interesting scroll. It contained what looked like the building plans for the Hall of the Dragon.

"Hey—originally there was only the main building," she said. "Look—there were no wings."

"Where did everyone live?" asked Chris.

"Well, it looks like the central room in the basement was the tai chi dojo, and everything else was on the third floor," said Sara. "Yeah, look—there were kitchens up there and living quarters and everything."

Katana and Chris spent the next half hour playing with Doc while Sara sifted through the rest of the materials. Katana figured out how the cat was able to get into and out of the top bunk. He had been climbing the curtains right behind the head of the bed.

Chris had great fun taking advantage of this new discovery. He dragged a shoestring—Doc's favorite toy—up and down the curtains. Doc followed. The only trouble was that the cat tried to climb down the curtains headfirst, and only made it partway before falling and tumbling across the floor.

"Well, now we know what DOC stands for!" he said.

"What?" asked Katana.

"Dumb Orange Cat!" said Chris. Katana punched him in the arm.

Sara said, "Whoa! This is interesting."

Katana and Chris left Doc at the top of the curtains and ran over to see what she'd found.

"This is an exercise to stimulate your prenatal chi!" said Sara.

Katana examined the diagram. It looked like the meditation exercise she'd found Master Nang doing every morning before her private lessons.

Katana and Chris sat down in full lotus position and followed Sara's instructions. She had them place their right hands palm-up, directly in front of the dantian. She told them to place their left hands, also palm-up, on top of their right. They had to touch the tips of their thumbs together, keeping their elbows out to the side.

"Now breathe in through your nose as deep as you can, hold your breath and push the air down to your dantian. Hold it for ten seconds, then exhale slowly through your mouth," Sara read from the manuscript.

Katana followed Sara's instructions. By the third breathing cycle, she felt like her chi was exploding inside her body. "I feel like I did the long form a few times!"

"This is unbelievable," Chris agreed. "I've never felt my chi flow this strong before."

By Thursday night, Sara had finished going through everything they'd brought upstairs. But she didn't find anything else interesting.

"I hope Sean finishes that translation soon—I'm dying to know what's in those memoirs!" said Katana.

Katana went to the team practices on Friday. The Eureka Challenge was fast approaching, so Sam and Fu worked the teams hard. Both workouts were strenuous enough that they drove the archives from Katana's mind.

Sam drilled them on kicking combinations and transitioning into sweeps. She made sure all the girls had at least a couple of turns sparring with the boys—she wanted to get the new girls on the team as much experience as she could against seasoned competitors.

When Katana got up to the wushu dojo, Master Fu said, "The uniforms are here! Check these out!" He held up one of the tops and turned it so everyone could see the back. It was the Hall of the Dragon's logo—a dragon jumping through a torii gate—but it was a simpler, stylized version. The torii gate was solid black. The dragon was red, and had the appearance of brush strokes. Katana thought it looked very sharp; from their reactions, the rest of the team agreed.

"Come on up and get one—I want you guys to change into these for practice tonight," said Master Fu. Katana changed right there—she was wearing shorts and a sport bra under her uniform. Everyone else ran out to the bathrooms.

Master Fu told them to roll up their sleeves. "They'll get in the way of your weapons if you're not careful," he said. "But they're stiff enough that once you roll them up, they'll stay that way."

Master Fu even had satin black belts for them to wear. Once they were in full uniform, they got in line to run through the demo.

They started with the team broken into two lines along the back edge of the room, facing the center. As the music started, one person from each line walked forward, meeting in the middle. They turned and walked toward the audience side by side.

The last two kids in each line—Tim and Donnie—didn't go all the way to the center. They stopped early and faced the audience without walking forward; they formed the crosspiece of a large letter T.

The team yelled out the introduction to the judges, then went into the opening choreography section. At the end, Katana and Dana did a tricking sequence while the kids in the broadsword set went to pick up their weapons.

Katana was anxious for the tournament. They'd been nailing the demo over and over again for a few weeks, and tonight was no exception. Practices were starting to feel repetitive—she wanted to do it for real.

Staff came out when broadsword was done. The kids did aerials past each other in the back corners, and Paul did a diving front roll over Jelly's butterfly twist. The set was perfect—they nailed their release skill, doing standing flash kicks as their staves soared overhead. The kids from broadsword returned for a quick tricking sequence to give Jelly time to put his staff down. Then he ran out and did the double backflip with Katana as Dana flash kicked past her.

The girls nailed their whip chain set. At the end, they spun the chains in one hand as they walked forward toward the audience. At the same time, the rest of the team got in position for the closer. The girls walked under the chains and slammed them on the floor behind them with a loud kiai.

Katana turned and nodded to Dana. They ran toward the

back of the stage, did an aerial and dropped their chains on the floor while they were upside down. The rest of the team ran past them—Jelly and Sara doing flash kicks—and got in position for their final bow. When they lined up and exited the stage, Master Fu yelled, "Awesome job, everyone!"

They did the full demo several more times and Master Fu had them perform their weapon sets individually. Jelly kept badgering Fu to add more cool moves into the demo—but Fu refused. He insisted that the way to beat Supernova was to drill the demo until they could do it in their sleep. He didn't want to add anything new so close to Eureka.

"After the first tournament, if you guys nail *everything*, I'll consider it," he said.

When Katana and Sara got back to their room after dinner that night, Sara had an e-mail from Sean. He'd finished his translation of Chang's memoir.

"I'll go get Chris," said Katana.

When they returned, Sara started reading to them.

"First of all, he says that this must be the first installment in a series. It only covers the period until Chang and Chow first came to California and started building the Hall," she said.

"Go on," said Katana.

"The first part talks about how Chow and Chang were at the Shaolin Temple together. Chow wanted to leave to start a temple in America. He wanted to let foreigners train, and not limit it to other Chinese. The headmaster refused. So Chow and Chang left anyway."

"Did they have to go through that crazy tunnel thing Sam was telling us about? With the burning coals at the end?" asked Chris.

"It doesn't say anything about that, so I assume not," said Sara.

"Well, Sam did say they stopped the practice hundreds of years ago—they must not have been doing it anymore by the time Chow and Chang came here," said Katana. "Keep going."

"I guess the other three masters that came with them were not from the temple in Henan—two were from Fukien and the third was from Shangdong. And the original arts they taught here were tai chi, chin-na, Northern long-fist, sanshou, and Southern crane fist."

"Wow—Master Fu wasn't kidding when he said the arts here have evolved over the years. Tai chi is like the only one that's been the same the whole time," said Chris.

"So when they say that Chow was the last Master of the Five Arts, they're not exactly talking about the five arts we have now," Katana observed.

"Yeah, and if Chow left the scroll for the next Master of the Five Arts... did he know that person wouldn't be mastering the same five?" asked Chris.

"This is interesting," said Sara. "It says here that Chow wanted to allow girls to train at the Hall, but Chang and the other masters wouldn't go along."

"You mean the Hall of the Dragon used to be all boys?" asked Chris.

"You know... now that I think about it, there weren't any girls at Shaka-In, were there?" asked Katana.

"That's true," said Sara. "I wonder if they allow girls to train at *any* of the other temples?"

Sara continued with Sean's translation. "Here it's talking about how the masters trained in a small dojo out in the forest while they were building the Hall..."

"That must be that old foundation we found out in the woods last year!" said Chris.

Katana felt her face growing warm—she'd known about this for ages. Master Osaka had told her about it when she went there to practice tai chi with him. But she'd never mentioned that experience to Sara or Chris. "You're right," she said, trying to act as if she didn't already know.

"Here it talks about moving into the actual Hall," Sara continued. "And it does say that the dojo in the basement was the original tai chi dojo. That's where the other masters trained with Master Chow.

"That's pretty much it, though," Sara concluded. "The last entry talks about how the Hall wasn't complete yet, but they were already living and training in it. There must be more volumes down in the archives somewhere."

"Yeah," said Katana, "there's tons more stuff down there. We only hit that one set of shelves on Halloween. I can't wait to see what else we find."

CHAPTER 16
MASTER SANTOS

Hotaka was slumped over in his chair, snoring quietly. His helmet sat on the desk beside him. He heard a noise, and sat bolt upright.

Hotaka was guarding the prisoners at the old factory building the Arashi had started using after the assassin infiltrated their warehouse. The prisoners stared at him fearfully from inside their makeshift pen. He must have dozed off—it was dark outside now. One lonely light bulb hanging from the ceiling provided the only light.

Hotaka heard the noise again. It was a metallic clanging that came from somewhere farther inside the building. He grabbed a flashlight from the desk and went to investigate. The prisoners cowered away from the edge of the pen as Hotaka passed. He smiled to himself, satisfied with the fear he'd instilled in them.

They'd erected the pen in the large storage room at the front of the building. The noise was coming from somewhere on the main plant floor. Hotaka walked the length of the production line where they used to can tuna before the plant had been abandoned. There was nothing here.

A moment after he returned to the storage room, Nori appeared behind a flash of light. Like Hotaka, he was wearing samurai armor. He carried a young boy over his shoulder, maybe seventeen years old.

Hotaka moved to the entrance of the pen. Removing the combination lock, he opened the door. Nori dropped the boy on the floor of the pen and Hotaka secured the lock.

"I don't want to hear his screaming when he wakes up," said Hotaka. "Make sure you break him in quickly."

Nori removed his helmet and grinned at him. "This one won't put up much of a fuss. His daddy beat him. He'll be submissive."

Hotaka grunted in reply, but then heard the clanging noise again. Nori turned in alarm.

"What was that?"

"Why don't you go look?" Hotaka suggested. "I couldn't find anything in there." He handed him the flashlight.

Nori placed his helmet on the desk next to Hotaka's and trudged off toward the plant floor. Hotaka saw him draw his sword right before he disappeared around the corner. He shook his head; Nori was a coward.

Hotaka retook his seat and put his feet up on the desk, closing his eyes. A few minutes passed and he began to doze off again. But his eyes snapped open when he heard several loud clanging sounds.

Nori screamed; the noise echoed through the factory. The prisoners looked around in terror.

Hotaka jumped to his feet, and dashed off to the production line. It was dark except for the beam of the flashlight, which was lying on the floor halfway across the room. Hotaka drew his sword and approached the light.

"Nori?" he called out.

There was no answer.

Hotaka bent down to pick up the flashlight, casting wary glances around the room. Sword in one hand, light in the other, he proceeded to the far side of the production line. He heard a gurgling sound coming from behind a large machine.

Hotaka moved slowly toward the source of the noise. Peering around the edge of the machine, he saw Nori lying flat on his back in a pool of blood.

"What happened?" Hotaka demanded.

"Assassin," Nori whispered.

But a moment later, his body vaporized in a cloud of steam. Hotaka backed away fearfully.

"You're next, Hotaka," a voice called out, echoing through the plant. It was male, but Hotaka didn't recognize it.

Hotaka looked around the room frantically, shining the flashlight into every corner. He could see nobody. Hotaka wanted to fade away from this place, but he could now feel Jaaku's will compelling him to stay and confront the assassin. Jaaku wanted to know who was doing this to his Arashi.

Hotaka moved across the room, holding the light and his sword in front of him. He advanced from one machine to another, peering behind each of them. Reaching the end of the room, he crept along the wall, shining his light across the plant.

Suddenly a figure appeared out of nowhere directly in front of him. Hotaka backpedaled, dropping the flashlight and nearly falling over. The light hit the ground, illuminating only the attacker's feet. Hotaka caught the glint of steel coming toward him. He raised his own sword in time to parry the assassin's thrust.

Hotaka raised his blade and sliced violently, but the assassin deflected his sword, cutting Hotaka's wrist. The assassin was hiding his energy somehow; neither his shen nor his aura was visible—making it impossible to sense his intent. In the darkness, Hotaka didn't see him thrust his sword. But he felt the cold steel penetrate his chest.

Hotaka dropped to his knees as the assassin withdrew his blade. Blood gushed from his wound. He stared up at his killer but couldn't see his face in the darkness.

Flashes of light erupted as other Arashi arrived on the scene. But it was too late. The assassin disappeared. Hotaka fell to the floor and writhed in pain as steam emanated from his body. Jaaku was taking his chi.

. . .

"GOOD MORNING, EVERYONE," said Master Nash. It was the beginning of their tai chi class on Monday morning, one week after Halloween. "I have several announcements today, so please pay close attention.

"To begin with, the first tournament of the season is upon us. We will be traveling to Eureka at the end of this month for the Eureka Challenge. I remind you that participation in the tournaments is a required part of your training here at the Hall. You may compete in whatever events you wish. Please feel free to talk to me or any of the other masters if you are uncertain which divisions you should do.

"Betsy and Ryan are passing out registration forms. It is your responsibility to fill these out and turn them in by the deadline. Your coaches will handle the registrations for the team events.

"In March we will be traveling to San Francisco for the Golden Gate Classic. Those of you who qualify will join the competition teams in May for the U.S. nationals. Nationals will take place in Washington, D.C. this year.

"Also, I am pleased to announce that Headmaster Santos from the Hall of the Tiger in Brazil will be joining us this weekend. Master Santos is a master in the art of Brazilian jiu jitsu. His seminar will begin Saturday at three, and I would ask you to arrive early enough to stretch and warm up ahead of time. And once again, please wear full uniform for this event."

As Katana had expected, Master Nash held her back for a few minutes at the end of class.

"Master Santos will be conducting your evaluation on Sunday. Please be here by eleven," he said.

"Do you have any idea what *this* evaluation will be like?" Katana asked.

"No, I do not," said Master Nash. "I discussed it with Master Santos, but he didn't sound like he had any definite plans yet. Don't worry—the headmaster is generally quite relaxed about things. I would expect something rather informal."

Sara made sure to get Chang's memoir back from Sean at study hall that day. Katana went with her and Chris to return everything to the archives that night. They went through several more shelves and brought up another box of interesting-looking documents to the girls' room.

For the rest of the week they pored over the new materials. This process was very slow, as Sara was the only one who could read any of it. Katana felt rather disappointed by the end of the week—they hadn't found anything worthwhile.

On Saturday afternoon, they traipsed up to the tai chi dojo for their seminar with Master Santos. Katana saw that, unlike Master Kim, Master Santos had chosen to travel alone. All the masters from the Hall of the Dragon were present, however.

Master Santos was taller than Master Nash. He had very dark hair and a bushy mustache. He wore a blue judo uniform, which was similar to a traditional karate uniform, but made of a much heavier material.

Master Nash lined everyone up. He introduced the headmaster, who in turn had everyone take a seat.

"Today we will be exploring the art of Brazilian jiu jitsu," he began. "Now whenever I give a seminar, someone always asks me how my art can come from Brazil, because of course everyone knows jiu jitsu is Japanese. So I will answer this question for you before we begin.

"Jiu jitsu flourished in Japan for countless centuries. It was the principal unarmed combat method of the samurai warriors. There were dozens of different jiu jitsu styles in Japan. Ultimately Master Ueshiba combined some of these methods to form the art of aikido, which some of you learn here at the Hall of the Dragon. Well, Master Kano also combined some of these different styles to create the art of judo.

"In the 1910s, Master Kano sent one of his students, Master Maeda, to spread judo throughout the world. Maeda ended up emigrating to Brazil, where he taught for many years. As you probably know, judo uses a lot of hip throws and flips to take an opponent to the ground. But part of the traditional judo curriculum also addresses how to keep fighting once you go to the mat. This little-known aspect of the art includes a variety of chokeholds and armbars.

"A man named Carlos Gracie began training with Master Maeda, and he taught the style to his brothers. Over the decades, the Gracie family developed and evolved the style and placed heavy emphasis on its ground fighting aspects. Ultimately they created a style that teaches you to dominate an opponent on the ground and force him to submit.

"Since those early days, many other masters have trained with various members of the Gracie family. They have spread the art of Brazilian jiu jitsu throughout the world.

"Over the next three hours, I will teach you some of the basics of my art. In jiu jitsu, we break a fight down into three separate phases. First, you must get your opponent to the ground. Next, you must gain a superior position—one that allows you to control the opponent's body throughout the fight. Finally you will apply a lock or hold and make your opponent submit."

Master Santos had everyone stand up and make a large circle around him. He called up Master Daniels to assist him.

"The first thing we want to do if someone is trying to punch us is avoid getting hit, right?" asked Master Santos. Everyone voiced their agreement. "So I do not want to stand here and trade punches with this guy. Master Daniels, please try to hit me."

Daniels took a swing at his head. But Master Santos ducked underneath Daniels' arm, lunged in and grabbed him in a big bear-hug. He buried his head below the man's shoulder blade.

"From here, I am safe—he cannot hit me or choke me," yelled Master Santos from the awkward position he was maintaining against Daniels' body. And sure enough, Master Daniels flailed around with both arms, trying futilely to reach Master Santos's head.

"Now I can pull the man to the ground," said Santos, and did exactly that. Master Daniels fell flat on his back. Santos immediately put him in the mount—straddling him with both legs like Sensei Mike had demonstrated over the summer.

"This is the first technique we will learn today," Master Santos concluded.

He got up and had everyone pair off with a partner. He

walked them through each step of the sequence he'd just demonstrated.

Katana worked with Sara. They had no trouble doing what Santos had shown them.

Once Santos had walked around the entire room and made sure everyone could do the move to his satisfaction, he called them together again.

"You have your man on the ground," he said. ("Man?" said Sara indignantly.) "Now we want to control him. The best position is the mount. But that is not your only option. What we will do now is learn how to get *out* of the mount."

He called Daniels over again. Master Santos lay down on the mat and instructed Daniels to get on top of him.

"There are many ways to get out of this. Usually, people will try to turn the man over and get *him* in the mount. And this is good, but you can also fight very effectively from your back, if you can free your legs.

"Right now, we are not in a good position. Master Daniels is heavier than me. He has all his weight on my hips, so I can't move very well," said Master Santos, trying to squirm around under Daniels' mass.

"What I want to do," he continued, "is turn my hips, like this, so I am sideways. This creates some space under his legs. Now I want to pull my bottom leg out from underneath him. Next, I'll go on my back again, and wrap my free leg around my opponent."

And indeed, Katana could see that he'd pulled one leg free and was now hooking it around Daniels' back.

"Once I am here, I can turn again, and free my other leg as well. Now I get that leg around him, and I hook my ankles together, pulling him into me. This position is called the guard. If you are on the ground and you are on your back, the guard is the best position. It gives you more control of your opponent than you have from his mount."

Master Santos had everyone pair off with their partners again, and walked them through the sequence.

Katana and Sara had a little difficulty with this move. They were both having trouble freeing their first leg. Master Santos pointed out that they weren't turning their hips sideways enough. Once Katana had corrected this, she had no problem getting Sara in the guard.

Master Santos gathered everyone together again. This time he demonstrated the same chokehold that Katana, Sara and Chris had learned from Sensei Mike. He performed the move on Master Daniels—who looked none too happy about it.

Master Santos had Daniels kneel down. He got behind him and wrapped one arm around his throat. He brought his other arm against the back of Daniels' neck and locked his arms together. Master Daniels tapped his hand frantically against Master Santos's leg.

Next, he showed them a simple armbar. Starting in the mount, he grabbed Daniels' arm and turned sideways, rolling onto his back on the mat, so that his legs were on top of Daniels. He pulled down on Daniels' wrist, and pushed his hips up under the back of Daniels' elbow—once again, Master Daniels tapped frantically.

Master Santos had everyone try both of these holds. He walked around again to make sure they were applying them correctly.

After that, he instructed everyone to do some free grappling with their partners. "I want you to apply what you have learned today. You will start on your knees, and try to get your opponent in the mount. If they put you in the mount, you will try to get them in your guard. You can also try to apply either the armbar or the chokehold."

Katana and Sara rolled around for a few minutes. Sara got Katana in an armbar one time. Katana was able to get Sara in the chokehold on their next turn. Katana didn't feel like she knew what she was doing, but still enjoyed the exercise tremendously.

Finally everyone sat back and watched Master Santos grapple with Master Daniels.

This sight reminded Katana of a boa constrictor squeezing its prey. Master Daniels struggled mightily, expending a vast amount of energy. And it seemed like Master Santos was toying with him. He would let Daniels get him in the mount, but then suddenly put him in an armbar. But he didn't force a submission. Instead, he rolled Daniels over and put him in the mount. Then he let Master Daniels start to get *him* in an armbar. But just as suddenly, he escaped the hold and put Daniels in his guard.

When Daniels turned his back to him, Master Santos put him in a chokehold. Katana wasn't sure what was going on, but it looked like Master Santos was extending his shen around Daniels. She could see tendrils of energy extending from him like she saw when she did chi fa with Master Nash. But the tendrils wrapped around Daniels like lengths of rope. Master Daniels struggled for a moment longer, began turning purple, and finally tapped out.

Master Santos concluded the seminar. He lined them up and thanked them for coming. Master Nash dismissed them for the evening.

Sam came over to Katana, Sara and Chris on the way down the stairs. She had to postpone sushi to Sunday night again—they were having another meeting with Master Nash. So after Katana and Sara went up to their room to shower, they joined their friends in the cafeteria for dinner.

"That was pretty cool," said Scott. "I've never grappled before."

"Yeah, Santos was way better than that Kim idiot we had last time," said Dana.

"That was awesome when he choked Daniels out!" Jelly exclaimed. "I'm gonna take aikido next year so I can do that to him!"

"Yeah, right," Sara retorted. "You're gonna take the class for a whole year just to choke him out once?"

"Nah, I'll choke him out every day!"

"I wonder why Daniels didn't fade out of it," said Scott.

"I'm sure he could have," said Katana, "but they'd probably agreed not to use the chen do."

"Hey, what events are you gonna do at Eureka this year?" Chris asked.

"Well, I'm sparring, obviously," said Katana. "I think I'm gonna do kata and weapons too."

"Wow—all three?" asked Sara. "And the team demo. You're gonna be busy this year!"

"I'm busy anyway," said Katana. "I might as well do them all. I'm psyched to do chains. I love doing that set with the butterfly twist."

"Yeah, you should do well with that," said Dana. "You'll have one more trick in the set than I will."

"Are you gonna compete with staff?" Katana asked Sara.

"I don't know... I wasn't going to, but if you're doing chains then maybe I will. I'm definitely not doing sparring, though. Yeah, kata and weapons, I think."

"I'm not doing weapons," said Chris. "My staff set still kinda sucks."

"Sure does!" Jelly agreed. Chris threw a pickle at him.

Katana felt a lot better about her evaluation with Master Santos the next morning now that she'd taken his seminar. He did seem pretty laid-back, just as Master Nash had said.

When Katana got up to the tai chi dojo Sunday morning, she found that it was only her, Master Nash and Master Santos.

"Good morning, Katana," said Master Santos.

"Hi," said Katana, shaking his hand.

"I understand you can do three of the chen do—that is very unusual for someone as young as yourself. I was just telling Master Nash that I've never heard of this before. We have two students at our temple in Brazil who can deflect intent, but none can do two of the chen do."

"Katana also trained with Master Nang recently," said Nash.

"She can now do some very interesting things with levitation as well."

"I've never been able to get levitation myself," said Master Santos. "We do not do much jumping in jiu jitsu. Katana, if you don't mind I would like to see you do the chen do that you know. First, if you would please throw a chi hit at me?"

She threw her hand out at Master Santos and shot a fireball directly at him.

Master Santos deflected it. "Very good. Now I will throw one at you, and I would like you to deflect it."

He threw his chi at her. Katana held out one hand, deflecting his energy into the chi around her.

"Excellent," said Master Santos. "And please levitate for me?"

Katana shot up into the air, did a triple backflip, and landed without landing, the way Master Nang had taught her. She stood there, hovering several inches above the ground.

Master Santos laughed out loud. "That is very impressive, Katana. Join me on the mat then. Let's see how much you remember from yesterday."

Master Santos got on his knees. "I have to grapple... with you?" Katana stammered.

Master Santos smiled. "Yes, Katana—don't worry, I'll go easy. I want to see how you react in an unfamiliar situation."

"Okay..." said Katana apprehensively. She dropped to her knees facing Master Santos.

Master Santos moved in immediately. He grabbed Katana by the shoulders and threw her to the mat. He had her in the mount the instant her back made contact with the floor.

Katana did the move Master Santos had taught them the previous afternoon. She got him in her guard—but definitely felt like he was letting her do it. Master Santos started to pin her arm against her neck. Katana pushed him away with her legs.

"Very good, Katana," he said. He somehow managed to squirm out of her guard. He got her in a side-control position. Katana struggled to turn him over; she wanted to get him in the mount. But suddenly he swung his leg over her and had *her* in the mount again instead.

Katana grabbed onto his shoulder with her left hand, brought her right hand up to his face, and pushed as hard as she could with her right leg—as Sensei Mike had taught her. And to her surprise she turned him right over.

He pulled her immediately into his guard. Katana struggled for a minute to escape—but she didn't know how to get out of this position. Suddenly she realized that Master Santos had managed to pin her arm against her head again. He was starting to apply some sort of choke. Katana had a brainwave; she brought her free hand down and pushed as fast as she could against the mat with her chi. This catapulted both her and Santos twenty feet into the air in a tangle of limbs.

Master Santos released Katana's arm. For an instant, she could see a look of shock on his face. Then he flailed around, looking for the ground—he had turned his back to her. She seized the opportunity. She flung one arm around his throat, pressed her other arm against the back of his neck and locked her arms together. By the time they crashed into the mat, she had him in a perfect chokehold.

And to her astonishment, Master Santos tapped her arm. She released him. He rolled onto his back and laughed out loud again. "Katana, that was brilliant," he said. "Totally against the rules, but brilliant nevertheless. I will have to return one day so you can teach me that trick!"

Master Nash dismissed her from the evaluation. Katana ran up to her room, expecting to meet Sara and Chris there. Finding the room empty, she went to the wushu dojo instead.

"Kat! How'd it go?" yelled Sara.

Jelly, Chris, Dana, Scott and Tim were there, too. They came over to find out how her evaluation had gone. She told them all about it.

"You choked him out? That's crazy!" Chris said when she was done.

"Yeah, but it was only cuz I surprised him with that levitation move," Katana replied. "He could've made me tap anytime he wanted."

They spent the rest of the afternoon working on tricks and their sets for the team demo. Then Katana, Sara and Chris took turns throwing their chi at Jelly, launching him into the foam pit. Katana thought there was absolutely no chance Jelly was ever going to learn how to deflect intent this way, but it was so much fun that she wasn't going to argue.

"Well, Santos was *way* cooler than Master Kim," said Sara. She did a backflip and shot Jelly across the room with her chi while she was upside down.

"He sure was," said Katana. "And honestly, being able to

choke someone out seems *way* more useful than those flying kicks Kim showed us."

Jelly climbed out of the foam pit. Katana did an aerial, throwing a fireball at him on her way over.

"It sounds like Master Nang was the coolest, though," said Chris. "I wish I coulda trained with him."

"Nang was the best," Katana agreed. "It was almost like he was a little kid trapped in an old man's body. He was a lot of fun."

Chris did a flash kick and shot his chi at Jelly while he was upside down. Katana was impressed. "Your flash kick's getting a lot cleaner," she said.

"It feels a lot better," he said. "Maybe one of these days you can show me how to do a gainer flash. Then *I* can start using it in sparring, too!"

They launched Jelly into the foam pit a few more times, until he decided he'd had enough for one day. "This doesn't seem like it's gonna work," he complained.

"You know, maybe you should try the sitting meditation exercise..." said Katana. But Sara shot her a warning look, shaking her head. Katana remembered that Jelly didn't know they'd been searching through the archives.

"What sitting meditation thingy?" Jelly asked.

Katana decided she could still teach it to him without telling him where she'd learned it. She had him sit down in full lotus position. She placed his hands one on top of the other, and talked him through the breathing pattern.

After a few cycles, Jelly said, "Whoa! I can feel my chi flowing like crazy! This is awesome—where'd you learn it?"

"Oh... um... Master Nang taught it to me," Katana stammered. Chris raised his eyebrows at her.

Jelly still couldn't do any more of the chen do. But Katana recommended that he practice the exercise on a regular basis. She figured it might help more than hitting him repeatedly with fireballs.

Katana went with Sara and Chris up to Sam's apartment for sushi a little later. She had to recount her evaluation with Master Santos again—Sam hadn't talked to Master Nash yet.

"You choked him out?!" she said when Katana finished.

"Yeah, in midair," Katana confirmed. "But I never woulda been able to do it if I hadn't used that levitation move."

"Hey, whatever works," said Sam. "You certainly have a flair for putting different techniques together in unexpected ways."

"How do you mean?" asked Katana.

"Well, think about it. First, you thought of forming a ball of energy to catch someone else's chi hit," said Sam.

"Yeah, and you almost killed Jason that time," muttered Chris.

"I did not!"

"Then you took a gainer flash kick from wushu and used it in sparring," Sam continued. "And now you used a levitation trick you learned from chi tao in a grappling match."

"Is that bad?" asked Katana.

"No, quite the contrary," said Sam. "It shows you have a talent for creative thinking. That's what set some of the great masters apart. Like Master Santos was saying—Kano and Ueshiba didn't create anything new, when you get right down to it. They only combined different things together in a way that no one had before."

"Speaking of creative thinking," said Sara, "Why didn't Daniels fade when Santos choked him out yesterday?"

"He tried," said Sam.

"Really?" asked Chris. "Why couldn't he do it?"

"Master Santos wasn't letting him," said Sam. "I just recently learned that technique myself. It turns out that if you envelop someone in your shen, and anchor your chi in place, you can stop them from fading."

"So that's what was happening!" said Katana. "I could see Santos wrapping him in his shen, but I had no idea what was going on."

"Anchor your chi... What does that mean?" asked Sara.

"When you fade, you basically project your chi to a different location," said Sam. "But if you lock your chi to the space you're already occupying, you can ground yourself there. As long as you wrap the other person in your shen as you do it, they can't fade away."

"Wow," said Sara.

"Hey, have there been any more Arashi murders?" asked Chris.

"We only know about two more incidents since Master Lee was attacked at the airport," said Sam. "The assassin took out two more Arashi in Japan, who were involved in that human trafficking ring. Apparently they'd set up shop in an old, abandoned factory. And it turns out one of the monks at the temple in Indonesia was an Arashi. The assassin tried to get him once before, but couldn't get inside the monastery. But then he got him when the monk was traveling."

"There's a temple in *Indonesia*?" asked Chris.

"Yes, there are many throughout Southeast Asia," said Sam.

"Do they have any idea who's doing this yet?" asked Sara.

"No, none," said Sam. "Whoever it is, they're covering their tracks very thoroughly."

CHAPTER 17

THE EUREKA CHALLENGE

With Master Santos's visit behind them, Katana spent every waking hour preparing for the upcoming tournament. She felt very strong with Kata Fourteen, and thought she might finally have a shot at defeating Becca Stratton. Sam worked them into the ground during their sparring team practices. Here as well, Katana was on top of her game. Michelle was the only one who provided Katana with much of a challenge—due only to her sheer aggressiveness. Katana had to stay on her toes to avoid eating one of Michelle's strikes. But no one else could touch Katana—boys or girls.

The performance team also continued to excel at every practice. Katana thought their demo had much more difficulty and much tighter choreography than it had the previous year. Jelly continued begging Master Fu to let them add more hard moves, but Master Fu held his ground. He renewed his promise, however, to add anything Jelly wanted as long as they nailed their performance in Eureka.

But Katana felt most excited for her double whip chain set. She'd never competed in weapons before and wanted to enter this division with a bang. She even gave up searching the archives in favor of scouring the internet for other tricks she could add. But she came up empty-handed. The butterfly twist to a split was the only trick she could find anyone doing with the weapon once the chains started spinning.

She spent the last weeks leading up to the event training the hardest she'd ever trained in her entire life. When they got to the Pacific Hotel in Eureka bright and early on the last Saturday of November, Katana was ready.

"Weapons first," she said as she walked around with Sara and Chris to find her ring. The convention hall looked much emptier that it had at nationals the previous spring. It was diminished somehow without the scaffolding for the ESPN cameras.

"This is gonna be interesting this year," said Chris. "Dana and Becca have owned this ring the past couple of years, but now it's gonna be the four of you against each other."

"Are you gonna stay and watch?" Sara asked.

"Obviously," said Chris. "The boys' ring won't be nearly as interesting—we already know the mighty midget's gonna win that one."

Katana started feeling nervous. Despite her training, she'd never done this set in front of an audience before—or judges. Once they'd found the ring, she went off to one side to run through her form. She didn't do any of the tricks; she just wanted to move the chains around. Once she'd walked through the set a few times she calmed down again. She was ready. Sara had also gone off to practice, so Katana went to talk to Becca.

"Katana! Hi!" said Becca, giving her a hug.

"Hey, Becca!"

"I'm so psyched you're doing weapons this year—Dana said you put a butterfly twist into your set?"

"Yeah," said Katana with a sigh. "I've been trying to think of more tricks I can add, but that's the only thing that works."

"Yeah, chains are hard that way."

"Our new wushu master is adding sport karate weapons—I started doing samurai sword with him. So maybe next year I'll compete with that instead. Who knows."

"It's a much easier weapon to trick with, that's for sure," said Becca.

The center judge started the ring. Katana gave Becca a high-five and wished her luck. They both got in line with the other girls.

Katana had just sat down again when the center judge called her back up—she had to go first. She knew that Dana *hated* going first, but at that moment, she liked the idea. This way she wouldn't get nervous again as she watched everyone else take their turns.

She strode to the front of the ring, one chain folded up in each hand, and dropped into a horse stance facing the judges.

"Representing the Hall of the Dragon," she yelled, "I am Katana Kahanu!"

She walked to the back corner of the ring. As she started her set, she could feel the judges and the other competitors melt away: it was only her and the chains.

She ran across the ring into her round-off and launched her flash kick. She threw the chains out before her feet hit the ground.

As she moved through the flowers she focused only on keeping the chains flowing smoothly—she knew she could go fast without even trying. She got up to her neck wrap and leg wrap, then did one more set of flowers before going into the monk move.

"Steady," she said to herself as she brought both chains together in her right hand. She grabbed her left foot and held it straight up. Five rotations, then she stalled the chains and fell into her split.

For an instant she became aware of all the crowd noise—then she powered up from her split and stepped around for the butterfly kicks. She completed three kicks with ease—one chain swinging underneath her kick as the other sailed overhead. On the fourth kick she brought her legs together and twisted over hard for the butterfly twist. She landed in a split again, her hands straight out to her sides. She kicked her back leg around and went into the body jumps.

When she finished her form and walked back to sit with Sara, she realized that a large crowd had gathered around their ring. They were cheering and shouting for her as she sat down.

"That was amazing, Kat," said Sara.

"It felt good," said Katana. "It felt really good."

The girl who went next did broadsword, but dropped her weapon when she did a backflip.

"That's rough," said Sara. "It sucks to be that good and then get disqualified."

The next girl did a samurai sword form—Katana didn't think she was very good. The judges called Becca.

Becca did something Katana had never seen—she entered the ring, and did a front flip down to one knee right in front of the judges.

"I didn't know you could do that!" said Katana. "You're allowed to do a trick when you go up for your presentation?"

"Yeah, I haven't seen anyone do it in a long time—but it's allowed. You just gotta be careful not to land on the judges. They deduct points for that," said Sara.

Becca shouted out her introduction, then walked to the back corner of the ring to start her form. Once again Katana was very impressed with her performance. As much as she'd liked the form Nathan had demonstrated that first day in Master Fu's class, Katana had never seen anyone else handle a set of nunchucks the way Becca did.

She was moving them faster than she had the previous year, and her release skills were much more difficult. She did one move where she sent one nunchuck spinning in the air. She spun around in a full circle herself before catching it again, then went right into the next move without the slightest hesitation. And as Becca went over in her flash kick, Katana noticed that she kept the nunchucks spinning on either side of her.

Right at the end of her form, Becca did something that totally surprised Katana. She went from an intricate set of weapon manipulations into a perfect gainer flash. Katana didn't know Becca could do that trick now—she hadn't been able to the previous year. But more than anything else, Katana realized that this was a trick she could do with her chains. Becca had kept the nunchucks spinning on each side of her again during the trick. That made Katana think of her chains.

Could this really work? The round-off made a regular flash kick impossible to do with chains—they'd stop spinning if she put her hands down. But she might be able to throw the gainer flash out of a flower sequence; that wouldn't require a round-off. She could keep one chain moving on either side of her as she went over. This was perfect. The only trouble would be getting high enough to avoid smashing the chains into the ground.

"That was awesome," said Katana, giving Becca a high-five as she sat down next to her. "I didn't know you had a gainer!"

"Yeah, I worked on it like crazy over the summer," said Becca. "I only got it like two or three weeks ago. My instructor didn't want me to do it today cuz I haven't been landing it consistently."

"Coulda fooled me..." said Sara. "That one was perfect."

The girl who went next did a spear set. Then the judges called Sara. "Here it goes," she said, getting up to walk into the ring.

Sara looked strong and confident. She nailed every move, landed all her tricks, and moved the staff around faster than ever.

The judges called Dana last.

"Go Dana!" Katana yelled at the top of her lungs.

Dana also opened with a flash kick. Her form was identical to Katana's, minus the butterfly twist. Katana thought she was flawless—and as usual she had a powerful stage presence. People from several of the surrounding rings came to watch.

Dana came back to the side of the ring when she was done. Katana, Sara and Becca gave her high-fives. Katana felt confident as they sat around waiting for the judges to figure out the places. Finally the center judge lined them up again.

"In fourth place," he yelled, "Sara Brown!"

"YES!" yelled Sara. She went up to take her place next to the judge.

"In third place, Dana Arlington!"

Dana walked up next to Sara.

"We have a tie for first place. Katana and Becca please come up."

"Don't you love ties?" asked Becca sarcastically. Katana and Becca stood before the judges.

The center judge yelled "Call!" He pointed to Katana along with one of the other judges—the other three judges pointed to Becca.

"In second place, Katana Kahanu, and in first place, Becca Stratton!"

The girls gave each other a hug. Then Katana and Sara went to find Chris in the throng.

"You shoulda won that, Kat," he said when they found him.

"Nah," Katana answered. "Becca was ridiculous. I'm gonna have to add more difficulty if I wanna beat her at Golden Gate."

"It's too bad you can't put more tricks in the set," said Sara. "You're already doing the hardest moves you can do with the weapon."

"Watching Becca, I realized there *is* another trick I can do!"

"What?" Chris asked.

"Gainer flash."

"Are you kidding me?" said Sara. "How the hell are you gonna do that with the chains moving... Oh! Like Becca did with the chucks!"

"Exactly," Katana replied. "I'm not sure how to go into it, but if I can figure that out, it should work perfectly."

The girls wished Chris luck with his kata and went off to find their own ring. Dana was not competing in kata. Katana figured this ring would come down to her, Sara and Becca.

But she was wrong: she'd forgotten about Michelle.

Michelle went up first. Katana was absolutely awestruck. She hadn't seen Michelle do kata before, as she didn't take Osaka's group classes anymore. Michelle was technically flawless, but when the event was done, Katana was certain that her power and stage presence were the things that had earned her first place. She had the loudest kiais of anyone in the entire tournament—Katana could see people clear across the room looking over to see who was making all the noise. And as she'd done every time Katana had seen her spar, Michelle underwent an incredible transformation when she was performing in front of the judges. She looked ferocious through her entire form.

Sara ended up in second. And after seeing Sara and Michelle perform, Katana was perfectly happy with third. Becca was relegated to fourth, which surprised everyone. She was the reigning grand champion from nationals the previous two years.

"Did you see Michelle?!" asked Sara as they went over to their sparring ring. "That was... I don't know what the hell to call it—I've never seen *anyone* do a kata that strong before."

"Yeah," Katana agreed. "I don't think anyone expected that."

Katana was, however, ready for Michelle in sparring. She got her gear on and thought about her strategy as she stretched. She knew Michelle would be her toughest competition. And she knew that as long as she kept her distancing right, she could win.

"Hey," said Becca when she came over to Katana a minute later. "Good luck up there."

"Yeah, you too!"

"You're so lucky your school has a team for this division," said Becca with a frown.

"Oh—yours doesn't?"

"No! I was so psyched when I heard there was going to be a girls' division, but I couldn't get the other girls from my school to spar! They're afraid to break a nail or something," said Becca, rolling her eyes.

The center judge was a heavyset man who wore his long, greasy hair in a ponytail. He lined them up for roll call. When he was done, he walked over to Katana. The other girls were sitting down around the ring. "I remember you from nationals last year," he said quietly. "Do me a favor—no levitation today, okay? It's against the rules, and gives you a totally unfair advantage. I don't wanna have to disqualify anyone."

"Uh... no problem," said Katana. She couldn't fathom how anyone could believe she'd done it intentionally.

She sat down next to Sara and asked, "Who is that guy?"

"Joe Rodriguez," said Sara. "I'm pretty sure he runs Golden Gate. Why?"

"He just lectured me about not using levitation!"

Master Rodriguez called Katana up for the very first match—against Michelle. They gave each other a hug before squaring off.

Katana usually waited for Michelle to make the first move. Today she decided to mix things up. When Master Rodriguez started the match, she launched in immediately with a hook kick. When Michelle dodged, Katana bounced forward on her base leg and snapped a roundhouse kick to her head. She was up 2-0.

Michelle took the initiative next. She managed to land a punch after nearly driving Katana out of the ring. Katana was still up 2-1.

They traded kicks for the next two rounds, bringing the score to 4-3. Then Michelle rushed in and Katana caught her with the leg scissors takedown. Katana won 6-3.

The judges called Sierra and Becca next.

Katana hadn't seen Becca spar in almost two years. But from what she remembered, she knew that Sierra would have her hands full.

Sure enough, Sierra was no match for Becca. Becca pulled out a win, 5-1.

Olivia went next against a girl Katana didn't recognize—she won her match 6-4. Two more girls fought after that. There were only eight girls in the ring, so they went to finals in the very next round.

Katana was called up first again. She went against the girl

who'd won the last match. Katana beat her easily, with a score of 5-1.

Becca and Olivia went next, and Katana finally found a way to tell the twins apart. They were both right-handed, but Sierra sparred with her right side forward and Olivia with her left. Katana couldn't believe she hadn't noticed this before—but at that moment it was throwing Becca for a loop. The twins' fighting styles were nearly identical, but with the opposite side forward. Katana could tell that Becca had grown accustomed to Sierra in her first match; she was anticipating moves from Olivia incorrectly. Katana almost thought Olivia was going to pull out a win when the match went to 4-3 in her favor. But Becca caught her with the leg scissors takedown to win 5-4.

The judges called Olivia and the girl who'd lost to Katana to fight for third and fourth place. Olivia won the match with ease.

Katana and Becca had to fight for first and second. The last time she'd sparred with Becca was the first time Katana had *ever* sparred in a tournament. It was her first year at the Hall of the Dragon. She'd lost to Becca badly that time. But she'd come a long way since then.

They got in the ring and gave each other a high-five. Master Rodriguez started the match.

Katana and Becca both started out very cautiously. They circled around each other, each gauging the other's reactions to a few feints.

Katana launched a kicking sequence. She started with a front kick into a roundhouse kick. When Becca dodged both of these,

Katana shot forward on her base leg and dropped an axe kick on the back of Becca's head. She took the lead, 2-0.

When they started again, Becca lunged in with a side kick. Katana knew she was going for the leg scissors takedown. Katana dropped immediately to sweep out Becca's other leg. But Becca jumped out of the way, avoiding Katana's sweep. She caught Katana in the head with a punch as Katana straightened up.

The score was 2-1 in Katana's favor.

As they started again, Katana wished she could use her gainer flash. But Becca wasn't big enough—it would never work. *And she'd promised Sam she'd save that move for nationals.*

Katana moved in for another kicking combination, but Becca dropped down as fast as lightning and swept out her base leg. Katana rolled out of the way as soon as she hit the floor, denying Becca any follow-up points. But Becca was now ahead, 3-2.

They traded kicks back and forth for the next two rounds, neither of them able to score. Finally they both moved in for a kick at the same time, jamming each other's legs. Katana pushed off her base leg and caught Becca with the leg scissors takedown. She tried to land a kick for the win once they'd hit the floor, but Becca rolled away too quickly. Katana was up, 4-3.

They went back and forth for a few more rounds, and Katana felt like the match might go on forever. But as Becca lunged in for a punch, Katana spun around and caught her in the back of the head with a hook kick. She won the match 6-3 and took first place.

"Good match!" said Katana, grabbing Becca in a hug. Master

Rodriguez called the four finalists up in their places and finished the ring.

"Good luck with the demo!" Becca yelled as Katana ran off to the stage with Sara. The girls found the rest of the team huddled around Master Fu.

"Let's go, everyone," he said, "this is it. You guys have been nailing this demo for weeks now. This one's going to be easy. Hit it tonight, and we'll go back and start adding harder elements for Golden Gate."

"YES!" said Jelly. "Come on guys, let's do this!"

The team went to stretch and warm up while they waited their turn. Katana recognized the first team to compete from both of the previous years' events. They did sport karate sets. Katana thought they were decent as far as their karate was concerned. But like some of the other teams Master Fu had shown them at the movie night, they didn't do much in the way of choreography. It was mostly one person at a time demonstrating a form or weapon set.

Team Strike Force went next. Katana thought they'd improved significantly from the previous year. They also did sport karate weapons. But while their martial arts skill was not any stronger than that of the first team, they had much better choreography and tricking skills. Katana also thought their stage presence had improved; they were louder and much more intense.

Katana started to get nervous again when they called the Hall of the Dragon to the stage. This would be the first time she'd ever performed the demo in front of an audience—or judges. As she took the stage she realized that there were way more people watching than there'd been for the other divisions. She'd always been in the audience, and had never thought about the fact that the other rings were done now. Literally everyone who was still at the tournament was watching the team demonstrations.

This was quite a bit more nerve-racking than Katana had imagined. In every other event, no matter how many people might gather to watch, her focus had always been on the competition at hand—whether that meant beating her opponent, or nailing her kata. But the whole point of the team demo division was to perform for a large audience. Katana realized that Master Fu was right—this was a whole different mindset.

Katana used one of the chi kung techniques she'd learned from the scrolls in the archives. She held both hands palm-down at waist level and focused on letting her chi flow along her lung meridian. Then she took several deep breaths. Immediately she could feel her heartbeat slowing and her nerves calming.

She was ready.

Katana put her chains in position at one edge of the stage and got in line for the demo. She was on the right, directly behind Sara. The music began and they started the performance.

Jelly and Sara walked forward, met in the middle, and turned to walk to the front of the stage, right in front of the judges.

Katana walked forward and met Dana in the center, then turned and moved forward. Katana stopped a few feet behind Sara and stood with her hands by her side. When they reached the cue in their music, Sara and Jelly stepped forward with one foot, blocked down with their lead hand and kiaied. The whole team shouted out, "Representing the Hall of the Dragon!"

Katana followed Sara's lead through the short choreography section, which consisted of pieces taken from some of their empty-hand wushu sets. Katana saw Donnie land his butterfly twist right next to her. That was her cue to start her tricking sequence with Dana while the rest of the team moved to the back of the stage.

Katana threw her aerial to the side of the stage as Donnie ran back, then she turned to face Dana. They ran past each other and did round-offs into back handsprings and flash kicks, landing in splits with their hands straight out to their sides. Katana swung her back leg around, rolled back on her shoulders and kicked to her feet. She and Dana ran forward and did front aerials past each other.

At the edge of the stage, Katana turned around and dropped to her knee. The kids doing broadsword came forward to start their set.

Katana picked up her chains in both hands. She could feel the bass from their music vibrating the stage. She watched the broadsword set—they looked stronger than ever.

When they were done, Scott and Donnie did their aerials past Sara and Tim in the back corners. Paul dove over Jelly as Jelly did his butterfly twist to the center of the stage. Jelly let out a loud kiai to start the staff set.

Katana started to fidget as she watched this—she knew it was Sara's first demo, too. She thought back to Jelly's first performance on this very stage, and the way he'd accidentally let go of his staff right after his release skill. But there was no such mishap today. They executed the beginning of the set perfectly. Then

Jelly, Sara and Tim threw their staves straight up into the air, did standing flash kicks, and caught the staves again without incident.

Katana got ready—she had to keep her weight on her right foot so she could spring into her aerial at just the right moment.

Staff left the stage as the kids from broadsword came back for a short tricking sequence. Katana watched Jelly put his staff down and run around to the other side of the stage. As he stepped into his aerial, Katana got to her feet and did her own aerial so that she and Jelly both hit the front corners at the same time.

This was it—the stage was clear. Katana nodded to Dana, who was now positioned diagonally across from her. Katana ran forward and did her double backflip as Dana ran past her into a flash kick. Katana and Jelly landed their flips, and Katana threw her chains out the moment her feet hit the floor.

Katana's nerves were gone—she felt calm and confident. She slammed out the first section of their whip chain set, right through the flowers, the neck wrap and the leg wrap. Then she brought her chains together in her right hand for the monk move. Katana lifted her left foot overhead just as Dana did, and counted out five rotations with the chains. Then she stalled the chains and fell to her split.

Katana kicked her leg around and did the full body jumps. As she kicked to her feet, she could see Dana out of the corner of her eye—they were perfectly synchronized. They turned toward the audience, did one set of flowers, and brought their chains together for the monk move again. They walked up to the judges, stepped under their chains and smashed them to the stage behind them.

Katana turned, ran toward the back of the stage as her teammates ran forward, and did an aerial. She dropped her chains on the stage as she went over. She landed and stepped into formation right behind Sara for their final bow.

She'd done it—along with her team, she'd nailed her first ever team performance. Katana thought this was the best feeling in the world—even better than winning an individual event. And she was certain they'd won. Strike Force had been good, but she knew her own team had totally outclassed them.

Sure enough, the judges announced the scores and the Hall of the Dragon took first by a wide margin.

"Awesome job, kids," yelled Master Fu, beaming at them as they left the stage. "Nicely done—that's what you gotta do it if you want to beat Supernova this year."

"Yeah!" yelled Jelly. "And now we get to add more stuff—you promised!"

"Yes, yes I did," said Master Fu. "You earned it. We'll start this week—so put some thought into what you want to do."

Katana went to collect her chains and her sparring gear. Chris came over to her and Sara as Katana packed her bag.

"That was amazing, you guys," he said. "The whole crowd went wild like over and over again."

"Really?" said Sara. "You know, I didn't notice the audience once we started!"

"Well, they cheered like mad when you guys did the release skill in staff, and they went insane for the double backflips. That was seriously the best demo I've ever seen."

"Better than Supernova?" asked Katana.

"Definitely," said Chris.

The three of them walked out to the buses together. Katana almost ran into Master Rodriguez on the way out the door.

"Good job today, Kahanu," he said. "See you at Golden Gate."

"Thanks!" said Katana, trying to smile.

"Who was that guy?" Chris asked once the man was out of earshot.

"Joe Rodriguez," said Sara, rolling her eyes. "He was Kat's center judge for sparring. He gave her this big lecture about not using levitation. I guess he saw her at nationals last year."

"Are you kidding me?" said Chris. "What a jerk!"

"Hey—how'd you do in sparring?" asked Katana when they sat down at the back of the bus.

"Good. I got second, but I lost to Mukon—he was amazing. He's way better under pressure than he is at practice."

"How'd Jimmy do?" asked Sara.

"He lost his first match—the kid was huge. Mukon beat him in finals though, and the kid ended up with third."

"Aw," said Katana. "Poor Jimmy!"

CHAPTER 18

MASTER CHATRI

Katana couldn't wait to get to the wushu dojo on Sunday. She was more excited than ever about her whip chain set after the Eureka Challenge. She'd lost to Becca, but felt like she now knew—finally—how to add a trick to her set that would put her over the top at Golden Gate. Dana was already there working on her butterfly twist when Katana walked in with Sara and Chris after breakfast.

"That looks a lot better," said Katana.

"Yeah, I'm getting there," Dana replied. "I can land it most of the time now, but I have no idea how to do it to a split."

"It's not that bad. You remember when we did the front aerials into splits last year?"

"Yeah," Dana said tentatively.

"It's like that—hold your first leg out when you're landing.

Don't let your feet touch before you hit the split," Katana explained.

"But what about the chains—how do you keep them going as you roll over?"

"Pull your hands in when you twist over—the chains just go," said Katana with a shrug.

"It must be from the centripetal force," said Sara.

"The what?" asked Chris.

"Centripetal force," Sara repeated. "When you're going around in a circle, the force of your body turning in the air pulls the chains along with you."

Katana tried to help Dana with the move. Instead of landing in a split, Dana kept putting her foot down, then sliding into it. Katana had her do the front aerial into a split the way Master Nash had taught them the previous year. Once Dana had done this a few times, she tried the butterfly twist again. Finally, she was able to land that in a split, too.

"Now I gotta do it with the chains."

"That's the easy part," Katana assured her.

Dana walked through the move a couple of times, then tried it for real. She stepped around like she did for the butterfly kicks, swung the chains and went into a perfect butterfly twist. She pulled her hands in as she started to twist and the chains went around with her.

Dana landed in her split and yelled, "YES!"

"WHOA!" yelled Jelly, who had just walked in. "You got it! You two have to show Fu so we can add it into the demo!"

"Hey, Kat—what about the gainer flash?" asked Chris. "Are you gonna try it with the chains today?"

"You're gonna do a gainer with the chains?!" asked Dana.

"I'm gonna try," said Katana. "You remember when Becca did one with her chucks yesterday? She kept them spinning the whole time, so I figure I should be able to do that with chains."

"Yeah, but chains are way longer, Kat," said Dana doubtfully. "You're gonna have to go wicked high or else you're gonna slam them into the floor. That wouldn't look too cool."

"One way to find out!" Katana picked up her chains. She walked to the center of the dojo and started spinning them. She figured she could start with flowers, then spin one chain forward on each side of her and go into the trick. But she tried it once, and wasn't able to get nearly high enough. She landed well, but the chains smashed into the floor, as Dana had predicted.

"Damn!" she yelled. She tried it a few more times, but couldn't generate the height she needed.

Dana walked through the flowers herself. "Kat, I think I've got it—try turning out of the flowers and spinning the chains *upward* when you kick your leg over. You should be able to get more momentum by turning into it. You'll probably get way more height!"

"Let me think about this for a minute..." Katana walked through what Dana had described. "Yeah, this is gonna work," she said.

She started with flowers again, then turned around, opened up the chains, and kicked over into her gainer flash. She landed it, turned around immediately, and went right back into flowers again. Her chains hadn't touched the floor.

"That's the coolest thing I've ever seen!" said Jelly. "We gotta get Fu to put *that* in the demo, too!"

"I wish I could do a gainer," said Dana. "Kat, you're gonna crush me at Golden Gate with that move!"

"You know," said Chris, "is there any reason you have to open your solo set with a flash kick?"

"Well, it's better than the aerial," said Katana with a shrug.

"That's not what I meant," Chris replied. "You've got that double back now..."

"That's true," Katana said pensively. "Yeah—if I open with the double back, and do the gainer flash right before the monk move..."

"Hey—you should do a trick when you go up to the judges, too," said Sara. "Like Becca did!"

"She's right, Kat—that was a strong opener for her. It definitely made her stand out," Dana agreed.

"I don't want to copy her though," said Katana. "I'd want to do it with a different trick."

"Well, you can't do any kind of backflip, cuz you'll land facing away from the judges," said Chris.

"Yeah, but a front aerial to a split would work," said Dana. "I can even do *that*. We'd have to run on an angle, and turn as we go in the air—that way we can land sideways in the split, right in front of the judges."

"This is awesome," said Katana. "One of you guys go up front and be the judge!"

Chris and Jelly ran to the front of the dojo and sat down on the floor. "Katana Kahanu, get your ass up here, fatty!" yelled Jelly.

Katana pretended she was at the tournament. She ran in an arc, did her front aerial and landed in a front split right in front of them.

"Representing the Hall of the Dragon," she yelled, "I am Katana Kahanu!"

She powered up, and strode to where the back corner of the ring would be.

She ran forward, and did her double backflip, throwing the chains out as she landed. She went through the flower section, and right after the leg wrap, threw the gainer flash. She landed, did the monk move, and finished the rest of the form exactly as she had at Eureka the previous day.

"Wow, Kat—that's insane," said Dana. "You're definitely going to nationals with that form. I can't double back *or* gainer flash."

"Well, I don't know about the double back," said Katana, "but you can probably get the gainer. You can do a standing back-flip, right?"

"Yeah," said Dana, "but the gainer's way harder, isn't it?"

"Honestly, the way I'm doing it—turning into it like that, it feels more like a regular standing flash," said Katana.

"That's true," said Jelly. "It's not much harder than a standing flash. Kat's right, Dana—you can probably get this."

Jelly helped Dana with the move for a while, and Katana went through her form again. She felt very confident with her set now.

She was certain that the extra tricks would give her the edge she needed in San Francisco.

Later that afternoon, after she finished her homework, Katana started thinking about the archive room again. They'd totally lost track of that with their preparations for Eureka. Katana knew there had to be more useful documents down there. She told Sara she wanted to start looking for more information again. After dinner they grabbed Chris and the three of them made their way down to the tunnels.

Although Sara was the only one who could read anything, Katana and Chris were getting good at discerning which documents were interesting and which were simply records or recipes or other mundane items. They collected a box load of material and headed up to the girls' room.

They spent the next thirty minutes sifting through everything. Finally, Katana struck pay dirt. "Hey guys, check this out!" she said.

"What is it?" asked Chris.

"I don't know, but it has meridian diagrams again—this one looks like the guy's throwing a fireball," said Katana.

Sara looked over the scrolls. "This whole thing is about how to do a chi hit. It explains how the chi is generated in your dantian and moves through your meridians and out your palms."

"That's not very useful—we know how to throw our chi already," Chris commented.

"Yeah, but it's still kinda cool to see how it works through the meridians and stuff," said Katana.

Sara looked it over for a few minutes then read it to Chris and Katana.

"So the chi travels along your palm meridian. It leaves your body and goes through the air until it hits whoever you threw it at," Katana summarized.

"That's all kind of obvious," said Chris.

"No, it's not obvious at all," said Katana. "In chi fa, you have to send your chi along your shen. But not when you throw a fireball."

"So what?" asked Chris.

"Well, for one thing, that means you can make your chi change directions in chi fa," said Sara. "Someone could levitate away from your chi hit, but if they tried that in chi fa, you could still hit them."

In the same box, Katana also found similar scrolls that dealt with deflecting intent, levitation and fading. "I wonder why there's nothing in here about the tai chi chen do," said Chris.

"Hmm... Well we know the tai chi one is way more complicated. Maybe that's stored on its own somewhere," suggested Katana.

They resumed their search. A few minutes later, Sara said, "Whoa! I've got it—it's another set of Chang's memoirs!"

Katana and Chris went over to get a look. "Volume two?" Katana asked.

"I think so," said Sara. "But Kat—this is like three more installments!"

"Looks like Fisher's gonna be busy for a while," said Chris.

"Yes he is," Sara said with a grin. "I'll bring these to him tomorrow in study hall."

It took them another hour to go through the rest of the documents they'd brought up. But they didn't find anything else that looked remotely interesting.

At the end of their tai chi practice the following morning, Master Nash announced that Master Chatri Benjawan would be arriving from Bangkok that weekend. And again he asked Katana to stay a moment after class.

"Katana, as you know, Master Chatri will be conducting your evaluation during his visit. Once again, you will need to be here Sunday morning at eleven.

"I should warn you, Katana, Master Chatri tends to be rather... stern. He is extremely powerful. In fact, he is one of the most advanced internal masters in the world, and he is very conscious of that fact. He has not told me how he plans to evaluate you, but I would expect that it will be rather more formal than what you did with Master Santos."

"Oh, great," said Katana. "Master Nash, is the chen do in hsing-i the same as in tai chi?"

"Yes, Katana, that is correct. The chen do in all three of the internal Chinese styles—including pakua—are the same."

"And aikido and jiu jitsu have the same chen do, too," said Katana. "How does that work—how can different arts have the same chen do?"

Master Nash considered this for a moment. "Imagine that you are climbing a mountain. You find a path that leads from the base all the way to the summit. When you arrive at the peak, you meet another climber who is getting there at the same time as you —but you did not see them on your way up the path. How did they get there?"

"Um... they took a different path?" asked Katana.

"Yes, precisely," said Master Nash. "Becoming a master—or learning a chen do—is something like climbing a mountain. There are many different paths, but the destination is the same."

"I guess that makes sense," said Katana. "But what exactly is the chen do in tai chi, anyway? I know that chi fa is part of it, but isn't holding the energy ball part of it, too?"

"Katana, the chen do of tai chi is the realization that all of the chen do are the same," said Master Nash with a smile.

"I don't get it..."

"One day you will, Katana. One day you will."

"Master Nash, is Master Chatri as powerful as you?" asked Katana.

He smiled. "Master Chatri and I are equals—although we arrived at the top of our mountain by very different paths. Oh, and speaking of different paths, I almost forgot to tell you about your evaluation with Master Tanaka!"

"I thought he refused to come here?" Katana asked.

"Indeed," Nash replied. "You will need to go to Shaka-In again. I have spoken with Mitch Brown. He has invited you and Chris to spend the winter recess with him and his family in Japan. If that is acceptable to you..."

"That's definitely acceptable!" said Katana with a big smile. She had thoroughly enjoyed her first visit to Japan and couldn't wait to go again.

"Excellent," said Master Nash. "As long as your aunt and Mr. Boyd's parents approve, Mitch will make the arrangements. You will go to Shaka-In while you are there, and Master Tanaka can conduct your evaluation in whatever manner he deems appropriate."

"Yeah... I'm sure *that's* gonna be interesting," Katana said.

"There is never a dull moment when Master Tanaka is involved," Nash agreed.

"Why is he so... eccentric?" Katana asked.

"Ah, Katana... truthfully, I don't know. Tanaka has always been unique. He is a good man, though. I trust him completely," said Master Nash. "But you are right—I am sure his evaluation will be unlike any of the others."

Sara brought the new volumes of Chang's memoirs to Sean at school later that day. She reminded him again to keep what he was doing to himself. Katana, Sara and Chris went back to the archive room every night that week, bringing up interesting materials one box at a time. They found nothing else worthwhile. Katana was sure, though, that other treasures were waiting for them—they'd yet to go through more than a quarter of the room's contents.

Katana found out from Sam on Friday that there would definitely be other girls' sparring teams at Golden Gate—unlike Eureka. Sam also announced that both the boys' and the girls' teams were in the lead for their divisions. The girls' matches had still earned them points even though no other teams had been present.

And Master Fu invited Jelly to present him with ideas for

additions to their demo. But the only elements Jelly suggested were the butterfly twists and gainer flash kicks in the whip chain set.

"Are you kidding me?" asked Master Fu. "Jelly—you hounded me for weeks to add harder skills. The only things you came up with are for a set you're not even in?!"

"Yeah... well..." Jelly stammered. "I wanna do more stuff, but I don't know what else to add! I was hoping *you'd* have some ideas!"

"All right," said Master Fu, shaking his head. "Girls, can you both do those tricks in your set?"

Katana and Dana showed him the butterfly twist—which they both did perfectly—and the gainer flash. Katana did it with ease, but Dana wasn't there yet. She could do a gainer, but when she tried to turn it into a flash kick, she didn't get as much height. She had to put her hands down. Of course, this wouldn't work with the chains.

Master Fu urged them to keep practicing both tricks. He told them he'd devise a way to incorporate them into the demo.

When Katana arrived in the tai chi dojo with Sara and Chris the next day for Master Chatri's seminar, she was pleased to see that Master Nakamura was there. Katana assumed that the other two people standing next to Nakamura were Master Chatri's assistants. They were dressed in uniforms very similar to those the masters wore at the Hall of the Dragon. Their pants were black, and their tops—which had frog buttons down the center—were a parchment color.

Master Chatri was a little shorter than Nash. His salt-and-pepper hair was trimmed very short, and his face seemed chiseled out of stone.

Master Nash lined everyone up. "It is my honor and great pleasure to introduce to you Master Chatri Benjawan from the Temple of the Golden Arhat in Bangkok, Thailand."

Everyone clapped for Master Chatri. He shook Master Nash's hand and addressed the whole room. Katana could see his aura glowing brightly around him—he did appear every bit as powerful as Master Nash.

"As I am sure Headmaster Nash has explained to you, at the Temple of the Golden Arhat we teach muay thai kickboxing and hsing-i. Today I will be introducing you to some basic hsing-i exercises.

"As you are all students of tai chi, you will probably find the movements of hsing-i somewhat familiar. In fact, the forms share some of the same postures. Also like tai chi, hsing-i is a purely internal art, thus all of the techniques, both external and internal, work directly with your chi. Hsing-i and tai chi are both extremely subtle and intricate arts and take a lifetime to master.

"The primary difference between the two is that while tai chi maintains the same slow, steady and relaxed pace throughout every movement, hsing-i builds its power slowly then releases it in a short, dynamic burst. Please observe."

Master Chatri began doing movements Katana recognized from the tai chi form. "When you do the Single Whip in tai chi," he said, going through the posture, "you keep your movement slow and soft.

"Now please watch how we do the same posture in hsing-i."

Master Chatri began the same sequence of movements again. "We build our power slowly as we begin the posture." Master Chatri then snapped both arms out. "Then we release the power and explode into the final position."

Master Chatri proceeded to teach them the beginning section of the hsing-i short form. The movement felt like a cross between tai chi and kempo. Master Chatri explained that the key was to stay loose initially, then hit the final position—which was always a push or a strike—moving the body like a whip.

Once Master Chatri had gone through the postures with the whole room a few times, he broke them down into smaller groups. He and his assistants—including Master Nakamura—worked more closely with each group.

They spent quite a while working on the form. Katana was in Master Chatri's group. He made sure everyone could execute each posture perfectly before moving on. Katana did find him rather strict—his very presence seemed to quell any sort of chatter or tomfoolery from the students. But at the same time she thought he was a very good teacher.

Chatri gathered everyone together again, and brought Master Nakamura up to the front of the room with him. "In hsing-i we also practice pushing hands, just as you do in tai chi. However the push is applied rather more aggressively. Please observe."

He began pushing hands with Master Nakamura. At first, Katana thought it looked identical to the tai chi exercise. Chatri and Nakamura held their wrists in light contact with each other, and tried to find each other's center. But suddenly Master Chatri shot his hands out in a short burst. He moved only a few inches, but sent Nakamura flying. She landed on her back on the mat. Katana wondered for a moment if Master Chatri knew chi tao.

Master Chatri broke them up into groups again. This time Katana worked with Master Nakamura. She had them pair off with a partner, and went around herself to work with everyone individually. This took a long time as there were more than twenty-five students in each group.

In the end, Master Chatri lined them up again. He had one of his assistants demonstrate the hsing-i long form. When he was done, Master Nash dismissed them for the evening.

"Chatri was all business, wasn't he?" said Chris when they got to dinner later that evening.

"Yeah, he didn't seem to have as much fun as Santos did," Sara observed.

"He was still a good teacher, though," said Katana. "And Nash was right—he's really powerful."

"I know—I could see his aura," said Sara. "It was as strong as Nash's!"

"Nash told me that he and Chatri are equals," said Katana. "It would be neat to see them do chi fa."

"He's evaluating you tomorrow?" Chris asked.

"Yeah, at eleven," Katana replied. "Nash said he'd probably be more formal, but he didn't seem too bad today."

"He doesn't seem like the type that would set you up to fail, at least—like that Kim guy," said Sara.

"I hope not," Katana agreed.

She returned to the tai chi dojo the following morning. Master Nakamura was there with Chatri and Nash.

"Good morning, Katana," said Master Chatri, shaking her hand. "I've been looking forward to meeting you. As you know, you have come to the attention of the headmasters because of your unusual abilities with the chen do.

"However, while it is your talent with chi manipulation that brought me here, I believe in evaluating the complete skills of a martial artist. Therefore I would like to see the full range of your abilities this morning. So please take a few minutes to warm up and stretch, and we will begin."

Over the next two hours, Master Chatri reviewed virtually everything Katana had ever learned in the martial arts—or at least everything he knew about. Master Nash had apparently neglected to mention the things she'd learned from the other headmasters —like chi tao and grappling.

Master Chatri had Master Nakamura run Katana through basics for a half hour first, then instructed her to perform all of her kata. Katana did her self-defense combinations on Master Nakamura next, and did fighting drills and sparring with her as well.

Katana also did her double whip chain set—Master Nash had brought up a set of chains for her to use. She did the form with her new moves in place. She also had to do both the short and long tai chi forms, and tai chi pushing hands with Master Nakamura.

Next, Master Chatri had her spar with Nakamura again, this time using the chen do. Katana wasn't sure it mattered, but followed Master Nash's lead and refrained from using any chi tao techniques. However she did have ample opportunity to deflect intent and throw fireballs. Master Nakamura was also quite adept at these skills, and kept Katana on her toes.

Finally Master Chatri said, "We are almost done, Katana. For your final demonstration of skill, I would like to see what you have learned so far in chi fa."

"Chi fa!" Katana blurted, looking pleadingly at Master Nash. "But I can hardly do it at all—I can't even play offense yet."

But Master Chatri assumed the stance, holding his hands out toward Katana.

Katana was *not* comfortable with this—she had no idea what Chatri expected. But she apparently had no choice.

She assumed her stance. As she turned her hands out toward Master Chatri, he extended his shen. He began sending chi at her immediately; balls of light came at her from all directions. Katana entered the lucid state of mind she always achieved in fighting drills. She deflected all the chi that came at her without allowing her conscious mind to interfere. But Master Chatri's attack was much more intense than anything Nash had thrown at her. She didn't think she'd be able to keep this up for very long.

Suddenly, the attack stopped. Not only had the pulses of light ceased, but Katana could no longer see Chatri's shen—or his aura. Nothing.

Katana was confused. Chatri's aura had been one of the brightest she'd ever seen. He held his stance for chi fa, his hands extended toward Katana. But he was totally dark.

What was going on? Was she imagining things?

A moment later, his shen reignited. Countless tendrils of energy extended everywhere, guiding chi pulses at her. She tried to deflect them, but was overwhelmed. Dozens of pulses smashed into her at once. She flew halfway across the room, only able to prevent herself from crashing by using levitation.

Katana was annoyed. Master Chatri had seemed perfectly reasonable until now. But what was the point of overpowering her in chi fa when she was only a beginner? This seemed more like something Master Kim would do. Nash looked equally unhappy when Katana walked back over to them.

"That will conclude your evaluation, Katana," said Master Chatri. "I have seen all I need to see."

Master Nash dismissed her, and Katana ran back up to her room.

"That took forever," said Sara as Katana walked in the door and collapsed on the couch. Doc jumped onto her stomach. She scratched his head absentmindedly.

"I'm exhausted!" said Katana. "Chatri made me do everything I know."

"*Everything*?" said Sara. "Define everything..."

"Everything—forms, combinations, sparring, tai chi, whip chain... He made me do chi fa, too, even though I told him I was no good. Sara, something really weird happened. He was throwing balls of light at me like Master Nash does, but all of a sudden, it stopped. I couldn't see his shen or his aura or anything. It was like someone turned off a switch."

"That's weird," said Sara with a frown. "I can see Nash's aura all the time now. Did it come back?"

"Yeah, it did. He threw like a million pulses at me and knocked me across the room!"

"Are you sure it wasn't Master Kim in disguise?" Sara asked sarcastically.

"That's what I was thinking..."

"Well forget about Chatri—Sean e-mailed me the translations of those new volumes," Sara said excitedly.

"Oh cool!" said Katana, pushing Doc off her stomach and getting back to her feet. "I'll get Chris!"

But as she opened the door, the cat ran between her legs, into the hall.

"Doc!" she yelled. "Get back here!"

"He's not a dog, Katana—he's not gonna come when you call him," Sara chided her.

Katana closed the door and walked down the hall to grab Doc. But as soon as she got near him, he ran farther down the hall, sniffing around and exploring this new landscape. They hadn't been letting him out of their room, and in recent weeks he'd started trying to escape.

Katana followed the cat down the stairs and through the hallway to the atrium. But when Doc got to the end of the corridor, he could go no farther—the doors were closed and there was no other way out.

"Gotcha!" said Katana as she picked him up. She was about to go back to her room when she heard voices from inside the lounge. It sounded like Master Nash and Osaka.

"I don't know what the man was thinking," she could hear Master Nash saying. "Katana and I both told him she was a beginner at chi fa, but he insisted on doing it anyway. Of course, Katana had no idea what was happening when he hid his shen."

"And he plans on failing her?" Osaka asked.

"So he says."

"Good," said Osaka. "Perhaps some of the others will follow his lead and we can put a stop to this insanity."

Katana was stunned. She stood there a minute longer but didn't hear another word that either of them might have said. Osaka *wanted* her to fail? Katana knew he'd been worried about her earlier in the term. She knew he didn't want her prying into Jaaku's past. But what possible reason could he have for wanting her to fail? She felt like she'd been slapped in the face.

She went to get Chris and the two of them walked to the girls' room. Katana told them what she'd overheard.

"Osaka wants you to fail?!" asked Chris. "That doesn't add up—you've always been his favorite!"

"I'm telling you, that's what he said!" She felt hurt and confused by his words.

"Why don't you ask him about it?" said Sara.

"Oh sure, tell him I was eavesdropping on his conversation with Nash, you mean?" Katana asked incredulously.

"Good point," said Sara with a frown. "Kat, I don't know what to tell you. That seems totally out of character."

"Yeah, well a lot of things have been out of character for him this year. I don't know what I did to make him feel this way," said Katana.

"I don't think you did anything, Kat," Chris consoled her. "He's been... I don't know, moody or something. I'm sure it's not you. But I wonder why Chatri's failing you," he added. "It almost seems like he was out to get you."

"Yeah, it does," said Katana with a sigh. "I still don't know what these stupid evaluations are about anyway. I mean, what's the point? It's like I'm a circus freak or something and they're coming to gawk at me."

"Hmm," said Sara, looking thoughtful.

"What?" Katana asked.

"It's nothing. Forget it," said Sara.

"No—what is it?" Katana insisted.

"I don't know, Kat," Sara said hesitantly. "But when Nash first told you about the evaluations, it sounded like the headmasters were only coming to see what you could do. But if Chatri is *failing* you—that would seem to mean there's something at stake, wouldn't it? How can you fail if it's not a test?"

"That's a good question," said Katana. "I hadn't thought about that—but you're right. Nash said they weren't testing me for rank or anything—but if I can fail, then there must be *something* on the line."

The three of them sat in silence for a few moments. Then suddenly Chris said, "Well, I have no idea what's going on with that, but I wanna read those new memoirs!"

"That's right!" said Sara. "I forgot!"

Sara opened her e-mail. "I guess there's not *too* much here. Sean says it goes on forever about mundane things that were going on at the Hall with some of the masters and the students and stuff. It does say that they were having problems with some of the people who lived in Eureka though..."

"What kind of problems?" Katana asked.

"Hang on..." said Sara, reading further along. "Wow—apparently there was a backlash against all the Chinese people living in California at the time. They were trying to make them leave and go back to China—they even passed laws limiting what they could do!"

"That sounds like racism to me..." said Chris.

"It *is* racism!" said Katana. "So much for the land of the free!"

"They tried to close the Hall of the Dragon," said Sara. "But apparently Master Chow was able to talk to some people and get them to back down. Oh, this is interesting—one of the masters did end up leaving. Chang says that Master Wang—the chin-na master—was angry about the laws that were being passed so he went back to China. The guy who replaced him was a chin-na master *and* a hsing-i master."

"Did he teach hsing-i when he got here?" Chris asked.

"Um... no," Sara said after she read a bit more. "Chang says that since they already had tai chi, they didn't want to add hsing-i. So the guy only taught chin-na. But Chang does say that he found out Chow was a hsing-i master, too. He'd never known about it before."

"Wait a minute—Chow was a master of *six* arts? Wasn't he supposed to be the Master of the *Five* Arts? How could he possibly master so many?" Katana asked.

"Chatri said that hsing-i and tai chi both take a lifetime to master," Chris added.

"Yeah—Chang was confused by it, too," said Sara. "He couldn't believe Chow had never told him about hsing-i before. But that's it—there's nothing else interesting in these volumes."

"I wonder how far his memoirs go?" said Chris.

"Me too," Katana agreed. "Hopefully they go all the way to when Chang took over—then maybe we can find out why Chow left a whole year before the battle with Jaaku."

When they went to Sam's apartment for sushi a little later, Katana wanted desperately to ask her about the conversation she'd overheard between Nash and Osaka. But she didn't want Sam to know she'd been eavesdropping—even if it had been unintentional.

"So Nash tells me Chatri put you through the ringer, Kat," Sam said as they sat down to eat.

"He sure did," said Katana, shaking her head. "He made me do everything I've ever learned. And when we did chi fa, his aura totally disappeared at one point—do you know how he did that?"

"I was just discussing it with Master Nash," said Sam. "It's similar to hiding your center in regular pushing hands. Instead of extending your shen, like you normally do in chi fa, you have to draw it in. Nash said only a handful of masters in the whole world can do it."

"Can Nash do it?" Sara asked.

"Yeah, he can," said Sam. "He always does it during pushing hands. It makes it impossible to anticipate where he's going to push."

"Can you do chi fa, Sam?" asked Katana.

"I can do defense, not offense," said Sam. "Sending your chi along your shen like that is very advanced."

"Is Chatri really as powerful as Nash?" asked Chris.

"That's what Master Nash says," said Sam. "I don't know though—I think he's just more modest than Chatri. When

Master Hua and I were at Shaolin, Liang told us that many believe Nash may be a match for the headmaster. If that's true, I don't think Chatri can possibly be his equal."

"That's so cool," said Chris. "Nash is the best."

"So Kat, are you looking forward to meeting with Tanaka again?" asked Sam with an amused grin.

"No, I'm not," said Katana. "He's too weird."

"Wait—when are you going to see Tanaka?" asked Sara. "You didn't tell us anything about this!"

"Oh crap!" said Katana. "I forgot—me and Chris are staying at your house for the whole winter recess, and Tanaka's gonna see me while I'm there!"

"I love how I'm always the last one to know these things," Chris muttered through a mouthful of sushi.

CHAPTER 19
ARASHI ATTACKS

As the end of the first term approached, the teachers at Lincoln increased the workload in anticipation of exams. Katana had no time to search the archives any further. Finishing her own work wasn't a problem, but Chris's troubles with math had achieved epic proportions. While he'd always struggled, he'd never been in danger of failing—until now. Chris had received dismal grades on their last two tests—both in D territory—and his highest grade to date had been a B+. If he didn't pass his final exam with at least a B he would miss honors for the term and his ongoing enrollment at the Hall of the Dragon would be in jeopardy. Things were so bad that Sara and Katana were both spending more time with Chris than they were on their own work.

"Even if he passes this term, he's going to be totally screwed next semester," Sara commented late one night after Chris had gone to bed. She and Katana were finishing up their own homework.

"I know," said Katana with a sigh. "We haven't gotten to trig yet."

At Katana's suggestion, Chris scheduled some tutoring sessions with Master Fu. This seemed to do the trick—Master Fu had been a math whiz in school. With his flair for teaching, he was finally able to get Chris to understand the concepts. Katana hoped it wasn't too late.

Katana found out from Chris that Jimmy was still interested in her, and had taken her rejection extremely personally. Katana felt horrible—she would've been willing to go out with Jimmy if she had any interest in having a boyfriend. She went with him to the last school dance of the term and used the time to talk to him more about her feelings. Jimmy told her that he'd been worried she was only refusing him because she was interested in someone else. But Katana pointed out that she hadn't gone out with *anyone* the entire term. That seemed to make him feel much better. Katana promised him that once she felt like being with someone, *she* would ask *him* out. Jimmy was walking on air after that.

Sam eased up a little during the last couple of sparring practices. She was very happy with their progress and didn't feel they were lacking in any major area. She spent all of their time running matches and sparring with each of them herself.

Master Fu, on the other hand, had gone the other way. Katana thought his drive to prepare them for Golden Gate had become almost maniacal. Dana still couldn't land a gainer flash with the chains, but Master Fu was able to add the butterfly twist right at the end of their set. They were now landing their twists in front of the judges in splits, then powering up and running toward the rear of the stage as before.

Fu also added a move into the staff set where the kids had to throw their staves to each other. They had major problems with this move at first, though. Jelly was supposed to throw it to Sara, but he overshot his target one time and hit Katana in the head. Tim got stressed out another time and forgot where he was throwing—he threw to Sara instead of Jelly. Of course, Sara was throwing her staff to Tim, so the two staves collided in midair. Sara was too busy watching the collision, and forgot to catch Jelly's staff. She got hit in the face.

Master Fu still didn't change the broadsword set, however. In fact, Scott, Paul and Donnie were working on samurai sword during their wushu classes. Master Fu told them he was definitely going to replace broadsword with samurai sword the following year. He was having them try all sorts of new moves with that weapon to see how they would look in the team demo.

Katana and Dana also continued learning samurai sword, but Master Fu wanted them to keep doing whip chain in the demo. Their training with the sword was a little more relaxed and fun than what the boys were doing. Katana was perfectly happy with this decision. She enjoyed working with the sword, but she didn't think she'd ever like another weapon as much as whip chain.

Jelly discovered that he was a natural with nunchucks. Master Fu had him working a lot with Nathan, the new boy who'd demonstrated the weapon back at their first wushu class of the term. Nathan would show off a few moves, and Jelly would try to copy him. Not only was Jelly able to duplicate every spin, finger roll and release skill with ease, he eventually started making up his own moves. Soon Nathan was copying *him*.

"I wanna do this weapon in the demo!" Jelly begged after every class.

"You will..." said Master Fu.

"YES!"

"Next year."

They had their last lessons of the term, and Katana and her friends spent their final weekend with their noses buried in their books. Katana breezed through her exams that week as always. But she looked over at Chris every few minutes during their algebra exam. Chris scratched away feverishly on his exam paper, but Katana couldn't tell from his body language how he was doing. She was worried. Chris's expulsion from the Hall of the Dragon was the last thing she wanted.

"How'd you do?" she asked when they went to their lockers after the exam.

"Good," Chris replied, only a little uncertainly. "I just realized that I screwed up that last problem... I think. But other than that I did all right. Master Fu's tutoring sessions helped a lot."

Katana went up to her room with Sara when they got back to the Hall. She packed everything for their trip to Japan—they were taking a flight first thing in the morning. After that, they collected Chris and Jimmy and went to sit at the sushi bar for dinner. Jimmy had started eating sushi as an excuse to spend more time with Katana.

"This is it," said Terry-san as they sat down on the stools. "The end of another term. How did everyone's exams go?"

Katana knew he was really asking about Chris.

"Good," Chris replied. "I'm pretty sure I made honors for the term."

"That is excellent news," said Terry-san with a smile.

"Where are you going for the holidays, Terry-san?" Sara asked.

"I will be here for the next week or so, then I will be going home to Japan for the rest of the recess. I will be staying at Shaka-In for part of the time—Master Tanaka insisted that I come and prepare sushi for him. Master Nash has been taunting him for months, telling him about the new rolls I've been making."

"You're still coming back here—aren't you?" asked Chris.

"Yeah," Katana added, "Tanaka's probably gonna try to keep you at Shaka-In permanently."

Terry-san laughed. "I am sure he will—but don't worry, I'll be back. The Hall of the Dragon is my home now."

"Hey, maybe I'll see you at Shaka-In when I go for my evaluation!" said Katana.

"Yes, perhaps," said Terry-san. "Master Tanaka is very excited for that—I think he has something special planned."

"I thought he wasn't telling you anything anymore?" said Sara.

"He has started talking about Katana's evaluations now that everyone else knows about them," said Terry-san. "There is still something else going on, however—I cannot figure out what. I am hoping to get it out of Master Tanaka while I am there."

The kids finished their sushi and headed back to their rooms. Katana was planning on getting to bed early. But as they walked across the student lounge, Master Nash came in from the other end. "Katana—are you ready?"

"Uh... ready for what?"

"Samantha didn't tell you?" said Master Nash, raising an eyebrow. "I am bringing you to Shaka-In."

"Now?"

"Yes—we will be fading there. Master Tanaka wants you to join the monks for their morning workout. You'll be staying at the temple for a couple of days. Gerald will bring your things to the airport with Sara and Chris tomorrow morning. They'll catch up with you there."

Katana looked back pleadingly at Sara, Chris and Jimmy as she followed Master Nash out the door. But Sara only shrugged her shoulders. Chris said, "See you tomorrow... I guess..."

Katana followed Master Nash through the atrium and out the main doors. "Take a deep breath, Katana," he said when they got to the fountain. "Ready?"

Before Katana could answer, Master Nash had put his arm around her shoulder, enveloping her in his shen. Although she'd done this before, she wasn't sure she'd ever get used to it. It was the strangest sensation—she felt at once as if she were being stretched and falling from a great height. The courtyard appeared to spin around her for a moment, then she was lost in a vortex of color and sound. Suddenly the falling sensation ceased. The torii gate in front of the Shaka-In temple came into focus.

Master Tanaka rushed over to them from the main building. He was carrying what appeared to be a bundle of dirty laundry.

"Welcome back, Katana," he said. "Quickly, come with me— I will show you to the guest house. You must change into your robes."

Master Tanaka pulled her along by one hand. Katana looked back forlornly at Master Nash. He smiled and waved. Katana saw him fade away in a brilliant flash of light.

Master Tanaka led Katana across the grounds to a small building next to the main temple.

"We have no girls at Shaka-In," he explained. "We use this building primarily as a guesthouse for female visitors."

He led her inside to a room at the end of the hall. "This is where Master Samantha stayed last year. Quickly now, get changed and meet me outside." Master Tanaka bustled out of the room, closing the door behind him.

Katana looked around the small room in dismay. There was nothing but a small cot and a dingy window that looked out on the grounds.

She changed out of her jeans and tried to figure out how to put on the robes. It turned out to be simple. There was a pair of gray pants that tied in the front. The top reminded Katana of an ugly, frayed dress. She tied the black belt around her waist and went back outside.

"Quickly, quickly—Master Suzuki has probably already started," said Master Tanaka, jogging across the grounds. Katana followed him. She wished she hadn't eaten quite so much sushi at dinner.

They ran into the temple. Master Tanaka led Katana down the hallway to the main dojo. Katana got in line near the back of the class.

Master Suzuki had indeed already started. He was leading the monks through basics. Katana got into a low horse stance and followed along. As during her last visit, Katana's thighs were burning by the time they finished.

Master Tanaka went to the front of the room and bowed to Master Suzuki. He turned and spoke to the monks in Japanese. Katana didn't know what he was saying. But suddenly they moved to the back of the dojo and knelt down. Katana started to follow, but Master Tanaka stopped her. "Katana, please come forward. I will be conducting your evaluation in two parts. Today we will do part one. You will demonstrate your skills before the monks of Shaka-In. Tomorrow morning we will proceed with part two."

"And what happens then?" Katana asked apprehensively.

"That will be a surprise," said Master Tanaka with a wide grin. "Katana, to start I would like you to perform a kata of your choice. Begin when you are ready."

Katana decided to use the same form she was competing with this year—Kata Fourteen. She bowed and took a deep breath, trying to calm her nerves. Then she did the form with the same intensity she had at Eureka.

Master Tanaka clapped for her when she was done. "That was very strong, Katana. Next I would like you to defend freestyle against Master Suzuki. Please use only external techniques for now."

Master Suzuki attacked her over and over again. Katana defended successfully, sending Master Suzuki to the mat every time.

"Now you will spar," said Master Tanaka, "and you may use any of the chen do in your repertoire."

Katana squared off with Master Suzuki. "Go!" yelled Tanaka.

Master Suzuki launched at her immediately with a kick to the head. Katana dropped to sweep his other leg. But Master Suzuki leaped several feet into the air—avoiding her sweep—and shot a fireball at her.

Katana held out one hand to deflect the fireball, then took to the air herself. She threw a kick to Master Suzuki's head mid-flight. He blocked it. The moment they landed Katana threw her chi at him. He deflected her fireball with ease. Katana rushed in with a kicking sequence—finishing with an axe kick to his head. Suzuki dodged.

When Katana backed off, Master Suzuki jumped in, catching her with the leg scissors takedown. Katana hit the mat, but rolled out of the way before he was able to land a kick.

They both kicked to their feet. Katana could see Master Suzuki preparing to throw another fireball. She formed a ball of energy in her arms, caught his fireball and threw the flaming mass back at him. The fireball streaked toward Master Suzuki like a comet. He got into a low horse stance, holding out both hands to deflect it. It looked like he was standing in a strong wind for an instant, then the last remnant hit him in the chest. He'd weakened it enough that it only pushed him back a few inches.

Katana ran forward, throwing a series of kicks at Master

Suzuki—all of which he deflected. He took the initiative next and came at Katana with a series of punches. Katana kept herself just out of Suzuki's reach. Then she dropped to a horse stance and threw a palm strike to his chest. She bounced her chi through her palm and sent Master Suzuki sailing through the air. Katana thought for a moment that he was going to crash into the wall. But she'd forgotten that he could levitate. Suzuki turned so that his feet hit first. He ran along the wall several steps before jumping gracefully to the floor.

"Very impressive," said Master Tanaka, clapping for her again as Master Suzuki returned to them. "You learned that last technique from Master Nang, I assume?"

Katana's heart skipped a beat—she didn't know if Nash wanted Tanaka to know about her training in chi tao. She'd never discussed it with him. But she hardly had a choice after her display.

"Yes," she said. "Master Nang taught me that."

"Very secretive, Master Nang," Master Tanaka commented. "I met him after he went to Shaolin. He refused to come here and conduct a seminar. Oh well—in any event, Katana, we are almost done. If you would please demonstrate your double whip chain set, then we will be dismissing everyone for breakfast..."

"But I didn't bring my chains—I didn't bring anything actually," said Katana.

Master Tanaka yelled something in Japanese to one of the monks at the back of the room. The monk ran up and handed Katana a set of chains.

Katana did her set exactly as she was planning to do it at

Golden Gate—she even did her front aerial into a split in the beginning. She landed facing the monks and yelled out her judges introduction. Why not, she thought. They couldn't understand a word she was saying.

She opened with her double backflip—generating gasps from some of the monks. She turned from the flowers into her gainer flash, then went into the monk move. One of the monks whistled when she spun both chains in the same hand.

When she fell into her split, she had a thought. She powered up and went into the butterfly kicks. But at the end of the butterfly twist, she dropped to her split again without actually landing. Instead she levitated several inches off the ground. This time the monks broke out in uproarious applause, until Master Tanaka gave them a stern look.

Katana dropped to the mat, kicked one leg around and did the full body jumps. When she finished the form, the monks cheered for her again. This time, Tanaka joined in.

"Very good, Katana," he said. "I've never seen anyone do a whip chain set quite like that before."

Master Suzuki lined everyone up and Katana joined them for their sitting meditation exercise. She used the technique she'd learned from the archives to stimulate her prenatal chi.

Finally Master Tanaka dismissed them for the morning. Katana walked with him to the main dormitory. She joined the monks for breakfast, although she wasn't hungry yet.

She spent most of the day with Master Tanaka. They took a walk through the forest around the temple grounds, talking again about Jaaku's history. Katana told him what she'd learned from

Sam and Master Nash. She told him about Jaaku and the Immortal Master being archenemies, and that Master Chow really had trained with the Immortal Master. She also told him about Jaaku learning dim mak from Master Tong.

By the end of the afternoon, Katana decided that she liked Master Tanaka. He was unusual, but he was also very humble and down to earth—unlike Master Kim and Master Chatri. He gave Katana the impression that he genuinely cared about the monks at his temple—and even about her.

She joined the monks for their evening workout right before dinner. After that she went back to the guesthouse and went to bed. She was very much looking forward to Chris and Sara's arrival—she didn't have a change of clothes or even her toothbrush.

But as much as she'd enjoyed her day at Shaka-In, she did not enjoy the night. The little cot was lumpy and uncomfortable; Katana had an awful time getting to sleep. She dozed off for a few minutes at a time, but couldn't fall into a deep sleep.

She woke up one time and thought that she must've heard a loud noise or had a bad dream—she was wide awake now. She felt like something was wrong—a sense of foreboding came over her. She looked out the little window, but couldn't see much through the grime.

Katana got out of bed. She pulled on her jeans, and walked down the hall, out to the grounds. The temple complex was awash in light—the moon was half full. She walked toward the temple, then across to the dormitory. The place was utterly deserted.

But Katana found this strange—she'd seen monks walking the grounds even during the morning and evening workouts. And the monk who'd shown them around over the summer had told them that they patrolled at all hours ever since the Arashi attacks earlier in the year.

She walked around the complex for a while longer, but found nothing amiss. She decided to go back to bed. But as she walked inside the guesthouse, she found herself standing face to face with a figure in samurai armor.

Katana yelled in surprise—instinctively throwing a massive fireball at the Arashi. She turned and bolted out the door.

She ran toward the dormitory—she had to wake the monks. But when she turned to look over her shoulder, the Arashi was right behind her. She could see from his shen that he was about to throw a fireball. She stopped only just in time—she turned and deflected the fireball an instant before it hit her.

She realized that normal strikes or kicks wouldn't do her much good. She couldn't get through the Arashi's armor. But in a flash of insight, she ran directly at him. She jumped into the air, pulling her knees into her chest. She kicked with both feet. At the moment her feet should have connected, however, the Arashi disappeared.

Katana landed on her side in the dirt. She sprang to her feet and looked around frantically, but couldn't see the Arashi.

She ran toward the dormitory again. But suddenly the Arashi appeared directly in front of her. He drew his sword and sliced it through the air, launching a line of fire at her. Katana tried to deflect the fire like a chi hit—it worked. The flame dissipated before it hit her.

The Arashi advanced—Katana didn't know what to do. He was standing between her and the dormitory. She bolted the other way, past the guesthouse, toward the burnt-out building. She stopped right in front of the structure—she was almost to the edge of the grounds.

She turned—the Arashi was almost on her. He threw another fireball. Katana gathered a ball of energy between her arms, caught his chi, and hurled it back at the Arashi. The tail streaming off the fireball was brighter than ever in the darkness. But the Arashi held out one hand and deflected it completely. Whoever this was, he was stronger than Master Suzuki.

The Arashi strode forward—Katana was cornered. There was nowhere else to run. Traipsing through the forest would only slow her down.

The Arashi lunged to grab her. Katana turned into him and grabbed his arm, flipping him onto the ground. She turned to run toward the dormitory again, but the Arashi grabbed her feet. Katana fell flat on her face.

She stood up at the same time as the Arashi. He lunged at her again—this time Katana punched him, bouncing her chi against his chest plate. The Arashi flew through the air. He smashed through the wall of the burnt-out building. Katana could hear a thud as he hit another wall somewhere inside.

She turned once again to run toward the dormitory—she needed to alert the monks. But then she heard a creaking sound, and a loud crash. The front of the building collapsed.

Katana watched in horror. The Arashi was still inside. She could hear a groan—the voice was male. "I am coming, Musashi —I will be with you soon..."

Katana recognized that voice—it was Tanaka.

She ran around to the other side of the building. Here, the structure had only partially collapsed. Katana climbed over the rubble. Sure enough, Master Tanaka was lying there on his back. His helmet had fallen off. An enormous wooden beam had fallen across his chest.

"What the hell!" Katana blurted out. "You're an Arashi?! I trusted you—Nash trusted you..."

"No, Katana," Master Tanaka wheezed. His voice sounded weaker now. "I am no Arashi. I was trying to..."

Katana didn't find out what it was he was trying to do. He closed his eyes and lost consciousness.

"Master Tanaka!" Katana screamed. "Master Tanaka!"

It was no use—he was out cold. Katana had to help him. But she didn't understand what was going on—was he really an Arashi? At that moment it didn't matter. He was trapped under the wooden beam and it was up to her to save him.

She got the best footing she could in the rubble, raised up her hand and drove her palm into the beam. She bounced her chi against the wood as fast as she could. The wood snapped in half with a loud pop.

Katana wedged her hands under Tanaka's upper arms. She tried to pull him out of the rubble. But between his weight and the awkward angle she had to pull from, she couldn't budge him.

"Damn!" she yelled as the building creaked ominously. But

then she remembered another lesson from her time with Master Nang.

Katana reached under Tanaka's arms again. She focused on pushing her chi against him very slowly. Finally she was able to pull him free. But as she slid his body out of the rubble, Katana heard a creaking noise farther inside the building. The rest of the structure was about to collapse.

She pulled him out and got him clear of the building just in time. It collapsed the rest of the way, a section of roof falling right where Master Tanaka had been trapped.

Katana bolted toward the dormitory to get help. She ran into Master Suzuki halfway there, accompanied by several other monks. Luckily one of them spoke English. Katana explained to him what had happened, and he translated for Master Suzuki.

"Master Suzuki says that Master Tanaka wanted to trick you into believing he was an Arashi, to see how you would react in a real confrontation," the monk explained. "He discussed his plan with Master Nash, and ordered the nightly patrols to stay inside the temple building during the exercise."

Katana understood. She explained that she hadn't been inside the guesthouse when Master Tanaka showed up. "His trick worked—I thought he really was an Arashi!"

Master Suzuki had Tanaka brought up to the medical building—although to Katana, it looked like little more than a hut. Like Nash, Master Suzuki was skilled in the healing arts. Master Tanaka had a concussion, two broken ribs, and a broken leg. But Master Suzuki assured everyone he'd make a full recovery.

Master Nash showed up a little later. "I warned him evaluating you in this manner could prove dangerous," he said to Katana. "But he insisted—he wanted to see how you would react in the face of a real attack. I guess he has his answer."

"Master Nash, at one point he threw a line of fire at me with his sword—I thought only the Arashi could do that?" said Katana.

"Tanaka played with that technique after the Arashi attacks here last year. We suspected that they were simply using the sword as a focal point for their chi—it turns out we were right. Tanaka was the one who figured out how to do it," Master Nash explained.

Sara and Chris showed up later that afternoon with Mr. Brown. They went to check in on Master Tanaka, but he was still out cold. Master Suzuki assured them, however, that he was in no danger and was simply asleep.

They went back to Sara's house. Katana was grateful for a hot shower and a change of clothes.

Mr. Brown updated them on the Arashi assassin after dinner that night. The FBI still didn't have any leads in the case. There'd been only one more attack—this time in China. Mr. Brown told them it was a master who taught near the monastery in Shanxi Province.

Katana went back to Shaka-In with Mr. Brown the next day. Tanaka was awake now and quite grateful to Katana for saving his life. Master Suzuki had told him everything that happened. Tanaka knew that if Katana had chosen to run for help, the building probably would've collapsed on him.

"Luckily for me, Katana, your skill with the chen do rivals that of Master Kosho," he said with a weak smile.

Katana was glad this experience was behind her. She enjoyed the next several days immensely, hanging out with Sara and Chris, free of any worry greater than what they'd be eating for Christmas dinner.

Katana and Chris went with Sara to her karate class several times a week for the remainder of the winter recess. Master Nakamura was there most days. She was home for the holidays, and was heading back to Bangkok a week before the kids were due back at the Hall of the Dragon.

They invited Katana, Sara and Chris to come in and train with Komatsu during the day a few times. He was getting ready for a big tournament in Tokyo the following month. Komatsu gave Katana a lot of pointers in her sparring technique. In return she tried to teach him the gainer flash. This turned out not to be so easy. He could already do a back handspring, and with Katana's help he learned how to do a backflip and a flash kick. But he needed the round-off to generate enough momentum to make it over backwards. He had no luck doing it from standing or walking forward.

Mr. Brown brought them up to Shaka-In one more time before they left so they could say goodbye to Master Tanaka. Katana was greatly relieved to see that he was on his feet again, albeit on crutches. Despite the fact that she'd *saved* his life, she knew that she was the one who'd put it in jeopardy in the first place.

When she told Sara about this, however, Sara said, "Yeah, well that's what he gets for masquerading as an Arashi! That was a stupid thing to do."

Mr. Brown brought them up to Tokyo by bullet train at the end of the recess. There, they boarded the plane back to San Francisco. As they made their way up the aisle to their seats, Katana saw Master Rodriguez putting his bag in the overhead compartment. Katana said hi to him, and he smiled at her. For a moment she didn't know if he recognized her.

"It's Katana, right?" he asked. "What brings you to Japan?"

"I stayed with my best friend for the holidays," she explained. "How about you?"

"My instructor lives in Tokyo," he said. "I try to come back a few times a year to train with him." The people behind her were pushing Katana up the aisle.

"See you at Golden Gate!" she said.

"Who was that?" Chris asked when they got to their seats.

"Joe Rodriguez," said Sara. "He's the guy who runs Golden Gate—remember he lectured Kat about not using levitation back at the tournament in Eureka?"

"Oh yeah," said Chris. "I remember. He was a jerk!"

"Well, that's it, isn't it, Kat?" said Sara.

"What?" Katana asked.

"Tanaka was your last evaluation, right?"

"Oh—no, actually. Remember, Nash said that the headmaster of Shaolin would probably evaluate me, too, when they come to California with their wonder kid," Katana replied.

"Hopefully *he* won't try to attack you in your sleep," Chris commented.

"Somehow I doubt it," said Sara. "Only Tanaka would do something crazy like that."

It was a ten-hour flight back to San Francisco. It felt to Katana like an eternity. She was uncomfortable and bored out of her mind. Fading with Master Nash to Shaka-In hadn't been pleasant either, but at least it was fast.

They finally got off the plane and went to collect their luggage. Katana spotted her suitcase on the conveyor belt. When she went to grab it, someone almost trampled her—it was Master Rodriguez.

"Oh, sorry!" he said.

Katana grabbed her suitcase and turned around to find Sara and Chris—instead an Arashi appeared in a flash of light not ten feet away. For an instant she had a crazy thought that it was Master Tanaka dressed in armor again—but the Arashi drew his sword and lunged at Master Rodriguez. He stabbed him in the chest, then turned and disappeared in another flash of light.

Several people screamed as Rodriguez hit the floor—there was blood everywhere.

Katana was stunned—within seconds a dozen airport security guards descended on the scene. They pushed people away from Rodriguez.

One of the guards came up to Katana. "Did you see anything? Did you see it happen?"

"Yes... I saw..." Katana stammered.

The guard grabbed her by one arm. "Come with me, please."

He escorted her to a room on the other side of the concourse. Several other guards were escorting people into the room as well.

As she sat there, Katana heard the other witnesses talking to each other.

"Did you see it?"

"I only saw him fall."

"I saw some whacko dressed in armor stab him with a sword!"

"There was no sword—someone shot him!"

Katana kept her mouth shut. Nobody else had seen the Arashi appear out of nowhere, and she was quite certain that none of them would know about the Arashi in the first place.

Nearly twenty minutes went by. Finally a man wearing a suit walked in with Master Nash.

"Master Nash!" Katana exclaimed, running over to him.

"Katana, come with us please," he said. He directed her out of the room.

The other witnesses were clamoring to leave as well. But the man in the suit said to them, "An FBI investigator will be here any minute now—he'll take your statements and then you'll be free to go."

"How did you get here so quickly?" Katana asked as she followed them to another room farther down the concourse.

"I was already here, Katana," said Master Nash. "Gerald fell ill, so I came to pick you up today."

Katana followed the two men into the room. They sat down at a conference table.

"Katana, this is agent MacGregor with the FBI. He wants to ask you some questions about what you saw today," said Master Nash.

"Hi, Katana," said MacGregor. "Please tell me what happened, from the beginning."

Katana told him everything, which wasn't very much.

"Katana, do you think it was an Arashi?" MacGregor asked when she was done.

"Definitely," she said. "He was wearing samurai armor, and he faded right in front of Rodriguez."

"Could you see his aura?" asked Master Nash.

Katana had to think about this for a minute. She was so used to seeing people's auras that she didn't consciously notice it anymore. But she *hadn't* seen an aura around this Arashi.

"No," she said. "Definitely not."

"Are you certain, Katana?" asked Master Nash. "Is it possible you just didn't notice it?"

"I'm certain," she replied. "The Arashi didn't have an aura."

MacGregor and Master Nash got up from the table. "Thank you, Jordan," said MacGregor, shaking his hand. "I'd better see how Vasquez is doing with the other witnesses."

He walked out of the room.

"It seems the assassin has struck again," Master Nash said with a long sigh.

"That was the assassin?!" asked Katana. "He's—the assassin is an Arashi?"

"So it would appear," said Master Nash with a frown. "It doesn't make much sense. But it would appear someone from inside Jaaku's organization has betrayed him."

"But if that was the assassin... was Master Rodriguez an Arashi?"

Master Nash let out a long sigh. "No, Katana, he was not. The Arashi stabbed him in the heart—he died almost instantly. But his body did *not* vaporize. It seems our assassin made a mistake."

Master Nash led her back into the concourse. There was an enormous crowd of police and media swarming through the airport. Katana followed Nash out to the parking lot. Chris and Sara were waiting for them in the school SUV. They sat in silence for the entire drive back to the Hall.

"This is crazy," said Chris when they got up to the girls' room. "The Arashi assassin is... an Arashi?!"

"That's what it looks like," said Katana.

"But how come you couldn't see his aura?" Sara asked. "He faded there, he was obviously an Arashi—his aura should have been really strong, right?"

"I would think," said Katana. "Unless he knew how to hide it."

"But didn't Sam say only a handful of masters in the whole world know how to do that?" asked Chris.

"Yeah," said Katana. "That's what she said."

"What I don't understand is why Jaaku doesn't just kill the assassin," said Sara. "He's got the prenatal chi of every Arashi, right? So can't he do the death touch on the assassin?"

"Apparently not," said Katana. "But I have no idea why."

CHAPTER 20
THE HEALING ARTS

Katana had a lot to think about over the next several days. Witnessing Rodriguez's murder had shaken her. She was having nightmares again. Instead of seeing her parents die, she dreamed about the assassin killing the people she cared about most—Chris and Sara, her aunt, and even Osaka.

On top of that, her anxiety about Jaaku returned in full force. She'd been busy enough during the first term that she hadn't thought about it much since her blowout with Chris. But being an eyewitness to one of the Arashi attacks brought the issue back to the forefront of her thoughts. Jaaku had to be stopped. She knew all too well that people were dying—countless people—so Jaaku could go on living. Yet seeing someone die at the hands of an Arashi—even one who wasn't acting at Jaaku's behest—made the situation much more real.

She also continued to feel bad for nearly killing Master Tanaka. But at the same time she derived grim satisfaction from the knowledge that she could now hold her own against an Arashi. She was no longer that frightened little girl who'd faced three of them in the tai chi dojo two years ago and been unable to defend herself. Tanaka wasn't a *real* Arashi, but she hadn't known that at the time. And he was certainly powerful.

She'd experienced two Arashi attacks in rapid succession—one real, one fake. But both had the effect of reigniting her drive for more power. Yes, she'd held her own against Master Tanaka, but she knew that wasn't enough. Jaaku was much more powerful than Tanaka, the Arashi, or even Master Nash.

The night they returned to the Hall of the Dragon, Katana dragged Chris and Sara back down to the archive room. There was an enormous amount of material they'd yet to explore. Katana still hoped to find something useful. But that night, at least, they came up empty-handed. Not a single box or crate contained anything that looked interesting enough to bring upstairs.

On Monday morning, Master Nash asked Katana to stay behind after tai chi.

"How are you doing?" he asked.

"Okay, I guess," she replied. "Seeing the Arashi attack was scary—I've been having nightmares about it."

"Witnessing such violence is always traumatic, Katana," said Master Nash. "You should consider seeing one of the counselors at Lincoln. As you know from Ms. Brown's experience last year, they can be quite helpful."

"That's not a bad idea," Katana answered thoughtfully. "When I first heard about the attacks, I thought someone out there was on our side—I thought it was good that someone was killing off the Arashi. But now... after seeing the attack, I'm not so sure. Whoever the assassin is, he has no *right* to go around killing people—no matter who they are."

"I agree," said Master Nash. "And this time he killed an innocent man."

"But I've also been thinking about that night with Tanaka—I almost killed *him*. And even though I thought he was an Arashi —if I *had* killed him, I wouldn't be any better than the assassin... would I?"

"Katana, there is a very big difference between those two cases. You were acting in self-defense, the assassin most certainly is not," said Master Nash.

"So killing someone in self-defense is okay? That still doesn't seem right to me..." said Katana.

"No, Katana, it's never 'okay.' But if someone attacks you with deadly force, you have the right, both legally and ethically, to respond in kind. Certainly killing your attacker is not desirable, but when faced with such a situation, it may be unavoidable."

"I guess you're right," said Katana. "And I wasn't *trying* to kill Tanaka—I was just trying to get away from him."

Master Nash looked at Katana for a long moment. "Katana, the other reason I wanted to talk to you is that it turns out you're going to have one more evaluation..."

"You mean with the headmaster of Shaolin?"

"No—the headmaster will not be here until the middle of

February. But there will be another master coming to the Hall of the Dragon this weekend. Master Dasari is a master of kokawa, which is indigenous to the Saharan region of Africa," Master Nash explained.

"Africa?! There's a temple in Africa?" Katana asked.

"No, there is not. Master Dasari turned up here during the winter recess. He has expressed an interest in joining the Shaolin temple network, but was uncertain how to approach the head-master. He heard that the Hall of the Dragon has always been the most... liberal of the temples, so he decided to approach us first.

"We talked for hours—he was very interested when he heard of your abilities. I proposed that he work with you while he's here. He was thrilled.

"You will be meeting with him this Saturday at eleven, here in the tai chi dojo. Like Master Nang, Master Dasari will be training you privately in his art," said Master Nash with a smile. "He was uncomfortable with a formal evaluation, so I suggested that a private lesson would be more to your liking anyway."

Master Nash was right—Katana was very excited about her lesson with Master Dasari that weekend. She'd never known that any martial arts had developed independently in Africa. She couldn't wait to see what it was like.

Later that morning, however, it was Chris's turn for some excitement. The kids got to their math class and the teacher handed back their final exams. Chris had earned an A, making honors for the term. In his excitement about avoiding expulsion from the Hall of the Dragon, he stood up on his chair and shouted for joy. The teacher was not amused. She gave him a detention.

"That was ridiculous," Chris said as they walked out the door after class. "Who punishes someone for being excited about making honor roll?"

"Apparently Mrs. Stevens does," Sara replied.

As it turned out, this wasn't the last of Chris's misfortunes that day. Chris, Sara and Katana were planning to go straight down to the archives after dinner. But Chris got held up on the way out of the cafeteria—Olivia wanted to talk to him.

Katana and Sara went downstairs without him. They'd plowed through several shelves, collecting a pile of interesting documents by the time Chris walked in. He was very grumpy.

"What's up?" Sara asked.

"Olivia broke up with me," he said, plopping down on a crate.

"Aw, that sucks!" said Katana. "Why'd she do it?"

"I don't know," Chris muttered.

"She must have given you a reason," said Sara.

"I guess she thinks I'm spending all my time with the two of you."

"That's nothing new," Katana observed.

"It is though," said Sara. "We've been spending loads more time together than usual, digging through all the crap down here, and then locked up in our room. I can see why she might find that a little suspicious..."

"Oh, well," said Chris. "You two find anything interesting yet?"

Chris joined in the search. Several minutes later Katana discovered a scroll that warranted closer inspection.

"Hey Sara," she said as she brought it over to where Sara was rummaging through a large crate. "What is this?"

Sara looked at it. "The title says 'Iron Shirt.'" She read through the scroll for a minute. "Hey—this is how Nang was able to do that thing with the spear in his throat!"

"We're definitely taking this," said Katana, throwing it in the pile. They put everything in a wooden crate and brought it upstairs.

"So how does the iron shirt work?" asked Chris once they'd locked themselves in the girls' room.

Sara pulled the scroll out of the crate. "You have to focus your chi on a given part of your body," she said tentatively. "You have to tense the muscles in the same spot."

Katana ran her fingers down her throat. "But there aren't any muscles there..."

"It doesn't matter," said Sara. "This says you have to tense the muscles in the same area, so for the throat, you would tighten your neck muscles. But you can do this to any area of your body. The scroll gives an example with your stomach. It says to tighten your abdominal muscles and focus your chi to your stomach. Then someone can punch you or stab you and it won't hurt."

"I wanna try this," said Katana. "There's no special breathing you have to do? No certain way of holding your arms or anything?"

"Nope!" said Sara. "Just tighten the muscles and focus your chi."

"I'm gonna try it with my stomach," said Katana. She took a deep breath, tightened her stomach muscles as much as she could, and focused her chi flow.

"Chris—punch me."

"Kat, I'm not gonna punch you in the stomach..."

Sara rolled her eyes. "Fine, I'll do it!"

She walked over and punched Katana. "Ow!" she yelled, shaking her hand.

"That was cool!" said Katana. "That didn't hurt at all!"

"It hurt me!" Sara retorted. "It felt like I punched a brick wall!"

"I wanna try this!" said Chris.

"No way—it's my turn," said Sara. "You were too squeamish to punch Kat, so I get to go next."

Chris didn't argue.

Sara focused for a minute. "All right, Kat—do it."

Katana decided to use a palm strike after seeing how painful it was for Sara. She wound up and hit Sara in the stomach.

"Abs of steel," Katana observed.

"Can I try now?" asked Chris.

"Yeah, I guess," said Sara.

Katana hit him with the same result.

"This is neat as hell," Chris declared.

"I wanna try it in the throat," said Katana.

"That's nuts, Kat," Sara replied. "The stomach's one thing, but getting hit in the throat could kill you if you do this wrong."

"Stop worrying," said Katana. She tightened the muscles in

371

her neck as much as possible, focused her chi in her throat, and then craned her neck. "Hit me."

"Kat—come on," pleaded Sara. "This is a bad idea."

"I'll do it," said Chris. He pulled his fist back, took a deep breath, and punched.

Katana smiled. "I didn't feel a thing." Chris shook his hand in pain. Neither Sara nor Chris wanted to risk attempting the throat shot, but they both tried it to the stomach again.

"Too bad we don't have a spear," said Katana. "I'd definitely try that trick Nang did now."

Chris had to serve his detention after school on Wednesday. Katana and Sara walked him to the office on their way to catch the bus.

"I still can't believe Stevens gave him a detention," said Katana as they continued outside.

"I guess," said Sara, "but Chris *did* look like an idiot jumping on his chair like that. He probably deserved it."

They had wushu that afternoon. Katana couldn't wait to get to class. Master Fu had started her and Dana on a new form with the samurai sword. It was the first sport karate form Katana had ever learned, and she was enjoying it immensely.

She also liked watching Paul, Donnie and Scott practice their routine. Master Fu had them working on a move where the three of them had to throw the swords to each other, similar to what the kids were doing in the demo with their staves. But they had to make the swords spin around like helicopter blades as they threw them, completing two full rotations in the air.

"That move is going to look amazing in the demo next year," said Dana.

Katana started to respond, but was suddenly overcome by a wave of anxiety. She felt dizzy and had to sit down. She thought she might faint. But her vision wasn't going dark—instead, she saw herself being shoved into the lockers at school by Ed Golia. She grabbed him, and threw him to the ground. Then Tommy Cosgrove punched her in the face. She threw her chi at him, knocking him into the lockers.

"Kat—are you okay?!" asked Dana.

"What? Oh, yeah..." said Katana, shaking her head. She got back to her feet. What had just happened? She knew Chris must have had a fight with Ed and Tommy. Somehow she'd seen it. She ran up to Chris and Jimmy's room as soon as Master Fu dismissed them for the day.

"Hey, Kat," said Jimmy when she walked in.

"Jimmy—did Chris come back yet?"

"Um... I don't think so," he said. "I just got back from Osaka's class—I haven't seen him. He had detention today, right?"

"Yeah, he did," said Katana.

She waited in their room, playing video games with Jimmy.

Finally Chris walked in. His lip was bleeding.

"Are you okay?!" asked Katana.

"Yeah," said Chris grumpily, throwing his book bag down on the floor and collapsing in his bed.

"What happened?!" asked Jimmy, abandoning the video game when he saw Chris's face.

"He got into a fight with Ed and Tommy," said Katana.

"Yeah—how'd you know?" asked Chris.

"I saw it..."

"You were at Lincoln?" asked Chris, clearly confused.

"No, dummy—I mean I saw it, like in my head. I was in Fu's class, and I blacked out or something. Ed pushed you into the lockers, and you threw him down. But then Tommy punched you in the face and you hit him with a fireball."

"Kat... how the hell do you know that?" Chris asked, sitting up now. "You actually saw the fight?"

"Yeah, I did," said Katana. "I wonder if it happened because our chi is mixed..."

"How is that possible?" asked Chris. Jimmy sat there looking at the two of them, totally dumbfounded.

"I don't know," said Katana. "But I bet it's like what happens with the twins... Sara was talking to Olivia one time, and she said that her and Sierra could sense when the other one was in trouble."

"That's right—Olivia told me about that. She said a dog chased her sister up a tree one time and she knew it even though she was miles away," said Chris. "Maybe we should ask Osaka about it. He was the one who told you about our chi being mixed in the first place. Maybe he'll know what happened."

"That's a good idea," Katana agreed. "I'll ask him during our private tomorrow. Hey—what was the fight about, anyway?"

"Golia was starting crap about Olivia breaking up with me," said Chris with a scowl. "I guess he heard it was because I was spending so much time locked in the room with you and Sara."

"Chris—you didn't *start* the fight... did you?"

"No..." Chris answered sheepishly. "I told Ed the real reason Olivia broke up with me... was because of all the time I was spending with his mother."

"Oh! Well, that would do it!" said Katana brightly. Jimmy sniggered loudly.

At the end of their private lesson on Thursday, Katana asked Osaka about the episode with Chris. Osaka looked from her to Chris for a moment. "This does not surprise me, Katana. If anything, I'm surprised it has never happened before. When your chi mixes with someone else's, a powerful link is formed. You can sense each other's emotions and moods, and sometimes see what the other is seeing. Usually the effect is only that profound during times of extreme stress—such as a fight," Osaka explained.

"That happens with Sierra and Olivia, too," said Sara. "But their chi isn't mixed the way Kat's and Chris's is... is it?"

"Not exactly," said Osaka. "Identical twins share the same prenatal chi, so they have a similar connection. But in Chris and Katana's case, *all* of their chi has mixed, so the effect will tend to be more pronounced."

"It's good to know I wasn't going crazy," said Katana.

The kids went down to search the archives again after dinner. Katana and Chris talked more about what Osaka told them while they worked.

"I bet the only reason it never happened before is because we were always *together* when something stressful happened," said Katana. "We were together when the Arashi came to steal the scroll, and when Jaaku showed up last year, too. And we've always been together when Ed and Tommy started crap with us—at least until now."

"Yeah, and nothing very exciting *ever* happened back in Vermont," Chris replied. "But you know, I think this *has* happened before."

"When?"

"Remember when you first said you were going to face Jaaku someday? Right after we found out the truth about your parents. I felt it too. I wonder if that was the same kind of thing, you know?" said Chris.

"You're right," said Katana. "That would make sense. And now that I think about it... that night at the dance, too, when you made out with Sierra. I felt all panicky right before you told us what happened. I must've been feeling what you were feeling."

Chris thought about it for a minute. "There was one other time," he said. "Last year, when you went to the Fall Ball, I had this picture in my head of the Arashi showing up. And that was when you went to the meeting and found out Sato was alive."

"That's true," Katana agreed. "I'd forgotten about that."

"Hey guys!" said Sara. "Check this out!"

"What is it?" asked Katana, moving closer to get a look.

Sara was skimming through a leather-bound manuscript. "The rest of this crate was full of financial records. But I found this at the bottom. I think it's a manual of the healing arts," she said. "Look—it has the meridian diagrams again, but this time there are lots of points drawn on each meridian. I think those are the points Nash must use for acupuncture and stuff."

Katana thumbed through the manuscript herself. "I think you're right."

Sara took the manual back and flipped to the beginning. "It says here that you have to use needles to get the full effect, but for a lot of the stuff you can *touch* the points—it calls them pressure points."

"We've got enough stuff here," said Katana. "Let's bring everything upstairs."

They had a close call on their way to the girls' room. Katana and Sara had just emerged from the stairwell into the short hallway that led to the main building. Master Daniels walked out of the student lounge.

"What are you girls up to?" he asked. "Students aren't allowed in the tunnels."

Katana pushed the door closed behind her, before Chris could walk through with the crate of documents.

"Um..." said Sara. "We were just..."

"Going for a walk," Katana finished for her.

Daniels stared at them for a moment. "Right. A walk. See that you keep your walking above ground from now on."

"We will!" said Sara. She and Katana walked past Daniels, up the steps.

"Oh crap," Katana exclaimed once they'd got to the third floor.

"We're screwed if he finds Chris," Sara replied.

But they had nothing to worry about. Chris walked in from the other end of the hall a moment later.

"How'd you avoid Daniels," Sara asked once they were inside the girls' room.

"I ran down the stairs when I heard his voice," said Chris. "Good thing, too—he opened the door and looked around for a minute. He didn't see me, though."

Katana dug the pressure point manuscript out of the crate. "Let's try something," she suggested.

"I don't know, Kat," said Sara. "There's a lot more text in this than there was in the other meridian manuscript. I can't read all of it. We should probably have Sean translate before we start playing with any of it."

"Yeah... good idea," Chris replied. "I'm betting some of this would be dangerous if you did it wrong."

Katana agreed—reluctantly. She was very eager to learn whatever techniques this document contained. Sara brought the manuscript to school the next day and gave it to Sean during study hall. At Katana's urging, he promised to get it translated as soon as possible.

Katana went up to the tai chi dojo on Saturday. Master Dasari was waiting for her with Master Nash. Master Dasari was only a little taller than Katana. He was nearly bald—his hair was so short, it almost looked like it had been painted on his skull. His skin tone was much darker than Master Nash's—he had the darkest complexion she'd ever seen. And he spoke with an accent that might have been French.

"Greetings, Katana," he said with a big smile as he shook her hand. "Master Nash has been telling me about some of the things you have learned with the other headmasters. I understand that you've had some training in Brazilian jiu jitsu?"

"Yes," said Katana. "I did some grappling with my instructor back home, and I learned a little more when Master Santos came here a few months ago."

"Excellent," replied Master Dasari. "In my art of kokawa, we do a form of wrestling that is very similar to Brazilian jiu jitsu."

"I never knew any martial arts came from Africa," said Katana.

"Oh yes," said Master Dasari, "there are many. As with the Chinese arts, some use strikes and kicks, and others, like kokawa, are based more on grappling skills."

"Does kokawa have a chen do?" Katana asked uncertainly.

"Yes, we fade, like most other jiu jitsu and judo styles. Please, join me on the mat, and let's see what you can do."

As Katana got down on her knees, she was immediately impressed with the strength of Master Dasari's aura. Chatri was stronger, but not by much.

Katana took the initiative. She grabbed Master Dasari and pulled him to the mat, swinging her leg over to put him in the mount. As she'd experienced with Master Santos, she felt like Dasari was letting her control the match. She tried to put him into the armbar she'd learned, and almost thought she had it—but suddenly Dasari rolled her over and put her in his guard.

They rolled around for a few minutes, until finally Katana was able to set up a chokehold. She was about to squeeze her arms together when Master Dasari pushed a spot on her elbow. It was excruciatingly painful. Katana felt like she'd smashed her funny bone. She released the chokehold reflexively, and in a flash Master Dasari had her in an armbar.

Katana tapped his leg, and Dasari released her.

"You move very fluently for someone who's only had a few lessons," Master Dasari complimented her.

"Thanks—what did you do to my elbow?" she asked. "That hurt a *lot!*"

"In kokawa, we study nerve endings in addition to grappling," Master Dasari explained. "As you can see, they can come in very useful in a wrestling match."

For the rest of the lesson, Master Dasari showed Katana dozens of different nerve endings. He pushed each one on her first, so she knew exactly where it was, then she applied it on him. Katana was amazed—there were nerve endings on both sides of the neck, down both arms, along both legs and at some points in the back. She wondered if these had any correlation to the pressure points they'd found in the new manuscript.

"Be careful, Katana," Master Dasari said at the end of the lesson. "Using these nerve endings is against the rules in most jiu jitsu and judo competitions."

Once Master Nash had dismissed her, Katana ran down to the wushu dojo; she knew that's where she'd find everyone.

"Hey, Kat—how'd it go?" asked Sara.

"It was really cool," said Katana. She showed Sara, Chris and Scott everything Dasari had taught her. The group had fun trying to hit each nerve ending. Scott proved much too ticklish for them to experiment on, however. Katana used Chris to demonstrate most of the points.

Dana and Jelly kept working on their weapon sets. Dana was still trying to get a gainer flash kick with the chains, and Jelly was working on a brand new move. He was jumping straight up and spinning around clockwise for three full rotations, kicking with his right leg on the final rotation.

"What's that move?" Katana asked him a while later.

"It's called a 1080—but I can't get it."

"It looks good to me..." said Katana.

"No—I can do the kick, but Fu wants me to do it when we throw the staves up in the air, instead of the standing flash," said Jelly. "And I can't get it!"

"Why not?" asked Katana.

"Cuz the kick makes me wicked dizzy," he replied. "I miss the staff every time."

Katana watched while he practiced. Sure enough, he landed the kick, but missed the stick by a wide margin. It crashed down on his head.

Katana went through her set with chains a few times. She felt totally confident, even with the new moves in place. She was getting excited for Golden Gate.

Sara was still working on her staff set, so Katana tried to teach Chris a gainer flash. But like Komatsu, he had great difficulty with this. His regular flash kick had continued to improve, but without the round-off, he couldn't get enough height to land the trick. He kept doing a back handspring instead.

They finished up and Katana went with Sara and Chris up to Sam's apartment.

"How'd it go with Dasari today?" she asked.

"Really good," said Katana. She told her about the lesson. "The nerve endings were cool," she concluded. "I'm sure he was letting me get him in the choke. But once he hit that spot on my elbow, I couldn't help letting go."

"Hmm," said Sam with a frown as she ate a piece of sushi.

"What?" asked Sara.

"I don't know—there's something about Dasari that doesn't sit well with me," she said.

"Like what?" asked Chris.

"I don't know—he seemed nice, but there's something up with him. I can't put my finger on it."

"He's pretty powerful," said Katana. "His aura's almost as strong as Chatri's."

"I know—I saw that too," said Sam. "Nash won't tell us much about him, but there's some connection between him and the Arashi."

"The Arashi?!" asked Sara. "You don't think he is one... do you?"

"No, I don't—it's not that," said Sam. "Nash said he has some contacts somehow, and he has a lot of information about the Arashi and Jaaku that we didn't know before. Of course, Nash won't tell us what that information might be. No—there's something else about him that's just off. For one thing, he calls chi 'chi.'"

Sara laughed. "Why is that bad?"

"Think about it. The martial arts that developed in Africa have no relationship to the Chinese arts—they developed totally independently. Chi is a Chinese word; wouldn't they have another word for it in Africa?"

"That's kinda thin, isn't it?" Chris said with a chuckle. "You dislike him cuz he doesn't have a different word for chi?"

"I didn't say I *dislike* him," said Sam. "I just don't know if I trust him."

"Well, I liked him," said Katana. "He was a good teacher—I wouldn't mind training with him again."

"You may get the chance, Kat. Nash says Dasari is going to be working with him and Mitch on the Arashi situation," said Sam. "He thinks Dasari may be able to help them figure out who the assassin is. I guess we'll be seeing more of him in the next several months."

The kids finished their sushi and went back up to the girls' room.

"That was weird," said Katana, collapsing on the couch. "I've never seen Sam react that way to anyone before."

"I know," said Chris. "I wonder what kind of information he had about the Arashi, though."

"Hey—come here, guys!" said Sara from her computer. "Sean's done translating the manuscript!"

Katana and Chris each pulled up a chair next to Sara.

"This is unbelievable..." said Sara, browsing through the e-mail. "It looks like this manuscript teaches you how to do the same stuff we learned in the chi kung manuscript—only it teaches you how to do it to someone else."

"Let's try something!" said Katana.

"We can't without the diagrams," Chris observed.

"Crap!" said Katana.

"Sean's online," said Sara. "I'm going to IM him and see if he'll bring it over. He's got his driver's license now."

Sean agreed. Twenty minutes later, Sara went downstairs to meet him in the atrium.

"This isn't a great idea," said Chris when she'd walked out of the room.

"Why not?" asked Katana.

"If Nash or someone catches Sara walking back inside with that manuscript, we're screwed."

But Sara made it upstairs without incident. She opened the text while simultaneously reading Sean's translation on the computer. "Here, this diagram shows you how to increase the flow of chi to someone's heart," she said.

"Chris, stand up," said Katana, getting to her feet.

"Wait a minute—you're gonna do this on *me*?" said Chris apprehensively. "What if something goes wrong... This could be dangerous, you two..."

"Oh come on," said Sara. "It's not dim mak—it's healing stuff. You'll be fine."

Chris reluctantly agreed to be the guinea pig. He stood still while Sara told Katana what to do.

"First, it says you have to relax and concentrate on increasing the flow of your own chi," said Sara. "It's even got something similar to that thing we found to stimulate your prenatal chi— only you don't have to sit down for this one."

"What do I do?" Katana asked.

"Hold your arms out at shoulder level. Keep your hands

palm-down, and your elbows slightly bent. Now sink your chi to your dantian, and take slow breaths in through your nose and out through your mouth."

Katana did what Sara said. Within a few breaths, the exercise did indeed stimulate her prenatal chi, if not as powerfully as the sitting meditation.

"Now what?" she asked.

"Uh... You have to push with your index finger on Chris's sternum—hey, this is right near the nerve ending you showed us!"

Katana put her finger on Chris's sternum and asked, "Is it the *same* place, or just near it?"

"Go up about another inch," said Sara.

"Got it, now what?"

"At the same time, you have to press with your other hand behind his ear lobe—this is also right next to one of the nerve endings, but a little closer to his ear," Sara explained.

"Got it," said Katana. She pushed on a spot behind Chris's ear while continuing to push on his sternum with her other hand.

"Whoa!" said Chris. "That's it—I can feel my heart beating like mad! This is exactly like that chi kung exercise we did."

Katana showed Sara how to do it on Chris, then Chris tried it on Katana.

"This is neat," said Katana. "Let's try something else."

Sara read through more of the document. "Here's one to augment vision."

She instructed Katana again. This time she had to place two fingers on the side of Chris's neck on two points that were right next to each other on separate meridians.

"Yep, everything's brighter," he said.

The three of them spent the rest of the night going through the manuscript. They learned how to augment each other's hearing, relax their nerves, stimulate the adrenal gland, and increase kidney function—and that was just the beginning. As with the chi kung manuscript they'd found the previous term, they could control virtually every bodily function by increasing the flow of chi to the relevant organ. By two in the morning, only a few techniques remained.

"Hey—this next one isn't like *anything* that was in the chi kung manuscript," said Sara. "It shows you how to feel a person's chi flow to see how strong it is."

"Cool—what do I do?" asked Katana.

"You have to put two fingers on his neck again," said Sara. "This time put your index finger on the same point we used to augment vision. But you have to put your middle finger down a little lower—on the auditory meridian."

Katana placed her fingers on Chris's neck.

"I don't feel anything this time," he said.

"I do!" said Katana. "Chris—this is incredible! I can feel your chi—it's like an electric current or something. It's really strong!"

"Well, that's good to know," said Chris with a smile. "I'd hate like hell to have weak chi!"

Once Sara and Chris had tried it, Sara went back to the manuscript. "I don't know if this next one's gonna do us any good—it's to revive someone who's unconscious."

Katana looked at Chris for a second. "No! No way—I know what you're thinking, Kat, and you can forget about it!"

"What?" Katana asked innocently.

"I am *not* letting you knock me out just so you can try this!"

Sara laughed, but Katana said, "No, of course not. But we can still try it, so we know how to do it."

"Yeah... all right," said Chris tentatively.

Sara read from the manuscript. "For this one, you have to press the point on the visual meridian below the one we just used, and use your other hand to push the brain meridian, below the base of the skull."

"Okay..." said Katana. She placed her hands accordingly. "Do you feel anything?"

"Yeah," said Chris. "My whole body is tingling—this is kinda weird."

Sara and Chris both tried it, then Sara opened the manuscript again. "This is it—we're on the last one," she said.

"What does it do?" Katana asked.

"It's to help someone who's paralyzed," said Sara.

"You're kidding me," said Chris. "I thought people got paralyzed when their spinal cord was injured—does this fix the spinal cord somehow?"

"No," said Sara tentatively. "It's talking about when you get paralyzed from your meridians getting overloaded."

"Your meridians getting overloaded... When that happened to Jason last year, he didn't get paralyzed—he lost consciousness," Katana replied doubtfully.

"I don't know, Kat. That's what it says here," Sara said with a shrug.

"Thompson paralyzed you with that dim mak move, Kat," said Chris. "Maybe that's what this is for."

"Maybe," agreed Katana. "Let's try it."

"For this one, you have to hit the heart meridian and the brain meridian at the same time," said Sara. "Put your right hand on the same spot we used to increase the heartbeat, and use your left hand to push the spot we used to revive someone who's unconscious."

Katana pushed the pressure points. Chris's body jerked violently—Katana took her hands away immediately. For a second she was worried he was having a seizure. But it happened only once and then he seemed fine.

"That was *not* pleasant," said Chris. "It felt like an electric shock or something."

Katana guided Sara through the technique. Once again Chris's body convulsed violently when she hit the pressure points. Then Sara showed Chris how to do it on Katana.

"I agree," she said. "That didn't feel good."

For the next week the three of them practiced everything they'd learned from the manuscript as much as possible. This earned them some strange looks from their friends, who had no idea what they were up to.

Ed and Tommy seized the opportunity when they found Chris and Sara in the hallway one day before study hall. Chris was pushing on pressure points on each side of Sara's neck to augment her hearing.

"Hey!" yelled Ed. "No making out in the hallway!"

"Aren't you jealous, Kahanu?" chided Tommy, pushing

Katana as they walked by.

The following weekend, when they were done working on their tricks and weapon sets, Katana had an idea. Jelly was still trying to learn more of the chen do, but hadn't made any progress. Even the exercise to stimulate the prenatal chi hadn't moved him any closer to his goal. But Katana realized she might finally know a way to help him.

"Hey, Jelly—come here a minute," she said.

"Yeah, what?"

"I have an idea. I think I might be able to get your chi to flow the right way for you to form a ball of energy."

"Um... how the hell are you gonna do that?" Jelly asked. Sara caught her eye and shook her head.

"Just come here," Katana insisted, waving Sara off. She remembered the manuscript they'd found about how the chen do worked, and she now knew how to increase someone's chi flow along the meridians that led to each hand.

She had Jelly sit down and start doing the sitting meditation exercise to stimulate his prenatal chi. Jelly sat in full lotus position, his hands on top of each other in his lap. While he was doing that, Katana pressed a point on the back of his neck with one hand, and a point partway down his left arm with the other.

Suddenly a small ball of chi formed in Jelly's hands.

"Holy crap!" he said. "How the hell are you doing that?!"

"Ninja magic," said Katana. Chris raised his eyebrows at her.

Jelly stood up and tried to form the ball on his own. Much to his dismay, he still couldn't manage it.

"This is ridiculous!" he yelled. "I'm never gonna get this—

everyone else can do a chi hit except for me! You can even *make me* do it, but I can't do it myself!"

Sara and Chris laughed as Jelly stomped up and down on both feet. He reminded Katana of a toddler throwing a temper tantrum.

CHAPTER 21

THE HEADMASTER OF SHAOLIN

"Could I please have your undivided attention for a few moments," said Master Nash at the beginning of their morning tai chi practice. It was a Friday morning in the middle of February. "Next weekend it will be our rare and singular honor to host the most powerful martial arts master in the world. Chan Su Ming, the Headmaster of the Shaolin Temple, will be arriving at the Hall of the Dragon on Friday.

"That evening we will be hosting a banquet in the headmaster's honor. On Saturday members of the headmaster's entourage will conduct a seminar and demonstration. Our wushu team will also perform for the headmaster's benefit.

"It is not by any means an everyday occurrence for the headmaster to visit one of the temples. Indeed, Master Chan has not been to the Hall of the Dragon in nearly twenty years. I would appreciate everyone's help in making this visit as smooth as possible. I must ask that you refrain from the usual noise and shenanigans that accompany a weekend at the Hall of the Dragon. And I expect you in full uniform for the event on Saturday."

"Evaluation on Sunday, I assume?" said Katana when Master Nash held her back at the end of class.

"Yes, Katana," Nash confirmed. "They're bringing the boy who can do three chen do—his name is Pai Lo. The headmaster will put you through an evaluation starting at eleven on Sunday. I will be present, of course, as will the other masters, to evaluate Pai Lo as the headmaster evaluates you."

"What should I expect?" asked Katana. "How is he going to run the evaluation?"

"Ah, Katana... Who knows. In the first place, the headmaster will probably not run it himself. He'll sit back and watch while his deputy, Master Liang puts you and Pai Lo through your paces.

"The headmaster has a reputation for changing his plans at the last minute. For instance, there wasn't going to be any demonstration or seminar when we first discussed his visit. Then two weeks ago he happened to mention that he would be adding those components. He only suggested three days ago that he wanted to see *our* team perform. Nelson almost had a coronary— I suspect your practice tonight will be grueling, to say the least.

"Be ready for anything, Katana," Master Nash concluded. "The headmaster has not shared his plans for your evaluation with me. Even if he had, I would expect those plans to change by next Sunday."

"Master Nash... why is the headmaster *really* so interested in me?" asked Katana. "I mean... what is the point of these evaluations? Are they leading up to something?"

"The headmaster derives an immense amount of pride from his role as the leader of the oldest hall of martial arts in the world. Over the centuries, nearly all of the most powerful masters have trained at Shaolin. I think it galls him that someone as strong as you should train anywhere else.

"The headmaster wants a good long look at what you can do, Katana. And I believe at some point he'll entice you to go to Shaolin as a disciple and continue your training there, under his supervision."

"Wow," said Katana. This was not something she'd considered. She thought it might be neat to visit Shaolin someday, but there was no way she wanted to be there long-term. "I wonder what it's like to train there..."

"I will not deny that it's an incredible experience," said Master Nash. "You cannot help but feel the history of the place."

"That's right—Mr. Brown told us that you trained there! I forgot about that!"

"Yes I did," said Master Nash with a smile. "I spent eighteen years at Shaolin. Master Chan was less than happy when I decided to leave. He tried very hard to convince me to stay."

"What's it like training with him—is he as powerful as everyone says?" asked Katana.

"Very much so," said Master Nash. "It is widely believed that he is the most powerful headmaster to preside over Shaolin since Li Shan."

"Who's that?"

"Li Shan was the headmaster during the middle half of the 1700s," Master Nash explained. "His chi was so strong that he could *see* people's meridians and the flow of a person's chi within his or her body."

"Like that Arashi two years ago," said Katana. "What was his name?"

"Togo," said Master Nash. "Yes, Togo was only the third person, that I know of, to possess that ability."

"Can Master Chan do it?" Katana asked.

"No, he cannot," said Master Nash. "But in other ways, his power exceeds that of Li Shan. Katana, the truth is that if you went to Shaolin, you would probably not spend very much time training with the headmaster himself. He teaches only the inner-most circle of monks. I did not train with him personally until I'd been at the temple for nine years," said Master Nash.

"Why doesn't he teach more?" asked Katana. "You teach everyone here..."

"The headmaster spends most of his time fulfilling the administrative duties of his position," said Master Nash. "In addition to being the headmaster of Shaolin, he sits at the head of the entire temple network.

"But sadly, I think the headmaster enjoys the power of his position perhaps more than is wise. He believes he is too important, too significant to train just anyone. Master Liang oversees the everyday training of the majority of the monks at Shaolin."

Master Nash looked at his watch. "I've held you up long enough, Katana—you'd better be off or you'll be late for school!"

Katana talked to Sara and Chris at breakfast about her conversation with Master Nash.

"So he didn't tell you what the evaluations are for, did he?" said Sara.

"I don't know," said Katana. "He said that he thinks the headmaster is gonna try to convince me to train at Shaolin. But I don't think Nash is telling me everything."

"Yeah..." said Chris. "That would explain why *he* is coming here, but what about the other headmasters?"

"Well, at least this explains why Osaka's been acting so strange," Sara observed.

"How so?" asked Katana.

"He doesn't want you to go to Shaolin! That's obvious, isn't it?"

But Katana wasn't so sure. She still felt like there was more going on than anyone was telling her.

Master Nash was right about their wushu practice—Master Fu made them go through the demo over and over again that night. Jelly still couldn't catch the staff consistently after his 1080 kick, but otherwise the team was nailing the show. But Master Fu demanded perfection. He told them they'd keep doing the demo until Jelly could catch the staff, or else he'd remove the 1080. The practice ran almost an hour late. When Jelly caught the staff during four consecutive run-throughs, Master Fu finally relented.

"Does the Shaolin Temple have a demo team?" Sara asked at the end of practice.

"No, team demos are unique to the U.S.," said Master Fu. "The monks will stick mostly to individual performances next weekend. But you'll see some of the best wushu athletes in the world. Nash said they're bringing Tan Zhi—he's the Chinese national champion in weapons. You guys are in for a real treat if he performs."

For the next week, the students at the Hall talked of little else than the upcoming visit from Shaolin. Master Nash even canceled regular lessons on Thursday. He was worried Master Fu would suffer a nervous breakdown if the performance team didn't have one last practice. Nash invited the entire school to watch them train.

Once again, Master Fu ran them through the demo over and over again. This time Jelly didn't miss the staff even once at the end of the 1080. Katana felt, as always, that the team performed with much more intensity for such a large audience than they ever did in regular practice.

Friday arrived. Katana and Sara ran straight up to their room after school to get ready for the banquet. Katana still had the dress she'd worn the previous year to the Fall Ball—it had been in tatters by the end of that night, but Leanna had been able to sew it up. Sara had brought three different dresses from home. She tried on each of them several times. Although she repeatedly asked Katana how she looked, Katana didn't think she was listening to her replies. Instead she seemed to be going through some deep internal debate as she looked at herself in the mirror. But eventually Sara settled on the blue dress that Katana had recommended from the start, and the girls headed downstairs.

When they arrived in the cafeteria, Katana was amazed at the transformation the room had undergone. The tables were covered with fancy tablecloths and set with fine china for a formal sit-down dinner. Huge floral arrangements adorned the center of each table and there was a fountain at the far end of the room.

"Um... what's everyone in line for?" asked Katana.

"They must be doing assigned seats," said Sara. "Look—the tables are numbered."

Sara was right. They got to the front of the line and Francine told them they were at table twelve. Katana and Sara were sitting with Chris, Jimmy, Dana, Paul, Jelly and Scott.

Master Nash was seated with the other masters at the head table in front of the windows. Katana thought he looked strange in a suit—she was so accustomed to seeing him in his martial arts attire. Yet that was nothing compared to Sam. She looked stunning in her red cocktail dress, but Katana almost didn't recognize her. She knew Sam hated dresses, and almost never wore them.

Once everyone had taken their seats, Master Nash stood up to address the whole room. "Everyone please stand to welcome our guests from the Shaolin Temple."

Getting to her feet, Katana looked across the room to see Gerald and another man open the doors from the student lounge. A procession of monks, twelve in all, entered the room, greeted by loud applause. They were dressed in the orange robes of Shaolin, their heads shaved bald—every one of them was male. They went to sit at the head table with the masters. The last was a boy who looked no older—or taller—than Jelly. Katana assumed he must be Pai Lo.

Master Nash addressed them again. "It is my deepest honor to introduce Headmaster Chan Su Ming." Everyone applauded a second time as Gerald and the other man opened the doors again.

Two enormous monks entered the room. They were so tall they could barely fit under the doorframe. Their robes left one side of their chests exposed. Katana thought they looked like bodybuilders.

Once they'd cleared the doorway, the headmaster came into view. He was no taller than Katana. He was bald, but had a white, pointy mustache and a narrow beard that hung down to his stomach. His aura was intense—it seemed to pulsate. Katana had never seen anyone so powerful.

"Who are the two giants?" asked Sara once Master Chan had taken his seat at the head table.

"They must be the headmaster's bodyguards," said Katana. "Remember—Sam told us about them."

"Why does the most powerful master in the world need bodyguards?" asked Chris.

"No idea," said Katana. "Probably just for show. It makes him look more important."

"Is that their wonder kid?" asked Sara.

"I think so," said Katana. "His name's Pai Lo, apparently."

"Hey, do we know *which* of the three chen do he can do?" asked Chris.

Katana thought about it for a moment and realized she had no idea. "I assume the same as me," she said. "Sam always says that fading is way harder than the others."

"Yeah, but Sam can fade and she can't levitate, so you never know," Sara pointed out.

After they had eaten their salad, Master Nash came over to Katana's table with one of the monks.

"Katana, this is Master Liang," he said. "He is the deputy headmaster at the Shaolin Temple. He will be acting as Master Chan's translator this weekend."

Katana stood up to shake his hand. "It is a great honor to meet you, Katana," said Liang. "Please come with me, and I can introduce you to the headmaster."

Katana followed Liang and Nash to the middle of the head table where the headmaster was seated with Pai Lo. One bodyguard was seated on each side of them.

They walked around behind the table. Master Liang said something to the headmaster in Chinese. The headmaster and Pai Lo both stood up. Master Liang said, "Katana, Headmaster Chan Su Ming."

Katana extended her hand, but the headmaster didn't take it. Instead he brought the palms of his hands together in front of his chest, nodding his head slightly. He said something to her in Chinese. Master Liang held his hand out toward the boy. "Katana, this is Pai Lo."

Pai Lo also brought his palms together in front of his chest and bowed. Katana did the same. She thought she could see a slight smirk on the boy's face.

Master Chan said something to her in Chinese. Although he spoke very quietly, his voice resonated above the din of conversation. She could hear him quite clearly.

"The headmaster says he is very pleased to finally meet you, Katana," said Master Liang. "He understands you will be taking part in the demonstration tomorrow and is very eager to see you perform."

Again, Katana thought she saw the slightest smirk flash across Pai Lo's face. It was gone the instant she looked at him directly.

"Thank you," she said to the headmaster.

Master Chan sat down again. Nash escorted Katana back to her table.

"What was that about?" asked Sara.

"Liang introduced me to the headmaster and the wonder kid," said Katana.

"The wonder kid has a staring problem," Jimmy commented with a scowl.

Katana looked over at the head table. The headmaster leaned over to say something to Pai Lo, who was looking directly at Katana.

"Yeah... I don't know what's up with that," she said.

"Well, you look really good in that dress, Kat," said Sara. "That's probably all it is."

Jimmy scowled again. "I don't think that's it," said Katana. "He was almost laughing at me when I was up there with Liang."

Katana tried not to look at the head table during the rest of dinner. But she could feel the weight of Pai Lo's stare almost the entire time.

After dessert, the masters and monks at the head table got to their feet. Nash asked everyone to quiet down, and then Master Chan addressed the room in Chinese.

Master Liang translated. "Headmaster Chan would like to

thank you for the warm welcome you have shown him this evening. He hopes that our visit this weekend will help forge stronger ties between the Shaolin Temple and the Hall of the Dragon. He knows that you are very fortunate to have Master Nash, one of the most powerful masters in the world as headmaster, yet no master is an island. Nash and the other headmasters are part of the Shaolin family, as are all of you. He looks forward to seeing you again at the performance and seminar tomorrow and wishes you a good night."

The headmaster and his entourage made their way out of the room. This time the bodyguards and Master Chan went first, followed by Pai Lo and then the rest of the monks.

Once the doors had closed behind them, Master Nash said, "That concludes the festivities for the evening. I will see you in the tai chi dojo tomorrow at three."

The next afternoon, Katana and Sara got dressed in their school uniforms. Master Fu had decided to use those for the demonstration instead of the new team uniforms. He thought the traditional Chinese outfits would be more appropriate in Master Chan's presence.

Katana and Sara went to collect Chris and Jimmy on their way up to the tai chi dojo. Katana noticed that while the masters from the Hall were there already, none of the monks had arrived yet. The masters were standing around the front of the room, talking to each other in hushed tones. Three chairs were set up against the middle of the front wall.

The kids sat down to stretch. Katana began to suspect that it was now well after three. The monks were still not there. Master

Nash kept looking at his watch, pacing back and forth at the front of the room.

Finally Katana caught a glimpse of orange through the far door. The monks had arrived in the front hallway.

Nash lined everyone up. The headmaster's entourage walked into the room. Master Chan, Master Liang and Pai Lo made their way to the front. The headmaster's bodyguards followed, each carrying a large Kwan dao. The rest of the monks walked to one end of the room. Master Chan, Master Liang and Pai Lo each sat in one of the chairs—the headmaster in the middle. The bodyguards took up positions on either side.

"Good afternoon, everyone," began Master Nash, with one final look at his watch. "Today you are in for a real treat. Our own wushu team will perform for Master Chan, and several of the monks from Shaolin will perform for us as well. After the demonstration, Master Liang will be teaching you one of the Master Forms of the Shaolin Temple. This is a form that Bodhidharma himself, the founder of Shaolin martial arts, first taught the monks centuries ago. Now if you would please move to the back of the room and take a seat, our performance team will go first."

Master Fu walked over to them as they set up their weapons for the demo. He looked even more nervous than Katana felt. He went around to each of them in turn and reminded them of the little details they'd been working on during their last couple of practices.

Finally they were ready. Katana lined up behind Sara. But their troubles began almost the instant the music started. Sara met Jelly in the center, but stumbled when she turned to face the masters.

Katana walked forward, met Dana in the middle, and turned to walk up behind Sara. Once they were in line, they shouted out their introduction: "Judges, we are the Hall of the Dragon!" But Katana could distinctly hear at least two of the other kids say "masters" instead of "judges." Master Fu had gone back and forth on this at their last practice. But he'd definitely decided to stick with "judges," because that was what they'd been saying in preparation for Golden Gate. Katana wasn't sure who'd said it wrong, but she knew it must have sounded goofy.

They made it through the short choreography sequence without incident. Katana did her aerial to one side as the rest of the team ran to the back. She nodded to Dana. They ran past each other, doing back handsprings into flash kicks, and landed in splits. Katana kicked to her feet. She ran past Dana again into her front aerial, then turned around, dropping to one knee next to her chains.

As she watched her teammates, she knew their demo was falling apart. Paul fumbled his landing on the aerial in the middle of the broadsword set, nearly crashing into Scott. Then during staff, Sara missed her catch when they threw the staves to each other. Jelly totally missed his 1080, landing on his back. The staff fell on top of him. He grabbed it and kicked to his feet to exit the stage.

But something was wrong—as the kids from broadsword came out for their tricking sequence, Katana could see Jelly limping to the side of the performance area. He looked at her and shook his head slightly.

Katana knew this meant he wouldn't be doing the double backflip with her. She did her aerial to the front corner, and turned to face Dana. Running forward, she decided at the last instant to do a flash kick instead of her double backflip—at least this way they would mirror each other.

But she was so used to doing the double backflip, it threw her timing off—the flash kick didn't take as long to complete. They were half a beat off through the whole first section of the whip chain set. Katana was on the leg wrap already by the time Dana did the neck wrap.

Katana lifted her leg into the air well before Dana on the monk move. She added two extra rotations with the chains so Dana could catch up. This did the trick. They landed their splits at the exact same time.

Katana kicked her leg around for the body jumps, in perfect time with Dana. They kicked to their feet and spun around for the butterfly twist. But then the worst thing imaginable happened. As they swung their chains around, Katana saw a glint of silver dart to the front of the room. Once she'd landed her twist in a full split, she realized that one of Dana's chains had broken. The spike had flown right at Master Chan, who'd caught it in one hand. The flag from Dana's chain hung limply from his fingers. Pai Lo smirked at Katana.

Katana and Dana got to their feet and threw their aerials as the rest of the team ran forward for their final bow. Katana felt awful. They'd totally bombed their demo in front of the Head-master of the Shaolin Temple.

The rest of the school got to their feet and applauded uproari-ously for them. Master Fu came over and tried to put a positive spin on things. "The opener was really good... And Kat, nice thinking taking out the double back—it would've looked totally out of place without Jelly."

But Katana knew they'd blown it. She could see the disappoint-ment written all over Master Fu's face, regardless of what he said.

Katana went with her teammates to sit at the back of the room with the rest of the school. Master Liang stood up. He called several monks to come up and perform individually.

One of the monks did a straight sword form that was unlike anything Katana had ever seen with that weapon. He moved the blade incredibly fast, sometimes in flowers, other times spinning over his head. The monk even did a release skill similar to what the performance team did with staves. He threw the sword in the air, did a standing aerial into a split, then caught the sword again.

Other monks came up and did forms with spears and broadswords, but when Master Liang called up Tan Zhi, Katana paid close attention. Master Fu had told them he was the Chinese national weapon champion, but had failed to mention the weapon he used: double whip chain.

Tan started the form with a flash kick. He did many of the elements from Katana's form, including the neck and leg wraps, the body jumps, the monk move and the butterfly twist to a split. And while he did *not* do a double backflip in the opener, nor any other tricks once the chains were spinning, what truly impressed Katana was the unbelievable speed of his weapon work. At no point during the flowers could Katana see the chains. In fact, they were moving so fast that she couldn't even make out the flags. She could see only the blurry white circles they painted in the air.

Katana and Dana looked at each other, mouths wide open. Although Katana thought she had slightly more difficulty in her form with the addition of the gainer flash, she knew Tan would crush her in competition. It looked like he was hardly trying, but the chains moved around him blindingly fast. Even his butterfly kicks made Katana's look slow.

When he finished, everyone gave him a standing ovation. Katana was glad she wouldn't have to face *him* at Golden Gate. Master Liang got to his feet again, this time inviting everyone to join him on the floor.

"Today I will be teaching you one of the oldest forms we practice at the Shaolin Temple. Indeed, as Master Nash mentioned, Bodhidharma himself taught this form to the monks centuries ago.

"Bodhidharma, or Ta Mo as he is called in Chinese, was born in southern India sometime in the late fifth century. We know very little for certain about Ta Mo, as records from that time are scarce and often inaccurate. In addition, myth and legend have mixed with reality over the centuries, making it difficult to separate fact from fiction.

"We do know that Buddhism had already spread from India to China by the time Ta Mo arrived at Shaolin. The temple had already existed for nearly half a century as a Buddhist monastery.

But Ta Mo brought a new kind of Buddhism, known as Chan Buddhism. While the monks at Shaolin prior to his arrival spent a great deal of time meditating and translating the great Indian scriptures into Chinese, they were weak and unhealthy. Ta Mo introduced a series of exercises to improve their physical fitness and cultivate their chi. Later he also taught the first set of martial arts forms ever practiced at the Shaolin Temple.

"The form I will be teaching you today has been passed down through the centuries. It is said to come from the original set that Ta Mo taught the monks. In fact, we call the form 'Ta Mo Fist.'"

Master Liang spent the next hour teaching them the form. Master Nash and Master Fu—who both knew the form already—walked around to help.

The form was simpler, somehow, than the other wushu forms Katana had learned. The movements were less flashy and more direct. Katana found it more similar to some of the kata she did in kempo. She liked it, though. It felt old, like a relic of martial arts history.

Once they'd completed the form, the monks followed Master Chan and his bodyguards out of the room. Master Nash dismissed everyone for the night.

"What the hell happened to you guys?!" asked Jimmy when they sat down for dinner that evening.

"I don't know," replied Jelly, looking totally dejected. "That demo sucked *so much*..."

"I can't believe my chain broke!" said Dana. "That's *never* happened to me before—it figures the first time is in front of the headmaster of the freaking Shaolin Temple!"

"Yeah, Fu said he's getting us both new chains before every tournament from now on," said Katana.

"That Tan guy was incredible," Chris observed. "No offense, you two, but he's *way* faster than you."

"Yeah, well he is the Chinese national champion, he'd better be fast," Dana retorted with a frown.

"I wonder how he got that way," said Katana. "I worked that weapon all summer, doing the pushups in the handstand and everything, but I'm slow as hell compared to him."

"Yeah, but the monks at Shaolin start training *way* younger than we do," said Paul. "And all they do is train all day. In China, they take kids away as young as three if they seem like they're going to be good at sports. They go to these schools where they can learn gymnastics or martial arts, or whatever. But they grow up training like eight hours a day.

"When they're older, the best of the best in the martial arts classes get to go to the Shaolin Temple. So that Tan guy, he's probably been doing martial arts since he was three, and whip chain since he was like ten. And he's probably spent at least six hours a day doing nothing but chains ever since."

"Wow," said Katana. "He'd better be good with that much training."

"Screw that," said Scott. "I like doing karate and everything, but not *that* much. Eight hours a day?! That's crazy."

"Yeah, and it'd cut into your video game time," Jimmy agreed.

Katana walked up to the tai chi dojo the next day with great trepidation. She'd hung out with Sara and Chris all morning, trying to get her mind off what was coming. Yet as inescapable as the evaluation was, the whole affair seemed utterly surreal. She was just Katana, a girl who loved doing karate. But she was about to be tested by the Headmaster of the Shaolin Temple, the most powerful master in the world.

Why was this happening? She still didn't understand what was going on. She was certain there was something Nash wasn't telling her. What it was, she couldn't guess.

She walked into the dojo to find that this time the headmaster, Master Liang and the two bodyguards were already there. They were seated at the front of the room again, as were all the masters from the Hall of the Dragon.

Pai Lo was down at the other end of the room warming up. He was finishing up the tai chi long form when Katana walked in, holding a brilliant ball of energy between his hands.

Master Nash walked over to her. "How do you feel?"

"Kinda nervous," she said with a little smile.

Master Nash smiled back at her. "Take a few minutes to stretch and warm up, and then we'll get started."

Katana sat down. Pai Lo went through an explosive empty-hand wushu set. In the middle of it he shot twenty feet into the air—clearly levitation was the third chen do he could do. He did a triple backflip, landing in a split.

Katana just stretched. She could feel her chi flowing very strong already—she didn't need to warm up. She was certain Pai Lo had only done his form to show off.

After a few minutes, Master Liang asked them to line up. Katana walked up to him and Pai Lo ran over from the other end of the room.

Master Liang spoke to Pai Lo in Chinese first, then addressed Katana. "We will be starting with forms. You will pick one that you feel best displays your skills."

"Can I do a kempo form, or does it have to be wushu?" Katana asked.

"I assume you will be demonstrating your double whip chain set when we get to weapons?" asked Master Liang.

"Yes..."

"Doing a kempo form will help to show the diversity of your skills," suggested Master Liang. He had them both go to the back of the room and kneel down, and returned to his seat. He called up Pai Lo first.

Pai Lo did the same form he'd been warming up with—minus the levitating triple backflip. The form was very dynamic, with lots of high kicks, low stances, sweeps and tricks. But he did only a single backflip where he'd levitated earlier. When it was Katana's turn, she did Kata Fourteen, with all the intensity she could muster.

They did weapons next. Pai Lo demonstrated a double broadsword form. Katana had never seen anyone use this weapon before. He started out with both swords in one hand, then separated them and went into a very fast flower sequence. He ran across the room, stabbing with both swords in rapid-fire succession. Then he launched himself into a front flip, landing on his back.

He kicked to his feet and spun the swords around in flowers, one on each side. The rest of the form contained a backflip and another move where he jumped into the air and flipped over, landing on his side. But the most impressive move, Katana thought, came right near the end of the form.

Pai Lo jumped straight up and lay out, as if he were lying in bed six feet in the air. Then he dropped, landing flat on his back. Katana thought she'd probably paralyze herself if she tried that. But Pai Lo kicked to his feet and finished the form.

It was Katana's turn.

She'd decided to do her chain set exactly as she was practicing it for Golden Gate, judges presentation and all. She didn't want any mishaps after the team demo.

She got to her feet and bowed. She ran into her front aerial, landing in a split right in front of the headmaster. "Representing the Hall of the Dragon, I am Katana!" she yelled. She powered up and walked back several steps.

Katana opened the form with her double backflip. She threw the chains out and went through the flower section as fast as she could, wishing she had Tan Zhi's speed.

After the neck and leg wraps, she turned, opened up both arms and kicked over into her gainer flash. She landed, turning right into the monk move. She brought the chains together in one hand and lifted her left leg over her head. Then she stalled the chains and fell into her split.

She powered up and went into her butterfly kicks, finishing with the butterfly twist into a split. After swinging one leg around, she did the body jumps and ended her form. She smiled at Pai Lo as she took her seat at the back of the room. He didn't smirk this time.

Master Liang brought them up together next and had them

do the tai chi long form. Katana was grateful for the chance to gather her energy again before they continued. The whip chain set always left her drained. By the end of the form she felt ready for anything.

Master Liang got to his feet again and said simply, "Now you will spar."

Katana looked around—it was just her, Pai Lo, the masters and the two bodyguards. There was no one else there. Was she going to spar with Sam? Or... surely she wasn't going to fight the bodyguards...

"Who will we be sparring?" she asked.

"Each other, of course," said Master Liang.

He brought them to the center of the room. "You may use any techniques you wish—internal or external." He instructed them to bow to each other. "Fight!"

Katana felt relieved—for a moment, she'd felt certain she was going to fight one of Chan's guards. But Pai Lo rushed in and she had no more time to think about it.

Pai Lo was very fast—it took everything Katana had to block or dodge his onslaught. But she dropped down and swept out his leg when he moved in for a roundhouse kick. This sent him sprawling on the mat.

He got back to his feet. Katana took the initiative. She launched at him with a series of kicks. She started with her triple combination, going from a front kick to a roundhouse and then finishing with an axe kick. But Pai Lo stayed just out of reach.

When she backed off, Pai Lo lunged in with a punch. Katana raised her arms to deflect, but the punch had been a feint. She realized an instant too late that he was using *her* signature move against her. He leaped into the air and slammed his foot into her rib cage, flipping himself over backwards. Katana wasn't nearly big enough for the gainer flash to work properly. She fell to the mat. Pai Lo managed to make it over only by using levitation.

The kick had knocked the wind out of her. But she had no time to catch her breath—Pai Lo threw a fireball at her. She deflected it, running forward to engage him again. But he vaulted into the air.

Katana followed. She shot straight up, catching him in the head with a roundhouse kick mid-flight. They exchanged kicks as they drifted back to the floor. Katana pushed off again the moment her feet hit the mat, jumping into the leg scissors takedown. She wrapped her legs around Pai Lo, twisted hard and slammed him to the floor.

She turned over for a kick to his head, but he scrambled to his feet too quickly. Katana jumped to her feet as well and threw a fireball at him. Pai Lo deflected it with ease.

They went back to external techniques, trading kicking combinations until Katana lunged forward with a punch. She bounced her chi against his chest.

Pai Lo sailed through the air. Katana wasted no time—she gathered her energy and threw a fireball. But Pai Lo used levitation to prevent himself from crashing. He formed a ball of energy before he'd even landed, catching Katana's chi with his own. He threw the flaming mass back at her—it streaked across the room like a comet.

Katana braced herself, holding out both hands. She bounced

her chi against the fireball. She'd had no time to think—she reacted instinctively, not knowing if it was possible to bounce so much energy this way.

It worked—the fireball shot back at Pai Lo. He tried to deflect it the normal way, but was overwhelmed. The fireball slammed into him full force. He flew halfway across the room, landing in a heap on the mat.

For an instant Katana expected him to jump to his feet and engage her again—but Pai Lo didn't move. She ran over to him at the same time as Nash and Liang.

Pai Lo was unconscious. Master Nash muttered, "Here we go again." He knelt down beside the boy and placed two fingers on his neck. Katana knew he was feeling his chi to see how strong it was.

Master Nash looked at Katana for a moment before speaking to Liang. "He'll be fine—his meridians have been overloaded. Give me a hand getting him down to the infirmary. I'd like to do acupuncture to restore his chi flow."

But Master Liang stood up and yelled something in Chinese. One of the bodyguards ran over. He lifted the boy up in his arms.

"We are done here for today, Katana," said Master Nash. "We will discuss this tomorrow morning." He led the bodyguard and Master Liang out of the room.

The other masters gathered at the front of the room, but Headmaster Chan remained seated, staring at Katana. She didn't know what made her do it, but Katana smiled at him and bowed before walking out the door.

CHAPTER 22
TRIPLE CROWN

"Headmaster Chan was very impressed, Katana," said Master Nash with a smile. It was Monday morning. They'd just finished their daily tai chi class.

Katana was relieved—she'd been worried she'd be in trouble for using the chi tao move against Pai Lo. Sara had insisted Pai Lo's use of the technique Katana had employed to knock Jason unconscious gave Katana the right to use any move she wanted. But Katana had worried anyway.

"He wasn't *happy*—but he was impressed," Master Nash continued.

"I can't believe he used the gainer flash against me," said Katana. "Did he know that was my signature move...?"

"Oh yes," said Master Nash. "The Shaolin Temple *does* have internet access, Katana; it's not nearly as spartan as Shaka-In.

From what I understand, Pai Lo saw you do that move online and spent the past several months perfecting it to use against you."

"Wait—so *he knew* we'd be sparring each other? That was a total surprise to me!"

"It appears that while the headmaster did not share his plans with me, he did share them with Pai Lo. I think he was stacking the deck as much as he possibly could," said Master Nash. "But as Master Nang refused to teach chi tao at Shaolin, the headmaster had no idea what new tricks you might have up your sleeve."

"Is it done now?" asked Katana. "The evaluations, I mean—there aren't going to be anymore, are there?"

"Katana, I will not lie to you, there may be one more... evaluation coming up. I don't know yet. But I promise you, as soon as I do know, I will tell you immediately."

"WHAT OTHER EVALUATION?!" asked Sara when they got to breakfast later that morning. "You've already been evaluated by every headmaster in the world—what the hell is going on, Kat?"

"Not a clue," she said, "but I *knew* something else was up. At least I'll find out soon—whatever it is."

For the next few weeks, both Sam and Master Fu went into overdrive preparing the teams for Golden Gate. Even Osaka seemed to have more enthusiasm for the event than usual. He had been hammering them on attack drills to get them ready for their third degree test, but he switched gears completely. He was now spending every class helping them prepare their kata for the tournament. But after the debacle at the demonstration, Master Fu was definitely the most determined to whip his team into shape for the competition.

Dana could finally do the gainer flash with the chains, but was nowhere near consistent with it yet. Master Fu wasn't willing to risk the move in the demo; Dana didn't argue.

Katana spent every weekend practicing for her individual events. She felt pretty sure Becca Stratton would be her primary competition in both the weapon and sparring divisions. And she thought Michelle would be her greatest opponent in kata. But it was her experience with Michelle that had taught her not to take anything for granted. She knew there very well might be someone out there—someone new to the circuit, perhaps, who could surprise her the way Michelle had at their first sparring practice.

Katana spent three to four hours every Saturday and Sunday doing her whip chain set, Kata Fourteen and sparring with Jimmy and Chris. She was exhausted by the end of every night. She found it difficult to imagine training for eight hours a day the way the monks at Shaolin purportedly did.

When the weekend of Golden Gate finally arrived, Katana was more excited—and more prepared—than she'd ever been for a tournament. "This is my year," she kept saying to Sara.

They boarded the buses right after school on Friday. A little over five hours later, they arrived at the Golden Gate Plaza Hotel in San Francisco. Katana and Sara checked into their room and went back downstairs to meet Chris, Jimmy and Sean Fisher in the restaurant.

"Hey!" said Sean. He gave Sara a kiss and a big hug as he got up to make room for the girls to sit down.

"You two saw each other at school today—get a room or something!" Katana chided. Jimmy stared at her. Everyone sat down again and the waitress came to take their order.

"Hey, are Ed and Tommy competing this weekend?" asked Chris when they finished.

"I think so," said Sean. "Sato hasn't been pushing the tournaments that much though. He wasn't even at the school all week. Sebastian was teaching again."

"I can't stand the moron twins," said Sara. "I hope they don't make nationals—at least we'll get a break from them there."

"Oh—I forgot to tell you guys," said Sean. "I told Sato about that day you got in the fight with them, Chris, and he really got on their cases. He told them to leave you alone, or he'd beat them with a stick!"

"Are you kidding me?!" asked Katana.

"Well, I think he was joking about the stick," said Sean, "but he was serious about them leaving you alone."

They talked about the tournament for a few minutes.

"What do you think, Kat," said Chris. "You going to nationals in three events, or what?"

"I hope so, but you never know. There might be someone competing tomorrow that we don't know about yet."

"You've got weapons in the bag, at least," said Sara. "It's been either Becca or Dana in that event the past three years, and your form is stronger than either of theirs now. I can't imagine anyone else is going to come along who can beat you three."

"And no one can touch you in sparring," said Jimmy. "Not after you fought in the boys' division last year."

"And what is that supposed to mean?!" asked Sara indignantly. "She *won* the boys' division, if you don't remember—and she woulda won nationals, too, if she hadn't levitated in the middle of her match!"

"I know!" said Jimmy defensively. "That's what I mean—if she can win the boys' division, the girls' division's gonna be easy!"

"Easy?!" asked Sara. Chris rolled his eyes at Katana. "Are you saying you think boys are better somehow? Cuz Kat's a girl—"

"I know she's a girl!" said Jimmy.

"—and none of the boys could *touch* her last year, so it seems to me like the *girls'* division is gonna be harder..."

Their food arrived. "It's okay, Sara," said Katana. "I know what Jimmy means. I feel good about all three of my events, but I still say it would be stupid to take anything for granted. Michelle totally shocked us at Eureka—something like that could happen again."

They discussed everyone's prospects for the weekend while they ate—Chris and Sean were doing sparring and kata, Jimmy sparring, and Sara weapons and kata. When they were done, they paid for their food and made their way out of the restaurant.

But no sooner had Katana set foot outside the door than she was accosted by Harvey Ryder—the reporter for the U.S. Sport Karate website.

"Ms. Kahanu," he called in his wheezy voice, practically pouncing on her. "I know you are going to be quite busy tomorrow—you are the favorite to win in your sparring event, not to mention weapons—so I was wondering if I could have a few minutes of your time now..."

Katana had forgotten about Harvey Ryder and the unique threat he represented to competitors at these events. The captain of the sparring team the previous year had told her that this man was so persistent for interviews that he had once caused someone to miss their ring.

"Yeah, I guess," said Katana with a sigh.

"Very good, very good—thank you, Ms. Kahanu, I promise not to keep you long. I've heard a rumor that you performed recently for the Headmaster of the Shaolin Temple—is this true?"

Katana was stunned—she had no idea people outside the temples would have any knowledge of what was going on with her evaluations. And she didn't know if anyone was *supposed* to know either.

"Um... yeah..." she stammered.

"Can you tell us what it was like?" Harvey asked.

Katana did her best to answer the question without being too truthful—she talked about doing her double whip chain set and Kata Fourteen. But she left out the part about sparring with a boy who could do three chen do and knocking him across the room by deflecting a fireball with a secret chi tao technique. She knew that most of the martial arts world didn't know about the chen do, and didn't think talking about it on the internet was such a wise idea.

Harvey talked to her more about her performance in Eureka and how she felt about Golden Gate. Finally he let her go.

"Well at least now he'll leave you alone tomorrow," said Sara as they walked up to their room. The boys had ditched them the moment they saw Harvey.

"Yeah, let's hope so," agreed Katana.

The girls got to bed early. They went back down to the restaurant first thing in the morning for a light breakfast. After they had eaten, they went into the convention center to find their weapons ring.

"Look—there's Becca!" said Sara. They ran over to the ring on the other side of the enormous room and both gave Becca a hug.

"You guys ready?" she asked them.

"Yeah," said Katana. "I'm feeling pretty good today. You?"

"I'm psyched," said Becca. "My gainer's consistent—I'm ready. Hey, where's Dana?"

"I don't know..." said Sara. Katana didn't know either—she hadn't seen her since they'd disembarked from the bus the previous night.

The three of them sat down to stretch. They kept an eye out for Dana, but she still hadn't turned up by the time the judges brought everyone up for roll call.

"Dana Arlington?" the center judge called out. "Dana Arlington? Okay... Jodi Attleboro..."

The center judge continued. Katana was now frantically looking around the room for Dana—she had no idea where she could be. But finally, as the judge got to the end of the list, Dana came running over.

"Are you Arlington?" the judge asked.

"Yeah—that's me!"

The girls sat down at the edge the ring. "Where were you?" Katana asked Dana. "We were getting worried!"

Dana had to say only one word: "Harvey."

"Yeah, he got me last night," said Katana.

"They've *got* to do something about that guy!" said Becca.

The ring started and Sara was called up first. "GO SARA!" yelled Katana at the top of her lungs as Sara started her form.

It seemed to Katana that Sara had adopted Becca's usual pattern—she was getting stronger at every event. Sara hadn't been that focused on getting ready for this tournament, but Katana was impressed with her staff form. She went very fast through the flowers, and nailed all of her tricks.

Katana, Dana and Becca gave her high-fives when she came back to sit down. As the next several girls went up, Katana knew Sara was the one to beat. Two girls did samurai sword, two did straight sword, and one did kamas, but Katana didn't think any of them were as good as Sara.

The judges called Dana next.

As Dana did her routine, Katana went through it in her head. When Dana got past the leg wrap, she shocked everyone—including Katana. She tried the gainer flash. Katana knew she hadn't planned on doing it. But she also knew Dana well enough to know that after watching Sara's form, she'd want to get as much of an advantage as she could.

Dana did it—it wasn't terribly high, but she got enough air to keep the chains spinning the whole time. Katana thought the move looked amazing—she couldn't wait to do it herself.

By the time Dana finished her form, a huge crowd had gathered around the ring. Katana figured a lot of people wanted to see if Dana would have a shot at recapturing her title after losing it to

Becca the previous year. The crowd burst into applause as Dana bowed and left the ring.

Katana knew that Dana had beaten Sara. She also knew that her own form would be a little less impressive now that Dana had done the gainer flash. That was the first time anyone on the entire circuit had *ever* done that trick with two chains in competition.

A few more girls went, and then it was Becca's turn. Becca did her front flip just like she had in Eureka, landing on one knee in front of the judges. Then she got up and stormed to the back corner of the ring—letting out a menacing kiai as she went. Katana knew this was going to be intense.

Becca started her form and launched into a giant flash kick, spinning her nunchucks as she went over. Becca's powerful stage presence drew more people to their ring as she performed every spin, finger roll and release skill to perfection. She did her gainer flash and got much higher than she had in Eureka—once again keeping the nunchucks spinning the whole time. Then she did a trick Katana couldn't ever remember seeing before. It looked something like a butterfly twist, but she went the other way around, kicking one leg up from underneath and rotating sideways. She even passed one nunchuck under her leg as she did the trick, catching it in her other hand.

She finished her form, bowing as she left the ring. The crowd went wild.

"What was that last trick?!" asked Katana, giving her a hug.

"It's called a corkscrew," said Becca. "I've been working on it for ages—I finally got it over winter break."

Katana was next—and the last one to go in their ring. She felt way more pressure now than she had when she went first in Eureka. Katana decided at that moment that she *definitely* preferred going first.

She had no time to calm her nerves. Taking a deep breath, she got up and bowed on her way into the ring. She ran in an arc, landing her front aerial in a split right in front of the judges.

"Representing the Hall of the Dragon," she yelled, "I am Katana!"

She powered up and marched to the back of the ring. As she started her form, she let out a loud kiai and ran into her double backflip. Katana threw her chains out before her feet hit the ground, all her focus on spinning them as fast as she possibly could. She nailed a huge gainer flash at the end of the flower section.

Katana still feared that Dana might have upstaged her by beating her to the punch with their new trick. But the overwhelming audience reaction when she finished her form allayed her concerns.

Sara and Dana both gave her a high-five when she returned to the edge of the ring. Becca just looked at her and said "Wow."

The girls waited anxiously for the judges to tabulate the scores.

"You're going to nationals," said Dana.

"I don't know," said Katana. "Your form was amazing—I can't believe you put the gainer in!"

"No, Kat—she's right," said Becca. "This one's yours."

Finally the judges were ready. The center judge yelled, "In fourth place... Sara Brown!"

Sara walked forward, staff in hand.

"In third place... Becca Stratton!"

Becca walked up and gave Sara a hug.

"In second place... Dana Arlington!"

Dana turned and gave Katana a hug. "I told you so!" She walked up to stand next to Becca and Sara.

"And in first place... Katana Kahanu!"

Katana couldn't believe it. She'd done it—it was her first year competing in weapons and she was going to nationals. She walked up and Sara, Dana and Becca pulled her into a group hug—just in time for Harvey Ryder's photographer to snap a picture.

The girls ran into Chris, Jimmy and Sean as they tried to cut through the crowd to their kata ring. "Holy crap—Kat, that was amazing!" said Chris, pulling her into a hug. "You're going to nationals!"

"I know!" said Katana, unable to stop smiling. "Good luck in kata!" she yelled as they got pushed along and separated by the crowd.

"You too!"

Katana, Sara and Becca arrived at their kata ring. The center judge was a tall man, somewhat chunky, with bright orange, balding hair. Katana recognized him from somewhere.

"Kat—it's that Griffin Lassater guy we met in Maine!" said Sara.

"You guys know him?" said Becca. "He's one of the guys who runs the whole circuit, isn't he?"

Master Lassater had spotted them. He came over to talk.

"Well—Katana, isn't it? You weren't kidding when you said

you knew how to use those chains, were you? My ring got over in time for me to watch you perform—your form was very impressive, I must say!"

"Oh, thanks!" said Katana.

"If you're anywhere near as good with your traditional work, I'm sure you'll be a shoo-in for kata today," he said with a wink. "Well, good luck, girls—I've got to get the ring together!"

Master Lassater returned to the judges table. Katana looked at Sara. "That's not exactly right, is it?" she asked. "He shouldn't be telling us how he thinks we're gonna do *before* we've competed, should he?"

"No surprise though, half these judges play favorites," said Becca.

Katana saw Michelle warming up on the other side of the ring. She went with Becca and Sara to say hello. Michelle got to her feet when she saw them. "Hi Katana, hi Sara!" she said with a big smile.

"Hey Michelle—this is Becca Stratton," said Katana. "You guys didn't get to meet at Eureka."

"Hi," said Becca, shaking her hand.

"It's such a pleasure to meet you," said Michelle. "I always used to watch you compete at this tournament, before I got my black belt. You were my inspiration when I was going up through the ranks—my dad even took me to nationals in Florida two years ago so I could watch you win!"

"Oh—wow—seriously?" said Becca. Katana could tell she was totally taken aback.

"Yeah," said Michelle, "I never imagined that someday I'd be in the same ring with you. "Well, I'd better finish stretching—good luck, you three!"

Katana followed Becca and Sara back across the ring. "Wow," said Becca. "I thought she'd be mean as hell after I saw her compete in Eureka! Is she always so nice?"

"Yeah, she is," said Sara. "She's only mean when she's in the ring. I don't know where it comes from..."

Master Lassater lined them up and got the ring underway. Katana went up third. It wasn't as good as going first, she thought, but certainly better than waiting until last.

She strode into the ring and called out her introduction to the judges. She turned around and walked to the back of the ring. As she looked down and saw Sara and Becca giving her thumbs-up, she had an idea. She stopped where she was, but didn't turn around to face the judges. She stood still for a few moments, gathering her energy, her back to the judges the entire time.

She could see Sara mouthing, "What are you doing!" and motioning for her to turn around. But Katana knew exactly what she was doing.

Suddenly she did turn around, explosively, and went into the first horse stance in her kata with an ear-splitting kiai. This had the desired effect—she definitely had the judges' attention. She'd never seen anyone start a form with their back to the judges before, and didn't think they had, either.

As she went through her form, the judges, the audience, the other competitors melted away. It was just Katana, alone in the ring. She went through Kata Fourteen with every ounce of intensity she possessed, throwing every move with all her power. She finished the form and hit her last stance with another loud kiai. Then she bowed and turned to leave the ring.

"You're on fire today," said Sara as she sat down next to her again.

"I loved how you started with your back to the judges—you mind if I do that?" asked Becca.

"Go for it!" said Katana.

Michelle went up after a few more girls. Once again Katana was blown away by her stage presence. Despite her own little addition to the beginning of her form, Katana felt certain that Michelle would make nationals.

Becca went next. Now that Katana could see how it looked, she liked the idea of starting the form with her back to the judges even more. She decided she'd use that approach from now on. Somehow it put a little more attitude into the presentation.

As always, Becca's form was even stronger than it had been in Eureka. But Katana couldn't help but feel that Michelle had the event in the bag. As good as Becca was, she still wasn't as intense as Michelle.

Sara ended up going last this time. When she was done, the judges turned around to figure out the places.

Katana was shocked when they called them up—she'd beaten Michelle and taken first place. She was going to nationals for kata, too. Michelle took second, Becca third and Sara fourth.

"You shoulda won that, Michelle," Katana said once Master Lassater had finished the ring.

"She's right," said Sara. "Kat was good, but you blew us away —Lassater threw the ring."

"It doesn't matter," said Michelle with a big smile. "I'm still gonna come to nationals and cheer you on, Kat!"

Katana thought the situation was totally unfair. It was clear to her that Master Lassater had, in fact, thrown the ring. She had absolutely no doubt that Michelle had turned in a stronger performance. Lassater had robbed her of her shot at nationals.

What was the point of competing, Katana asked herself, if a judge would play favorites like that? She tried not to think about it. Their sparring ring was next and she needed to focus.

Katana followed Michelle, Sara and Becca across the room to their ring. She got her gear on and tried to keep her body warm. She wanted this event almost as much as weapons after making it to nationals the previous year only to be disqualified.

She looked around and saw that Sam was right—there were a lot more girls in this ring and it looked like there were three or four other teams as well. But she was also right that none of the girls appeared large enough for the gainer flash. She'd definitely be saving it for nationals.

Katana was glad to find she didn't know any of the judges in this ring. At least she wouldn't win *this* event unfairly. They did roll call and started the ring right away.

Katana got called up first—against Becca. They walked into the ring and gave each other a hug. The center judge had them bow to each other and square off.

Suddenly, Katana realized that if she beat Becca in this match, Becca wouldn't make nationals in *any* of her events. As far as Katana knew, Becca had never failed to make nationals before. Katana felt bad, but there was nothing she could do.

They started fighting, and Katana moved in right away with her triple combination. She snapped her foot from the round-house to the axe kick as fast as she could. Becca didn't dodge fast enough. Katana caught her in the side of the head and the match went to 2-0.

They started again and this time Becca took the initiative. She launched at Katana with a ferocious barrage of kicks. Katana dropped immediately, sweeping out Becca's other leg. Katana was up 4-0.

When they started again, the girls danced around each other for a minute, each of them feinting with a kick. Then suddenly Becca jumped into the air and caught Katana with her legs. She slammed her to the floor with the leg scissors takedown. Katana rolled away before Becca could get any more points. Katana was still up 4-2.

In the beginning of the next round, Katana moved in very aggressively with a kicking sequence. Becca tried to sweep out her base leg. But Katana saw this in time and was able to jump over her sweeping leg. She landed a punch when Becca straightened up. Katana won the match 5-2.

Michelle went up next and destroyed her opponent—she won the match 5-0. The other girl failed to throw a single kick or strike, so aggressive was Michelle's onslaught. Sierra won her first match as well. But Olivia lost badly to a very aggressive girl whose uniform back read "Team Tigress."

Katana thought the girls from Team Tigress were the strong-est. In the end, two girls from that team advanced to finals along with Katana and Michelle. But Katana and Michelle both beat their opponents and had to face each other in the final match.

"Good luck, Kat," said Michelle, giving Katana a hug.

The match began. Michelle faked with a kick, then rushed in for a punch. Katana was ready for her. She snapped a roundhouse kick to Michelle's head. She was in the lead, 2-0.

Michelle won the next round, though, sweeping Katana's leg out as Katana moved in for another roundhouse kick. But as Katana got to her feet, she paid attention to a thought that had been nagging at her consciousness since the first match.

Katana was going to let Michelle win.

She knew this was a crazy idea, but she wanted to do something to make up for Lassater's bad call. And she also knew that since it was down to the two of them for the final match, their team would go to nationals regardless of who won.

Michelle was good enough that Katana didn't have to do much to give her the win. Michelle surprised her with a leg scissors takedown. Katana hesitated for just a moment when she hit the floor—but this gave Michelle the time she needed to land a follow-up kick. Michelle won the match 6-4.

The judges finished the ring. Katana congratulated Michelle, then ran off with Sara to get ready for the team demo.

"You threw that match, didn't you?" said Sara once they were out of earshot. "You *let* Michelle beat you!"

"Was it that obvious?" Katana asked with a frown. "I didn't think anyone would notice."

"Nobody else did," said Sara. "But I could tell. You stayed still a second longer than you normally do when she took you down. Why'd you do it?"

"It makes up for Lassater's ring, doesn't it? And we're going to nationals anyway, so it doesn't matter."

When they got to the other side of the stage and found the rest of the team, Master Fu sat them down for a little pep talk. "This is it, everyone. We were a little shaky in front of the headmaster..."

"A little shaky?!" asked Paul. "We sucked!"

Everyone laughed. "You're right, we did suck," said Master Fu. "I was trying to be nice. But you guys have nailed the demo at every practice since then. So forget the headmaster, forget the audience and do what you do. And no improvs, anyone," he added with a look at Dana. "Stick to what we've done in practice!"

"I won't change a thing, I promise," she said with a smile. "I wouldn't risk it for the whole team like that."

At that moment, Master Lassater took the stage to address the room at large.

"Before we get started with the team demo competition," he began, "I wanted to take a few minutes to honor the life and memory of Master Joe Rodriguez.

"Master Rodriguez ran the Golden Gate Classic for nearly thirty years. Through his hard work and dedication to the event, it has grown to be one of the best-run tournaments anywhere on the circuit. So many of the stars of the sport karate world over these many years got their start right here, on this stage.

"When Master Rodriguez passed away this winter, his family

lost a terrific father and husband, and the sport lost a legendary competitor, coach and promoter. I know Joe will be missed by all who knew him. I would like to ask everyone to bow their heads for a moment of silence as we reflect on the impact Master Rodriguez had on our lives."

Katana looked around the room. She wondered if Master Lassater knew the truth—that an Arashi had murdered Master Rodriguez. The assassin had made a mistake—Master Rodriguez was no Arashi. But as Katana looked around, she began to wonder if one of the other judges might be an Arashi—perhaps one of them would be the assassin's next target.

But Katana had no more time to think about it. Master Lassater announced that the demo competition was about to start. The Hall of the Dragon was first. Katana walked up the stairs to the stage with her teammates to set up their weapons and get in line for the demo.

As in Eureka, Katana had butterflies in her stomach. She took a deep, steadying breath, but had no opportunity to do any chi kung exercises.

"Don't trip this time," she hissed at Sara when the music started.

"Shut up," Sara whispered back. She walked forward to meet Jelly in the middle of the stage.

This time they got through their opening without any mistakes. By the time Katana did her aerial to the side of the stage she felt strong and confident. They were going to nail it today, she just knew it.

Katana did her tricking sequence with Dana, then dropped to

one knee next to her chains. She moved the chains around to make sure she had each handle securely between her thumb and forefinger. Then she watched as her teammates pulled off their broadsword set without a hitch. Paul did his diving front roll over Jelly's butterfly twist and Katana had to stop herself from cheering along with the audience.

Staff went perfectly as well. Nobody dropped when they threw the staves to each other. And Jelly landed a clean 1080, catching his staff without any outward sign of dizziness.

Katana got ready as the kids from broadsword came out to trick. Jelly ran to the back of the stage, dropped his staff, and walked to the front corner.

Katana stood up and threw her aerial, then nodded to Dana. They ran diagonally across the stage toward each other. Katana and Jelly did their double backflips, landing together at the same moment Dana landed her flash kick.

The girls flew through their double whip chain set. They got up to the monk move, each holding one foot overhead as they spun the chains in one hand, then dropped to the floor in their splits.

After body jumps, they did their butterfly twists toward the judges. When they landed in their splits Katana couldn't help but glance at Dana's chains to make sure both spikes were still attached. They got to their feet again and ran toward the back of the stage, dropping their chains as they went over in their aerials. Their teammates ran past them toward the audience.

They'd done it. They'd nailed the demo that they'd bombed so badly in front of the Shaolin monks. Katana was smiling ear to ear as they turned to exit the stage. She could hear the audience roar its approval. Master Fu met them at the bottom of the stairs, giving them high-fives as they went by.

"Great job, everyone!"

The judges scored them very high—two of them even awarded perfect 10s. Katana felt great. But she knew the next team wasn't feeling so good. They looked extremely nervous as they set up their demo. Katana couldn't blame them—her team had turned in a performance that would be extremely difficult to beat.

Two more teams went before Strike Force took the stage. Their performance was strong, but Katana knew they couldn't touch the Hall of the Dragon. Not today.

Katana was right. Her team won and was going to nationals. She wondered if Strike Force would make it too—it depended on how they'd done in comparison to the second place teams from the other regions. But it didn't matter. She knew that going into nationals, their main competition was bound to be Supernova.

CHAPTER 23

MASTER LASSATER

Katana thought her day had gone extremely well. She'd won her weapon and kata events, and her team had won the team demo division. And despite her loss to Michelle in sparring, she'd still be going to nationals for three individual and two team divisions. As good as it had felt to win her weapons event, nothing could compare to winning team demo—especially after the fiasco they'd endured together in front of Master Chan.

No, she couldn't have asked for a better day than this.

"I still can't believe you let Michelle beat you in sparring," Sara said as they gathered up their bags and their weapons.

"What?!" asked Chris, who had come over to congratulate them. "You let Michelle win? Why?"

Katana told him what Lassater had done.

"You still go to nationals, though, right?" asked Jelly.

"Yeah, exactly," said Katana.

The four of them walked out of the convention hall and made their way across the lobby.

"You won in weapons, I assume?" Chris asked.

"Of course," said Jelly with a smile. "But Paul was *really* good —he had to go first, and I was worried he was gonna beat me this time."

"How'd you guys do in sparring?" Katana asked as they walked out the door to the parking lot.

"Not bad," said Chris. "Greg took first again, and Jimmy and me had to fight for third and fourth. He beat me, but we'll all go to nationals since we won as a team."

No sooner had they made it into the parking lot than Katana heard a wheezy voice behind her. "Ms. Kahanu... could I have a word?" She turned around to see Harvey Ryder waddling over to them.

"Sure," said Katana. "The buses aren't here yet—why not!"

"Very good," said Harvey. "Ms. Kahanu, I must say as impressed as I was with your performance in weapons and kata today, I was rather surprised to see you lose the sparring division, especially to a newcomer like Ms. Summers. You were the favorite to win that event after your stellar performance last year and your first event in Eureka. Do you think you underestimated Ms. Summers?"

"No, not at all," said Katana. "Michelle's really good. I was trying my best, but she was better today."

Sara raised an eyebrow.

"Well, it was a surprise to see you win in your weapon and

kata events—you faced some very stiff competition from Ms. Arlington and Ms. Stratton in weapons. What do you think put you over the top against those two veterans?"

Katana thought this was a stupid question. Who knew?

"Well... um... I know I've been working hard on my whip chain set, I spent a lot of time adding new tricks into it this year. I guess today was my day."

"Yes, it would seem so," said Harvey. "Well your tricks were stronger than Ms. Arlington's, anyway, and I imagine you both beat Ms. Stratton because of the difficulty of your weapon. What about kata—how did you feel about your surprise victory there?"

"Not so good," said Katana with total honesty. "Michelle should have won that—she was the best in the ring by a lot."

Harvey asked Katana a series of increasingly irrelevant questions for the next several minutes. A steady stream of people walked out the doors, giving them a wide berth. Katana could tell nobody wanted to get caught by Harvey.

Finally the buses arrived. Katana managed to pull herself away.

"Man, that guy can talk!" said Jelly. "He blabbed my ear off about my weapons ring the whole time I was watching sparring!"

They made it only halfway to the buses before someone else wanted to talk to Katana. This time it was Master Lassater.

"I was very impressed with you today, Katana," he said with a smile. "Your star seems to be rising on the circuit—I expect you will do quite well at nationals this year."

Yeah, Katana thought, *as long as I have you for a judge...* "Thanks," she said.

Suddenly there was a flash of light. A figure in samurai armor appeared out of nowhere, right in front of Katana. He pushed her to the pavement and drew his blade.

The Arashi reached back with the sword, aiming a thrust at Lassater. Katana threw a massive fireball—it smashed into the Arashi an instant before his blade found its target. He flew through the air, landing flat on his back. Katana sprang to her feet. Lassater was on the ground—he'd lost his balance backpedaling away from the Arashi. Several people screamed, running from the commotion.

Lassater regained his feet. The Arashi advanced on him again. Lassater threw out both hands, shooting a fireball at the Arashi. The Arashi deflected it with one hand, raising his sword again with the other.

Katana rushed forward, slamming both hands into the Arashi's chest—she bounced her chi and sent him flying across the parking lot. He crashed into a nearby car and smashed the window, setting off the alarm.

"Katana—get out of here!" yelled Lassater. The Arashi regained his feet and ran toward them. Katana realized she could see neither his aura nor his shen. It was the assassin.

Then in an instant of horrible insight, she realized something else. "You're... You're an Arashi!" she said, backing away from Lassater.

"Run!" he yelled. The assassin was almost on them. Lassater was his target, and Katana was standing directly in between them. She looked back and forth between Lassater and the assassin in a moment of indecision. Then she threw another fireball at the assassin.

He deflected it this time, stopping his advance. "Get out of the way," he yelled, his voice muffled through his mask. "It's him I want. This isn't your fight—MOVE!"

Katana thought the man spoke with an accent—but she had no time to think about it. She heard a rumble of thunder. Suddenly there were dozens of bright flashes all around her. The parking lot was full of Arashi, all of them now advancing on her position.

Chaos engulfed the scene—people were screaming everywhere, running out of the parking lot. Master Nash ran out of the hotel. "Katana! What's going on—"

But apparently Nash saw the Arashi now converging on Katana. He vanished, reappearing right next to her. He grabbed her and faded to the buses.

"Stay here!" he yelled, disappearing again.

"KATANA!" yelled Sara, right next to her with Jelly and Chris.

Katana watched in horror—Osaka, Sam and Fu had now joined Nash, engaging the Arashi. It was very hard to tell what was going on. Katana could see Lassater fighting alongside the masters, but could no longer tell which of the Arashi was the assassin. She tried to find the one without an aura, but with so many of them running around, it was impossible to pick him out.

Just then Sam jumped into the air and kicked an Arashi in the chest. She knocked him into a car, but another Arashi came from behind, hitting her with his chi. Sam was down.

"NO!" Katana screamed, running into the fray to help Sam.

"Katana—NO!" yelled Sara. Katana didn't listen. Sara looked desperately at Chris and Jelly for a moment, then the three of them chased after her.

As Katana ran over, Sam got up on her knees. But the Arashi had raised his sword. Katana threw a fireball, knocking him to the pavement.

Sam regained her feet. "Katana—get out of here!"

But at that moment, Katana saw an Arashi fade out of nowhere, right next to Lassater. The Arashi had no aura.

Katana ignored Sam. She ran toward Lassater—the assassin had grabbed him from behind, drawing his sword again.

An Arashi grabbed Katana, pulling her around. She struggled for a moment, then saw Jelly, Chris and Sara moving toward her. The Arashi held out one hand and threw a fireball at Jelly.

"NO!" Katana yelled.

Jelly cringed and screamed like a little girl, but held his hands in front of him. He deflected the fireball. Chris and Sara stared in amazement.

Katana grabbed the Arashi's arm, turned and flipped him onto the pavement.

He sprang to his feet, ready to grab Katana again. Jelly yelled "HEY!" He threw a fireball at the Arashi. It knocked him to the ground.

Katana turned to run toward Lassater again—he'd escaped the assassin's hold. He was trying to keep his distance, dodging repeated sword thrusts. Katana threw her chi at the assassin—but she was an instant too late. The Arashi impaled Lassater with his blade.

"NO!" Katana screamed. The assassin vanished in a flash of light. Katana ran to Lassater's side. He'd fallen to the ground, propped up against a car. He was covered in blood. His eyes were closed and he seemed to be unconscious.

Katana dropped to her knees. She placed two fingers against the side of Lassater's neck. His chi was barely flowing; she couldn't feel a pulse.

Without thinking, she pushed a pressure point on his sternum with one hand, a point behind his ear with the other. She knew this was the right combination to increase the chi flow to his heart.

It seemed to work. Lassater opened his eyes partially and looked up at her. "Katana..." His voice was weak.

Katana kept pushing the pressure points—she had to save him.

"Katana!" It was Master Nash. He knelt down on the other side of Lassater. He saw what Katana was doing, and held two fingers to the side of Lassater's neck. "It's too late, Katana—there's nothing you can do."

Lassater's eyes closed again.

"No," whispered Katana. "No..."

"It's over, Katana. The assassin is very accurate with his blade. He punctured Lassater's heart, as he did with Rodriguez. There's nothing you can do."

A hissing sound emanated from Lassater's body. Katana

sprang to her feet, backing away. Nash stood up as well. Lassater's body vaporized in a thick cloud of smoke.

"He really was an Arashi..." said Katana.

"Yes," said Nash with a sigh. "We heard a rumor last year that someone on the tournament committee was an Arashi. The assassin must've heard the same rumor, and mistakenly concluded it was Rodriguez. It would seem this time he guessed correctly."

Katana looked around, suddenly fearful. "Where are the other Arashi—there were tons of them a minute ago..."

"They faded away the moment Lassater fell," Nash replied with a frown. Katana, I'm going to take you back to the Hall—I want Doctor Hubble to get a look at you."

"I... I'm fine," said Katana, but looking down saw that she was covered in blood. "It's not mine—really, I'm fine, Master Nash."

"I'd rather be safe than sorry," he said, putting his arm around her. The scene went blurry for an instant, then she could see the infirmary at the Hall of the Dragon. The last rays of sunlight were streaming in through the windows.

Master Nash walked her to one of the beds. Once Doctor Hubble had come over, Nash said, "I have to go back to San Francisco and talk to the FBI. They should be there by now. You can go to your room and clean up once Doctor Hubble makes sure you're okay—but we need to talk when I return."

Master Nash disappeared in a flash of light.

Doctor Hubble didn't keep Katana long. She took her vital

signs, made sure she didn't have any puncture wounds, and let her go.

Katana ran up to her room and showered. She walked out on the balcony in time to watch the sun set over the ocean. Her head was swimming with visions of what she'd witnessed. The tournament seemed like it was ages ago—in reality, only an hour and a half had gone by since she walked out of the hotel with Chris, Jelly and Sara.

Master Lassater had been an Arashi... he'd been the assassin's intended target when he killed Master Rodriguez. Katana still couldn't believe it. Why did other Arashi show up this time? That hadn't happened at the airport. Katana felt like there was a lot going on that she didn't understand.

She went back inside and lay down on the couch when it started getting dark. Doc jumped up on her stomach. She scratched him behind his ears as the events of the night kept replaying in her mind.

There was a knock at the door—Katana jumped. It was Master Nash.

She followed him up to his suite in silence. He led her into his sitting room this time. They each took a seat on one side of the table.

"Have you eaten?" he asked.

"No, actually. I'm starving," said Katana. Master Nash called in an order for sushi.

"Where's everyone else—Sara and Chris..." asked Katana.

"They're on their way back," said Master Nash. "The other

masters got everyone loaded onto the buses right after I faded here with you. They should be back in a couple more hours.

"Katana, where did you learn the healing arts?" he asked with a bemused smile. "You have surprised me on more than one occasion with your aptitude for manipulating chi. But I am finding it difficult to believe that you could've learned how to push chi along the heart meridian without some guidance."

"Oh... um..." Katana stammered. She felt like Master Nash was staring right through her. "Well... Last year, when we were playing hide-and-seek down in the tunnels at Halloween..." She felt foolish. "Um... we, well, I found these scrolls and... stuff. So this year when we went to play hide-and-seek again, I figured I'd look through it to see if there was anything about Jaaku..."

"Hmm," said Master Nash, looking somewhat surprised. "Was there?"

Katana laughed. "No! But I did find all sorts of stuff about chi kung, and history stuff from when the Hall was first being built... And we found this manuscript about the healing arts— wait, you don't know what's down there?"

"No—sadly our archives are a disaster. Each headmaster since Chow and Chang has left various documents behind, but nobody has ever organized any of it," Master Nash explained. "Katana, if the manuscript you found is the one I'm thinking, surely it wasn't in English—how were you able to read it?"

"Oh! Well, Sara was able to read some of it, but we had Sean —her boyfriend, he goes to Lincoln and he's fluent in Chinese— we had him translate the stuff for us."

"I see," said Master Nash, whose amusement seemed to be growing by the minute.

"Master Nash, what happened tonight—why did the Arashi show up like that?"

Master Nash's smile faded almost instantly.

"You noticed, I assume, that once again the assassin had no aura?"

"Yeah, I saw that," said Katana.

Master Nash rubbed his hands over his face and sat back in his chair. "Ah, where to begin... Jaaku has taken the prenatal chi of all the Arashi. As you already know, Jaaku can use that connection to compel the Arashi to do his bidding. The connection goes two ways. Jaaku can also sense strong emotion from the Arashi. He can tell when one of them is in danger. In every one of the assassin's attacks, prior to this one, the attack happened in an instant. The assassin faded in, killed his target, and faded away again immediately.

"This time, it took much longer. The Arashi faded in, and from what Ms. Brown, Mr. Boyd and Mr. Gallo tell me, you attacked him before he had a shot at Lassater."

"Yeah, I did..." said Katana. "But what does that have to do with the other Arashi showing up?"

"Everything!" said Nash. "Lassater was an Arashi—Jaaku could sense that he was in grave danger. He summoned the other Arashi to the scene. Jaaku is able to share power with the Arashi through his connection with them—all of the Arashi can fade, for example, even if they could not do so before becoming Arashi. Jaaku can also implant a vision in their minds of where he wants them to go. Thus they can fade to places they have never been before. Normally this is impossible.

"In every other instance, the attack was already over and the Arashi dead before Jaaku had time to summon any of his servants. But not this time—you delayed the attack. In effect, you gave Jaaku the time he needed to call the other Arashi to Lassater's defense.

"We've been expecting this," Nash continued. "At some point the assassin's perfect record was bound to break. We knew it was only a matter of time before something would prolong one of the attacks, and Jaaku would be able to send his Arashi to capture the assassin."

"But the assassin got away," said Katana.

"Yes, he did," said Master Nash. "The assassin faded away the moment I grabbed you, when I first walked outside. In the chaos of the ensuing battle, none of us knew where he'd gone—apparently the other Arashi lost track of him as well. I assume he faded somewhere nearby, and waited until Lassater was alone again."

"But the assassin is an Arashi," said Katana. "Jaaku should know who it is—why doesn't he use his connection to do the death touch? Why hasn't he killed the assassin?"

There was a knock at the door; it was Gerty with their sushi. Nash brought two large trays back to the table.

Katana began eating. "That is the crux of the whole problem," said Nash. "As you know, this particular Arashi has learned to hide his shen. He must be using that technique to block his chi from Jaaku—to temporarily close his connection with him. This would render him invisible to Jaaku, essentially, while he carries out the attacks."

"I thought hardly anyone knew how to do that," said Katana. "Hide their shen, I mean?"

"That is true," said Master Nash. "Besides myself, and Master Chatri, only Headmaster Chan, Master Dasari and Master Nang can do that technique. Oh, and Master Sato now, as well."

"Sato?!" asked Katana, incredulous. She didn't think he was in the same league as the others.

"I began teaching Master Sato how to hide his shen after he showed up here with Jaaku last June," said Nash. "We surmised that it would help him block the connection with Jaaku, making it easier for him to operate as a spy. We didn't know for sure that it would work until he tried it."

"Do you think Sato might be the assassin?" asked Katana.

"No," said Nash. "Nor do I think it is any of the other masters. Someone else must have figured out the technique."

They ate in silence for a few minutes. Then Katana said, "Oh —Jelly can do three of the chen do now!" She told him what Jelly had done in the battle.

Master Nash looked at her in surprise. "Oh, the headmaster is going to *love* this," he said sarcastically. "Now we have *two* students who can do three of the chen do..." He sat back in his chair and let out a long sigh.

"Is Jelly going to be evaluated now, too?" Katana asked with a wry smile.

"No, I doubt it," said Master Nash. "If anything this will only serve to heighten the headmaster's interest in *you*, Katana."

"Me?! Why would he be more interested in me because *someone else* got a third chen do? That doesn't make any sense..."

"It is very rare for anyone your age to learn a chen do," said Master Nash.

"Yeah, I know that already," said Katana.

"It is exponentially rarer for a student your age to master *two* of the chen do, and yet we now have... *five* students who can do two—or even three."

"That is pretty strange, but I don't see what..."

"Katana, you seem to be the focal point," said Master Nash.

"What does that mean..?"

"Jason Beecher, Chris Boyd, Sara Brown, and now Stephen Gallo—all of them can do two or more chen do, and all of them have been very close to you during their time at the Hall of the Dragon," said Master Nash. "The headmaster believes there may be a connection. That is what sparked his interest in you—not *your* abilities, but the abilities of so many people around you."

"But... How... What does that have to do with *me*?"

"Katana, think about Jaaku's connection with his Arashi. He is able to share power with them using that connection. The headmaster initially suggested that *you* may know dim mak, and that you were transferring power to your friends the same way that Jaaku shares power with his Arashi."

"You've got to be kidding me... How am I supposed to have learned dim mak... That's... insane!"

"I agree, Katana," said Master Nash. "And I don't think the headmaster ever truly believed it. Chan heard about your abilities and found out that others around you were also growing powerful. He began to suspect there might be *some* connection. He offered up the dim mak theory, I'm sure, only because it provided him with a reasonable excuse to demand that I bring you to Shaolin. At the end of the day, Katana, what he wanted was to see you for himself, to see firsthand what you could do."

"Well, he's had his chance—he saw what I can do when he was here," said Katana. "Master Nash... Do you think there *is* a connection between me having three chen do... and the others getting them, too?"

"Maybe," said Master Nash pensively. "Or perhaps it is mere coincidence. Don't let it trouble you too much. Well, I think we are about done here—all that remains is the matter of your punishment."

"My punishment?!" asked Katana. "For what?"

"Well, for trespassing, of course," said Master Nash with a smile. "You didn't have permission to go digging through the archives, Katana. Nor did Mr. Boyd or Ms. Brown. I'm afraid I cannot allow that transgression to be free of consequences."

"But... We didn't harm anything—we put everything back where we found it..."

Master Nash continued as if Katana hadn't spoken. "I'm a big believer in making the punishment fit the crime, however. I think an appropriate consequence in this instance would be for you and your cohorts to organize and catalog the archives..."

Katana was stunned. "You're kidding! You're going to punish me by letting me dig through the rest of the archives?"

"This is no small task, Katana—the archives are in terrible disarray. I looked through them last year when we found out that

Sato was breaking in. It's going to take you weeks to do this properly."

"This is still the best punishment I've ever had," Katana replied. "The only problem is that we can't read everything. It's all in Chinese!"

"Ah yes. Perhaps we'll extend this punishment to your translator as well—what was his name again? Mr..."

"Fisher," said Katana with a smile. "Sean Fisher. But he doesn't go to the Hall of the Dragon. We were bringing stuff to him at Lincoln..."

"No problem," said Master Nash. "I will speak with Principal Hennessey and make the necessary arrangements."

Katana went back up to her room and waited for Sara and Chris to return. It was nearly eleven when they walked in. Katana told them about her conversation with Master Nash.

"Sato *must* be the assassin!" Chris interrupted. "If he knows how to hide his shen, it's gotta be him!"

"That's what I was thinking," said Katana. "And the assassin *did* have an accent."

"It would make sense," said Sara. "Jaaku made him an Arashi against his will. He's probably killing off the rest of the Arashi to get revenge. But Nash doesn't think it's him?"

"No, he doesn't," said Katana.

"But it could be Chatri, Chan, Dasari, or Nang," said Chris. "They know how to hide their shen, too."

Katana went on with her story.

"Wait a minute," said Sara when Katana was done. "You

mean the headmaster thinks the only reason *we* can do the chen do is because *you* can do them?"

"I guess," said Katana. "That's crazy, right? But it *is* weird that so many of us have this power. The Shaolin Temple has one kid who can do three chen do, and none who can do two. And the temple in Brazil only has like two kids who can do *any* of the chen do—Santos told me that when he was here. Maybe there is some connection."

"There *is* a connection—with me and you, anyway," said Chris thoughtfully. "Our chi is mixed."

"Yeah, but Kat can do the chen do on me and Jelly and Jason," Sara observed. "So we know *our* chi hasn't mixed with hers. That can't be it."

"Right, and not only that, but Jelly almost had his first one before he ever came to the Hall of the Dragon," said Katana. "Remember, Sara? The first day we met, he told us his instructor sent him here because he was close to getting levitation. So I definitely didn't have anything to do with *that*."

"That's true..." said Chris.

"Oh—I almost forgot. Nash is punishing us for going through the archives," said Katana.

"How the hell did he find out about that?" said Chris.

"I tried to save Lassater," said Katana. "After the Arashi stabbed him. His chi was weak, and his heart stopped. I tried to increase his chi flow, the way we learned in the manuscript. Nash came over while I was doing it."

"Ah," said Sara. "Yeah, it's not like you could learn that just anywhere. So what's the punishment?"

Katana smiled. "We have to 'organize and catalog' the archives!"

Sara looked excited. "You're joking!" said Chris.

"We get in trouble for going through the archives and the punishment is that we get to go through the archives *more?*" said Sara. "Nash is the best—wait a minute, how are we going to figure out what all that stuff says—it's in Chinese!"

"Oh—he's gonna talk to Hennessey. Sean's gonna help, too!"

CHAPTER 24
MASTER CHOW

Katana had an awful time getting to sleep that night. She kept seeing the Arashi stab Master Lassater over and over again. She went over the whole night in her head, trying to think of some way she might've been able to save him.

But this time the assassin got it right, she reminded herself—Lassater really was an Arashi. Yet he still hadn't deserved to die like that. Jaaku had taken Sato's prenatal chi against his will; perhaps that had happened to Lassater as well. Maybe he'd never wanted to be an Arashi, but had been trapped somehow, forced into it like Sato. He'd seemed so nice—even if it had been unfair of him to throw Katana's kata ring.

Katana finally drifted off to sleep, but visions of the Arashi attack invaded her nightmares, too. She saw Lassater's face vaporize, replaced by Jaaku's skeletal features and pale, green eyes. But then Jaaku was gone and it was the Master Chan lying there on the pavement, a puncture wound in his chest.

The next day, Katana joined her friends in the wushu dojo. Although they practiced their tricks and weapon sets for a little while, Katana, Chris and Sara spent most of the time taking turns fighting with Jelly. Now that he could project his chi and deflect intent, all he wanted to do was spar with the chen do.

Katana especially had a great time with this. The two of them chased each other around the dojo—throwing fireballs, levitating, and using their chi to toss each other across the room. Katana was grateful for this activity—it got her mind off of everything that had happened the previous night.

Later that afternoon, Katana, Sara and Chris began the monumental task that awaited them in the archives. Chris brought his laptop and they started out by going through the materials they'd already explored. They cleared off several shelves and began sorting the documents into different categories. Chris recorded everything in a spreadsheet as they went.

For the next few weeks, Katana felt like she was living in the tunnels. The project was bigger than she'd realized—they discovered that the archives spilled into several adjoining rooms. They piled some things up in the hallways temporarily because there wasn't enough empty shelf space to do the job otherwise.

Sean Fisher joined them most evenings. He translated anything that Sara couldn't read for the purpose of cataloging it. But they also found more volumes of Chang's memoirs, and Sean spent much of his time translating those.

One evening during their last week of classes before spring

break, Sara stumbled upon a manuscript that seemed to explain the chen do of tai chi. "This is weird," she said. "It looks like this explains *all* of the chen do... but it makes it sound like they're all part of tai chi."

Sean examined the document, and he agreed with Sara. "Yeah, this basically says that all of the chen do are the same..."

"That's what Nash told me," said Katana, "but he didn't explain what it meant."

Sean skimmed through the manuscript for a few minutes. "I guess that to get the chen do of tai chi, you have to have total control of your chi and your shen. With that level of control, you can automatically throw fireballs and deflect intent and levitate and fade."

"So someone who can do the chen do of tai chi can do all of the chen do?" Chris asked.

"Yeah, according to this," Sean confirmed.

"Does it explain chi fa?" asked Katana.

"Um, yeah it does," said Sean. "It's kinda long, though."

Sean spent a few minutes reading, then explained it to Katana.

"It describes exactly which meridians you have to use to project small amounts of chi along your shen. When you throw a fireball, you send your chi down the meridians in your arms. But in chi fa, you have to allow chi to flow along the auditory and brainstem meridians, and then out into your shen. It sounds pretty hard though—this says that if you send *too much* chi, it won't work."

"Wow," said Chris.

Katana got to her tai chi class with Master Nash the next afternoon and told him what she'd found.

"Ah yes," he said. "I'd always wondered if we had copies of those documents in our archives. I long suspected that Master Chow would have brought them from Shaolin."

"We found manuscripts about the other chen do, too," said Katana. "Months ago. Did they come from Shaolin?"

"Yes, they did," replied Nash. "Do you remember when I told you about Li Shan?" Katana nodded. "Well, Li Shan was the author of those documents. Because he was able to see the flow of chi along people's meridians, he was the first person to map out precisely how the chen do work. Li Shan was also the author of the manuscript from which you learned the healing arts. He was the greatest healer who ever lived—he did much to expand acupuncture and acupressure. I'm sure that the headmaster of Shaolin at the time had no idea that Chow took copies of those documents—he never would have granted permission."

"Why not?" asked Katana.

"The Shaolin Temple has always been very protective of Li Shan's work," Master Nash explained. "Just as Master Nang didn't want to teach the Shaolin monks the secrets of chi tao, so too have the headmasters of Shaolin kept the teachings of Li Shan a closely guarded treasure."

They worked primarily on pushing hands that day. Katana had only recently been able to feel where Betsy was going to push, and where her center was. Betsy still beat her most of the time if Katana kept her eyes closed, but Katana had managed to pull out her first couple of wins.

At the end of class that day, Master Nash did chi fa with her as well. They'd been doing this periodically. While Katana continued to get stronger at defense, she didn't feel like she was any closer to learning offense.

But as she assumed the posture and Nash extended his shen, Katana thought about what she'd read in Li Shan's manuscript the night before. She tried to focus on increasing her chi flow along her auditory and brainstem meridians.

Suddenly a pulse of light shot from her shen. It hit Nash in the chest, knocking him over.

"Well done!" he said, getting back to his feet. "I was *not* expecting that!"

The other students stopped what they were doing to come over and watch. Katana and Master Nash resumed their stances and started the exercise again.

"This time, Katana, I am not going to play offense. I want you to feel where my shen is, and project your chi through any holes you can find," said Master Nash.

Katana wasn't sure she could repeat what she'd done. But as Nash's shen extended out in all directions, she tried again to project her chi along the appropriate meridians. And it worked— she shot another pulse of chi. This time, Nash deflected it with ease.

"Good, Katana. Now extend your shen in all directions. Don't focus so much on one spot—that makes your chi much easier to deflect."

She wasn't sure how to do what he was asking. Nonetheless, she tried to extend her awareness more broadly, like she did when she played defense. This made it easier to send a pulse of chi. She could direct it more slowly, too, subtly changing its course as Nash responded.

After a while—long after the class was due to finish—Nash dismissed the rest of the students. He and Katana continued working on chi fa late into the night. By the time she ran up to her room, she'd been able to send multiple pulses at Nash at the same time.

"You did it—you got offense?" asked Sara. It was nearly midnight and Katana hadn't even started her homework.

"Yeah! He was able to block it, of course—I'm not very good yet, but I got it! Did you guys find anything else in the archives?"

"Nah, not really," Sara said through a yawn. "We found some more history stuff—it wasn't Chang's memoirs this time, though. I don't know who it was, but someone started writing down lists of all the students who were training here, and what classes they were taking—it was pretty boring."

Katana was up nearly all night doing her homework. She was exhausted at school the next day, but she didn't mind—her breakthrough with chi fa was well worth it.

By the time spring break arrived in the middle of April, the kids had cataloged most of the materials in the archives. They'd finally hit their stride—Katana and Sara did most of the physical digging, while Sean was in charge of translating. Chris entered everything in the computer, keeping track of what they found and where they put it.

But the task started to feel like a punishment as the rest of the school went out on the grounds every day to play soccer or Frisbee, or across Highway 101 to the beach. Katana thought if they stepped it up now that they had entire days free, they might finish the project before the week was over. She wanted to have at least a few days to enjoy herself like the rest of their friends.

Unlike the rest of the school, they continued getting up before five every morning. The four of them spent every waking hour plowing through the archives. They took breaks only for meals and worked late into the night. Late Thursday afternoon, they got to the very last shelf.

Sara pulled out a crate, immediately removing a thick, leather-bound manuscript. "Another memoir," she said halfheartedly to the room in general.

They'd found more of Chang's memoirs, but none had yielded anything interesting. The others had lost their enthusiasm, but Katana remained optimistic. She knew this latest find would probably cover Chow's departure from the Hall of the Dragon—she was hopeful she'd finally learn what happened all those years ago. Sean got to work translating the memoirs while the girls kept digging through the crates.

About an hour later, Sean found something. "Hey—whoa— this is big, come here!" he said.

Katana's heart skipped a beat. "What is it—what'd you find?"

"It's right at the end," said Sean. "He said that Jaaku showed up and attacked the school!"

"No way!" said Sara.

"You've got to be kidding!" said Chris.

"Wait—why did he attack?" asked Katana.

"Here—hang on," said Sean, skimming through the rest of

the entry. "Whoa—Chang says that Jaaku showed up and demanded that Chow come out. Chow refused. Chang wanted to fight—he thought that with all five of the masters, they could take Jaaku. But Chow refused. So the masters and the students stayed inside the Hall. Chang says something about an escape tunnel..."

"What escape tunnel?" asked Sara.

"Oh, never mind," Sean replied. "I guess when they were building the Hall, one of the masters wanted there to be an escape tunnel in case they were ever attacked. He talked about having it extend into the forest somewhere. But they never built it. Anyway, the attack went on for days—Jaaku kept trying to break in, but he couldn't no matter what he tried. He even threw lightning bolts at the front doors. Finally after like a whole week, Chow told Chang he was leaving."

"What? Why?" asked Katana.

"Chow told him it was the only way to stop the attack. Chang didn't understand. He was angry—he said that was crazy and they should fight. But Chow said no. He told Chang he'd have to take over as headmaster. Then he walked out the front doors. Jaaku tried to grab him, but Chow faded away. Jaaku stayed for another few days, camped out in front of the school, but Chow didn't come back.

"This last part is strange... it's Chang's very last entry. He says he can't understand why Jaaku wanted Chow so badly. But he also says he was suspicious that Chow wasn't who he said he was. Chang didn't understand how Chow could've mastered so many arts... Wow, he says Chow didn't look like he'd aged the whole time that Chang knew him.

"Guys, Chang says that *Chow might have been the Immortal Master!*"

"Kat, where are you going?" Sara asked. Katana had stood up and was walking right out of the archive room.

"To get some answers," she said.

She went straight up to Master Nash's suite and knocked on the door.

"Katana, what can I do for you?" Master Nash asked when he opened the door.

"I have some questions—about Master Chow," she said. He invited her into his sitting room.

"We're almost done with the archives," she said, sitting down in one of the chairs. "There's like one more shelf... We found Chang's memoirs from back when the Hall was founded."

"Oh," said Nash, sitting down in his chair. "I didn't realize Chang kept any memoirs prior to becoming headmaster."

"He did—we read a bunch of them back in the fall. But we just found the last set. In his final entry he says that Jaaku attacked the Hall of the Dragon! He demanded that Chow surrender himself."

Master Nash suddenly looked very serious. "Go on."

"Master Nash, Chang says he thinks *Chow was the Immortal Master!* First of all, it turns out that Chow had mastered *six* arts, not five—he was a hsing-i master, too. And hsing-i and tai chi are both supposed to take a lifetime to master—how did Chow master both? And Chang says that Chow hardly aged the whole time he knew him—which was like thirty years, apparently... You told me that you have loads of information about Chow in the books and scrolls you have in your conference room... So... Is it true? Was Chow really the Immortal Master?"

Master Nash looked at Katana for a long moment before he answered. "Yes," he said finally. "Master Chow was the Immortal Master."

Katana was shocked. She thought for sure that Master Nash would deny it, that he'd have some other explanation—although what it might have been, she had no idea. But she couldn't believe this was true.

"But... the *Immortal Master*... How can anyone be immortal?"

"I do not know the answer to that, Katana," said Nash with a frown.

"And what did Jaaku want with him?" Katana asked. "Why did he attack the Hall?"

"Katana, as you know, Jaaku has sought for centuries to become truly immortal. When he first encountered the Immortal Master in Japan, the Immortal Master was called Kushan. Jaaku tried to persuade Kushan to teach him the secret to immortality. Kushan refused. Jaaku attacked; he tried to defeat him and force him to divulge the secret. But the two were an even match—neither could defeat the other.

"It was at that point that Jaaku went to China and found Master Tong. He studied with Tong for many years, learning the secrets of dim mak. He realized then that he could use the death touch to extend his own life. As long as he kept taking chi from others, his own chi would never run out—or so he thought, at least at first.

"But as Jaaku's life extended well beyond the years of any mortal human, he ceased *being* human. Using the death touch so much corrupted his meridians. It disfigured him terribly. He now appears as you have seen him: little more than a living skeleton.

"When Jaaku left Japan to find Master Tong, Kushan left Japan as well—never to be heard from again. Of course, Kushan was the Immortal Master, and he'd simply taken another identity. He went back to China, and took the name Chow. He trained at Shaolin and ultimately came to California to found the Hall of the Dragon."

"We read about that," said Katana. "We read in Chang's memoirs that Chow talked to him about starting a temple in America. It listed the other masters that went with them."

"And did the memoirs talk about the difficulties they eventually had with the locals?" asked Master Nash. "The attempts that were made to rid the area of the large Chinese population that had built up?"

"Yeah!" said Katana. "Chang did talk about that—he said that one of the masters left because he was upset about the new laws they were passing... What was his name..."

"Master Wang," said Nash.

"Yeah! Master Wang—he left and another guy took his place and that's when Chang found out that Chow knew hsing-i!"

"Katana, Master Wang eventually sought out Jaaku to learn dim mak. Jaaku learned about Chow and the Hall of the Dragon from Master Wang. He figured out that Chow must have been the Immortal Master. That is when he came here and attacked the school."

"But... What made him think that Chow would be any more willing to teach him the secret of immortality than he'd been before?" asked Katana.

"Much had changed since their last encounter," explained Master Nash. "Jaaku was much more powerful by that time. He'd learned to control the chi of everything around him..."

"You mean he could throw lightning," said Katana.

"Yes, and he knew the death touch," said Master Nash. "Jaaku believed that if he took the chi of the Immortal Master, he himself would become truly immortal. It would no longer matter how Chow had achieved it."

"Is that true—was he right? Would he become immortal if he took Chow's chi?"

"I don't know," said Master Nash. "He didn't succeed, of course. As you read in Chang's memoirs, Chow decided to leave. He knew that as long as he stayed at the Hall of the Dragon, they would never be free of Jaaku's attacks. Chow left so that the other masters and the students could live in peace. Then, as you know, he organized the attack against Jaaku. He rallied the government and the temples in Japan. Chang joined them and they attacked Taiyou."

"That explains why it took a whole year," said Katana.

"What did?" asked Nash.

"Sam told us that Chow left here in 1868 to go fight Jaaku," Katana explained. "But Tanaka told me that the battle at Taiyou was in 1869."

"Ah," said Nash. "Yes, that does make sense. And of course you know that neither Jaaku nor Chow died in that battle, as was commonly believed."

"Yes, Tanaka told me that Chow didn't die there," said Katana. "What was the secret, then? How did Chow really become immortal?"

"Nobody knows," said Master Nash.

"Wait—you told me that Chow *trained* with the Immortal Master—how is that possible if he *was* the Immortal Master?!"

Master Nash chuckled softly. "You've got me, Katana," he said. "I was not entirely truthful. But in a sense, what I said was accurate. Chow was more advanced in the internal arts than any other master who'd ever trained at Shaolin. He had mastered tai chi, and hsing-i, as you know, but he had also mastered pakua, the third great internal art. He pushed the limits of chi manipulation, going beyond what any other master had ever done. In fact, it was he who first discovered chi fa. As he was creating new facets to the martial arts he practiced, he was in effect his own teacher."

"Was he able to control the chi around him, like Jaaku does? Could he throw lightning?" Katana asked.

"Hmm... Now that you mention it, I have no idea," said Master Nash. "Nothing in our records mentions anything about that."

"So it's possible Jaaku became more powerful than him," said Katana.

"That is indeed possible."

"What about the scroll!" said Katana. "Chow left that behind and it was supposed to hold the secret to immortality... That's how Chow knew the secret! He *was* the Immortal Master... but how are you supposed to learn anything from a blank scroll?"

"Ah, Katana, I don't know the answer to that question, either. I do know, however, that Chow did expect that someone would come along one day who *could* learn the secret from the scroll. He left a document for his successors, for every headmaster of the Hall of the Dragon to follow him, which outlined his expectations for the scroll.

"Chow was very clear on this point. He wrote that the next Master of the Five Arts would be able to understand the scroll and learn the secret to immortality. But I believe that the explanation may be somewhat backwards. I believe that the person who could figure out the scroll would *become* the next Master of the Five Arts. As you have already begun to suspect, Master Chow was only able to master so many arts *because* he had lived so long. So for anyone else to master five arts—or more—they would already have to know the secret."

"You saw the scroll—was it really blank?" asked Katana.

"Yes, it was just a blank piece of paper," said Master Nash. "I thought perhaps Chow had used invisible ink, or maybe a message was encoded there by some other secret means—none of these ideas were correct.

"The Scroll of the Five Masters was a *blank piece of paper.*"

"Then how..."

"I don't know how anyone could learn from that, Katana, but I am certain of one thing. Chow believed with every fiber of his being that *someone* would come along who could figure it out."

"But Osaka destroyed the scroll when Jaaku attacked last year," said Katana. "So now what happens? If Chow was right and someone does turn up who could've understood it, they'll never figure out the secret, because the scroll doesn't exist anymore!"

"That is what Jaaku believes," said Nash. "He took the scroll literally, as I did at first. But a blank scroll is only an idea."

"Oh..." said Katana. "It's like you said last year—the scroll was a koan."

Master Nash smiled at her.

CHAPTER 25
THE CHEN DO MASTER

"Let me see if I've got this straight," said Chris when Katana returned to the tunnels and told Sara, Chris and Sean everything she'd learned from Master Nash. "Jaaku was a samurai warrior in Japan. At some point, he ran into the Immortal Master and tried to learn the secret of immortality..."

"But the Immortal Master wouldn't teach him, so they fought," said Sara. "But Jaaku couldn't beat him, so then he went to China to learn dim mak from Master Tong."

"Right," said Chris. "Then he killed Tong, and went back to Japan and set himself up in a temple... what was it called again?"

"Taiyou," said Sara. "The Temple of the Sun. And Jaaku trained his Arashi there."

"And meanwhile the Immortal Master—he started going by the name of Chow, and he went to the Shaolin Temple, and got

Chang and the other masters to join him, and they went off to America to start the Hall of the Dragon," Chris continued.

"And then Master Wang left California to go back to China. He found Jaaku to learn dim mak from him, told him about Chow and the Hall of the Dragon, and Jaaku figured out that Chow was the Immortal Master," said Sara.

"Right, and so Jaaku came here and attacked the place to try to get to Chow—to take his chi? Jaaku believed that if he took the Immortal Master's chi, he would become immortal?" asked Chris.

"That's what Nash said," Katana confirmed.

"So Chow left," said Sara, "and then him and Chang and the headmasters in Japan attacked Taiyou, and Jaaku left..."

"And went to Tibet for thirty years," said Chris.

"And then eventually showed up in Hawaii," added Sara.

The three of them stared at each other for a moment.

"And that's the whole story," said Katana.

They finished cataloging everything on that last shelf shortly thereafter, and spent another hour and a half going through their work, making sure they hadn't missed anything. But Katana couldn't stop thinking about Master Chow. He really was the Immortal Master. He'd fought Jaaku more than once, but had never been able to beat him. He was immortal, and possibly the most powerful master who'd ever trained at Shaolin, yet he couldn't defeat Jaaku.

What chance would Katana have when her day came to confront Jaaku? Was he invincible? It certainly sounded like he might be—he was the only one who knew the death touch. And he was the only one who could use the chi around him as a weapon.

Katana, Sara and Chris were able to enjoy the last three days of vacation before it was time to get back to their normal routine. They spent most of Friday outside on the grounds, and went to the beach on Saturday. It was unseasonably warm, but the water was still much too cold to go swimming.

Katana went back to school on Monday feeling like she finally knew everything she was going to find out about Jaaku and the Immortal Master. She still did not know much about Jaaku's early years, before he went to China. Nor did she know where he'd been for all those years after he left Tibet, before turning up in Hawaii. But she was ready to accept that she might never learn those parts of the story.

Jelly became more boisterous than ever at school now that he could do three of the chen do. In addition to levitating all over the place, he'd now started throwing fireballs at Katana whenever nobody else was around. Katana became very leery of walking down empty corridors. Jelly always seemed to know when she was coming, and would jump out of empty classrooms to ambush her.

He had also started instigating fights with Ed Golia and Tommy Cosgrove. He would taunt them to the point of getting physical. But when one of them would try to push him or grab him, he would deflect their intent, causing them to fall feebly to the ground. Katana, Sara and Chris were enjoying this facet of Jelly's newfound power immensely.

Katana decided she wasn't going to let Jelly have *all* the fun, however. Now that she could play offense in chi fa, she decided a little extra practice was in order. She made it a point to knock Ed Golia down with a pulse of chi whenever she saw him in the halls. The fact that he could see no more than a flash of light made the activity all the more enjoyable.

Chris's struggle with math began anew as their class covered trigonometric identities. Katana was fascinated by the idea that two totally different functions could actually be the same. She spent hours one weekend memorizing and figuring out as many of the formulas as she could. She found some instances where three or even four functions that looked totally different were equivalent. But Chris was totally stymied by this concept. "These functions look *nothing* alike!" he complained. "How the hell can they be the same? And if they *are* the same, then why do we need all of them!"

The weekend of U.S. nationals was fast approaching. Both Sam and Master Fu had increased the intensity of their practices to unprecedented levels. Sam told Katana during her private lesson one Tuesday afternoon that she knew Katana had lost intentionally to Michelle. She said she understood Katana's motive, but at the same time made her promise not to do it again at nationals.

"Don't worry," said Katana. "I'm not planning on it. I'm winning that title this year."

After Dana's success with the gainer flash in her whip chain set at Golden Gate, Master Fu decided to add that element into the team demo for nationals. But he wasn't willing to make any further changes or additions to the demo this late in the season.

Katana was okay with that—she thought their show was incredibly strong. After Master Fu showed them Supernova's performance at their regional event, Katana felt very confident that the Hall would regain the national championship. As long as they didn't repeat the performance they'd given for the headmaster of Shaolin...

"LET'S GET STARTED, EVERYONE," said Master Nash as he sat down at the head of the large table in his conference room. All the masters were there this morning. They had their laptops open on the table—except for Master Dasari. He had no laptop, and sat with the fingers of both hands interlaced in his lap.

"Sam, Fu, nationals are this week. Your teams are ready?"

"We're ready," said Sam. "The girls' team is in first place going into the tournament, and the boys are in second. Team Tornado beat our boys by one point. But if we go head to head with them in D.C., we'll probably win. The other teams in Tornado's division are nowhere near as strong as Strike Force—that's the only reason they're ahead."

"Excellent," said Master Nash. "You confirmed that Katana threw her match against Michelle?"

Osaka raised an eyebrow at this. "Yes," replied Sam. "She thought Lassater gave her the win over Michelle in kata unfairly. So she let Michelle win sparring to settle the score."

"I'm glad she retains her sense of fair play despite her ongoing success," said Master Nash. "But make sure she doesn't pull that stunt at nationals! Fu, how about your team? Will we be depriving Supernova of a repeat?"

"No doubt about it," said Master Fu with a smile. "As long as the headmaster of Shaolin doesn't show up in the audience, the title's as good as ours."

The others chuckled. "No, I don't think there's much chance of Chan showing up in D.C.," said Nash. "He will almost certainly make an appearance at the Games this summer, however."

"But there's no team competition at the Games," said Master Fu. "So I have no worries there!"

"True," said Master Nash with a nod. "Dasari, do you have any news?"

"Unfortunately not," said Master Dasari. "The assassin has been quiet since the attack at the tournament, as far as my contacts know."

"Mitch said the same thing—the Arashi have continued their state of inactivity, and there have been no further attacks in Japan," Nash replied. "Sato confirms that Jaaku was incensed when the Arashi failed to capture the assassin in San Francisco. Because of Katana's intervention, this was the first attack to become prolonged in any way—but Jaaku missed his chance."

"We're certain, then, that by hiding his shen, the assassin can prevent Jaaku from finding him? From knowing his identity?" asked Master Fu.

"I know of no other means by which the assassin would be able to block that connection," said Nash.

"It's still possible the assassin is *not* an Arashi," said Sam.

"That's hardly likely," said Master Daniels. "Who else do we know that walks around in samurai armor, wielding a sword?"

"Maybe the assassin wants everyone to *think* he's an Arashi to throw people off his trail," Sam replied.

"I highly doubt that," said Master Nash. "According to Sato, Jaaku seems convinced the assassin is an Arashi. I have a feeling he's probably right. I've spoken to Chan about this. He's going to get Master Lu to come here to meet with Sato and Dasari. Maybe we'll get somewhere if the three of them put their heads together."

"You still don't think *Sato* is the assassin?" asked Fu.

"I've known Master Sato for thirty years," said Osaka. "He says it's not him. I believe him."

"This brings me to the next item on our agenda," said Nash. "Katana and the Shaolin Temple. We are moving forward with the plan. Katana will go to Shaolin in June to test for master."

"The other headmasters gave her the go-ahead?" asked Sam.

"Not all of them," said Master Nash. "But Santos, Nang and Tanaka approved. The Code of Bodhidharma says three headmasters must consent, and that provision has now been fulfilled."

"What about the others?" asked Master Fu. "Kim and Chatri —what did they say?"

"They both failed her," said Master Nash.

"What's Kim playing at—Katana *beat him* in a sparring match!" said Sam.

"Yes, but he claims the technique she used is not officially endorsed by the temples for sparring and should therefore disqualify her from consideration," said Master Nash.

"Yeah, right," said Sam, rolling her eyes. "He's just embarrassed that a fifteen-year-old girl was able to beat him."

"What about Chatri?" asked Master Fu.

"He insists that Katana did not display true mastery during her evaluation with him. He believes that her inability to adapt when he hid his shen should disqualify her," said Master Nash with a shrug.

"Yet she used a chi tao technique in a grappling match with Santos," said Sam, "and defeated Tanaka when she believed she was being attacked by an Arashi. Mastery is supposed to mean that the techniques of a given art have permeated your being. Based on everything Katana has done in the past two years, I don't see how anyone could argue that she doesn't understand the chen do on that level. And as far as Kim—she's not testing for master in tae kwon do, she's testing to be a chen do master. It's irrelevant that she didn't follow the official sparring rules!"

"This is a moot point," said Osaka. "Three headmasters have endorsed this action, so Katana will go to Shaolin regardless of what Kim and Chatri say."

"Well... I guess," said Sam. "But I still don't see why those two are being jerks."

"I am sure they're not voicing the *real* reasons for their rejections," said Master Daniels. "The truth is that there is no way a fifteen-year-old girl should be testing for master! I don't care how many chen do she can do..."

"Enough," said Master Nash. "Osaka is right. This action is going forward; the time for debate is behind us. What we must do now is prepare Katana for the exam. And she must still test for her third degree in kempo—Osaka, is she still on track?"

"We could test her tomorrow and she would pass," said Osaka with a grim smile.

"Very well then," concluded Master Nash. "The degree test will be here on Saturday, June ninth. Assuming Katana passes that, we will take her to Shaolin the following Saturday and she will test as a master of Shaolin."

The other masters' reactions to this were markedly different. Sam smiled and Master Fu nodded, but Master Daniels and Osaka shook their heads.

"I should give Katana the news—do we know where I'd be likely to find her at this time on a Saturday?" asked Master Nash.

"Wushu dojo," said Sam. "With Sara, Chris, Jelly, Scott and Dana. I guarantee it."

Master Fu laughed. "Do they ever stop doing karate?"

"Not that I know of," said Sam.

"They are just like three other students I remember from many years ago," said Osaka, with a wink at Sam.

AT THAT MOMENT, Katana was indeed in the wushu dojo with her friends. She and Dana had been practicing flowers. More than the monk move, more than the butterfly twist, even more than the gainer flash, they'd been practicing flowers for weeks now, trying to go as fast as Tan Zhi, the Chinese national champion. The two of them had even resumed doing pushups in a handstand. Katana figured that the stronger they could make their chests and shoulders, the faster they'd be able to go.

Jelly was practicing his staff set. When Katana grew tired of flowers, she sat down to watch him. He did his 1080 perfectly, catching the staff and flowing right into the next move.

She decided she wanted to try a 1080 herself. Despite all the tricks she now had in her arsenal, she'd never tried anything that involved spinning more than 360 degrees. She tried it once, but fell right over, landing on her butt with a thump.

Jelly laughed at her. "Oh, that was smooth!" he chided. "You're doing it wrong, anyway—you gotta launch off of both feet."

He helped her with it for a minute, but then Master Nash walked in.

"I'm sorry Katana, I didn't mean to interrupt," he said when she stopped working with Jelly to walk over to him.

"I wasn't getting it anyway."

Master Nash looked around the room. The others had stopped what they were doing to watch the two of them. "Why don't we take a walk?"

Katana followed him out the back doors, into the Zen rock garden. They sat down on a bench at the far end of the garden.

"Katana, do you recall right after the headmaster's visit, when I told you there may be one more evaluation?" asked Master Nash.

"Yeah…" said Katana uncertainly. "So there definitely is one?"

"After a fashion…" said Master Nash. "Katana, you are going to the Shaolin Temple in June. You will test for master."

Katana thought he was joking. "Come on—I'm only a second degree. I can't test for master," she said with a small laugh.

"Are you familiar with Bodhidharma?" asked Master Nash.

"Yeah—Liang talked about him, right? He was the founder of the Shaolin Temple or something?"

"Not exactly the founder, no," said Master Nash. "He was the monk who came from India and introduced the monks of Shaolin to a series of chi kung exercises and simple forms. Bodhidharma went on to be the headmaster of Shaolin for several decades. He oversaw the establishment of the first few temples beyond the original in Henan Province. And during his time he established the rules governing the monks' training and promotion to disciple and master. Those rules are written down in a long scroll known as the Code of Bodhidharma.

"In the Code, Bodhidharma stipulated that any disciple who could attain third degree in any art and also learn three or more of the chen do could test for master. Such a disciple would not become a master of any particular art. Instead he would become a master of the chen do."

"You're serious. This isn't a joke..." said Katana. This was the most ridiculous thing she'd ever heard.

"No, this is not a joke. Katana, as I told you a few weeks ago, the headmaster heard of your abilities last year, and the fact that so many around you were learning the chen do, and he became obsessed with meeting you. I refused to bring you to Shaolin. That's when he concocted his theory about your being a dim mak master. And when I failed to fall for that excuse, the headmaster brought up the Code.

"The rule for a disciple testing as a chen do master has *never* been used. And again, I do not think the headmaster truly cares about the Code. What he is after is you. The Code states that anyone testing for master must do so at the original Shaolin Temple, in Henan. Of course, that rule hasn't been used for over a hundred years. But since you will be the first-ever chen do master, the headmaster insists that we must observe the old rules and bring you to Henan Province. Once you are there, the head-master will, of course, finally have you within his grasp. He will do anything in his power to convince you to remain at Shaolin and train with him—or train with Liang, anyway. I doubt he intends to train you personally."

"But they don't allow girls there—how would that work?" asked Katana.

"As you can see, the headmaster will bend any rule to suit his purposes, Katana. He wants you so badly that he would not hesi-tate to break with that particular tradition. It galls him that someone as powerful as you should train anywhere else. And in addition, he is determined to understand how, by what mecha-nism those around you have learned the chen do. He is convinced it is through some connection they share with you."

"Well, there's no way I'm staying at Shaolin," said Katana. "This is my home—my friends are here."

"I have told the headmaster you'd feel that way, yet he persists," said Master Nash, shaking his head.

"Well... what is the test going to be like?" Katana asked. She still couldn't believe this was happening.

"I suspect your test will be similar in nature to the evaluation you had with him, or the master's exams we run here. Although I doubt he will have you spar with Pai Lo again—that didn't work out so well for him last time."

"Oh—is Pai Lo going to be testing, too?" asked Katana.

"Yes, he is—all of the headmasters except for Tanaka endorsed him," said Master Nash. "Tanaka said that you were out of his league. He didn't want to embarrass Pai Lo by making him take the test with you."

"Did all of the headmasters endorse me?" asked Katana. She felt like she already knew the answer to this question.

"Tanaka, Nang and Santos gave you the most glowing of recommendations," said Master Nash. "But Chatri and Kim demurred. They felt you weren't ready to become a master. But don't take it personally. I think they're simply unwilling to accept that a fifteen-year-old girl could possibly qualify."

"That's not much a surprise from those two," said Katana.

Everyone else had left the wushu dojo by the time Katana finished with Master Nash. She went up to her room. As expected, Sara and Chris were waiting to find out what Nash had wanted.

"They're testing you for master?!" they both asked when Katana gave them the news.

"Yeah—a chen do master," she said. She explained everything about the Code of Bodhidharma and the headmaster's real motives. Sara and Chris both seemed as blown away by everything as Katana felt. They went down to Sam's apartment that evening for sushi, and Katana told Sam about her conversation with Nash, too.

"Are you excited?" asked Sam with a big smile. "You're going to be the first female ever to test for master at the Shaolin Temple. This is huge."

"I don't know..." said Katana apprehensively. "It seems kinda crazy. I mean, the headmaster is only doing this because he wants to try to get me to train there. He thinks I'm doing something to make everyone around me get the chen do," she said, nodding to Sara and Chris.

"Oh, so what," said Sam. "You're obviously not going to stay there. And regardless of the headmaster's *real* motives, you're still going to become a master. Your parents would be so proud."

"Well, I have to pass the thing first, don't I?" said Katana.

"Don't start this again!" said Chris.

"What?" asked Katana, confused.

"It's your first black belt test all over again—remember how badly you were freaking out about that? Don't worry—you dealt with every single thing the other headmasters threw at you. Hell, Tanaka even pretended to be an Arashi and attacked you in the middle of the night, and you still kicked his ass! I don't imagine Chan's going to come up with anything you can't pass just as easily."

They laughed, but Katana asked, "Sam, is this what Osaka's been so upset about all year? Me testing for master?"

Sam hesitated a moment too long. "I don't know, Kat..."

"It is, isn't it?" said Katana. "Why on earth would he be against this? He's been my instructor since I was six years old—I would figure he'd be excited for me."

"Yes, Katana, you're right. Osaka is dead set against you going to Shaolin for this test. In fact, he's still hoping to put a stop to it. But I don't know the reason for it. Maybe he's just being a little old-fashioned... Daniels is totally against it, too, because he doesn't believe any teenager should be allowed to test for master. It's never been done, and he doesn't want that to change."

"Oh, so Osaka thinks I can't do it? He thinks I'm not good enough or something, because I'm a kid? After everything I went through this year—with Tanaka and the real Arashi, he doesn't think I deserve to take a simple test?"

"I don't know if that's it, Kat—but something's definitely bothering him. He hasn't been the same, ever since we first found out this was going to happen. I'm sure he doesn't have anything against you—he adores you, there's no way it's personal. If anything, I think he wants to keep you away from the headmaster. Maybe he's afraid you might decide to stay there... I don't know."

But Katana wasn't convinced. Osaka had been acting extremely strange toward her all year. First he'd refused to tell her *anything* about Jaaku's history, then he'd said he hoped the other headmasters would fail her. She knew it was utterly ridiculous that Master Chan wanted to test her just so he could try to get her to stay at Shaolin. But at the same time, she was excited to have a shot at becoming a master. She couldn't understand what Osaka's issue was, and she wanted to get to the bottom of it, right away.

When they walked out of Sam's apartment that night, Chris and Sara headed toward the stairs. Katana went the other way.

"Kat—where are you going?" asked Sara when she realized Katana wasn't with them.

Katana didn't answer. She walked to Osaka's door and knocked. But there was no answer. She knocked again, more loudly. But Osaka wasn't there.

"I want to know what the *hell* is going on with him, right now," said Katana when they got back up to the girls' room a few minutes later. "Why wouldn't he support me? Why would he want me to fail?"

"Ask him during our private on Thursday," Chris suggested. "I'm sure there's a good reason for the way he's acting—he's always supported you, in everything."

"I'm not waiting that long," said Katana.

CHAPTER 26

THE FORGOTTEN ARCHIVE

Katana woke up the next morning before dawn. She was tired and restless; she hadn't slept well. She wanted to talk to Osaka as soon as possible. And she thought she knew exactly where to find him at this hour. After taking off her pajamas, she threw on a pair of shorts and a sports bra. She pulled her sneakers on and exited her room as quietly as possible to avoid waking Sara.

Katana hadn't been to the old dojo in the woods since the beginning of the school year. She hadn't practiced tai chi there during spring break because she'd been so busy cataloging the archives. But she hoped Osaka might be there, back to his old routine.

She was disappointed. The dojo was deserted.

As she was already there and awake anyway, Katana decided

to practice. She began the long form, immediately forming a ball of energy between her arms. And as during her last visit here, she could feel her own energy reverberating against the chi of the forest.

She thought about Osaka as she moved through the postures. What possible reason could he have for not wanting her to test for master? Osaka himself had always said that to become a master, the student had to absorb the art in her very bones. Hadn't Katana proved, time and again that she could use the chen do instinctively?

Like Sam had said months ago, Katana had a talent for using the chen do in ways nobody would've anticipated. She'd nearly killed her boyfriend the year before—or thought she had, anyway—trying a technique she'd come up with on her own, without any instruction. And she'd learned everything Master Nang taught her with ease, getting nearly every technique the very first time she'd tried it. She'd used chi tao against Master Santos during her evaluation, and had used it again against Master Tanaka—whom she'd thought at the time was a real Arashi.

Not to mention the fact that she'd fought the Arashi assassin, using the chen do, and had held her own. And she could play both offense *and* defense in chi fa now. Only the masters knew how to do that.

Didn't all of this prove that she deserved a shot at testing for master herself?

And on top of everything else, she'd learned so much about chi in the archives. She knew how to control the flow of chi along her meridians; she could use pressure points to control the flow of someone else's chi; she had learned Iron Shirt chi kung...

The archives... Katana stopped in the middle of her form, looking around at the old stone foundation. She knew this was where the original masters had trained before the construction of the Hall itself was complete. Chang had talked about one of the masters wanting to build an escape tunnel out to the forest. They hadn't done it by the time Chow left—did they ever do it? Did the tunnels extend out here, under the old dojo?

Katana walked all over the foundation, trying to discern if there was anything underneath. There were no holes or openings.

She jumped off and walked around the perimeter, through the underbrush, to examine the sides of the structure. Finally she found something. On the side farthest from the Hall, there was a large crack.

She squatted down to get a closer look. Sure enough, there appeared to be an open space underneath the concrete. It looked like a large room, but there was so little light seeping through the opening that she couldn't tell for sure.

She thought about trying to squeeze herself through the crack to see what might be down there, but thought better of it. The opening wasn't big enough for her. Even if she did manage to squeeze through it, she didn't know how she'd get out again. The last thing she needed was to be trapped underground in the woods.

She walked around farther out from the foundation. About thirty feet from the back corner, she stumbled upon something.

Partially buried under decades of leaves and brush was a raised concrete frame with a wooden hatchway. Much of the wood had rotted away; Katana pulled apart what little remained. But it was no good. There appeared to be a stairway that led underground, but the roof had long since caved in.

But maybe there was another way into that room...

Katana ran back to the Hall. She went down to the tunnels, making her way to the eastern wall. She searched along its length. This proved difficult, as there was no one room or hallway that spanned the entire back of the building. She had to keep doubling back to find a way to the next section of wall in some other room or corridor.

Finally, as she walked along a dimly lit corridor in the back corner of the building, she discovered something intriguing. There was a door—a rickety looking, wooden door, constructed of several planks, hanging on rusty hinges. She tried to peer around its edge, but couldn't see a thing.

What could be back here? She was certain this was the very back wall of the main building. She tried to pull at the padlock, but although rusty, it was solid.

Katana had a thought. She sunk her chi into her dantian, and took a deep breath. Then she hit the plank to which the lock was affixed with the palm of her hand. She bounced her chi against the wood, splitting it in two. She had to break the plank again below the lock, but she was able to pull the broken wood away. The door swung open.

There was a tunnel—it reminded Katana of an old mine

shaft. Wooden beams rose from the floor on each side, supporting thick timbers across the ceiling.

Katana hesitated for a moment—the tunnel didn't exactly seem safe. She wondered if it might collapse at any minute. But she set out to see if her suspicion was right—she was guessing she'd found the escape tunnel. And she was willing to bet it led to the room under the old dojo. After everything she'd found in the archives, she wondered if there might be more secrets waiting for her there.

The tunnel became pitch black very quickly once she'd moved beyond the light of the corridor. Using the chi kung exercise to enhance her vision, she could make out a small pinprick of light at the end of the tunnel.

She walked for what seemed an eternity—she stumbled a few times, as the earthen floor was strewn with small rocks and debris. Despite her augmented vision, there was hardly any light in this tunnel. But finally she found the end.

The light she could see came from a tiny crack in the wall. Feeling the surface with both hands, she realized it was solid concrete. Someone went to great lengths to seal off this chamber.

Katana gathered her energy. Striking the wall with the palm of her hand, she felt and heard it crack. It took several more shots, but she was able to create a hole large enough to climb through. She felt like she was breaking into a tomb.

Inside was a large room—there was a shaft of sunlight streaming down from an opening near the ceiling. This must have been the crack she'd found on the side of the foundation. As dark as the room had appeared from the outside, now that her eyes were used to the pitch-blackness of the tunnel, it seemed blindingly bright.

There was a lot of debris strewn about this room as well—loose rocks and pieces of timber. She could see the entrance to the short tunnel that led to the hatchway. On the far side of the space was an old weapon rack.

Katana walked across the room to investigate. There was a straight sword in a scabbard—it appeared to have rusted through, though, as Katana couldn't pry the sword out. There was an enormous, extremely heavy-looking Kwan dao, but Katana didn't dare touch it—some of the wooden handle had rotted away.

There was also a samurai sword and a set of double broadswords. Katana was able to pull these out of their scabbards —all three blades were in excellent shape. The broadswords were very heavy—much heavier than the performance swords the wushu team used. Katana assumed they were real swords that had once been used in combat. She returned the blades to their scabbards, leaving them in the rack where she'd found them.

Then she saw it. In the corner adjacent to the door was a wooden crate. Other than the weapons, it was the only item in the room. She tried to pry off the top, but it wouldn't budge. Instead, she broke the top planks and ripped them aside.

The crate was loaded with straw. Katana rifled through it and found a book—a black, leather-bound manuscript with a single character on the cover. Although she didn't know Chinese or Japanese, she'd seen enough from the archives to recognize that word. It was the character for chi.

She browsed through the pages. It looked similar to the manual of healing arts they'd found. There were diagrams of the human body on each page that clearly showed meridians and various pressure points. Katana could not, however, read the short descriptions next to each diagram.

She dug through the rest of the straw to make sure there was nothing else in the crate. The book had been its only contents. She made her way back down the dark tunnel and up to her room.

"Sara—wake up!" she yelled once she'd closed the door.

Sara sat up in bed, looking groggy. "I'm awake—what's up?"

"Check this out," said Katana, handing Sara the manuscript.

A look of dawning comprehension came over Sara's face as she thumbed through the pages. "Katana—do you know what this is!?"

"I have a pretty good idea," Katana replied with a mischievous smile. "I'm gonna go get Chris."

She ran downstairs and banged on the door. Jimmy answered, looking Katana up and down, suddenly wide-eyed. She hadn't changed out of her shorts and sports bra, and she was covered in dirt and sweat. She couldn't comprehend how Jimmy could possibly find her attractive in this state. But she finally got around him, dragged Chris out of bed, and brought him upstairs.

"What the hell did you wake me up so early for?" Chris asked grumpily.

Sara handed him the manuscript. He browsed through it. "Who cares—it's another copy of the healing arts book. Wait—

where'd you find it, I thought we'd gone through everything in the archives?"

"No—it's not the healing arts," said Sara. "Look again."

Chris was confused. He opened up to a page that showed the heart meridian. He pointed at the diagram. "Yeah it is—see, this is the thing to increase chi to the heart... Wait, this is wrong—that's not the right pressure point... No way! It can't be... Is this... Is this what I think it is?!"

"The dim mak manuscript?" asked Katana.

"Yeah—is it?" asked Chris. "Holy crap..."

"What does that one do," asked Katana, taking the book back from Chris. "Is it the opposite of the healing arts—does it *stop* the chi from flowing to the heart?"

Sara stood next to Katana and read the description. "Yeah, Kat, that's exactly what it does. You hit the exact same point on the back of the neck that we used to increase chi flow, but then you hit this other point, in the ribs. It reverses the chi flow along the heart meridian."

"How can you read it that clearly?" asked Chris. "Isn't it in Chinese?"

Sara frowned. "No. This is straight kanji—it's Japanese."

"I wanna try it," said Katana.

Sara and Chris both stared at her in disbelief.

"Are you kidding?" said Sara. "Kat—this is *dim mak*. You wanna try dim mak?!"

"Yeah, I do," she said. "Chris, come here." Chris backed away, looking at her like she'd gone mad.

"No way—Kat, this is nuts! We can't start doing dim mak—we should bring this... this thing straight to Nash!"

"No," said Katana. "Well, yes, I'll bring it to Nash, but I wanna learn what's in here first. This is what I've been looking for all year. I'm not just gonna hand it over."

"Kat... You haven't been looking for *this*—the dim mak manuscript... What are you saying?" asked Sara, looking very worried.

"No, obviously not that specifically, but *something* I might be able to use against Jaaku! I told you what Nash said—even the Immortal Master wasn't as strong as him. Jaaku can control the chi around him and he can do the death touch—the Immortal Master couldn't do either. Guys, this is finally something that might make me strong enough to fight him! I've got to do it, can't you see that?!"

Sara and Chris looked at each other, then back at Katana. She knew she had them.

"You said you can read it, right?" Katana asked Sara.

"Yeah, perfectly," said Sara.

"So we'll know exactly what we're doing. Remember when Golia used that move against me last year in the tournament?"

"Yeah, and I remember how much you said it hurt," said Chris. "You almost passed out."

"Right, but Nash said that was only because Golia held it for so long. Remember? When Thompson and Van Heldon were doing it on each other at the beach, they didn't hurt each other that badly. If we do the moves, but don't hold them very long, we should be fine."

"I see where you're going with this..." said Chris.

Sara looked back and forth at the two of them for a minute. "Are you two both nuts?" But before either of them could answer, she added, "Yeah, you are—and so am I." She took the manuscript from Katana. "Chris, you're gonna have to be the guinea pig again."

"Yeah, I figured," he said.

"What do I do?" asked Katana.

"Hang on... it's like the other technique, but with a different pressure point. Push on the same point behind his ear. With your other hand, you have to hit the point that's two farther along the heart meridian from the one on the sternum," said Sara. "But it says to use the palm of your hand on the heart meridian—the chi flow in your palm is stronger than your finger, so it makes the effect stronger."

"Hmm..." said Katana. "I'm gonna try it with my finger first, that way it's not too severe." She applied the pressure points. "Do you feel anything?"

"No," said Chris. "Not a thing."

Katana tried using the palm of her hand. This time Chris reacted. "It's not that bad—I only felt a small twinge in my ribs."

"This was how it was when Van Heldon tried it the first time, remember?" asked Katana. "He wasn't able to do much, but when Thompson did it on him, he doubled right over."

"Maybe you have to stimulate your prenatal chi first," suggested Sara. "When we did the healing arts stuff, that was the first thing you were supposed to do."

"Good point," said Katana. She held her hands in front of her at shoulder level, palm-down, and took slow, deep breaths. She focused on sinking her chi into her dantian. It worked—her chi flow increased dramatically.

She tried the move on Chris again. This time he yelped in pain, doubling over like they'd seen Van Heldon do that night on the beach so long ago.

"Yeah, that was it," said Chris with a smile. "That hurt like hell!"

Katana talked Sara through it next, and then Chris did it on Katana.

"OW!" she yelled, pulling away from Chris almost the instant he touched her. "That's exactly what Golia did to me!"

"Kat... I don't remember him pushing behind your ear like this," said Sara doubtfully. "I just remember him ramming his palm into your chest."

Katana thought about this for a moment. "No—he did put his other hand here. He had me by the hair. I thought he was just pulling me closer—but he must've been hitting the pressure point at the same time."

"And when we saw them on the beach, they were putting one hand on the other person's shoulder—I thought they were just holding each other still..." said Sara.

"So this move causes all that pain," Chris said thoughtfully, "because what you're really doing is..."

"Reversing the chi flow to the heart," said Sara, finishing for him.

"That means... if Golia had held the move long enough... I could have died?" asked Katana.

"Are you sure you wanna keep messing with this stuff?" asked Chris.

Katana wasn't so certain anymore. For an instant, she had an impulse to do exactly what Chris had said a few minutes earlier—bring the book directly to Master Nash. But she didn't want to give up this opportunity.

"This is really, really dangerous stuff we're playing with here, Kat," said Sara. "Reversing the chi flow to the heart—if we mess something up, one of us could end up... dead."

"I know," said Katana. She sat down on the couch, arching her head back and staring at the ceiling. "I'm scared to try it. But I feel like I have to. This is the first thing we've found that has any chance of working against Jaaku."

"Kat, you're getting more and more powerful by the day, practically," said Chris, as he and Sara sat down in the chairs on either side of her. "By the time you do face him, you'll probably be strong enough..."

"How?" asked Katana.

"Well, you can do the chi fa thing now," said Sara.

"So can Nash—and so could Chow. Chow invented it! But he wasn't strong enough to beat Jaaku. Nash said the death touch was one of two things that made Jaaku *stronger* than the Immortal Master," Katana said, sitting up straight.

"But we're not even talking about the death touch," said Chris. "We're only talking about normal dim mak moves here..."

"Yeah, but it looks like even the normal moves can kill," said Sara.

"Definitely," Katana agreed. "And that's why I need to learn them. Guys, when I confront Jaaku, it's not going to be a sparring match. There isn't going to be a judge stopping the fight if Jaaku gets a point. It's going to be a fight to the death, and you both know it. This is the first thing we've found that can possibly help me."

"Kat, you're talking about killing someone," said Chris. "Think about that for a minute."

"I get it," Katana replied. "But it's not like I'm ever going to use this on anyone besides Jaaku."

"Obviously," said Chris, "but this is still incredibly serious. You're going to be using the exact same tool that Jaaku uses to kill."

"So you're saying you don't think I should learn any of this stuff?"

"No..." Chris said pensively. "I'm just saying you need to think about what you're doing here before you do it."

Katana decided to sleep on it. Sara hid the manuscript in her suitcase; they didn't go back to it for the rest of that day.

When they got to the tai chi dojo the following morning, Master Nash had them take a seat. "This weekend, those of you who earned enough points in Eureka and San Francisco will be joining our competition teams as they travel to Washington, D.C. for the U.S. nationals. Master Daniels and Master Osaka will be staying behind to hold down the fort," he began.

"This summer, the World Games of Martial Arts will be taking place in Beijing. The Games do not have team divisions, however the winners of the individual kata, weapon and sparring events at nationals this weekend will have the opportunity to represent the United States and compete against the rest of the world. This event takes place only once every four years, so this is an extraordinary opportunity and honor for those who go.

"The Games are the most prestigious event in the world for martial artists of all styles. And it represents the highest caliber of competition imaginable—national champions from dozens of countries participate in the Games. Should any of you qualify, it will be an experience you will remember for the rest of your life."

Breakfast that morning was much louder than usual from the buzz about the World Games.

"I bet that kid from Shaolin who did the whip chains is gonna be there," said Jelly in between mouthfuls of toast.

"Tan Zhi?" asked Dana. "Definitely."

"Yeah, but Kat'll beat him," said Jimmy, looking at her with a big smile on his face.

"Psh, whatever!" said Katana. "Even if I go to the Games, there's no way I can touch him! Did you see how fast he was?"

"I bet Komatsu will be there, too," said Sara.

"Who's that?" asked Paul.

"He's the Japanese national champion in sparring," said Chris. "Kat beat him when we went to visit Sara's school in Japan."

The whole table stopped to look at her. "You beat the Japanese national champion?!" asked Scott, clearly impressed.

"Guys, I only beat him because he wasn't trying and I used the gainer flash. When we went back again this winter he kicked my ass!" said Katana.

Katana and Sara ran up to their room to get changed after

school that day. When they got to the wushu dojo the talk about the Games continued. Master Fu was telling a bunch of the kids about the way Tan Zhi had beaten the reigning champion in weapons four years earlier.

"Maybe there'll be another upset this year," he concluded, looking right at Katana.

Katana and Dana worked on their samurai sword form that day. Katana felt like she was making progress, but still lacked the fluency she had with her chains.

Paul, Scott and Donnie, however, were getting quite good. They were working on a variety of complicated spins and release skills. And Jelly was good enough with the nunchucks that Katana thought he could give Becca Stratton a run for her money. She couldn't wait to see what their demo would look like the following year.

Katana was a little worried about Dana. She'd been doing the gainer flash in the whip chain set perfectly for weeks after Golden Gate. But more recently she'd become much less consistent. She still nailed it about half the time, but sometimes dumped the trick completely. Katana hoped she'd get it back in time for nationals.

When the lesson was over, everyone headed downstairs. Sara and Chris made their way toward the cafeteria, but Katana went across the atrium toward the kempo dojo instead.

"Where are you going?" asked Sara. Katana didn't answer.

She walked into the room. Osaka was kneeling down in front of the altar, taking off his belt.

"Osaka," Katana called from the doorway, "can I talk to you for a minute?"

He stood and turned. "Yes, Katana, what's on your mind," he asked, walking across the room to her.

"Master Nash told me about what's happening at the Shaolin Temple—about my mastery test," she began uncertainly. It had never been hard to talk to him before. "And... Well, Sam told me you're totally against it. I was just... wondering why?"

Osaka stood there looking at her for several moments. "I'm sorry, Katana, this isn't something I can discuss," he said finally. He walked past her, toward the door.

"You don't think I'm good enough to be a master," Katana said to his back.

Osaka stopped, turning to face her. "Katana, you are already more powerful than many masters I've met. It's not a question of your being good enough."

"Then what is it?" asked Katana. "Why do you want to deny me this? You've been my teacher since I was six years old. You've always supported me before. Why not now?"

Osaka looked down at the floor, shaking his head. "I'm sorry, Katana," he said very quietly, then turned again and strode out of the room.

Katana stood there for several minutes, staring after him. "I'm sorry, Katana," was all he could say? He could provide her with no reason, no explanation for his stance in this matter?

Katana went to dinner. She told Chris and Sara about her conversation with Osaka. She also told them that she'd made up her mind about the dim mak manuscript. She intended to move forward, and learn everything she could from it. They went straight to the girls' room after dinner.

"Let's start from the beginning," said Sara, digging the volume out of her suitcase.

Katana, Chris and Sara spent the next few hours going through the manuscript, one technique at a time. They went very slowly and carefully—all three were well aware of how dangerous this was, and wanted to make sure not to make any mistakes.

Much like the chi kung and healing arts documents, the dim mak manuscript taught how to control the flow of chi to virtually every organ in the body—only instead of increasing that flow, it taught how to diminish or even reverse it.

Every technique they tried that night caused pain in some way. They were careful to hold each move for only a moment or two, to avoid causing any lasting damage.

They each tried a technique to stop the flow of chi to the kidneys, and in fact this caused a sharp pain in Chris's back when Katana applied it. They had a scare when they tried the technique that reversed the flow of chi to the lungs. Suddenly Chris couldn't breathe—he started turning blue. Katana immediately did the technique from the healing arts to increase lung capacity. Chris took a deep breath. He and Sara decided to skip that particular move.

They also learned how to reverse the flow of chi to the liver and the intestines. Both techniques caused great amounts of pain in the affected region.

On Tuesday night they forged ahead. They learned how to reverse the flow of chi to the stomach—Chris nearly vomited when Katana tried that technique—and the pancreas. But when they got to the next page, Chris refused to let Katana try the move described there.

"Come on, Chris, it's not like it'll make you vomit... or stop breathing..." pleaded Katana.

"No—no way!" said Chris, backing away from her. "The bladder, Kat—I'm gonna end up pissing myself!"

Sara laughed. Katana moved forward, trying to grab Chris. But he jumped over the couch to get away from her.

"Forget it, Kat!" he said, laughing himself now, but totally serious. "We're *not* doing this one!"

"How am I going to learn if you won't let me try it?" she asked.

"Try it on Sara then!" said Chris.

"No way," said Sara. "You're not doing that on me!"

"Give it up, Kat—it's not like this one's gonna be useful against Jaaku anyway! You're not gonna beat him by making him wet his pants!" said Chris.

"Does samurai armor even have pants?" Sara asked.

Katana was determined to learn this technique, however. She decided she knew the perfect test subject.

"Ed Golia?!" asked Sara at breakfast the next morning when Katana told her what she was planning. "I'd pay money to see him wet himself, but how are you going to get close enough to try it?"

"You'll see," said Katana enigmatically.

But she couldn't find Ed anywhere that morning. She usually ran into him at least once by the time they finished their morning classes, but not today. She did see him at lunch, but the cafeteria was much too crowded for what she was planning.

Finally an opportunity presented itself. It was the end of the day. Katana was walking with Sara and Chris, down an empty hallway on their way to the library for study hall. They went around the corner and nearly walked right into Ed and Tommy. Before they had a chance to hurl any insults at them, Katana dropped her backpack and stood right in front of Ed.

He backed up nervously. "Wha... What are you doing, Kahanu?" Katana hadn't given up her habit of knocking him over with a pulse of chi whenever she saw him.

"Well, Ed," she said in a voice as sultry and sensuous as she could manage, "I had this dream about you last night..."

"Uh... really?" Ed said stupidly. He stopped backing away.

Katana put one hand around his neck and brought her face in close to his, giving a little giggle. Chris's eyes bulged at this display. "Oh yeah," she cooed. "And I realized, I think I like you, Ed..."

"Oh... Uh... You do?"

Katana ran her other hand down his chest. "Yeah, I do." Now she had him. With her left hand, she pressed the back of his neck, and with her right, a point on his abdomen along the bladder meridian.

"OW!" yelled Ed. "What are you doing?!"

He tried to back away, but Katana was able to hold him still long enough to achieve the desired effect. A large wet spot appeared in the front of his pants.

Sara and Chris laughed so hard they nearly fell over. Katana finally let go. Ed started to run away, but slid in the small puddle of urine that had formed between his feet. He fell over flat on his back.

Tommy laughed out loud. "I don't believe it! YOU PISSED YOURSELF!" Ed regained his feet and ran down the hall.

Katana, Sara and Chris laughed themselves breathless repeatedly throughout the rest of the afternoon. But when they arrived in the girls' room after dinner, they sobered almost instantly. The innocuous-looking manuscript reminded them immediately of the gravity of what they were doing.

"Right," said Sara as she opened the book. "The next technique... Oh—it's the one Thompson used when he kidnapped you!"

"When he paralyzed me?" Katana asked.

"Yeah," said Sara. "But this says it's only temporary. You have to *hit* the back of the neck this time—you can't just touch it. And you have to use your index finger and your middle finger to hit two points at the same time."

"This sounds complicated," Katana observed.

Sara walked her through it, and in minutes, she was able to smack the two points on the back of Chris's neck, paralyzing him. Once he could move again, he and Sara tried the technique on each other as well.

"Oh no," said Sara when she read the next page in the manuscript. "This one causes permanent paralysis."

"Yeah, we're not doing this one," said Chris, waving his hand in the air. "What's next?"

"Wait," said Katana. *"Permanent* paralysis? Define permanent?"

"Well, it says the person will remain paralyzed until someone restores their meridian system."

"We know how to do that," said Katana.

"We do?" asked Chris uncertainly. "Oh yeah, we do! That was in the healing arts manuscript! I don't remember it, though..."

"I do," said Katana. She did it on Chris once to make sure. And just like before, Chris's body jerked violently when she pushed the necessary points.

"You wanna try the paralysis move now, don't you?" said Chris.

"Yeah, I do," replied Katana.

Chris let out a long sigh. "Let's do it."

Sara read the directions to Katana. She pushed the pressure points—one on the shoulder and one in the side of the neck. Chris froze, still as a statue.

The girls stood there and stared at him in amazement for a moment—he wasn't moving. "That's enough, Kat," said Sara. "This is scary—make him better!"

Katana pressed the points to restore his meridians again. This time instead of jerking violently, Chris's entire body went limp. He nearly fell to the floor before the girls caught him and helped him into a chair.

"Are you okay?!" asked Sara.

"Yeah, I'm fine," said Chris, a little shaky. "That was messed up—I couldn't move. Everything started to go dark. I think I would've passed out if you hadn't revived me when you did."

"Kat, I don't know if we should go any further," said Sara. "This stuff keeps getting scarier..."

"We might as well do the rest," said Chris. "We've gone this far."

Neither Chris nor Sara wanted to try the paralysis move, though, so they moved on.

The next technique caused blindness, the one after that, deafness. Katana practiced the techniques they'd learned from the healing arts to restore these functions before they tried the dim mak moves. She remembered each technique flawlessly. Sara read the directions, and Katana applied the dim mak move to make Chris blind. Immediately, she restored his vision. She repeated the process with his hearing.

"Three more techniques," said Sara. "This next one... Oh no, this one knocks you out. Kat—we shouldn't try this. This could be so dangerous—what if you knock him out and then can't revive him?"

"We know a technique to revive someone," Chris pointed out. "Let's do it—but Kat, do the one to revive me first, please—to make sure you remember how."

Katana remembered the technique perfectly. She pressed the point on the side of Chris's neck along the visual meridian, and one at the base of his skull along the brain meridian.

"Yeah, that's it," said Chris. "I'm tingling all over, just like last time. Let's do it—but don't leave me out for too long, okay?"

"Chris, lie down," suggested Katana. "If you're gonna pass out, I don't want you to fall and hit your head."

"Yeah, good idea," said Chris. He stretched out on the floor.

"You have to push the point along the heart meridian on his left shoulder," Sara read from the manuscript. "And at the same time smack the point on the back of the neck—the one on the brainstem meridian that we used for temporary paralysis."

"Oh," said Katana. "Chris, you gotta roll over—I can't hit your neck if you're on your back."

Chris turned over and Katana tried it. She pushed a finger into his shoulder, and smacked the back of his neck. Nothing seemed to happen.

"Do you feel anything?" she asked.

Chris didn't answer.

"He's out, Kat—bring him back, I don't like this," said Sara, her voice a little higher than usual.

"Yeah..."

Katana rolled Chris onto his back—his head lolled eerily to one side. She pressed a point on the side of his neck with one hand, reaching under his head with the other hand to push the point at the base of his skull.

Nothing happened.

"Oh no—CHRIS!" Sara screamed.

Chris opened his eyes. "Did you do it?" he asked groggily.

Sara collapsed in a chair. "Kat, this is scary as hell. I don't wanna do any more tonight. Let's leave the rest for tomorrow, okay?"

Katana couldn't agree more. For an instant she'd thought she wouldn't be able to revive Chris. That scared her in a way that none of the other techniques had.

Thursday night after dinner they went straight to the girls' room again. Sara opened the manuscript, skipping to the end. "We're almost done—only two more techniques."

"What are they?" asked Katana. "One of them must be the death touch—we're obviously not trying that."

Sara flipped back and forth a few times between the last couple of pages, looking confused.

"What's wrong?" asked Chris.

"Well... I don't know," said Sara. "Neither one of these says anything about the death touch. One says 'chi flow,' and the other says 'merge prenatal chi.'"

"Chi flow..." said Katana. "Maybe this is something like the move in the healing arts where you can feel the other person's chi?"

"What about 'merge prenatal chi'?" Chris asked. "Could *that* be the death touch?"

"Must be," said Katana. "When Jaaku takes an Arashi, he absorbs the person's prenatal chi into his own dantian, right? And I know for sure he can use that connection to do the death touch."

"Kat, I don't think we should try either one of these," said Sara fearfully. "You have to do almost the exact same thing for both of them. Either one could be the death touch."

Katana looked at Chris. There was no way she was willing to try either move unless she could be certain what they did. It was much too great a risk.

"You're right," said Katana. "Let's do this—we're leaving tomorrow for D.C. Take the manuscript with you. Think about it more over the weekend. See if you can figure out for sure what these two techniques do. If you can, we'll try the one that's *not* the death touch when we get back."

"Sounds like a plan," said Chris. But Katana could tell Sara wasn't so crazy about the idea.

For the rest of the night they went back through the other techniques to make sure they remembered everything. Finally they decided to get to bed early as they had a flight to catch first thing the next morning.

CHAPTER 27

U.S. NATIONALS

During their entire plane ride the next morning all Katana could think about was the dim mak manuscript. She went through every technique in her head; she remembered them all perfectly.

The manuscript changed everything. This one little book gave her, at last, the kind of power she could use to defeat Jaaku. She knew very well how dangerous this power was, and she would never dream of using it against anyone but Jaaku—her little experiment on Ed Golia notwithstanding.

But for the first time she had a tool, a weapon in her fight against the enemy—a fight she knew without any doubt loomed somewhere just over the horizon—that gave her a chance of defeating him. She could reverse the chi flow to his heart or render him unconscious with a touch. And in a few short days she would know how to do the death touch. There would be no way to try it, but the knowledge at least would be hers.

This idea scared her to the core, yet it was also comforting. She now had, for the very first time, a glimmer of hope, a possibility of victory in that unavoidable confrontation.

Once they'd landed in Washington and boarded the bus that would take them to the Presidential Hotel, all thought of Jaaku and the dim mak manuscript was driven from her mind. She was about to compete in the U.S. nationals—in all three of her individual divisions as well as both team divisions. Katana hadn't given a moment's thought to her preparations.

She *had* spent hours every weekend working on her whip chain set and Kata Fourteen, and sparring with Chris. And both Sam and Master Fu had been working them into the ground every Friday for weeks getting ready for the tournament. But in the past week, between finding out she'd be testing for master and discovering the dim mak manuscript, Katana's usual flow going into a tournament had been totally disrupted.

Normally, during that last week she'd think of nothing but the competition. In addition to the physical practice during her lessons, she'd go through everything mentally over and over again —in her classes at Lincoln, during meals and as she went to sleep each night. But she hadn't done that this time. Instead, she'd been mentally reviewing the dim mak manuscript or trying to imagine what her test at Shaolin might be like.

But this was it. They arrived at the hotel and she had only a couple of hours to check in, eat and prepare for the first event. The tournament would be starting at three.

She arrived at the convention hall with Sara and stopped in her tracks just inside the doors. Master Lassater had told them this place was much bigger than the hotel in Eureka, but had failed to convey any comprehension of its true size. The ceilings were probably twice as high as those in the dojo at the Hall. The room was so wide that Katana couldn't make out the faces of the people standing near the opposite wall.

They walked around to look for the weapons ring. Katana realized that these rings were much larger than usual. She'd had to be careful at Eureka and Golden Gate not to get too close to the edge of her ring for fear of hitting someone with her chains. She wouldn't have that issue here.

The stage was set up near the back wall. There were scaffolding towers halfway across the room for the spotlights and television cameras. Katana hoped she'd be on that stage the next night, performing on national television in at least one of her events.

Master Nash came over to them a minute later. "Katana—listen to me very carefully. Harvey Ryder just interviewed me..."

"I thought he only bugged the competitors!" said Katana in disbelief.

"Well, he was asking about *you*. Katana, somehow he has heard a rumor that you will be going to Shaolin to test for master. I'm sure at some point this weekend he'll interview you as well. If he asks you about Shaolin, it is imperative that you deny the rumor!"

"What—why?"

"I can't get into it right now, but tell him that you're only

KEN WARNER

going to visit—the headmaster invited you to the temple after your performance back in February. Do *not* let him know the truth, Katana!"

Master Nash ran off again. Katana looked at Sara, her eyes wide with surprise. Sara merely shrugged.

It took them several more minutes to locate the weapons ring. When they finally found it, they had a bit of a surprise: Becca Stratton was there to greet them.

"What are you doing here?!" asked Katana.

"What do you think I'm doing here—I came to cheer you on! You made nationals in *three* events—I wouldn't miss this for the world," she replied.

"No," said Katana. "I only made it in kata and weapons, remember? Michelle beat me in sparring."

"Oh, whatever—you still get to compete!" said Becca. "Hey, who else from the Hall made nationals this time?"

"Other than the two teams, Jelly made it for weapons..." said Sara.

"Jelly—he's the short kid that does staff?"

Katana and Sara both laughed.

"Yeah, that's him," said Sara.

The room became steadily more crowded while Katana stretched and warmed up. The judges arrived and the center judge lined everyone up for roll call. There were eleven other girls here —including Katana, one from each of the twelve national regions. All but one of the others were using sport karate weapons—staves, nunchucks, kamas and samurai swords. The last girl had a set of double broadswords.

516

The judge finished roll call. "We will be eliminating down to one competitor. The winner of this ring will compete tomorrow night in grands against the winner from the fourteen- and fifteen-year-old boys' ring, and the boy and girl winners from the sixteen- and seventeen-year-old division. Good luck, all of you."

Katana grew nervous. She remembered vividly how good everyone in this ring had been the previous year. But Becca had won then—and Katana had beaten her at Golden Gate this year. She could do this.

The judges started the event. Katana became more and more nervous as each successive competitor took her turn: every one of them was amazing. One girl dropped her samurai sword during an incredibly difficult sequence. She'd released the sword spinning in the air as she spun around herself, and had been unable to catch it. The girl was disqualified, but everyone else performed flawlessly.

Katana was called up near the end—only two other girls remained.

She got up and took a deep breath—she could feel the butterflies in her stomach. She'd done the chi kung exercise to calm her nerves while she waited her turn, but it had worn off every time another competitor came up.

Katana ran forward in an arc toward the judges, doing a front aerial to a split. None of the other competitors had entered the ring with a trick.

"Representing the Hall of the Dragon, I am Katana!" she yelled. She pushed to her feet and walked forcefully to the back corner of the ring. As she started her set she could feel her nerves melting away, her energy level rising.

She ran across the ring into her double backflip. The crowd reacted shrilly as she landed. But then the crowd faded away and it was just her and the chains.

Katana focused on keeping the chains steady through the flower section. She and Dana had worked on their speed every weekend—it was paying off. Katana felt like she was almost as fast as Tan Zhi now.

She got to the leg wrap and neck wrap, turned around, opened her chains and threw the gainer flash. One more cycle of flowers, and she brought her chains together in one hand for the monk move, carefully lifting her left foot over her head. Five revolutions and she stalled the chains, falling to her split. She was vaguely aware of the crowd roaring its approval.

Katana pushed to her feet, did her butterfly kicks, and went into the butterfly twist. She landed in her split. Sara and Becca were screaming for her at the opposite side of the ring.

She was almost there. Katana kicked her back leg around and did her body jumps. Finally, she kicked up to finish her form.

Sara and Becca gave her a hug when she exited the ring. They both said they were certain Katana would win. Katana didn't want to take anything for granted, but she knew she'd turned in an extremely strong performance.

The last two girls performed and the judges went to figure out the scores. Dana ran over with Chris and Jimmy.

"We missed it!" said Dana. "Fu was making me do the gainer

flash over and over again—he's still worried I'm going to miss it. How'd you do?"

"Kat kicked ass," said Sara. "I think she's got it."

"Jelly won his ring," said Chris. "He's going to grands."

"Not that that's a big surprise," added Jimmy.

The center judge lined them up again.

"I want to congratulate you on some amazing performances," he said. "The top three scores were only one tenth of a point apart from each other. Advancing to grands tomorrow night will be... Katana Kahanu!"

Sara, Becca, Dana and Chris went wild as Katana walked up to shake hands with the center judge. Katana felt great—even if she lost all her other events, she'd still take the stage for weapons.

"Kata next," said Chris as he went with the girls to find Katana's ring. Katana had only a few minutes to stretch before they started. The judges did roll call, and Katana was called up first. She was relieved.

She marched to the front of the ring and yelled out her introduction. Then she walked backwards, keeping her eyes on the center judge the whole time. She let out the loudest, meanest kiai she could manage.

She got to the back of the ring and turned her back to the judges as she'd done in San Francisco. Her friends were right in front of her, cheering her on. Katana stuck her tongue out at them. She turned around and started her form.

Katana focused on hitting every stance perfectly, slamming every strike and kick as hard as she could. It felt good. She knew when she was done that at the very least, she'd set the bar extremely high for everyone else. Her friends gave her high-fives as she left the ring.

Katana was totally relaxed watching the other girls perform. But when the last competitor was called up, Katana thought for a moment that one of the boys had mistakenly entered the ring. The girl looked very masculine. She was over six feet tall and built like a small mountain. She wore a red gi top with the letters "MKA" screen-printed in white on the back. Katana didn't think she was nearly as sharp as the other girls had been, but she had an amazing amount of power. Her presentation was nearly as fierce as Michelle's. Katana knew she'd never want to get hit by this girl —she could probably knock her halfway across the room.

"There's no way that girl's only fifteen!" said Sara. "She's... huge!"

"She could be sixteen," said Becca. "I turned sixteen in December, and I'm still in this division."

"She'd be huge even if she were eighteen," muttered Chris.

When the girl was done, the judges went to calculate the scores.

"This is the same as the weapons, right?" Katana asked Becca. "Whoever wins goes to grands against the boy from our division, and the boy and girl from the older division?"

"Yeah," said Becca, nodding her head. "It's exactly like weapons."

The center judge lined them up again. "Going to grands, for girls' fourteen- and fifteen-year-old kata, will be... Katana Kahanu!"

Katana turned to look at her friends. Becca, Sara and Dana

screamed, grabbing her in a hug before letting her go up to shake the judge's hand.

Only then did Katana see Michelle on the far side of the ring. Standing next to her was a man Katana assumed to be her father. Katana ran over to her. "That should've been you up there!"

"I don't think so, Kat," replied Michelle. "You were amazing at Golden Gate—you earned your place here. I hope you beat them all tomorrow night! Oh—this is my dad."

"Hi," said Katana with a smile.

"Hello, Katana," said Mr. Summers, shaking her hand. "Michelle's told me about you. You were her inspiration in sparring last year when you competed with the boys. But I don't want to hold you up—you two had better get to your sparring ring."

Chris and Jimmy went off to their own sparring ring. Dana, Becca and Sara went with Katana and Michelle to find Sierra and Olivia.

When they arrived at their ring, Katana noticed that the big girl from her kata event was in her sparring ring, too. It appeared her whole team was here—several other girls wore red gi tops with MKA on the back. Katana wondered where they were from.

Because everyone from the top sparring teams earned a chance to compete at nationals, there were far more girls for sparring than there'd been in weapons or kata. The judge explained that they'd eliminate down to four competitors. The finalists would fight in grands the following night.

The center judge started the ring. "First match," he called out, "Sierra Gonzalez and Mildred Kane." It was the big girl from

MKA. Katana gave Sierra a high-five and wished her luck. But she didn't think Sierra stood a chance.

The match began. Sierra moved in very aggressively. She started with a front kick to roundhouse kick combination. Mildred batted her leg away as if swatting a fly. She punched Sierra in the face, knocking her to the floor. The other girls from MKA chanted "Milton, Milton!"

"Milton..." said Sara, looking thoughtful. "Milton... Karate Academy—Kat do you think they're from that school Sensei Mike told us about?"

"Yeah—where that kid goes who was picking on Billy," said Katana. "I think you're right."

The match started again. Sierra still looked dazed. Mildred threw a front kick at her ribs. Although Sierra blocked it, Mildred got her kick through anyway, knocking Sierra out of the ring. Mildred was up 3-0.

Sierra managed to land a kick in her next round, but only because she moved so much faster than Mildred. She'd launched it the instant the judge said "Go." But it wasn't enough. Mildred landed another kick in the following round, winning the match 5-2.

Sierra had been eliminated.

Two more matches went, then it was Michelle's turn. Her opponent was a full head taller, but it didn't seem to matter. Michelle was so aggressive, the girl didn't have a chance to throw a single punch or kick. Michelle won the match 5-0, advancing to the next round.

Olivia also advanced, although her match was much tougher.

She and the other girl went several rounds without the judges agreeing on a single point. Olivia ended up with a bloody nose, but pulled out the win 6-4.

Katana went next. Her opponent was the same size and very aggressive. She jumped at Katana with an overhead strike the moment the match started. Katana dodged, using her back leg to catch her in the ribs with a hook kick.

Katana opened with her three-kick combination in the next round. She landed the roundhouse kick and the axe kick, moving ahead 4-0.

The other girl landed a big hook kick to Katana's head in the round after that, earning two points. She tried the same kick again in the following round, but Katana dropped, sweeping out her other leg. Katana won the match 6-2. She advanced with Michelle and Olivia.

Katana was called up first in the next round—she hardly thought this was fair, as she'd just fought in the last match. Her opponent, a girl from MKA, had fought in one of the very first matches. She'd had much more time to rest.

The girl was extremely aggressive. She launched a barrage of punches as soon as they started, driving Katana right out of the ring. Katana was down, 1-0.

Katana kept her weight on her back leg as they set up for the next round. She snapped a roundhouse kick to the girl's head the moment the match started. Katana was up 2-1.

The girl didn't learn her lesson. She continued to rush in, so Katana snapped a kick to her head every time. She won the match 6-1.

Michelle also advanced—once again her opponent failed to score a single point. But Olivia was knocked out of the running. Her opponent was much taller, and Olivia couldn't get through her kicks.

"One more match and we go to grands," said Katana.

"I know," said Michelle with a frown. "I hope I don't have to spar with Mildred—I don't know if I can beat her."

"You can," said Katana. "Do what Sierra did when she landed that one kick. She's big, but you're *way* faster." But neither of them had to face Mildred. Katana and Michelle both won their next matches with ease, advancing to grands along with Mildred and another girl from MKA.

"Hey," said Sara as they left the ring to get ready for team demo, "with only two teams in grands..."

"Whoever wins first place wins the team competition, too," Katana finished for her.

"Yeah," said Sara. "So no pressure or anything, Kat!"

They arrived at the stage to find Dana in a heated argument with Master Fu.

"I can do the gainer! I can't believe you're taking it out!" Dana yelled.

"I know you can do it, but it's not worth the risk tonight," said Fu. "Did you see Supernova warming up? They're *not* going to make any mistakes. Our demo is just as strong without that one move—we don't need it. We only need to make it to grands, and we can do that *without* the gainer."

"But I can *do this*! Give me a chance..."

"Dana, here's the deal. We can make grands without the

gainer. If we keep it in—hang on—if we keep it in, and you *nail* it, we're no better off than we are without it. But if we keep it in and you miss it, then we lose *everything*! It's not worth the risk. If it's close going into tomorrow night, we'll put it in for grands."

Dana stormed off. Master Fu walked over to Katana and Sara.

"We're taking the gainer out, Kat—go from the leg wrap into the monk move."

"Got it," said Katana. Master Fu smiled and patted her on the shoulder before running off to follow Dana.

Katana knew Dana always performed better under pressure. She thought if Master Fu let them do it, Dana was virtually guaranteed to land the gainer flash. But she wasn't about to argue.

Katana and Sara went with the rest of the team to warm up on their weapons. Dana joined them a few minutes later. She walked through her set with Katana a couple of times. Several other teams were warming up as well. Strike Force hadn't scored well enough against the Hall of the Dragon to make it to nationals, so they weren't present. In fact, Supernova was the only team Katana recognized from the previous year.

A few minutes later the judges told everyone they were starting the event. "Taking the stage will be the team demonstration event," someone announced over the PA system. "The top three teams will advance to grands tomorrow night."

The first few teams to go up were good, but Katana knew they weren't at the same level as her team and Supernova. They had great martial arts, but the choreography was either weak or nonexistent.

Supernova went next.

Katana continued to be impressed. They still weren't doing double backflips, but they executed every trick they did do perfectly. The team used sport karate weapons—they had a staff set, followed by samurai swords. Then a boy did nunchucks, while two girls framed him with an empty-hand set. As always their choreography was very well designed. Their transitions to and from the stage were smooth, integrating tricks in a way that was very exciting to watch. There was something on stage every second of the demo.

After the next two teams had gone, the center judge called the Hall of the Dragon to the stage. Katana had no doubt that Supernova was the team to beat. They took the stage, set up their weapons, and got in line to wait for their music to start.

"Dana still looks pissed," Katana whispered to the back of Sara's head.

The music began. Sara walked forward to meet Jelly in the middle of the stage. They turned to walk up to the judges. Katana and Dana followed. They hit the cue in the music and shouted out their introduction.

They executed their opening choreography sequence flawlessly; Katana and Dana threw their tricks. Katana watched from the edge of the stage as first broadsword, then staff nailed their sets.

Katana started to fidget—chains were next.

The kids from broadsword did their tricking sequence while Jelly dropped his staff at the back of the stage. Then he and Katana did their aerials to the front corners.

Katana could tell Dana was still furious as they launched into their tricks. Katana and Jelly both landed their double backflips at the same time Dana landed her flash kick.

The girls flew through the beginning of chains, but Katana knew something was wrong when they got to the monk move. Dana was spinning both chains in one hand, but they were wobbling. Katana wasn't sure, but it looked like she'd grabbed the handles badly. They lifted their legs over their heads. As they stalled the weapon to drop into their splits, Dana's chains smashed together.

Katana thought they'd be okay. By the time Dana's chains hit, they'd been finishing the move anyway. She wondered if the judges had even noticed. They finished the performance and the audience roared its approval. The entire crowd got to its feet, giving them a standing ovation.

They held their final formation to wait for the judges' scores. They were high. Katana didn't remember Supernova's numbers, but she was certain they'd scored higher than anyone else. They would definitely be going to grands.

"We tied Supernova!" Sara said as they left the stage. "Tomorrow night should be interesting."

Dana brushed past them, throwing her chains on the ground. Master Fu walked over to them, smiling ear to ear. "Dana— what's wrong? You guys nailed it!"

"I BLEW IT!" Dana yelled.

Master Fu looked confused. "What are you talking about— you guys were perfect!"

"The chains—they smashed together on monk!"

"I didn't see that..." said Master Fu.

"They did," said Katana. "But it was right as we dropped into the splits. We had to stop the chains anyway."

"See?" said Master Fu, but Dana didn't reply. She picked up her chains and stormed off again. Master Fu walked around, congratulating the rest of the team.

Katana and Sara met up with Chris and Jimmy. The four of them went off to the hotel restaurant for a late dinner.

"How'd you guys do in sparring?" Katana asked.

"Really good," said Chris. "Me and Jimmy made it to finals. I don't know who the other two kids are—one's from like Georgia I think, and the other one's from Chicago."

"Wow," said Sara. "So as long as one of you makes it to the final match, our team wins."

"Yeah—how'd it go in the girls' ring?" asked Jimmy. "You won, I assume?"

"Yeah," said Katana. "Me and Michelle are going into grands with these two girls from MKA—Chris, they're from that school in Milton Sensei Mike told us about!"

"The place that kid goes to—the one who was picking on Billy?"

"That's the school," said Katana.

"Hey, how'd Jason and them do—did we make it to grands in the older division, too?" Sara asked.

"Jason made it," said Chris. "Matt and Jeff got eliminated. Jason was ridiculous—this kid kicked him in the face in his first match. He had a bloody nose and he lost a tooth—the other kid got disqualified for excessive contact. But Jason kept going. I don't think his nose stopped bleeding until his third match!"

"Hey—where's Fisher?" Jimmy asked.

"Oh, he didn't make nationals," said Sara with a frown. "He wanted to come and watch but his dad wouldn't pay for the trip if he wasn't competing."

"That sucks," said Jimmy.

"Yeah, that is kinda crappy," Katana agreed. "Becca came to watch—and she's not even going out with anyone who's here."

"I know," said Sara indignantly. "Apparently her parents aren't cheap!"

CHAPTER 28
NIGHT OF CHAMPIONS

After dinner Katana and Sara went up to their room. Sara pulled out the dim mak manuscript. She sat on her bed and flipped to the end. She stared at it for a good twenty minutes, going back and forth between the last two pages, before Katana finally asked, "So what do you think?"

Sara sighed, put the book down and flopped over on her back. "I think the last one is the death touch."

"Good. Then what about the one before it?"

"That's the thing, Kat—I don't think it does *anything*. I mean, in both of them, you have to put your hand on the prime meridian—right over the dantian itself. And you have to connect your chi to the other person's."

"Connect your chi...?" Katana asked.

"Yeah," said Sara. "You actually make a connection—you plug your meridians into theirs. In the first move, you establish the link, and that's it. It doesn't say to do anything else. But in the second one, you take their prenatal chi into your own dantian."

"Then that *must* be the death touch," said Katana.

"I guess..." said Sara doubtfully.

"How could it not be?" asked Katana.

"No, it is," said Sara. "I'm sure of it. What's making me uncomfortable is that I have no idea what that first technique is supposed to do. You just connect your chi to theirs—and that's it? I mean, what's the point?"

"So it's exactly the same as the other one, except you don't take their prenatal chi?" asked Katana.

"No—that's the other weird thing. You have to push against the prime meridian with one hand for both techniques. But the first one uses a point in the back along the lung meridian. For the second one, you have to push a point in the back of the neck along the brain meridian."

"Well maybe that first one is... I don't know, like I said last night. Maybe it's to feel the flow of their chi, like that move in the healing arts," said Katana. "It seems like every other technique in there has an analogous move in the dim mak manuscript. That's the only one we haven't seen yet."

"Yeah, but in the healing arts, you're trying to *help* the other person. All the dim mak moves are for *hurting* them—why would you need to know how strong their chi is to do that?"

"Hmm," said Katana. "Good point."

. . .

THE UNDER-BLACK BELT events took place the next day, so Katana and Sara spent most of their day at the pool with Chris, Jimmy, Jelly and Becca. Jelly told them that Master Fu was making Dana work on her gainer all day.

The girls told Chris what Sara had figured out from the dim mak manuscript—they had to be careful not to let the others hear. That proved difficult where Jimmy was concerned. He seemed incapable of taking his eyes off Katana while she was wearing her bikini.

Chris agreed that the second move had to be the death touch. "Jaaku must use that move to take someone's prenatal chi. Once he's got it, he can take the rest of their chi, too. And anyway, it would makes sense to leave the chen do for last, wouldn't it?"

"Yeah, but then what does the other move do?" asked Sara. "It *also* connects your chi to the other person's. Could dim mak have *two* chen do?"

"Sam said that dim mak only has one chen do—taking chi," said Chris.

Chris thought they should try the first move. Sara was afraid. They were in agreement, however, that it would have to wait until they returned to the Hall of the Dragon.

They grabbed an early dinner at the hotel restaurant late that afternoon, and headed back to the convention hall for grands. Katana was much more nervous now than she'd been the night before. This was the first time she'd ever made it to grands— much less in four separate events.

Like the previous year, Katana thought she was walking into a rock concert rather than a karate tournament. The room was dim except for the lights on the stage. The scaffolding towers reminded her of a beehive with the camera crews and lighting technicians getting ready for the show.

They had also set up enormous curtains along the back of the stage. They extended past the edges, blocking off a separate area for the competitors to warm up.

Once Katana got backstage with Sara, Chris and Jimmy, it felt like a karate tournament again. The competitors were warming up and getting ready, many of them running through their weapon routines. Katana saw Jelly and went to warm up with him.

"This is your first time in grands, right?" he asked.

"Yeah," said Katana with a weak smile.

"It's way scarier—having all those people watching and the cameras and the spotlights..."

"Stop!" said Katana. "I'm nervous enough already!"

One of the judges came backstage to let everyone know the order of events. Weapons would go first, starting with the younger divisions. A few minutes later he came back for the first set of competitors.

Katana stayed backstage, walking through her set a few times. She didn't know anyone in this division and wanted to stay focused on her own form.

Master Fu came in a few minutes later to talk to her and Jelly, reminding them to stay calm. "Do it like you do in training," he said. "The audience doesn't exist—focus on your weapon."

The judge came back again to tell them the fourteen- and fifteen-year-olds were up next. A minute later, Katana could hear the roar of the crowd as the emcee announced the winner of the younger division.

It was time. Katana went with Jelly and an older boy and girl to the edge of the stage.

The emcee called Jelly first. He ran up the short set of stairs. Katana thought the butterflies in her stomach were going to punch holes right through her abdomen.

Jelly was amazing—Katana hadn't had a chance to watch him compete all year, as her own ring had always been at the same time. Like Dana, Jelly seemed to thrive under pressure. He flew through his set faster than ever, landing every trick perfectly. Katana thought for an instant that he was going to miss the staff at the end of his 1080. But he grabbed it by the very tip and finished the form without incident.

The emcee called Katana next. She gave Jelly a high-five as they passed each other on the stairs.

This was scary. There were at least a thousand people watching and the spotlights were blazing. Katana felt surreal walking onto the stage, like she was in a totally different world, separate from everyone in the audience.

She ran forward into her front aerial, landing in a split right at the edge of the stage. The judges looked up at her. They were seated at a table directly in front of her.

"Judges! Representing the Hall of the Dragon, I am Katana!"

She pushed to her feet and walked to the back corner of the stage.

As she started her form, she could once again feel her nerves disappearing, turning into energy. Katana took a deep breath and ran toward the front corner. She did her round-off and launched her double backflip.

The crowd cheered and screamed. She landed, throwing her chains out to go into flowers. For whatever reason, Katana was much more conscious of the audience than she normally was. They roared again when she threw her gainer flash. But the cheering continued uninterrupted for the rest of her form. Through the monk move, the butterfly kicks and the butterfly twist, the crowd only grew louder. When she landed in her split again, she could hear a section of the audience chanting her name —"Katana, Katana!"

She kicked her back leg around and did the body jumps, one chain gliding effortlessly underneath her as the other circled above. She kicked to her feet and finished the form.

The audience rose to its feet as Katana made her final bow. It only took a few seconds for the judges to show their scores. Two of them awarded her perfect 10s. She swelled with happiness as the crowd grew deafeningly loud.

Katana was thrilled—she didn't care if she won at this point. She knew she'd nailed her form in her first-ever performance at grands. Jelly gave her a high-five as she went down the stairs. Katana headed backstage.

"Aren't you gonna watch the other kids?" Jelly called after her.

"Nah," said Katana. "I gotta get ready for kata."

Katana walked through her form twice. She was oblivious to the crowd noise emanating from the other side of the curtains, until suddenly Jelly came running over to her.

"Get out here!" he said, dragging her by the arm. "You WON!"

Katana was elated. She bounded up the stairs to the stage. "And here she is, her first time in the night show at U.S. nationals," the emcee announced. "Our fourteen- through seventeen-year-old black belt weapons grand champion, Katana Kahanu!"

Katana ran over to shake hands with the judges before going to stand with the emcee. He handed her an enormous crystal cup on a marble base. Jelly returned to the stage with the other two finalists so the photographer could get a group picture. After that, Katana and Jelly ran backstage again.

Sam came over, pulling Katana into a hug. "Not bad for your first time in grands," she said, glowing with pride. "Are you ready for kata?"

"Yeah, I got it," said Katana. She couldn't stop smiling.

Katana went through the form once just to make sure. Sam suggested a couple of places for extra kiais to enhance her intensity. Katana felt a surge of regret that Osaka wasn't the one giving her pointers instead of Sam. She knew he wasn't into the tournaments like the other masters, but he had been her teacher, her mentor, from the very beginning. As much as she liked Sam, she felt like he was the one who should be with her now. Was his absence from this event simply an extension of whatever else was going on? She felt abandoned.

The thirteen and under division went first, then it was Katana's turn again. She was called up first for the fourteen-through seventeen-year-olds.

She took the stage again, bowing to the judges. She stormed forward and called out her introduction.

Like she'd done the night before, she walked backwards with a menacing kiai, then turned around when she got to the back of the stage. As she stared at the curtain, her back to the judges, the audience noise diminished to total quiet.

She turned around, slamming the first move of her kata with a loud kiai. The situation felt even more surreal than it had for weapons. Now this enormous crowd sat in utter silence. During her entire form, Katana was the only one who made a sound.

She executed the final move, her kiai echoing through the cavernous room. The audience erupted—Katana could hear her friends chanting her name. She held her last pose as she awaited the judges' scores. This time she'd achieved *three* perfect 10s.

She ran back down the stairs and arrived backstage to find Betsy waiting for her.

"Kat, that was amazing—I don't want to go out there now!"

"You made grands?! I didn't know," said Katana.

"Yeah, it's my first time... This is so nerve-racking!"

"But I thought you won the tai chi division the last couple of years..."

"I did, but they don't put tai chi in grands," Betsy explained. "It's not exciting enough for the night show, I guess."

Katana watched Betsy's performance. She wasn't terribly intense, but her movement was incredibly sharp and her stances were perfect. Katana cheered along with the crowd when she was done.

But as well as Betsy had done, the night belonged to Katana.

The emcee called her back to the stage and she collected a second cup to add to her collection. After the group photo, Katana ran backstage again. Sam came over to her, Michelle in tow.

"Wow, nice job, Kat," said Sam. "We need to get you two ready for sparring. We have a few minutes—they're going to do the thirteen and under division first. Listen, one of you is going to fight that monster from MKA..."

"Mildred?" asked Katana.

"Yes, Mildred," Sam replied. "Here's the deal—whichever one of you fights her, you can't give her a chance to throw anything. She's too strong—she'll go right through your block. But she's slow, so I want you to be aggressive and keep moving in as soon as the match starts."

Katana thought this was excellent advice.

She put on her gear and bounced around to keep her body warm. Once they'd finished the thirteen and under group, the judges called Katana's division to the stage. Katana didn't feel nervous this time—she was eager to spar with Mildred.

But the judges called Michelle and Mildred first.

Michelle heeded Sam's advice. The instant the match started, she rushed in, scoring with a punch to Mildred's head. But this approach cost her in the second round. Mildred turned away from Michelle to throw a back kick, launching Michelle into the air. Mildred was up 2-1.

Mildred adopted Michelle's strategy when the next round began. Michelle rushed in for a punch, but Mildred threw a front kick the moment the judge said "Go." She sent Michelle airborne once again.

Michelle tried to start with a kick after that, snapping her roundhouse to Mildred's head. But Mildred batted her leg out of the way and punched her in the face. She won the match 5-1.

Katana was next. The other girl from MKA wasn't nearly as large as Mildred. Katana started the match very aggressively. She threw a roundhouse kick to the girl's head, which she blocked, then snapped her leg around the other way for a hook kick. Katana's second kick connected, knocking the girl's headgear off.

When the match started again, the other girl rushed in with a kick. Katana was ready—she swept out her leg, rolling over immediately to land a kick to her head. She won the match 6-0.

The girl had to go again right away to spar with Michelle for third and fourth place. And while Michelle took a little longer to beat her than Katana had, she still pulled out a win 5-2.

This was it. Katana now had to fight Mildred for first and second place.

As the judge called them into the ring, the audience noise rose to fever pitch. One large group started chanting "Milton! Milton!" On the other side of the room, the kids from the Hall of the Dragon countered with a chant of their own: "Katana! Katana!"

The match started. Katana danced around Mildred, feinting with a couple of kicks to gauge her reaction. Each time Mildred moved to block. Finally Katana faked with a front kick, then snapped her leg around to catch her in the face with a round-house kick.

The next round started and Mildred took the initiative. She

rushed Katana with a barrage of punches—Katana was able to dodge, but Mildred drove her right out of the ring.

As they began again, Katana kept her weight on her back leg. She snapped a roundhouse kick to Mildred's head when Mildred rushed her again. But Mildred was ready. She batted Katana's leg out of the way and punched her in the head.

Katana saw stars—she nearly fell over from the force of the punch. When they started again, she stepped badly, taking Mildred's front kick to her ribs. It knocked the wind out of her. Mildred was now up 3-2.

Katana was in trouble. For the next couple of rounds, she eased up and played very defensively. Her head was still spinning from Mildred's punch and she'd yet to fully regain her breath. She danced just outside of Mildred's reach, giving herself a chance to regroup.

When they started again, Katana was ready. Mildred rushed in with a punch. Katana sprang into the air for the leg scissors take-down. But when she caught Mildred with her legs, nothing happened. Katana twisted over as hard as she could, but Mildred was too large. She didn't budge. Katana slid down her body, landing on the floor. She scrambled out of the way in time to avoid a punch to her head.

Katana decided enough was enough. The match resumed, and she went straight into her gainer flash. Katana faked with a punch, which Mildred tried to block. But Katana was already airborne. She planted her foot in Mildred's rib cage, kicking over hard. She flipped over backwards, landing perfectly.

Katana earned two points. But Mildred was so stout that the

gainer hadn't moved her back at all. And that gave Katana the idea for her next move.

She was up 4-3, but still felt woozy from Mildred's first punch. She wanted to end this quickly.

The judge started the match and the crowd roared. The people chanting "Katana!" overpowered those chanting "Milton!" Katana went into the ridiculous kick she'd learned from Master Kim's seminar so many months ago.

She jumped into the air and threw a flying side kick at Mildred's chest. As expected, Mildred batted Katana's leg out of the way. But Katana was counting on that reaction. She twisted hard, kicking her other leg around. She caught Mildred in the side of the head with a huge hook kick.

Katana landed as Mildred staggered backward several feet. She looked like she was about to pummel Katana. But the center judge stopped the match and awarded Katana two points.

She won 6-3.

The crowd went wild. Katana had won her third straight event in grands, winning team sparring for the Hall of the Dragon in the process. Sam and Michelle ran over, grabbing her in a hug. The emcee presented her with her third cup of the evening. It took several minutes for the commotion to die down before they could start the next event.

There hadn't been enough girls in the sixteen- and seventeen-year-old division to hold grands, so the boys took the stage next. The thirteen and under division went first. Katana hung out with Chris and Jimmy backstage while they warmed up.

Jimmy ended up fighting first. He won his match and the kids from the Hall cheered wildly again. They were now guaranteed a win in the boys' team division regardless of the outcome of the remaining matches. But Chris won his match as well—he would have to spar with Jimmy for first and second.

The match for third and fourth place went next. Katana watched with Chris and Jimmy. When their turn came, she kissed them both on the cheek for good luck. Jimmy held his hand to his face in surprise, looking back at her as he climbed the stairs to the stage. He tripped over the top step and fell flat on his face. A chorus of laughter rose from the audience. Katana felt horrible, but Jimmy seemed focused again by the time the judge started the fight.

Chris and Jimmy were an even match. They always sparred at practice and could anticipate each other's tactics almost perfectly. Katana thought their bout might go on forever. But finally Jimmy caught Chris with the leg scissors takedown, winning 6-4.

Jason Beecher won for the sixteen- and seventeen-year-old division. But the Hall of the Dragon didn't win the team division for his age group. The two boys who took second and third were from the same team. Jason's win wasn't enough to overtake them.

Katana stayed by the stage long enough to congratulate Jason, then ran behind the curtain to join the rest of the performance team. Team demo was the last event of the night.

Master Fu gave them a big pep talk. Katana could tell Dana was even angrier than she'd been the night before. She had apparently spent a good part of the day working the gainer flash with her chains, but Master Fu still didn't feel she was consistent enough to risk adding it to the demo.

When Master Fu was done, they walked toward the stage. Katana almost walked right into Sean Fisher. "Sean!" yelled Sara, running over to grab him in a big hug. "I thought your dad wouldn't let you come!"

"I got him to change his mind last minute," said Sean. "I just got here like an hour ago!"

The emcee announced the division. He called Supernova to the stage first. They performed with even more intensity than they had the night before. Katana already thought her team would have a tough time beating them. But then the worst happened. Two of the kids ran from the back of the stage after their last weapon set and did side-by-side double backflips.

Katana couldn't believe it—they'd clearly practiced this move for ages, given how perfectly they landed it. But they'd saved it for grands.

Dana freaked out. She yelled at Master Fu, demanding that they add the gainer flash into the demo. Master Fu had to take her backstage to calm her down. Luckily, the third team was called to the stage next, leaving the Hall of the Dragon for last. Katana went backstage to see what was going on.

"Fine!" said Master Fu as Katana walked over. "I give up— we'll add it back in. You'd better land it!"

"I will, I swear," said Dana. She gave Master Fu a big hug before running back to the stage. Katana thought she could make out the faintest blush on Fu's face.

"So we're doing the gainer?" she asked.

"You're doing the gainer," he confirmed with a sigh.

"Awesome!"

It was time. Katana took the stage with her teammates. They set up their weapons and lined up in their opening formation. Dana was glowing with excitement. And that excitement proved contagious. The team did everything a little better than they had the night before. The tricks were a little bigger, the weapons moved a bit faster and the presentation was more intense.

When Katana and Dana got to the gainer flash, Dana flipped higher than ever. They both landed the trick perfectly, their chains spinning the entire time. They finished the set and ran to the back of the stage, dropping their chains as they went over in their aerials.

The team hit their final formation and awaited the judges' scores. The crowd erupted. The Hall of the Dragon had edged out Supernova by a tenth of a point to regain the national title.

"YEAH!" Dana screamed as they went backstage. She held the cup over her head. "I *told* you I could do it, Fu!"

"Yes you did," said Master Fu, winking at Katana. "Yes you did."

Suddenly, Katana realized this had been his plan all along. Certainly he knew better than anyone how much Dana shined under pressure. He knew she could land the gainer in front of an audience, no matter how inconsistent she was in practice. Fu probably took the trick out of the demo Friday night precisely because he knew how excited Dana would be to add it back in on Saturday.

The man was definitely a genius, Katana decided.

CHAPTER 29

THE DEATH TOUCH

K atana was exhausted. A full weekend of competing had sapped her energy. She wanted nothing more at that moment than a good night's sleep. But the reporters from ESPN and Black Belt magazine had other ideas. It turned out Katana was the first competitor in twenty years to win grands in weapons, kata *and* sparring.

She spent a good ten minutes with each of them. Harvey Ryder caught her as she tried to get out of the main doors of the convention hall. As Master Nash had warned, he asked about her upcoming trip to Shaolin.

"I heard a rumor you're going to be testing for master while you're there," said Harvey.

Katana laughed. "Where did you hear *that*?!"

"On our website, of course," Harvey replied with a wheeze. "One of our members from Korea posted in the forum. He heard from Master Kim that the Shaolin Temple is getting ready to test an American girl for master. It wasn't too hard to figure out *which* American girl that would be."

"That's ridiculous," said Katana, rolling her eyes in what she hoped was a convincing manner. "The headmaster invited me to visit the temple when I performed for him a few months ago."

"Yeah," Sara agreed. "She's just gonna be another tourist."

Finally they managed to escape, and the girls went up to their room. Katana was spent.

It had been a good weekend, she reflected as she drifted off to sleep that night. Three individual grands and two team grands. And now she had the World Games to look forward to sometime in the summer.

But when they returned to the Hall the next day, there was only one thing on Katana's mind. "This is it," she said to Sara and Chris. They were in the girls' room, right after dinner. "I wanna try that last move from the manuscript."

"Kat," said Sara, "I don't think you should. I've been worrying about this all day. We have *no idea* what that move does." Doc jumped onto the bed next to Sara. He rubbed his head against her leg.

"We know it's not the death touch," said Chris before Katana had a chance to reply. "Why not try it?"

Sara continued to protest. But Chris insisted that, as he was the guinea pig, Sara had nothing to worry about. Sara took the book out of her suitcase and opened it to the next to last page.

"There's not much to it. Put one palm flat against his dantian. With your other hand push against the point on the lung meridian, right under his shoulder blade."

Katana did as Sara instructed. Nothing happened. Sara read the directions again, and Katana tried it a second time.

"This one's a dud," said Chris with a shrug.

"You're sure you don't feel anything?" Katana asked.

"Not a thing."

Katana stimulated her prenatal chi and tried the technique a third time. But still, nothing happened.

"Chris, take your shirt off," Katana suggested after a few minutes.

"What—why?"

"Well, if I'm supposed to be connecting my chi to yours, maybe there needs to be direct contact. Maybe clothes get in the way."

"Uh... okay," said Chris, pulling his shirt off. He and Sara both blushed slightly.

Katana tried the technique a fourth time. She placed her right hand against his dantian, reaching around his back with her left. But again nothing happened.

"This doesn't make any sense," she said in frustration. "Why would there be a move in there that doesn't do anything?"

Sara looked at her for a minute. "Try it on me."

"No," said Katana. "I don't want to make you do something you're afraid of."

"Just try it." Sara stood up, taking off her shirt—Chris turned around immediately. "I'm wearing a sports bra, idiot," said Sara, blushing again.

"Oh..."

Katana thought this was futile. The move didn't seem to do anything. But she gave it a try. She placed one hand over Sara's dantian and pushed against the point below her shoulder blade with the other.

"Holy crap!" For an instant, Katana could feel Sara's chi. It was, in fact, similar to the move in the healing arts manual. But this time, Sara's chi was *connecting* to hers—it was as if Katana's meridians were extending into Sara's body. She could feel Sara's chi beginning to bleed into her own.

But in the next instant, something went horribly wrong. Sara let out a little squeal. She went rigid. Katana broke the connection immediately. Sara's eyes rolled into her head, and her body went totally limp. Katana barely caught her in time. Chris helped her ease Sara's body to the floor.

"Oh no..." Katana attempted to revive Sara. Nothing happened. She tried again and again, but it was no use—Sara wouldn't come around.

"SARA!" Katana screamed.

"I'm gonna go get Nash..." said Chris. He ran out of the room.

Doc walked over to investigate. He rubbed his head against Sara's face. Katana brought two fingers to Sara's neck to feel her chi—there was nothing.

"NO!"

Only a few seconds had gone by—not nearly enough time for Chris to make it to the south wing and back. But Master Nash and Osaka came running into the room with Chris right behind them.

Nash dropped to his knees next to Sara. He pressed two fingers to Sara's neck.

"What happened?" he asked, his expression grave as he rose to his feet.

"We..." Katana sobbed. Chris handed him the dim mak manuscript.

Nash flipped through the book. "No..."

"What is it?" asked Osaka, taking the book from him. He examined the page where Nash had stopped. Osaka's expression turned to stone.

"The infirmary, *now*," said Nash.

"What is it?" asked Katana, panic-stricken. "What did I do?"

They didn't answer.

Master Nash squatted down, picked up Sara's limp form, and carried her from the room. Katana, Chris and Osaka followed him to the infirmary.

"What happened?!" asked Doctor Hubble when they arrived. Nash placed Sara gently in one of the beds.

"She needs acupuncture," said Nash, running off with Doctor Hubble to fetch the needles.

Osaka went to the head of the bed. He pressed a point on the side of Sara's neck and another at the base of her skull. Katana knew he was trying to revive her. It didn't work any better for him than it had for her.

Nash came back with his needles. He began inserting them in Sara's neck and chest.

"Where did you get this," Osaka asked with a quiet fury Katana had never heard in his voice. He was holding up the manuscript.

"We... I..." Katana stammered.

"WHERE?!"

"In the tunnels!" Katana said. "I was out at the old dojo doing tai chi... I remembered the archives and I thought there might be more underneath... I found a tunnel... The manuscript was there —in a crate..."

"What were you thinking?! This is the *dim mak manuscript*!"

"I know—what did I do? Is she going to be okay?"

"This is the technique you did?" Osaka asked, holding the book open to the next to last page.

"Yes," Katana whimpered.

"The death touch," said Osaka, his voice full of accusation.

"NO!" Katana screamed. "No—it can't be—the last one..."

"You fool!" Osaka yelled. "Dim mak has *two chen do*! One transfers the victim's prenatal chi into your dantian—the other siphons out *all* of the victim's chi."

"No..." Katana sobbed. She dropped to her knees at the side of Sara's bed, taking her limp hand into her own, pressing it to her forehead. "No..."

"How did this manuscript come to be under the old dojo?" asked Nash, as he inserted more needles. "I had no idea there were any tunnels under there."

"Neither did I," Osaka agreed. "Chang must have had it built after Chow left."

"Is she... is she dead?" asked Chris, tears streaming down his face.

Master Nash looked at him across the bed. "She lives," he said. "But I don't know for how long."

"No..." Katana sobbed again.

"But how can she still be alive if that was the... the death touch?" Chris asked.

"Chris, please tell us exactly what happened," said Osaka. He was looking down at Katana, a mixture of rage and pity on his face.

"We went through the other moves last week... We learned the healing arts months ago. Everything in... in this book was like that, but it used different points. The night before nationals... we were down to the last two techniques. We decided to wait to try them until we got back—we knew one of them had to be the death touch...

"We had no idea both of them were, I swear," said Chris pleadingly. "We figured the second one was, so we decided to try the first one today.... Katana tried it on me first—but it didn't work!"

"It didn't work?" Osaka asked, looking away from Katana for the first time.

"No—she tried it like four times. Nothing happened. Was that because our chi is mixed?"

Osaka looked at Master Nash. "Now we know."

"Yes, Chris," said Master Nash. "When you do a chen do, your chi interacts directly with your opponent's. Because your chi has mixed so completely with Katana's, you cannot use *any* of the chen do against each other."

"But all the other moves in the dim mak manuscript worked," said Chris. "And all the stuff in the healing arts manual, too—she did all of them on me..."

"None of those are chen do," said Osaka. "Your chi doesn't need to interact for them to work. It's like pushing water around inside a balloon—you're not touching the water. But when you do a chen do, you touch the other person's chi with your own. It would be like touching the water inside the balloon."

Nash finished inserting the last few needles. "Chris, how long did Katana hold the points when she did the death touch?"

Katana sobbed loudly at these words.

"I don't know..." said Chris. "Not very long. Sara went stiff the second Katana touched her. Kat let go right away."

"That is the only reason she's alive," said Master Nash. "If Katana had held the technique for a moment longer, Sara would already be dead."

"Is she going to make it?" Chris asked.

Master Nash didn't answer immediately. He looked down at Sara for a minute, then back at Chris. "I don't know," he said quietly. "I've never treated a victim of the death touch before. But her chi is weaker than Master Hua's was last year, when Jaaku hit him with the lightning."

"I need to talk to Katana," said Osaka. "Alone."

Master Nash escorted Chris from the room. Osaka stared down at Katana for several minutes.

She couldn't believe what was happening. This wasn't real; it couldn't be. It was some sort of twisted nightmare. There was no way Sara could be lying here, near death... There was no way that Katana could have done this to her. She loved Sara like a sister; she would never do anything to hurt her.

"What were you thinking?" Osaka asked for the second time. "After your experience with the healing arts, you clearly knew enough to figure out what this was," he said, still holding the manuscript.

Of course she'd known what it was. But she did not know that dim mak had *two* chen do. It was so obvious to her now. Jaaku had one technique to take all of a person's chi, and another to take only their prenatal chi.

"We thought there was only one chen do," Katana pleaded. *"Sam told us there was only one..."*

"Don't you dare try to blame anyone else for your actions," Osaka said icily.

He was right. Katana knew this was no one's fault but her own.

"You were obsessed. All year you were obsessed with Jaaku, with attaining more power. I told you to let it go. Yet you refused to listen. Look where it has led you."

"I wasn't obsessing anymore, I swear," said Katana, tears streaming down her face.

"Then explain this!" said Osaka. "Explain why, when you found the dim mak manuscript, you tried every move—*on your best friends*! Why you didn't bring this book to me or Master Nash immediately!"

"I have to defeat him," Katana said quietly. "This was the

only way. Not even the Immortal Master was strong enough to beat him. This was the only way."

"So in your quest to become stronger than Jaaku, you killed your best friend."

"No..."

"This makes you no better than him," said Osaka, the bitterness oozing from his voice.

"No..."

"All Jaaku does is take. He lives only because he takes—no one, nothing matters to him more than his own wretched life. He went to Tong in his quest for power, and he killed him. Jesse Thompson left Hawaii in *his* quest for power. He betrayed your father to Jaaku. And now you have sunk to their level..."

"No..."

"In your own pursuit of greater power, you have taken Sara's life. Was it worth it, Katana?"

"No! I didn't want to take her life—I'd never take anyone's life!" Katana got to her feet, looking at Osaka for the first time. "I didn't know! I didn't know it was the death touch! I'd never use it —against anyone!"

"You failed, Katana. You lost control of your emotions, instead allowing your obsession to control *you*.

"Chan wants to test you, Katana—yet you are no master. Not in my eyes. You don't deserve that title when you have so clearly failed to master yourself."

"Why did you turn against me?" Katana asked, crying uncontrollably. "All year you've been against me—you don't want me to go to Shaolin, you wouldn't tell me about Jaaku—you even wanted me to fail my evaluations! Why?"

All the blood drained from Osaka's face. "You wouldn't understand, would you?" he whispered, a tear sliding down his cheek. He tossed the dim mak manuscript at Katana's feet. She stared at him. Osaka turned and strode from the room.

CHAPTER 30
THE ARASHI ASSASSIN

Katana stayed by Sara's side all night. Chris came back, too, and fell asleep in the next bed. But Katana sat on the floor, holding Sara's hand.

Katana drifted off to sleep eventually and woke up at dawn, sprawled out on the cold stone floor. She stood up immediately and tried to feel Sara's chi—still nothing.

Nash came in a little later and woke Chris. He told the kids they needed to get ready to go to school; he promised he would take care of Sara the best he could.

But Katana had no intention of leaving. Chris left the infirmary to go up to his room. Katana stayed.

Sara's parents arrived late Monday afternoon. They ran to their daughter, one on either side of the bed. Mr. Brown took Sara's hand in both of his, tears streaming down his cheeks. Mrs.

Brown hunched over Sara's body, hugging her, sobbing uncontrollably.

Katana turned to look away. She felt like she was invading their privacy. Listening to Mrs. Brown's sobs, she started crying again herself.

A few minutes later Katana jumped when she felt someone's hand on her shoulder. It was Mr. Brown.

"Are you okay?" he asked.

Was *she* okay? This wasn't the question she was expecting. She sobbed. Mr. Brown pulled her into a hug. Katana cried into his chest and he patted her softly on the back of the head. She didn't think she deserved his sympathy.

Then she had a horrible thought—did they not realize she was the one who'd caused Sara to be lying on that bed, unconscious and near death?

But Mr. Brown whispered, "It was an accident, Katana. Jordan explained everything. It was an accident."

He let her go. Mrs. Brown walked over to her.

"Katana!" she sobbed, lifting her hands toward her. Katana thought for an instant Mrs. Brown was going to strangle her, but she pulled her into a hug too.

"This must be so awful for you," said Mrs. Brown. Katana couldn't believe this woman could feel sympathy for her, rather than hatred.

Chris, Jimmy and Sean Fisher came up to visit that night. Jimmy had brought up a tray of food from the cafeteria. He tried to get Katana to eat something. She hadn't eaten since dinner the previous evening, but she wasn't hungry.

Sean took Sara's hand in his, speaking softly to her in Chinese. Katana cried.

Mr. and Mrs. Brown went to stay in the guest quarters that night. And again, Chris and Katana stayed in the infirmary with Sara.

Chris explained to her that Master Nash didn't want anyone else to know what had really happened. Nobody knew they'd found the dim mak manuscript, and nobody knew Katana had done the death touch on Sara. Instead, Chris told her, the story was that Katana had experimented with some moves they'd learned in the healing arts manual, and something had gone wrong.

Katana didn't care what they told people. This cover story was close enough to the truth anyway.

All week, Master Nash and the Browns tried to convince Katana that she needed to go to school, but Katana refused to leave Sara's side. She finally had something to eat on Tuesday night—Jimmy kept bringing her trays at breakfast and dinner.

Sean Fisher came by every night. He talked to Sara, sometimes in English, sometimes in Chinese. But there was absolutely no change in Sara's condition.

Master Nash checked up on her a few times a day, sometimes inserting needles in different places, sometimes removing them completely. Nothing he did had any effect. He couldn't explain how she was still alive—but he was certain it wasn't from anything he was doing.

Osaka didn't visit at all. Katana knew something had ruptured between them. She felt like her connection with him, which had somehow felt damaged all year, was now severed completely. And she didn't understand.

But if he thought that this experience would deter her from her quest to defeat Jaaku, he was wrong. She had a lot of time to think about it, and she was more determined than ever. If Sara had to die, Katana was going to make certain it wasn't for nothing. She had the knowledge now; she had the power to defeat Jaaku. Katana intended to use it.

Again and again, Master Nash tried to convince Katana that she needed to go to school, go back to her routine. Jelly, Dana, Scott, Jimmy and Paul came by to visit Sara, too—and they tried to remove Katana from the infirmary as well. Sam even got in on the act, trying to entice Katana to come with her to try some of Terry-san's latest creations. But Katana refused. She would stay with Sara until the end.

Mr. and Mrs. Brown were there every day, and Jimmy and Sean came to visit every night. Chris slept in the infirmary, but went to school during the day. He tried to bring Katana the work she was missing—it was the next to last week of classes—but the last thing on Katana's mind was schoolwork.

Her best friend was dying before her very eyes. Katana knew there was no hope. Sara's meridian system was disrupted even worse than Master Hua's had been the previous year. Only four days had gone by before he passed away.

Yet by Saturday night, when Master Nash came to check up on her, Sara was still inexplicably clinging to life. The Browns had gone with Chris and Sean to get something to eat, and it was just Katana and Master Nash.

"She's lasted this long," said Katana. "Do you think she might pull through after all?"

Master Nash only shook his head slightly. "I don't understand how she is still alive," he said. "But it cannot last indefinitely. Her chi has been almost totally depleted."

Katana felt the little glimmer of hope she'd been nurturing extinguish itself.

"Katana, there is someone here who would like to see you," said Master Nash.

"Who is it?"

"Master Dasari," said Nash. "He's been overseas the past several weeks, but he's here to meet with Sato and Master Lu. I told him what happened—well, he doesn't know about the manuscript; I told him our cover story. He wanted to talk to you about it."

"There's nothing to talk about," said Katana.

"Mmm. I told him you wouldn't want to see him," said Master Nash. "He wanted to talk to you about Jaaku. It turns out Dasari knows where he was for those missing decades. But I said that..."

"What! Where?"

"Well, you'll have to talk to him about that. He's waiting down in the atrium."

Katana recognized this for the ploy that it was. Master Nash knew Katana wouldn't be able to resist finding out this crucial information about Jaaku's past. She understood that this was simply the latest of his many attempts to extricate her from the infirmary.

But ploy or not, she had to know.

She turned to Sara, taking her hand in her own. "I'll be back soon," she said, and kissed her on the forehead.

As Katana followed Master Nash down the stairs, he said something very strange.

"Katana, I want you to know, I already know *everything* Dasari is going to tell you. And I trust him completely."

"Um... okay," she said, totally confused.

They got to the atrium and met Dasari. Master Nash escorted them to the front doors. As Katana walked outside with Master Dasari, she saw Master Sato walking toward them from the fountain, with a man she didn't recognize.

"Sato, Lu," said Master Nash, holding the door open for the two men.

Master Lu nodded to them as he walked past. Katana glanced back, and as Sato walked over the threshold, he looked at her, his eyes wide with surprise.

"Master Nash tells me you have been conducting some research," said Master Dasari.

"What?" said Katana, still distracted by Sato. "Oh—I guess you could say that."

"Why don't we walk to the beach?" he said.

"Sure."

They walked in silence, partway down the gravel driveway, and across the brick walkway through the woods. Katana could see the sun getting lower in the sky as they traversed the pedestrian bridge over Highway 101.

They walked across the grass to the top of the stairs that led to the beach. Katana thought of Master Hua, his memorial stone standing sentinel a little farther along. She followed Dasari down the stairs.

"We have so little water in the Sahara," said Master Dasari. "Every time I see the ocean, it seems like a miracle." They walked along the beach a short distance. Katana could no longer contain her curiosity.

"Master Nash says you know where Jaaku was, after he left Tibet."

"I do," said Master Dasari. "Jaaku was in Africa."

"Africa?!" asked Katana, totally surprised.

"Yes, in my home country of Niger, to be precise," said Master Dasari.

"He was there the whole time, after he left Tibet?" asked Katana.

"Yes, until he went to China, when his Arashi found out about the Scroll of the Five Masters."

"Why did he go to Africa?"

"As you know, when Jaaku left Japan, he fled to Tibet. There he learned the secrets of the Tibetan monks. But then he heard about the African martial arts. He came at first, I believe, to learn all that he could. Jaaku had already mastered the chen do of the Asian martial arts. He discovered in Tibet secrets not known to the Chinese or Japanese masters. Jaaku must have thought the African martial arts would harbor other unknown treasures.

"How great his disappointment must have been when he discovered the African masters had no more knowledge of chi than the Asian masters. There were no new secrets for Jaaku in Africa."

"Then why did he stay?"

"For one thing, Jaaku needed a new base for his financial empire. As a samurai lord, he controlled vast wealth. But he lost it all when he was driven from Japan. In Africa, he found he could take control of the diamond trade. The Arashi had always been involved in organized crime so it was simple for him to set up a new operation in Africa. He had countless hundreds of nameless, faceless souls he could enslave to work in the mines, with his Arashi controlling everything.

"This also provided him with an endless supply of victims whose chi he could steal," said Dasari with a scowl. "I learned from Master Nang that Tibet was too sparsely populated. When Jaaku kidnapped someone to take their chi, people noticed. Yet people disappeared in and around the diamond mines all the time. Nobody noticed and nobody cared. Jaaku could go on stealing the chi he needed with impunity."

Katana shivered at the thought. Then she remembered something Sam had said when Master Dasari had first come to visit.

"Why do you call chi 'chi'?" she asked.

Dasari laughed. "What else would I call it?"

"Well, that's a Chinese word. I thought the African martial arts developed on their own? Wouldn't there be a different word for chi?"

"Ah, again, we come back to Jaaku," said Dasari. "When he first came to my home in Niger, in the desert, he found a thriving martial arts community. The people of my village had passed down their art of kokawa for generations. Jaaku trained with them, learned their art, and taught them many things in return. He showed them how to use their chi in ways they'd never imagined before. And my people adopted some of the language he used—thus we call our internal energy 'chi.' And our greatest masters learned chi fa—and called it by that name, because they learned it from Jaaku, and that was what he called it," explained Dasari.

"I can't imagine Jaaku *teaching* anyone," said Katana.

"He did so only to gain my people's trust," said Dasari. "Once he had it, he ensnared them and used them to raise the next generation of Arashi. My people built the temple where he resided, deep in the desert. From there, Jaaku commanded his empire for a hundred years."

Master Dasari sat down in the sand. Katana took a seat next to him. She looked out at the ocean, the sun nearing the horizon now, and listened to the sound of the surf.

"How did you get started in martial arts?" she asked.

"My twin brother and I learned from our father," Dasari replied with a smile. "We used to wrestle each other all the time, so my father decided we might as well learn how to do it properly, with some technique. He began training us when we were only three years old."

"Did you learn any chen do?" she asked.

"Oh yes," said Dasari. "By the time we were twelve, we were running around the village, throwing fireballs at each other. We could both deflect intent as well. I learned to levitate just before we turned sixteen. Oh, my brother was so jealous. I would leap up walls and he couldn't follow! But he learned, too, only a few weeks later. Then he chased me up the walls.

"Our mother used to yell at us when we got too rowdy. She said she was worried what the other villagers would think—no one else we knew could do any of the chen do. But my father used to say, 'Let them play—they are young boys, growing into strong men.' He was never able to manipulate his chi that way. I think he was proud to see us growing so powerful. But he died soon after that. Our mother was left to raise us alone.

"Soon, we found a new teacher. One of the villagers, Dotie, was a kokawa master, and he *could* do the chen do," said Master Dasari. "He was an old man, and had lived in our village his entire life.

"He talked to my brother and me one day, and began training us. Dotie taught us to use our chi to do wondrous things—we started learning chi fa when we were seventeen."

"You could do offense?" Katana asked excitedly.

"It took a while, but yes," said Master Dasari. "We could project our chi along our shen. That is when Dotie offered to take us to *his* teacher. He explained that his master was so powerful, he could manipulate the chi of another man simply by touching him."

"Jaaku. He was talking about Jaaku," said Katana.

"Yes," said Master Dasari. "We'd heard stories about Jaaku, and how evil he was. But Dotie made him sound like a benevolent teacher. He assured us the stories were not accurate. So we went to meet Dotie's master.

"Jaaku told us he had to connect his chi to ours to teach us how to control an opponent's energy. We were young and foolish —we agreed."

Katana sprang to her feet, backing away from Master Dasari. "You're an Arashi!"

Dasari sat there, smiling up at her, seemingly amused at her sudden alarm. "Yes, Katana, I am an Arashi. Believe me, it is a mistake I regret every day of my life."

"Nash knows." It wasn't a question. She realized this was what Nash had been talking about on the way down the stairs. Katana sat down again, feeling slightly foolish.

"Yes, Nash knows," said Master Dasari. "When Jaaku left Africa, he forgot about us. For the first time since he took my chi, I was free. I traveled around the world, trying to find other masters as powerful as Jaaku. I thought perhaps there was a way to take back my chi, to sever the link with Jaaku."

"Is there?" asked Katana.

"No, there is not. But as I searched, I heard of the Shaolin Temple. And I learned about the other halls. I found out that Master Nash was widely thought to be as powerful as the head-master of Shaolin, but much more open-minded. That is when I approached him, after Christmas.

"He told me about the Arashi assassin, and I thought I could help. Jaaku has forgotten about his Arashi in Africa, but we still have contact with his agents in Japan and China. I tried to learn more from them about the assassin's activities. I attempted to figure out his identity. But I have searched for months with no success. This assassin has covered his trail very well."

"What is it like?" asked Katana. "What is it like having your connection to Jaaku?"

"I can feel what he feels," said Master Dasari quietly. "When he was searching for the meaning of the scroll, even though he'd left us behind, I could feel his obsession. I could *see* the scroll—it was like a bad dream that didn't stop when I was awake. *I* wanted to understand; *I* felt a burning desire to unlock its secret.

"But that was nothing—Jaaku was not focused on me. He had no reason to believe there would be any pertinent documents in Africa. For the Arashi in China and Japan, it would have been much worse. He would have focused his obsession on them, especially those who were near the temples."

"So it's impossible to stop yourself, when Jaaku wants you to do something?" Katana asked.

"Yes, if he focuses his will on you," said Master Dasari. "But my brother and I learned to hide our shen. We found that this weakened our connection to Jaaku. Although we could still feel his will, it was no longer overpowering. We could function—even when he was focused directly on us.

"We did our best to sabotage his operations—we destroyed one of his diamond mines. And we convinced others to join us. Only my brother and I could hide our shen, so it was more difficult—and more dangerous—for the others. When they defied him, he knew it instantly. He could take their chi from any distance.

"One day, before he left for China, Jaaku found out that my brother was one of the leaders of the resistance. He took his chi. My brother vaporized before my eyes..."

Master Dasari sniffled, wiping his eyes with one hand. Katana looked away. The sun had slipped below the horizon and dusk was upon them.

"You were twins..." said Katana. "Were you able to sense things from each other? Could you feel when your brother was in danger?"

"Yes," said Master Dasari. "The connection we had was similar to the one with Jaaku, but not as strong. If I was separated from my brother, and he was happy, I would feel a twinge of happiness myself. Or if he was in danger, I could sense it.

"When we were little, my brother went away with my father. They were far away, in the south of Niger. My brother woke up in the middle of the night—there were lions prowling near the camp. I could see it. I woke up myself, and I could feel my brother's fear. For a few moments, I could see what he was seeing. But then it passed. With Jaaku, it never passes.

"Jaaku is evil, Katana. He uses men as tools, and does not value human life. He takes chi any way he can. And he is obsessed, always, with his drive for greater power. When he was searching for the meaning of the scroll, it was all I could think about, day and night. There was no relief.

"That kind of lust for power, Katana, is never healthy. I was drawn to Jaaku by the desire to enhance my skills. Dotie showed my brother and me so much, and I wanted more. When he offered to take us to his master, it did not occur to me to refuse. I knew the stories about Jaaku, I had heard the warnings, but I ignored them. Jaaku could give us more power, so I took the bait.

"Jaaku tricked us. He didn't tell us how much control he would have over us. Yet had we not been so hungry, my brother and I, we wouldn't have walked into his trap in the first place. We would have listened to the warnings; we would have paid attention to the stories. Both of us knew better, Katana. But we forgot everything in our quest for more power.

"I think you understand what I am talking about," he said with a sly smile.

"I do," said Katana, thinking of Sara lying in her bed back in the infirmary.

"You knew better when you tried those moves on your friend, as I knew better when I went to Jaaku," said Master Dasari, his smile gone. "Learn from this mistake, Katana."

At that moment, there was a flash of light, not twenty feet away. They sprang to their feet. It was an Arashi—he threw a fireball at Katana, knocking her through the air.

Katana landed on the sand, flat on her back. She jumped to her feet again, in time to see the Arashi lunge at Dasari with his sword. The Arashi was hiding his shen—and so was Dasari. Dasari faded away, reappearing directly behind the Arashi. He flung his arm around the Arashi's neck, but the Arashi flipped him over—Dasari was down. The Arashi raised his sword.

Dasari hooked one foot around the Arashi's ankle, pushing against his knee with his other foot. He knocked the Arashi to the ground. But as Dasari sprang to his feet, the Arashi faded away.

Dasari looked around frantically. "Katana—run! It's the assassin—go back to the school!"

The assassin appeared again, right behind Dasari. He stabbed as Dasari turned to face him. The sword pricked Dasari's arm.

Katana threw a fireball. It hit the assassin in the chest,

knocking him off his feet. But the assassin faded again, appearing right behind Dasari.

Dasari was ready for him. The assassin tried to stab him; Dasari dodged. He grabbed the assassin's arm, flipping him onto the ground. The sword flew from his hand when he hit the sand. Dasari dove on top of him, locking him in the mount.

Katana could see Dasari's shen again—he was enveloping the assassin to prevent him from fading. The assassin struggled to get out of the mount. Dasari tried to put him in a chokehold. But as Dasari brought his head down, the assassin caught him in the temple with an elbow.

Katana could tell Dasari was dazed—he lost control of his shen. The assassin faded away.

Katana looked around frantically to see where he'd go next. She didn't have to wait long—he appeared right in front of her, advancing on Dasari. Katana took one step, jumped up and kicked him in the back with both feet. She landed hard on her side; the assassin fell forward, landing on his face.

They both regained their feet; the assassin advanced on *her* now.

"Fool!" he yelled at Katana. "He's an Arashi!"

Dasari was on his hands and knees, behind the assassin. He crept toward the sword lying in the sand.

Katana ran forward, jumped into the air and slammed her right foot into the assassin's chest plate. She turned over mid-flight, swinging her left leg around. Her foot connected with his head, knocking his helmet off.

The assassin staggered. Dasari grabbed the sword. He lunged, stabbing the Arashi in the back. The blade protruded from the man's chest.

The assassin fell to his knees. Katana got a look at his face—it was Master Lu.

"You!" Katana screamed.

Suddenly, Dasari ran forward, grabbed Lu by the shoulders and spun him around. He lowered his face to Lu's. "Look at me! I'm the one who stabbed you! Me!"

Lu's aura began to glow. He'd been hiding it, but he was losing control. Katana could see the wispy tendrils of his shen extend around him, fading as he grew weaker. Blood was pouring from the wound in his back.

A moment later, she heard a hissing sound. Lu's body vaporized before her eyes.

Dasari dropped the empty armor. "Go," he said, fear in his eyes. "Go to Nash, tell him what happened here."

"You're coming with me, aren't you?" Katana asked.

"No," he said. "I have to go to Jaaku."

"Jaaku?! But why!"

"Lu saw me," he said. "He saw my face, and only *my* face as he lost control of his shen. That means Jaaku saw me."

And then it hit her—by turning Lu away from Katana, Dasari had saved her. "If he saw me..." she said, her voice quavering with fear.

"Exactly," said Dasari. "If Lu was still looking at you when he lost control, Jaaku would have seen you. He would have come looking for you. I have to leave now, Katana! Go—go to Nash!"

And with that, Dasari faded away in a brilliant flash of light.

CHAPTER 31

SACRIFICE

Katana hurtled up the stairs to the top of the cliff. Osaka and Nash ran toward her from the pedestrian bridge.

"Katana!" yelled Master Nash.

"What happened?" asked Osaka.

Katana told them about the attack.

"Lu..." said Master Nash, incredulous. "Sato tried to convince me it was *Dasari*."

"Lu knew how to hide his shen?" asked Osaka.

"Chan must have taught him," Nash replied. "It would've been nice of him to mention that."

Osaka went down to the beach to collect Lu's armor and sword. Nash faded with Katana back to the Hall. They appeared in the infirmary.

Chris was sitting in a chair next to Sara's bed. He ran over to see what had happened. Doctor Hubble looked Katana over, but she was fine.

Nash went to check up with Osaka. Katana sat down with Chris in the chairs next to Sara's bed. She told him everything.

"So Lu's the one who killed all those Arashi?!" he said when she was done.

"Yeah, and apparently he knew how to hide his shen," said Katana. "Nash thinks Master Chan must have taught him."

"What's going to happen to Dasari now?" asked Chris.

"I don't know," said Katana. "I'm sure Jaaku's going to wonder what Dasari was doing here."

"Dasari seemed like a smart guy. Maybe he'll tell Jaaku he was hunting the Arashi assassin. He was, actually, so he can just leave out the part about helping the good guys!"

Katana looked down at Sara. "How is she?"

"No change," said Chris. "Her parents went to bed a few minutes ago."

"She's not going to make it," Katana said quietly.

"I know."

They both spent the day Sunday sitting with Sara. Katana begrudgingly went over some of the work she'd missed at school. Their final week of classes was upon them; exams would be the following week. Katana also realized their test for third degree black belt was that Saturday. She had difficulty getting herself to care about any of it.

But finally she decided to return to school and get some practice time before her test. She went to Lincoln and attended her lessons at the Hall of the Dragon. But she and Chris continued to sleep in the infirmary. They both ate their meals there and spent every moment they could spare at Sara's bedside.

Yet despite her best effort, Katana found it impossible to keep her mind off of Sara when she wasn't with her. She might die any day now.

There must be a way to save her, Katana thought. There had to be. But Dasari had said he'd searched the whole world for a way to reverse the *other* chen do of dim mak. He'd come up empty—there was no way he could take his chi back.

The private lesson with Osaka that Thursday was very awkward. He reviewed all of Chris and Katana's material—every kata and combination, as well as attack drills. He told them they were ready to test for third degree. But his demeanor toward Katana was cold and distant. Katana felt like she was suffering two deaths at the same time—the death of her best friend, and the death of her relationship with Osaka.

Katana spent more time crying than she ever had in her entire life. She cried herself to sleep at night and found herself crying at random points during the day as well. Katana was incredibly thankful that she still had Chris. She was losing Sara and Osaka—she thought she might go insane if she lost Chris, too.

Sam and Master Fu canceled the team practices on Friday, instead inviting everyone to visit Sara. Master Fu informed Katana that she'd be testing for her first degree in wushu the next day, in addition to her third degree in kempo. At least she wouldn't be alone—Fu also told Dana, Paul and Scott that they'd be testing for their second degrees. Katana cried when she found out that Fu had wanted to test Sara, too.

Then Sam told Chris and Jimmy that they'd be testing for their second degrees in tae kwon do. "Is this your new favorite pastime?" asked Chris. "Giving people a single day's notice for a black belt test?"

Saturday afternoon Katana went up to the tai chi dojo with everyone else. She didn't know how she was going to pass—her heart wasn't into it. But she did basics and went through her kata with everyone else. They did combinations as a group—Katana and Dana worked together—then they sat down along the back wall.

Katana wasn't paying any attention to the test. She was lost in thoughts of everything that she'd learned about Jaaku and dim mak. Her knowledge now was substantially greater than it had been at the beginning of the year. She knew Jaaku's entire history. And she could perform every technique in the dim mak manuscript. She never imagined she'd *ever* know this much when she conducted her research the previous summer.

Master Nash had to call Katana's name three times before she heard him. It was her turn to perform the advanced kata. She went through the forms with as much intensity as she could muster.

Katana sat down again and racked her brains. She tried to remember if there was anything in the healing arts manual that might help Sara. This was ridiculous, of course—if there were, surely Nash or Osaka would have thought of it by now.

She felt so helpless. Despite everything she'd learned—the techniques from Master Nang, chi fa from Master Nash, the healing arts, all the chi kung—even dim mak—there was nothing she could do to help Sara.

Sam called Katana for attack drills. She worked with Betsy, who was testing for her second degree in kempo. They both had a turn using external techniques, then Katana had to go again, using only the chen do.

Katana sat down when she was done. She thought back to the day she'd met Sara. She'd woken to the sight of her opening the door, struggling with her suitcases. Sara had a lot more clothes than she did—Katana thought about the dresses in Sara's closet. She started crying. Now Sara would never get the chance to attend a formal.

Master Fu called Katana next. She wiped her eyes and performed her double whip chain set. Luckily, she could do it in her sleep. She had to do her empty-hand forms as well, and even her samurai sword set. This confused her, as it wasn't wushu. But Fu explained that the sport karate forms would count as extra credit. Katana really had to concentrate to do this set—she didn't know it nearly as well as chains. But she got through it, and then had a break again.

Katana felt empty. There was about to be a huge hole in her heart. Sara was the best friend she'd ever had, next to Chris.

She went up next to spar with Sam. Katana had sparred with her on both of her previous tests as well. But it hadn't been a requirement then—now it was. She had to spar with a master to make third degree.

They squared off, and fought with only external techniques

at first. Katana's head was in a fog. She was certain it was only her extensive tournament experience that got her through the match.

They fought with the chen do next. At one point, Katana used chi fa to send several pulses of chi at Sam. Sam faded away, but Katana redirected her chi and hit her anyway.

Katana was vaguely aware of Chris going up to spar with Sam next. Then the test was over. The next thing she knew, Master Nash was shaking her hand. "Congratulations, Katana. You are a third degree black belt today."

Chris wanted a shower, but Katana went straight to the infirmary. She removed her uniform top and draped it over a chair. Katana sat down, taking Sara's hand in her own. She was surprised the Browns weren't there—but then remembered it was dinnertime. They were probably down in the cafeteria.

"I did it," she said. "I got my third degree. I guess I'll be going to Shaolin next week…"

Or would Osaka talk Nash and Chan out of it? She didn't care anymore. All that mattered was Sara. Katana would give anything to keep her alive.

"I don't want you to die," she said, sobbing. She pressed her lips to the back of Sara's hand. Tears streamed down her face.

Was there nothing she could do?

Katana thought back to the night it had happened, going over the death touch in her head. She'd pushed the pressure points and made the connection instantly. Katana had felt Sara's chi as if it had been her own.

Then it hit her. If she could use that connection to *take* chi, could she use it to *give* chi as well?

The dim mak manuscript didn't specify. It only gave instructions for establishing the connection—it gave no indication of how to use it. Of course, Jaaku would have used the connection only to *take* chi. But Katana hadn't *done* anything. Sara's chi had started flowing into Katana's meridians of its own accord. Could it go the other way?

Katana knew what she had to do. She could establish the connection again, this time forcing the chi to flow the other way. Katana could give her chi to Sara.

Her heart skipped a beat. She could do this; she could save Sara.

Katana got to her feet. She reached down with her left hand, pressing her palm against Sara's dantian. Then she slid her right hand under Sara's back—but abruptly she stopped.

What would happen to *her* if she gave Sara her chi? Would she effectively do the death touch in reverse, killing herself in the process?

Katana was prepared to take that risk. If saving Sara meant sacrificing her own life... So be it. Sara was worth it.

She forced her right hand farther under Sara's back, pushing the point under her shoulder blade. Again, she felt the connection instantly. Sara's chi was almost gone. Katana could feel her own chi flowing vibrantly. She focused on sending it through her connection with Sara, into her dantian.

Katana looked into Sara's face, searching for some sign that this was working. She could feel Sara's chi getting stronger—her own chi, actually, flowing through Sara's meridians.

Everything started to go dark. It wasn't working—she was going to die for nothing...

Suddenly, Sara's eyes fluttered. They opened—only partway, but Katana could make out the brown of her irises. In the next instant, all was black. Katana knew no more.

CHAPTER 32
THE SHAOLIN TEMPLE

Katana's limp body slumped to the floor. Sara's eyes bulged—she tried to sit up, but was too weak to manage it.

"Katana!" she said quietly, her voice weak and raspy. Katana didn't move. Sara tried to scream, but achieved only a hoarse whisper.

Doctor Hubble came to check up on her. She spotted Katana lying on the floor. Hubble ran over and squatted next to Katana, checking her pulse.

"She's alive," said Hubble. Sara dropped her head back to the pillow, tears streaming down her face.

Doctor Hubble managed to pick Katana up from the floor. She laid her in the bed next to Sara's—the same one in which Katana had been sleeping for the past two weeks.

Hubble ran to her office to call Master Nash. He appeared in the infirmary a minute later with Sam and Osaka.

"Sara—what happened?" asked Nash.

"I don't know," Sara whispered. "I woke up and Katana was doing something. Her hand was on my stomach—she was doing that dim mak move... What am I doing here? How long was I out?"

Nash looked very concerned. He went to the head of Katana's bed and pressed two fingers against the side of her neck.

"What the hell?" asked Sam, looking totally dumbfounded.

Master Nash breathed a sigh of relief. "She's fine—her meridians were overloaded." He touched the side of her neck and below the base of her skull. Several seconds went by and nothing happened. But finally Katana's eyes fluttered open.

KATANA'S VISION WAS BLURRY. She rubbed her eyes and looked around. Then she remembered.

"Sara!" She tried to sit up, looking over at Sara's bed.

"I'm here, Kat," said Sara, smiling at her.

Master Nash pushed Katana back into bed.

"Rest," he said. "But tell us what happened—what did you do?"

Katana felt tears of joy sliding down her cheeks—she'd done it. Sara was alive.

"I... I did the death touch again..."

"What?!" asked Sam.

"What do you mean?" said Master Nash. "You did the death touch—on Sara?"

"Yeah—the manuscript only says to make a connection. I figured if I could use it to give Sara my chi..."

"You gave Sara your chi...?" asked Sam, looking more confused than ever. "Nash... How is that possible...? How is Katana alive?"

Master Nash looked a silent question at Osaka—he merely shrugged in response. "Katana, what you did was incredibly dangerous," said Nash. "Doing the death touch in reverse... You could have killed yourself."

"I know... But I had to do it. I couldn't let Sara die—not like this. But it worked! And... I'm not dead," Katana said, beaming around at them.

"Far from it," said Master Nash. "You managed to overload your own meridian system, but you're going to be fine."

Within minutes, the infirmary became quite crowded, as first Sara's parents, and then all of her friends arrived. Chris, Jimmy, Jelly, Dana, Scott, Paul, Sierra, Olivia and Michelle came to see for themselves that Sara was conscious, no longer in any danger.

Once everyone had cleared out later that night, Katana and Chris filled Sara in on everything she'd missed. Sara remembered nothing after volunteering to let Katana try the dim mak move on her.

"So that really was the death touch," said Sara, her voice a little stronger now. "That's so freakin' scary... What do you think is gonna to happen to Dasari now?"

"I don't know," said Katana. "I think he'll be all right. Jaaku will probably be happy that he got rid of the assassin for him."

Sara reached out to Katana. She took Sara's hand in both of hers.

"You saved my life, Kat," she said, a tear streaming down her cheek. "You could have died, you know."

"I had to," said Katana. "It was because of me that you needed saving in the first place."

"You know... I was thinking. You really do deserve to be a chen do master now," said Sara.

"Why's that?" Katana asked.

"Well... with the death touch, that's *four* chen do you can do now. And you used the fourth one in a way that nobody else ever did. Isn't that what all the great masters did, according to Sam? Put things together in a way that nobody had before?"

"Wow," said Chris, looking thoughtful. "She's right, Kat. Jaaku's the only other person who can do the death touch. God knows *he'd* never think of using it this way."

Sara was very weak. She was able to sit up in bed the next day, and Doctor Hubble had her walk up and down the infirmary once on Tuesday. But she was far too feeble to take her exams at Lincoln—or their AP test in biology. Principal Hennessey made arrangements with all of her teachers to make up the exams. She would have to wait a year to make up the AP test, however.

What upset Sara most was missing her test for third degree. But Master Nash assured her she could test privately once she recovered.

Katana returned to her routine, and moved back into her

room. She had no trouble with her exams, but she was worried about her upcoming trip to Shaolin.

Katana had an early dinner on Saturday. It was Sara's first day out of the infirmary, so Katana went with her and Chris to eat at the sushi bar with Terry-san. Her friends wished her luck, and she went to meet Master Nash out in the courtyard.

"Ready, Katana?" he asked.

"As ready as I'll ever be."

He put his arm around her, and everything started spinning. She felt like she was being stretched out, head to toe, and falling fast; all was a kaleidoscope of color.

Suddenly her feet hit solid ground. She looked around in amazement.

The sloping green tile roof and red brick walls of the Shaolin Temple loomed before her. Katana was in the middle of a stone courtyard, with trees spaced out at large intervals. There was an enormous foo dog on each side of the steps leading to the temple entrance. And there at the top of the stairs stood Headmaster Chan Su Ming, his two huge bodyguards standing sentinel beside him.

Dozens of monks stood in two lines, forming an alleyway leading to the stairs. They all wore the orange robes of Shaolin. Some held large weapons or banners.

It was morning here. All was silent except the birds chirping in the trees. Sunlight streamed through the leaves.

"Is the candidate ready?" asked a voice behind Katana.

She turned to see Master Liang. Pai Lo stood next to him, looking terrified.

"Liang—what's going on?" asked Master Nash. He looked around, from the headmaster, to the monks, and back to Liang again. Nash appeared scared, too.

"The headmaster has decided to observe the old customs for this occasion," said Master Liang with a grim smile.

"The old customs?" said Katana, her heart suddenly beating a mile a minute. "You mean... the hall of death thing?"

"You and Pai Lo will undergo a centuries-old rite today, Katana," said Master Liang very seriously. "You will follow the path prescribed by Ta Mo himself for monks who wish to test for master."

"Liang—this is unacceptable," said Nash. "Chan said *nothing* about this—he told me it would be a simple evaluation!"

"The headmaster's decision is final."

Master Nash pulled Katana aside.

"Katana..."

There was a bright flash of light. Osaka appeared next to Liang. He walked over to Nash and Katana. "What is going on?"

"Chan is using the old rite," said Master Nash. "I should have known."

"Is it as bad as Sam told us—do you really have to lift that urn?" Katana asked apprehensively. Master Nash rolled up his sleeves. Katana could see a tiger and a dragon branded into his forearms. "But you got through it—Sam said that people died in there..."

"They do," said Master Nash. He pulled up the top of his uniform. Katana could see an angry red scar in the side of his rib cage.

"The Hall of Wooden Men, Katana," he said. "I didn't get out of the way in time. I was impaled with a spear. I made it through the test, and I moved the urn, but I paid a price. My right lung collapsed. I was coughing up blood by the time it was over. If Chan hadn't brought me to the infirmary immediately, I would have died."

"But... Sam said they haven't used the old rite in hundreds of years..." said Katana.

"They hadn't. But the headmaster didn't want me to leave Shaolin. He said my training was incomplete. He would only let me go if I could pass the test. Katana, I cannot let you do this. I'm going to call the whole thing off."

"That will mean leaving Shaolin," Osaka pointed out.

"If the headmaster is going to force us into this position, so be it," said Master Nash. He took a step toward the temple.

"Master Nash—wait," said Katana, grabbing him by the elbow. "We can't leave Shaolin. I'll take the test."

"Katana, you have no idea what you're saying," said Master Nash, looking at her with pity in his eyes. "I barely made it out alive. I guarantee you Chan *expects* you to fail. Then he'll lord his knowledge over you. He'll tell you that if you stay at Shaolin, you can learn the secrets you need to pass the test."

"I can do it," said Katana. "I'm meant to do it." She only realized it as the words parted her lips. But she knew suddenly, somehow, that this was the right course of action.

"Katana..."

"She's right," said Osaka quietly.

"What?" asked Master Nash, totally surprised. "Osaka—

you're the one who's tried to keep her from Chan all along. What are you playing at? We *cannot* let her go in there..."

"I was wrong," said Osaka, looking at Katana. Was that pride she saw in his face? "She can do this—we have no choice, Jordan. You know the fate that awaits us. We can delay it no longer. We're going to need access to the archives at Shaolin. Katana can do this."

Master Nash stared at Osaka for a moment, then looked at Katana with fear in his eyes. "Katana, you're going to battle the headmaster's bodyguards first."

"Both of them?!" she asked apprehensively.

"Yes, both of them," said Master Nash. "Next, you'll have to have to fight your way through an alleyway of monks—nine on each side. They'll be waiting for you inside the temple. If you make it through that, you will enter the Hall of Wooden Men. The dummies are activated by your body weight. And at the end of the Hall..."

"Is the urn with the burning coals," Katana finished for him. She looked Nash in the eye and nodded.

They walked back to Liang and Pai Lo.

"She will proceed?" asked Master Liang.

"I will," said Katana.

Liang nodded. "You will start with the headmaster's guards. Pai Lo will go first."

"Wait," said Katana. "What are the rules? I assume we're not going for points..."

"Ah, no," said Liang. "You will fight until you—or they—can fight no more."

Pai Lo walked forward, entering the alley between the monks. The bodyguards walked down the steps. Katana had forgotten how large they were—they towered over Pai Lo. They had to be seven feet tall, their bare arms as thick as tree trunks.

Pai Lo let out a loud kiai—he ran forward and leaped into the air. He turned sideways into a split kick, each foot connecting with the head of a bodyguard.

This had no visible effect. He landed on his feet, and rushed at one of the guards, throwing a spinning kick. The guard caught Pai Lo's leg and tossed him across the courtyard like a rag doll. Pai Lo levitated to avoid crashing into the stone.

The guards moved forward. One threw a fireball at Pai Lo. He caught it in his arms, spun around and threw it back, then threw his own chi at the second guard. The fireballs slammed into the guards. They both stumbled back a foot or two, but a moment later resumed their advance.

Pai Lo shot straight up, ten feet into the air. He spun around hard and slammed his foot into the face of one guard—Katana could see blood and several teeth fly out of his mouth. But the other guard grabbed Pai Lo, pulling him into a bear hug.

Pai Lo struggled mightily, but couldn't escape. The guard he'd kicked looked dazed, but strode forward. He punched Pai Lo in the head and knocked him out. The first guard dropped Pai Lo's limp body to the ground. They turned and bowed to Headmaster Chan.

One of the monks ran out and picked up Pai Lo. He carried him out of sight.

"It is your turn," said Liang.

Katana looked at Master Nash, who shook his head slightly, and at Osaka, who nodded. She walked up the alley between the two lines of monks.

The guards strode forward to meet her. Katana wasted no time—she ran forward and did her gainer flash on the first guard. She kicked him in the ribs, flipping herself over backwards. She landed on her feet only to discover she hadn't moved him an inch.

The second guard grabbed her from behind, lifting her off her feet. The first guard moved in to punch her in the head. Katana kicked with both legs, pushing him back. She thrashed against her captor's hold and jammed her knuckle into the nerve ending in his elbow—he flinched, loosening his grip enough for Katana to wriggle free.

She dropped to the ground and backed away, trying to think of what to do next. The guards advanced. Katana leaped into the air, kicking one of them in the chest. She twisted around, smashing a hook kick into his jaw with her other foot.

He staggered back, but the other guard lunged at her. Katana levitated, flipping upside down over his head. She twisted around in midair and threw her arm around his throat as her body swung down behind him. Katana pushed her other arm against the back of his neck, applying a chokehold. She wrapped her legs around his torso and held on for dear life.

Katana squeezed as hard as she could, hoping to knock him out. The guard thrashed around violently, trying to shake her off. He tried to pry her arms away with both hands. Katana held on.

The other guard moved in, but couldn't get close—his partner was flailing too wildly. Katana extended her shen, and hit the other guard with a dozen pulses of chi. He flew through the air and landed on the stone behind one line of monks.

The first guard continued to jerk violently. Katana could see the blood vessels bulging from his forehead, but she didn't let go. Finally he fell to his knees. He continued desperately trying to pry Katana's arms from his neck. But his body went limp and he slumped over, Katana still on top of him.

She held on a few moments longer to make sure he was out. She let go when she saw the other guard running toward her.

Katana got to her feet, striding forward to meet him.

The guard threw a fireball. Katana caught it, spun around and hurled it right back at him. She continued her advance.

But the guard formed a ball of energy in his arms. He caught the fireball and threw the enormous flaming mass back at her again. It streaked toward her, a tail of flame streaming behind it.

Katana dropped to a horse stance, held out both hands, and bounced her chi against the fireball. It rebounded, slamming into the guard. He flew several yards, crashing down on the stone.

Katana was on him before he could regain his feet—she threw another fireball. But he levitated away before it hit him.

They were at the end of the alley now, near the stairs. Katana ran up a couple of steps, leaping into the air. She slammed a side kick into the guard's ribs mid-flight, then spun around, smashing him in the head with her other foot.

They each landed on the ground, behind one line of monks. The guard was bleeding profusely from the nose. He threw another fireball.

Katana deflected it. She extended her shen, slamming him

with a dozen pulses of chi. He sailed through the air, this time crashing into the temple wall with a crunching noise.

He landed on the ground in a heap, but sprang to his feet. Katana hit him with an enormous fireball. It smashed him into the brick wall. This time his head snapped back, hitting the wall with a cracking sound. He slumped to the ground and moved no more.

Katana walked away. The monks in the line closest to her had turned around to watch the battle. But now they turned back, facing the other line of monks again.

Chan stared at her from the top of the stairs. He turned and went inside.

Master Liang walked over to Katana. "Come with me." He led her through the line of monks, up the stairs into the temple.

After the brilliant sunlight outside, the interior of the temple seemed dark. It took a few moments for Katana's eyes to adjust. Liang led her down the entrance hall, which was lined with ornate statues. They arrived at a set of large wooden doors, one carved with an elaborate Chinese dragon, the other a tiger. Liang pulled open one door, motioning Katana into the room.

It was a large training hall, with high, vaulted ceilings and a stone floor. Two lines of monks formed another alleyway leading to a set of doors at the back of the room. The monks stood with their feet together, the palms of their hands pressed together in front of their chests.

"I will meet you behind those doors," said Master Liang. He left the way they'd come in, closing the door softly behind him.

Katana stood still as stone, gazing up and down both lines of monks. They didn't move; they hardly seemed to breathe. But when Katana took a step forward, the first two monks kiaied loudly and jumped at her.

The one on her right lunged at her with a punch—Katana sidestepped. She grabbed him by the wrist with one hand, pushing against the back of his elbow with the other and tossed him into the second monk.

They came at her again. One of them jumped, throwing a kick at her head. Katana stayed out of range, then spun around and caught him in the head with a hook kick. He fell to the floor. The other monk tried to tackle her. Katana dove out of the way, going into a front roll toward the doors.

This was a mistake. As she moved between each pair of monks, they attacked. She now had six monks coming at her at once. She shot ten feet into the air, and threw a fireball straight down at the floor. She hit one monk in the face—he collapsed as the others jumped out of the way. Katana landed and all five monks advanced.

A melee ensued. Katana felt like a small tornado. As each monk attacked, she defended—throwing strikes and kicks everywhere, flipping one monk into another. When two monks came at her at once, she would deflect the intent of one so she could fight the other. There seemed to be no end to the onslaught. Finally Katana leaped into the air, flipped over their heads and landed at the doors where she'd come in.

She extended her shen. As the monks rushed in, she hit them all with several pulses of chi. They went flying, landing on their backs on the stone floor. One crashed into one of the monks still standing in line. Their skulls collided and they both fell to the floor, unconscious.

The other four ran at Katana. She threw a fireball at one, then leaped into the air, spinning around and slamming her foot into the face of another. Katana landed and the third monk grabbed her from behind—Katana flipped him. As he went over, his feet smashed the fourth monk in the face.

She decided to make a run for it. But as she dashed toward the second set of doors, all the remaining monks jumped at her. They were blocking her escape. She turned and ran back to the front doors. The monks followed. Katana ran up the wall, kicked hard and sailed over their heads, landing at the back of the room. She scrambled out the door, and pulled it shut behind her.

Master Liang was standing there. "Follow me."

They were in a dark hall. A spiral stone staircase led down to the depths of the temple. Katana followed Liang around and around, into the darkness. They finally emerged into an ancient-looking chamber, no larger than Katana's room back at the Hall. The ceiling was so low she could push against it with her palms.

There was a stone door on the far wall, attached with great rusty hinges. It was held shut with an iron bar that latched into the wall. A giant foo dog stood on each side, nearly as tall as the ceiling. The only light came from several torches burning on the walls.

Liang walked across the room. He lifted the latch and opened the door. Inside was dark. "The Hall of Wooden Men," he said.

Slowly, Katana walked over to him. "I have to go in there?" She knew it to be a stupid question.

Liang didn't reply. He just stood there, holding the door open.

Katana stepped inside. Liang shut the door behind her. She heard the latch close with an ominous clang.

It was pitch dark—Katana couldn't see a thing. She sank her chi to her dantian, and let the energy flow along her visual meridian.

It was still dark, but she could see now by the light seeping under the door. She was standing at the end of a long, stone corridor. It was only slightly wider than her arm span. The ceiling was veiled in darkness. The walls rose at least three times Katana's height, but she couldn't see beyond that. She could make out large recessed openings along both sides of the corridor. In the two closest to her, she could see the outlines of wooden dummies. At the far end of the corridor, which might have been a hundred miles away, Katana could perceive a faint, red glow.

Katana took a tentative step forward. She heard a faint click, and the dummy on her right shot forward. Its wooden arm swung around, slamming into her ribs. It knocked her breathless and threw her into the stone door.

Katana relaxed her stomach, allowing her chi to flow along her lung meridian. Warm air rushed into her chest.

Katana crept very carefully around the dummy, which was now blocking her way. She took a deep breath. All the muscles in her body were taut, ready for action. She took a step down the hallway.

Another click—something moved. Katana shot straight up. She kicked her feet against one wall and jammed her palms into the other. Katana held herself up, her body spanning the corridor, by pushing against the walls with her hands and feet. She looked down. A dummy had sprung, propelling its wooden fist across the corridor. Katana thought it would have gone right through her if she hadn't moved.

She climbed down and perched herself on the wooden shoulders. That was only the second dummy. This was proving much more difficult than she'd imagined. Going one dummy at a time meant she'd have 106 more chances of being impaled or crushed.

Katana had a better idea. She squatted like a cat ready to pounce. Then she leaped as hard as she could, bouncing her chi against the dummy, and hurtled through the air. She flew down the dark corridor. Katana went into a front flip and landed without landing. She pushed her chi against the stone floor, levitating in place.

It worked—no wooden attackers jumped out of the wall. But now what was she supposed to do? She was standing there, holding herself a few inches off the floor. She couldn't quite reach either wall. The only way she could go any farther was to put her feet on the floor. And as soon as she did that, another dummy would attack.

She had no choice. Katana focused with all her might on listening for another click—she had no idea which side the dummy would come from. Gently, she let her feet come to rest on the floor.

There was a click to her left. Katana shifted her hips out of the way—a spear grazed her stomach. But the dummy wasn't far behind—it pummeled her, smashing her into the wall.

She was pinned. Blood trickled down her abdomen. She couldn't move her legs, because her pelvis was stuck between the dummy and the stone. Her torso was pinned as well—the wooden chest held her flat against the wall. She had difficulty drawing breath.

But she could move her arms.

Katana reached around behind the dummy. She could feel the wooden pole that had propelled it forward. She drew her hand back, focused her chi, and then smacked her palm into the pole, bouncing her chi against the wood. It snapped.

Katana caught the dummy before it fell—had it hit the ground, it could've activated another. She leaned it against the wall.

Katana took a minute to catch her breath. Then she sprang into the air, sailing farther down the hallway. Again, she landed without landing. She used her chi to augment her hearing, and let her feet slip to the floor.

She heard the click. In the split second it took to perceive the attack, Katana tightened her neck muscles and focused her chi. The dummy swung a giant Kwan dao, slamming the blade into her neck. The force of the blow nearly toppled her over—she had to grab the dummy to hold herself up.

That had been close. She brought her fingers to her neck—no blood.

She was getting closer—the red glow at the end of the corridor had shape now. It was circular. Katana was certain she knew what it was. She would deal with that problem when she got there.

Katana leaped forward a third time. But she lost her balance when she landed, stepping hard on the stone. She saw a glint of metal—she tightened her stomach and concentrated her chi. The spear slammed into her abdomen, knocking her into the opposite wall. Then the dummy flew forward.

Katana flung out her hands, blasting her chi into the wooden torso—it shattered into a million pieces.

This needed to stop. Katana decided to try something different. She sprang forward again, diving through the air. But this time when she started to descend, she turned sideways. Katana kicked her feet hard into the walls—one in front, the other behind, catching herself in a split above the recessed openings in each wall. She couldn't hold it—she was sliding. Katana pushed her chi through her feet, into the stone. She came to a stop.

She shot a fireball at the floor. A wooden man flew out of one wall. Katana jumped down, landing next to the dummy. The end of the corridor was in sight. And the red glow was indeed coming from a large urn.

Katana sprang through the air one more time, kicking her legs out again as she started to descend. And again, she suspended herself partway up the walls in a split. She shot another fireball at the floor. This time the dummy swung a long-handled axe across the corridor. Katana dropped, landing behind the weapon.

This was it—she could reach the end of the tunnel with one more jump. She sprang forward, flipped over, and landed without landing right in front of the urn. The heat was intense.

Katana looked around carefully; she was in a small chamber. She couldn't see any wooden men—there were no recessed openings in these walls. But she was taking no chances. She let her feet slip to the ground, ready for another attack—but none came.

Katana was drenched in sweat. Her body ached, and the cut in her belly was throbbing. But she was almost there—all she had to do was move the urn, and she'd be free. She could see the hole in the wall that was meant to provide her escape. The urn was blocking it completely.

But moving the urn was no small task. It was huge—it came up to her chest. She peered over the rim and saw the hot coals inside. It was so wide she'd barely be able to get her arms around it—if she could endure the heat. She also saw the brands on each side—a tiger on the right, a dragon on the left.

She looked around, trying to find another way out of the chamber. There was none. She thought of smashing her way out —she could break the bricks in the wall and climb to safety. But she was afraid that if she did that, the chamber would collapse on top of her. Katana felt lightheaded from the heat and blood loss. She had to get out of here soon.

Katana was going to have to move the urn. But how? She thought back to the lesson with Master Nang, when she'd lifted Master Daniels by one arm. Of course, Daniels hadn't been filled with burning coals. And she couldn't lift the urn, even using her chi, without coming into physical contact with it.

She knew what she had to do.

Katana squatted down, right in front of the urn—she had to squint her eyes almost shut to shield them from the heat. She reached around with both arms, took a deep breath, and pressed her forearms against the brands. The tiger and the dragon burned into her flesh. The pain was unimaginable—she screamed. Katana focused her chi, pushing it slowly into the urn.

She stood a little straighter, lifting the urn off the floor, and waddled over to one side. The chamber flooded with light. She lowered the urn very carefully—she didn't want to spill the coals. It hit the ground with a metallic thud. Katana backed away cautiously. The opening in the wall wasn't very big—she had to get on her hands and knees to clamber through. But she did it.

She'd made it out alive. Blood was oozing down her abdomen, the searing pain in her forearms was unbearable, and she was covered in soot and sweat. Her uniform was in tatters— there was a hole where the spear had grazed her stomach, two more where the brands had touched her skin. But she was free.

Sunlight dazzled her as she looked around. She was standing on a grassy hillside, sparsely covered with trees. The chamber from which she'd emerged was embedded in the earth, only the outer wall fully exposed. She could see the temple, far above, at the top of the hill. Mountains surrounded her.

"Very impressive," said a voice to her left.

Katana turned. It was Master Chan. He stood with his palms pressed together in front of his long, white beard.

"I didn't think you'd make it out on your own." His English was perfect, no trace of an accent.

"You wanted me to die in there, is that it?" Katana asked, unable to keep the contempt from her voice.

"We would not have let you die," he said calmly. "So tell me, how did you do it? How did you get through the Hall of Wooden Men unscathed?"

He called this unscathed? She wasn't about to argue—but she realized he still didn't know what she'd learned from Nang.

"It's a secret," she said, more boldly than she felt.

"Yes, I thought Nang might teach you a way to pass the test. And I see from the ease with which you dispatched my guards that Nash has taught you chi fa as well. Yet they could hardly provide a true test of your abilities, not knowing that particular skill themselves. Let us see how you fare against a more worthy opponent."

Chan assumed the stance for chi fa. Was he kidding? He wanted her to do chi fa after what she'd endured? Chan extended his shen and shot a dozen pulses of chi at her.

Katana extended her shen, and deflected his chi. Chan played rougher than Nash ever had, but Katana held her own. He shot balls of light at her from all directions, but she didn't allow her focus to narrow. She deflected them all.

She reached out, the tendrils of her shen intertwining with his, and sent pulses of chi at him from every angle. Back and forth they fought, wave after wave of chi flowing through the air between them.

Suddenly it stopped—Chan's aura disappeared; his shen evaporated. Katana's chi passed through him as if he were a ghost.

She dropped her hands and stood up straight. But Chan's shen exploded, extending all around her. He hit her from every direction at once—a brilliant sphere of light imploded into her. Katana flew through the air, slamming into the wall of the chamber. Her head hit the stone and she saw stars.

She slumped to the ground. Chan walked toward her, his

shen still extended. Katana got to her hands and knees. She held one hand out and shot a fireball at him. He faded away.

Katana got back to her feet; she couldn't see him anywhere. She stepped forward and suddenly felt his hands on her—he'd faded right behind her. He grabbed her left shoulder with one hand, pulling her closer. Chan pushed two fingers into the side of her neck.

With a sudden rush of fear, Katana froze. His hands were on the exact spots necessary to cause permanent paralysis. What the hell was going on? There was no way the headmaster of Shaolin could possibly know dim mak. It had to be a coincidence—she had to be imagining things.

But she stood perfectly still, just in case.

"Your skill is formidable, young one," said Chan, letting her go. "But you still have much to learn."

Katana turned to face him. "And I suppose you're going to tell me that if I stay here and train with you, you'll teach me secrets I can't learn anywhere else?" Katana asked, her voice full of scorn.

"You presume too much. Disciples do not train with the headmaster until they've trained at Shaolin for many years. But yes, eventually, I would train you myself. There is knowledge at Shaolin that you will find nowhere else in the world. The scrolls of Li Shan, for example..."

Katana felt rebellious. "You mean the scrolls that map out the chen do? I've read them already—I've studied them all. Chow brought copies to the Hall of the Dragon."

"You mean the copies he *stole*?" said Chan, his voice dripping with sarcasm. "Oh yes, I know about those. Master Wang came back to Shaolin after he left Chow. Before he went to find Jaaku, Wang told the headmaster that Chow had stolen the scrolls. But I was not referring to the chen do scrolls, nor the manual of the healing arts. I am talking about the scrolls that reveal Chow's deepest secret.

"Li Shan discovered the mechanism of Chow's immortality—Chow himself hadn't understood it. Li Shan promised Chow he would reveal the information to no one. But when Chow left Shaolin to go to Japan as Kushan in 1733, Li Shan knew he had to record what he had discovered. He couldn't let that knowledge be lost.

"Li Shan authored several more scrolls, explaining Chow's unique gift. Chow never knew he wrote them—nobody did. Only the headmasters of Shaolin have ever been aware of their existence."

Chan laughed. "If Jaaku had known that we possessed those documents, when he was trying to figure out the Scroll of the Five Masters—he would have besieged Shaolin and never rested until he had them."

"You have scrolls here that explain how Chow became immortal?!" Katana hated to admit it, but Chan *had* piqued her interest.

"Oh yes," he said, clearly aware that he'd gained an advantage. "No one alive knows they exist. They are not kept in the archives —oh, no. The scrolls of Li Shan never leave the headmaster's chambers. So you are going to have to stay here, if you ever want to learn Chow's secret."

"Chow is still out there, somewhere," said Katana. "I could find him and learn the secret from him directly."

"Silly girl, Chow is dead," said Chan.

"How do you know that?"

"Chow—Kushan—whatever you wish to call him—he came to Shaolin again, after the battle of Taiyou in 1869. Chow revealed to the headmaster that he was the Immortal Master. But he told the headmaster he was going to take his own life. Chow feared that Jaaku was still alive. He knew that if Jaaku ever caught him, he could steal his chi, and become truly immortal. In the end, Chow was both a thief and a coward. The most powerful internal master ever to train at Shaolin, they called him. Yet he chose to run away, to end his life to prevent Jaaku from stealing his immortality."

"That doesn't make him a coward," said Katana. "It makes him a hero."

"A hero? A hero would have confronted Jaaku and rid the world of that evil once and for all. Instead Chow chose to leave that problem to those he left behind.

"So I say again, if you want to learn the secret of the Immortal Master, you will have to stay at Shaolin."

CHAPTER 33

FOREBODING

"How are you feeling, *Master Kahanu*?" Osaka asked with an ironic smile.

The truth was Katana hurt all over. The wound in her abdomen was throbbing; the burns on her forearms were still searing despite the ice packs now wrapped around them; the cuts on her hands stung and she had dozens of other scrapes and bruises all over her body.

And she'd never felt better. The ordeal of the test was behind her, Sara was alive and Katana was a master.

"People aren't really going to call me that, are they?" she asked with a smile.

"Not if you don't want them to," said Osaka.

Chan had walked her back to the courtyard, where Liang and Master Nash had met her and escorted her to the infirmary. The doctors had tended her wounds, and Osaka had come to see her.

He had offered to give her a tour of the grounds, and she couldn't refuse. She was fascinated by the history—hundreds of years of martial arts history—that had unfolded here.

They were walking around the Pagoda Forest—a graveyard of hundreds of stone and brick pagodas. Osaka had explained that they contained the cremated remains of generations upon generations of noteworthy Shaolin monks.

"Katana," said Osaka, somewhat hesitantly. "You need to know... Jaaku will be coming for you."

Katana already knew this. But hearing Osaka say it seemed to make it a hard fact, no longer just a gut feeling. But why was he telling her this? Why now?

"How do you know?"

"Jaaku will hear that the Shaolin Temple has promoted a fifteen-year-old to master. And when he does, he'll want to add you to his Arashi. Nang and Dasari both said that when Jaaku resided in their countries, he was on the lookout for young people with extraordinary talent."

"Why?" Katana asked.

"Why does Jaaku do any of the things he does?" said Osaka. "More power. When he takes someone's chi, he adds their power to his own. That's why he came for your father. When Jesse found Jaaku, he told him about Adrian. Jaaku wasted no time— he went to Hawaii to take your father, to make him an Arashi."

Osaka let out a long sigh. "In hindsight, I almost wish Jordan *had* brought you here when Chan accused you of knowing dim mak. Perhaps that way, we could have avoided the current situation."

"Chan doesn't know I found the manuscript, does he?" Katana asked. She hadn't thought about this.

"Ah, no—definitely not," said Osaka. "The only people who know about that, besides the two of us, are Samantha, Jordan, Chris, Sara and of course, Sara's parents—already too many, if you ask me."

Katana thought about everything for a minute. "So is that why you didn't want me to test? Because you knew Jaaku would find out about me?"

"That's correct, Katana," Osaka confirmed. "It was clear that Chan only brought up the Code of Bodhidharma to force Nash to bring you here. But he'd backed Jordan into a corner. The only way he could refuse was to leave the temple network altogether.

"And that's exactly what I insisted he do," said Osaka. "I wanted to protect you at any cost. But matters grew worse. Chan announced that five other headmasters would be evaluating you in advance of your trip to Shaolin. After Kim's visit, my very worst fears were realized. Master Lee was an Arashi. If he'd made it back to Korea, and reported to Jaaku, it no longer would have mattered if you tested. Jaaku would have already been aware of your existence and your power. But of course, Master Lu made sure that didn't happen."

"That's why you wanted me to fail the evaluations," said Katana quietly. "You were trying to protect me."

"How did you know about that?"

Katana felt her face growing warm. "I overheard you talking to Master Nash one day—Nash said that Chatri was going to fail me, and you said you hoped the others would follow his lead."

"I'm very sorry for that, Katana. I know how that must have sounded—but you are correct. I only wanted to stop you from going to Shaolin. If you never went, there was still the possibility of preventing Jaaku from finding out about you."

"But Osaka," said Katana, "he would have found out no matter what. That Harvey Ryder guy said that there was a rumor about me on the internet. Some guy in Korea posted on their website that a girl from America was going to test for master at Shaolin. And when I went to Japan, Tanaka already knew about me and the chen do—the monks were practically asking for my autograph! Everyone knew—even Sara's instructor. It's not like I've been a carefully guarded secret. Even if I didn't come to Shaolin, Jaaku was bound to find out about me anyway."

"The monks at Shaka-In knew you could do three chen do?!" asked Osaka, sounding totally surprised. "I need to have a little chat with Tanaka."

"Why didn't you want me looking into Jaaku's past?" Katana asked.

"Ah, Katana... Samantha came to me after she talked to you on the beach that night. She told me that you were obsessing about Jaaku, that you were afraid you'd have to face him one day. That was my fault."

"What? Your fault—how?"

"Our chi has mixed, yours and mine," said Osaka. "As your chi has mixed with Chris's."

"But... that's impossible—I can do the chen do against you! All those times you attacked for me in class, I could deflect your intent..."

"Our chi has not mixed *completely*, but it has mixed enough that we can feel each other's thoughts. I first became worried that Jaaku might find out about you the moment you learned to levitate. In fact, you could say that I became obsessed with this fear. I didn't want to lose you to Jaaku.

"When Samantha told me that you were becoming consumed with, essentially, the same fear, I knew I had to put a stop to it. I knew that you were feeling my emotions, because of our connection. From that moment on, I hid my shen—I made sure you couldn't sense my fear any longer."

"But if I was feeling your thoughts... Can you feel mine, too?"

"Yes. When you did the death touch on Sara, I saw it happen. I went to get Jordan and we ran up to your room," Osaka explained. "And I knew when Lu attacked you and Dasari."

"Then why didn't you fade to the beach?" asked Katana.

"Unfortunately, that is an advantage Jaaku has over us," said Osaka. "Jordan and I can only fade to a place we know well enough to see in our mind's eye. Neither of us could fade to you when Lu attacked because, frankly, neither of us has ever spent much time on the beach. Jaaku, on the other hand, can fade to any place he can see through the eyes of his Arashi."

"That would be a useful power to have," Katana observed.

"Indeed," Osaka agreed. "Believe me, it has occurred to me to try imitating Jaaku's ability. I *tried* to fade to the beach that night. But I couldn't do it."

"Why does it work for Jaaku, but not anyone else?" Katana asked.

"The nature of his connection is different," said Osaka.

"Jaaku has taken the prenatal chi of his Arashi—*taken* it—that is an important distinction, Katana. The connection you and I share, and that you share with Chris, exists because we have *given* our chi to each other. I do not own you the way Jaaku possesses the Arashi. Thus I cannot *take* your knowledge or your vision the way Jaaku can take those things from his servants."

"Osaka... I had dreams about my parents—last summer," said Katana, tearing up. "I saw them die. How is that possible? I couldn't have been feeling their thoughts—they've been dead for years."

"Yes—Samantha told me about this," said Osaka. "I'm afraid that is my fault as well, Katana. I've had that same nightmare for fifteen years. It comes and it goes, but I had it almost every night last summer."

"Then... What I saw really happened?"

"Yes, Katana, it did. I saw it *as it happened*. I was at the top of the cliff when your parents' car went over the edge. Adrian and I shared the same connection that I have with you. I saw everything that happened in that car exactly as Adrian was seeing it. And because of *our* connection, you saw it as well."

"He reached for her," said Katana, tears streaming down her face. "It was like he was trying to grab her. Osaka... Could my dad... Could he fade?"

"Yes, Katana, he could. He'd only learned to do it the week before. He hadn't yet been able to fade with someone else."

"Then he was trying to get my mom to fade out of the car with her..."

"Yes, I think that's exactly what he was doing. This is crucial for you to understand, Katana. Your father could have faded out of that car alone. But his only thought was for your mother.

"When you did the death touch on Sara, I thought I'd lost you. I thought you'd gone down the same path as Jesse, when he left to find Jaaku. The same path that Jaaku himself had gone down, when he went to learn dim mak.

"But I was wrong. You turned around a week later and used the death touch to *save* Sara. You chose to sacrifice yourself for her. I knew then that you were a true master.

"It is critical that you understand this, Katana. This is a choice that Jaaku would never make—that it would never occur to him to make. Or Jesse, for that matter. They only ever choose to take, never to give, never to contribute. If either of *them* had been in the car that night, they would have saved only themselves."

"What about Lu?" asked Katana. "I bet he probably thought *he* was contributing by getting rid of those Arashi."

"Lu acted out of revenge," said Osaka, "for what Jaaku had done to him. In the end, his desire for revenge destroyed him."

"Why didn't Chan tell you about teaching Lu to hide his shen?"

Osaka sighed. "As it turns out, Chan did *not* teach him that."

"What?" said Katana. "Then who did?"

"We don't know."

They walked in silence for a minute.

"Why did you change your mind about the test?" Katana asked. "When you got here, and you told Nash I had to take it?"

"When you saved Sara, that changed everything," said Osaka.

"I realized I couldn't protect you forever. I'd been obsessed with hiding you from Jaaku—I tried for a year to prevent you from taking this test. Yet you became a master right before my eyes. If you are meant to confront Jaaku, that's what will happen. I cannot stop it—the best I can do is prepare you for the fight."

They walked past the edge of the Pagoda Forest, and partway down the grassy slope beyond. The two of them sat down next to each other. Katana stared out at the mountains.

"Chan told me the Immortal Master is dead," she said after a few minutes.

"Oh?" said Osaka.

"Yeah—he said he took his own life so Jaaku would never be able to take his chi. I guess after the battle at Taiyou, Chow came to Shaolin and told the headmaster he was going to do it."

"Well... It appears Chan knows more than we realized," said Osaka.

"And Chan *did* try to get me to stay," said Katana. "He told me about the scrolls of Li Shan."

"Did you tell him you'd already read the copies that Chow brought to the Hall of the Dragon?" Osaka asked with a bemused smile.

"Hey! How'd you know?"

"I figured you wouldn't be able to resist."

"Well, that's exactly what I told him," said Katana. "But he said that Li Shan wrote a dozen more scrolls that Chow never knew about. He said that Li Shan figured out how Chow became immortal."

"That's very interesting," said Osaka. "Did he elaborate?"

"No, he didn't—he said I'd have to stay at Shaolin if I wanted to learn Chow's secret." said Katana. "But I turned him down."

"Yes, we knew one way or another, Chan would try to get you to stay," said Osaka. "That was the reason he made you go through the ancient rite, I am sure. He never thought you'd pass. Undoubtedly he planned to tell you, when you failed, that if you stayed at Shaolin you could learn the skills you'd need to take the test again.

"You foiled his plans, of course, by passing the first time. Oh, he must have been desperate at that point to find some way to entice you. I'm sure he never would have told you about the scrolls otherwise."

"Yeah—he said that only the headmasters of Shaolin knew about Li Shan's later scrolls," Katana agreed. "But... he also said that if Jaaku ever found out about them, he would attack Shaolin and never stop until he took them. If that's true, why would he risk telling me? What if I went and told Jaaku?"

"Chan knows that won't happen," said Osaka. "He knew you would tell me, and Jordan, but he also knows that we are just as committed to defeating Jaaku as he is.

"No, Chan would not have told you about the scrolls if he thought there was any possibility of Jaaku finding out. The very existence of dim mak is the shame of Shaolin. Every headmaster since Li Shan has been committed to eradicating that particular evil from the world."

"Sam mentioned something about this," said Katana. "A Shaolin master discovered dim mak and wrote the manuscript, right?"

"Exactly," said Osaka. "Master Tong. He was Li Shan's student. Tong learned the healing arts and all the chen do from Li Shan. Yet he twisted that knowledge and put it to evil use. Li Shan failed to stop him."

"But we have the dim mak manuscript now," said Katana. "And besides Jaaku, I'm the only one who knows the death touch. So if we defeat Jaaku and destroy the manuscript, that will be the end of dim mak..."

"No, Katana, it will not," said Osaka.

"Why not?"

"The manuscript you found under the old dojo is *not* the original. The copy you found is in Japanese. The original would be in Chinese."

"But... Then where did our copy come from?" asked Katana, totally confused.

"That's a good question," said Osaka. "But here's what I believe happened. I think that Jaaku himself wrote the copy that you found, to make sure the knowledge was never lost. He wouldn't have trusted the secret of the death touch to anyone else, so he must have inscribed it himself. I believe that Chang must have snatched the manuscript from Taiyou before the temple was destroyed. Jaaku would have hidden it in his inner chamber—in all likelihood, nobody else knew it existed. Chang must have searched the chamber. He found the manuscript and hid it under the abandoned dojo behind the Hall. After that, he probably forgot about it."

"And what happened to the original?" asked Katana.

"I'm afraid I have no idea," said Osaka. "Jaaku either lost it, destroyed it, or never had it to begin with. Liang told Samantha that when the monks of Shaolin raided Tong's temple in the desert, after Jaaku killed him, the manuscript was gone. We assumed that Jaaku took it.

"I think it unlikely that Jaaku would destroy it. My guess is that he simply never had it in the first place."

"Then the original is still out there somewhere," said Katana.

"So it would seem," Osaka agreed.

"WE KNOW EVERYTHING, now, don't we?" said Sara. "The whole story of Jaaku and the Immortal Master."

She was sitting on her bed, next to Katana. Chris was sitting in Katana's desk chair, facing the girls. Katana had told them about her test, and her conversations with Chan and Osaka.

"Let me make sure I've got everything straight," said Chris. "Jaaku was a samurai warrior in Japan, and somehow he found the Immortal Master. He tried to get the Immortal Master to teach him the secret to immortality, but the Immortal Master refused."

"Right, but Li Shan figured out the secret," Katana interjected. "And he wrote it down in those scrolls that Chan's got."

"Don't interrupt!" said Chris, screwing up his forehead in an attempt to regain his train of thought. "So Jaaku went to China and found Master Tong to learn dim mak..."

"Which Tong was able to figure out because he was a student of Li Shan, and he learned the healing arts from him," added Sara.

"Stop!" Chris yelled. "Jaaku killed Tong, and the original dim mak manuscript disappeared. And then Jaaku went to Japan and took over Taiyou, where he started the Arashi. And he wrote down a new copy of the dim mak manuscript.

"In the meantime, the Immortal Master—who people knew as Chow at this point—was at Shaolin and he took some other masters and came to America to start the Hall of the Dragon. But then when Master Wang left, he went to Jaaku and told him that he knew where the Immortal Master was. So then Jaaku attacked the Hall of the Dragon to try to get Chow..."

"Because now that he knew the death touch, he could take Chow's chi and become immortal," said Katana.

"Right—but then Chow left, and went with Chang and the headmasters in Japan to kick Jaaku out of Taiyou," said Chris.

"And Chang took the new dim mak manuscript and hid it under the old dojo," said Sara.

"And then Chow took his own life to make sure Jaaku could never take his chi," said Katana.

"Let me do this!" said Chris. "Jaaku left Japan and went to Tibet, and learned all that crap from the Tibetan monks... Then he went to Africa, and that's where he was for a hundred years. But he came back when he found out about the Scroll of the Five Masters."

"Which Osaka destroyed, so no one can ever learn the secret of immortality," said Sara.

"Right, except that the headmaster of Shaolin has the scrolls of Li Shan. And they contain the information," said Katana.

"And now..." Chris stopped and looked at Katana. "And now

Jaaku is going to be coming for *you* when he finds out the Shaolin Temple promoted you to master."

The three of them sat in silence for a minute, contemplating Chris's last words.

There was a loud bang on the door. Chris and Katana both jumped and Sara squealed.

It was Jimmy—he barged in a second later when nobody answered.

"Hey! You're back—did you make it? Did you pass?"

Katana sighed. "Yeah, I did."

"So you're a master now?!"

"Yeah, I guess I am," said Katana.

"Awesome! So do you wanna go out with me now?"

Katana looked from Sara to Chris in disbelief. But the two of them only smiled, then turned away, pretending to be deaf.

"Yeah," said Katana with a smile. "Sure."

"YES!" yelled Jimmy. He walked over to where she was sitting. But Doc ran out from under the sofa, cutting across his path. Jimmy stumbled trying to avoid stepping on the cat. He tripped and fell over, smashing his head on Katana's desk.

"Jimmy!" Katana yelled. The three of them jumped up to see if he was okay.

Jimmy was on the floor, lying flat on his back. Sara squatted down next to him.

"Kat—he's unconscious!" she said.

"Idiot," said Chris, shaking his head.

Katana got down on her knees. She pushed her fingers against the side of his neck and the base of his skull.

Jimmy opened his eyes and said, a little groggily, "Kat... will you go out with me now?"

Katana laughed. "I already am, you fool!"

As she pressed her lips to his, she realized that Sam was right. These really were going to be some of the best years of her life. She intended to live them to their fullest.

To be continued...

Milton Keynes UK
Ingram Content Group UK Ltd.
UKHW010118270324
439993UK00003B/103/J